A PROMISE OF TRUST

"I will deal gently, Nicolaa," he said, his voice as soft as carded wool.

The words, the words of promise, whispered against the tattered edge of her soul. What a promise it was, to be treated gently. Had she said she would not succumb to a single well-turned phrase or the beauty of a gentle smile? The lost girl she had been cried out in her far-off corner for it to be so. With a phrase, he had resurrected her, she who had been dead and unlamented for so many years. To trust, to believe that a promise would be kept, a vow honored. How sweet a temptation. How tempting to believe.

"Allow yourself to trust me," he said, taking her hand in his, his touch solid and substantial, giving weight to his soft command. "I will not betray."

"I do not know you," she said, suddenly wanting to know him better, taking a single, treacherous step toward belief.

"I am your husband and your lord," he said. "I am worthy of your trust, lady."

THE
Willing Wife

CLAUDIA
DAIN

LEISURE BOOKS   NEW YORK CITY

A LEISURE BOOK®

October 2002

Published by

Dorchester Publishing Co., Inc.
276 Fifth Avenue
New York, NY 10001

ISBN 0-8439-5111-7

The name "Leisure Books" and the stylized "L" with design are
trademarks of Dorchester Publishing Co., Inc.

Printed in the United States of America.

Visit us on the web at www.dorchesterpub.com.

To Alicia Condon,
who gives me the freedom to find my way through
the story. Thank you for your patience and your trust.

THE Willing Wife

Chapter One

England, 1155
Lammas

"I want neither lands nor wife," Rowland grumbled.

"A sorry state, since you now have both," William said.

"Talk to the king, William; you have his ear," Rowland said.

"I may have his ear, but I want to keep my head. I will not argue his choice of gifts."

"This is no gift," Rowland said, looking off into the distance.

"It could be," William said softly, his eyes on his friend's dark profile.

It was just before Lammas, the beginning of the autumn season, and the woods were still cloaked in green. That would change soon enough. Even now, the wind had lost its summer softness; the season had turned. As Rowland's life had turned.

William looked around him at the lands Henry had gifted him at the beginning of the year. Greneforde was his home and his destiny, the prize he had striven for in battle upon battle. With the land had come a wife, as was so often the way of things in this world. As Rowland now knew for himself. The difference between them was that William had been hungry for his gift of land and legacy; Rowland was hungry only for battle. It was a rare irony that his battle skills had earned him his present misery.

Rowland spoke true: he wanted no wife. Yet he had one, and there was no escaping a gift when King Henry II was the giver. Nay, Rowland must claim the woman as wife.

"They say she is fair, her hair red as fire," William offered, knowing it would make no difference.

Rowland did not answer. He looked off into the distance of the wood bordering the plain that surrounded Greneforde. The leaves were green on the trees, but the scrub at the edges of the field was tinged with the faint yellow of autumn and fluttering in protest against a wind gone suddenly sharp.

They said she was fair. What mattered fair in a woman? Lubias had possessed the heart of a lion . . . and love? She had loved more deeply than ten wives. That had been fair. Other men might yearn for beauty; he yearned for Lubias. He wanted no other, only Lubias, and Lubias was lost to him. He would not soil her memory by linking his name to another, not even for the king.

"Will you leave Henry and his England, Rowland?" William asked, reading the direction of his friend's thoughts.

The Willing Wife

"How far will you go to escape a wife who has been ordered to marry as surely as you?"

To leave England was to leave William. Rowland turned to look at his comrade. They were closer than brothers, bonded by ties deeper than friendship. William would not leave England. England was the home he had fought for all those years and through all those battles in which they had formed their bond. William would not leave, not when Cathryn was in England.

Rowland's thoughts skipped to the girl he had been commanded to marry, and settled there. William had chosen his words well, as was his way. This girl had been ordered to marry, as had he. She would be trembling with fear and masking the fear with resolve, bound by law and honor to do her duty to her king. It was within his will to refuse Henry, even to leave William, but could he abandon a frightened girl, repudiating her from a distance?

His heart was not so hardened.

He was trapped, as William had known, but friend that he was, he had let him come to the realization on his own.

"What is her name?" he asked, looking at the sky and the long clouds that lay like tattered blankets on the tree-tops.

"Nicolaa," William said, smiling. "Nicolaa of Cheneteberie."

"His name?" Nicolaa asked the messenger.

"Rowland," he answered.

"And where does this one hail from?"

"Aquitaine, lady, though he is called Rowland the Dark."

Nicolaa ignored the tremor she felt at that remark. "And

3

why is this Rowland of Aquitaine dark?" *Jesus, let it not be for his temper*. She clasped her hands together in a firm embrace. She had heard of him; he was companion to William le Brouillard, their devotion to each other as well known as Jonathan's to David in far-off and long-ago Jerusalem. As David was the better known in the biblical tale, so was William; of Rowland she knew only that he carried the reputation of unblemished devotion and that he had once been married. Well, who had not?

"His complexion is dark, lady, his hair and eyes black as well."

Nicolaa breathed out slowly in relief. A man of dark coloring, a simple explanation.

"When does he come?" she asked.

The messenger coughed and shifted his weight from foot to foot.

"You were not told," she said calmly. Rowland the Dark was not eager or he would have come on the heels of the messenger. "It matters not," she said when the messenger could only look about in embarrassment. "I shall be waiting, whenever he comes."

The messenger left at her nod, leaving her to resume her tapestry. It was a more pleasing occupation than hearing that she would marry, and a more fruitful one. She was thankful to bend again to her tapestry, bending her thoughts away from the knowledge that a husband was coming to claim her. Creating tapestries was the thread that bound her life with meaning, and her many homes were lined with them. This room, the solar of Weregrave, boasted three of delightful intricacy, though small in size. They warmed her as nothing else could, not even a husband's embrace.

4

The women under her care continued with their needles, up and down, sharp and slender, the thread the deepest blue. Silently. Diligently. Determinedly. A husband had been announced, yet none commented on it. They knew well enough how greatly she disliked talking about future husbands.

Heads bent against curiosity or concern, they worked, each concentrating on her tiny section of the whole, their hands never still in the staccato rhythm of their combined effort. It would be a beautiful tapestry, though the image was unclear now. In time, the outline would take form and the colors give life to the fabric in their hands. It was a worthy way to fill the hours that defined a life.

Nicolaa kept her eyes downward, forcing her mind to stillness, forcing herself to think only of the cloth and the thread and the design. Forcing herself to think nothing of the man who was to come and claim her. She was well versed in not thinking of husbands.

This man, this Rowland the Dark of Aquitaine, was yet another. No different. Another man to burst in amongst them, shouldering his way, hurling deep-throated commands. Another man to proudly claim the lands she held as his own. Another man to wed and bed and tolerate. Until he went his way, as did they all, and she was left with her ladies and her tapestries and the serene solitude of managing her own domain.

Rowland the Dark was just another husband, neither her first nor her last.

He came with the rain, seeking out his betrothed. He came with his squire and two men-at-arms, expecting nothing more than a woman who would bend to his will. In that, he had misjudged.

Jean de Gaugie was welcomed within her hall, for she could do no less, though she would have preferred to keep him without her walls. The laws of courtesy would not allow it. Nicolaa kept Beatrice within the safety of the solar as she met with the man who had come to view his betrothed. Edward, Weregrave's bailiff, stood at her side, his presence most welcome.

"Good morrow, lady," Jean said, his eyes scanning her hall, measuring its worth. He would have done better to study her, to determine her mettle. But he did not.

"Good day," she said, studying him, this man who had been pledged to Beatrice. He had seen his prime a few years past, though he carried himself with the air of a man who had no doubts as to his capabilities or worth. Men were wont to carry that self-appraisal, though they be days from the grave. Unfortunately, Jean looked years from that, though who could tell what God would decide. A man might die choking on his supper.

"I have come to collect Beatrice. The time of our betrothal grows long. I would say our vows with all haste," he said.

Nicolaa studied the man and did not answer him with all the haste he seemed to prefer. She did not like the look of him any better now than she had before, not when paired with gentle Beatrice. Beatrice, her girlhood barely past, had not the skills to keep this man under her control. The difference of age between them was too great, the difference of temperament even greater. Beatrice would blossom under a gentle hand. Jean did not appear to see the need for gentleness, not even with the woman who fostered his bride. He was not pleased that Nicolaa did not cower at his look or his commands.

"Beatrice is young yet, and not ready for the rigors and responsibilities of marriage," she said. "I advise you both to wait until she is more fully come into her season."

"When last I saw her, she looked ripe enough," Jean said.

Jean de Gaugie was a forceful man in manner and in speech, and he did not look the sort to have any patience with a woman's needs or even her desires. Yet what man did? Nay, she would not give shy Beatrice over to this man's keeping, not yet. She had more to teach Beatrice of men before she gave her into Jean's callused hands.

"Yet she has need of more time to learn the skills that will serve you best in your many holdings. Is that not what fostering is for, to train and teach so that we each may excel at our God-given duties upon this earth? I cannot believe you would want a wife who is unready for her role. She is to be a mother to your children, is that not so? Would you have a child to lead your children?"

Jean strode across the hall to stand more closely upon her. She did not flinch; nor did she back away from his aggression, as she knew had been his intent. She was no woman to run from a man.

"I do not seek your counsel on this, lady," he said softly, only his eyes revealing the hardness of his heart. "I am come to collect my bride."

"I do not answer to you, my lord," she said. "Beatrice's fostering has been arranged by her father's word. That is the contract I must defend. If you would seek a wife, go to her father and demand Beatrice of him. I only follow the course he has laid out for me in the care and training of Beatrice."

His squire looked ready to burst with laughter at such a rebuke, though he also had the look of a man who had been well tutored in the cost of such an action with such a lord. She had met Baron de Gaugie once before when he had come to peruse his bride just after the betrothal contracts had been signed by her father. Nicolaa had not been impressed with him then and she was less disposed to think well of him now. Of Beatrice he had only one thought: of how soon he could make her his possession. Such a man would not deal gently with his wife in the isolation of his hall if he would not now deal courteously with Nicolaa in the security of hers.

"You follow the contracts most carefully, Lady Nicolaa," Jean said. "A worthy trait."

"Thank you, my lord," she said.

"Will you not offer me the courtesy of welcome and hospitality, lady? I am come far and would refresh myself," he said, attempting to chastise her. It was a failed effort. He could not touch her.

"Of course," she said. "Take your ease here within Weregrave. There is no need to hasten away simply because Beatrice is unavailable to your will," she said, taking some small joy in the turning of the knife. He could not take Beatrice against her will or the will of the girl's father. With only four men to back him, he could not take her from within the very center of Weregrave. Beatrice was safe. Nicolaa could be at ease with him in her domain; he was powerless to inflict harm or to force his will, those two skills at which men most excelled.

The table was arrayed, and the food, light fare only of cheese and bread and wine, was laid out for him. With

Beatrice and the others safely behind the solar wall, Nicolaa entertained her unwelcome guest.

"You have been married before, my lord?" she asked, keeping her eyes on her food.

"Yea," he answered around a mouthful of bread, "six times before. God has seen fit to leave me with a hall full of babes but no mother to do for them all that is in a mother's province."

"Six wives?" Nicolaa asked. "Six? That is a mighty number, Baron de Gaugie. How is it that you have lost yourself six women given into your keeping?"

Her eyes skipped to his squire, so silent and so still at the mention of the six women who had found themselves given into Jean's care. His youthful face revealed nothing. So carefully, it revealed nothing.

"Can I answer for God?" Jean said, looking askance at her, wiping the crumbs off on the cloth. "I do not claim to know the mind and will of God, lady. He takes whom He chooses, at the hour of His pleasing."

"Aye, that is so," she said. "Man's days are numbered, even to the hour."

Even to the hour. But could she give Beatrice over to a man who had such a loose grip on the women of his name and his house? She had no choice in that; it was a matter that had been arranged between her father and her betrothed, a contract most firm. Yet she could delay it and would.

Let Beatrice have time. It was a great gift, the gift of time. She knew that well, she whose own betrothed would come upon his whim. Let Rowland the Dark delay; it was only a gift to her.

9

Chapter Two

Michaelmas

He came to her holding of Weregrave before Michaelmas, as the summer was dying away leaf by leaf, to leave all bare and exposed to the dark of winter. It was fitting. She found she could even smile at the poetry of it.

He had come unheralded, a full month and more since the arrangements had been made, courtesy of King Henry II. She bore Henry no animosity for the match he had contracted; Stephen in his day had done her the same service. She was much married. But for her betrothed to come unheralded? Was he so poor in regard or worldly wealth then?

"Is he within the walls, Edward?" she asked her bailiff.

"Aye, lady. He awaits you in the ward."

"Not in the hall?" It was his right. Many a man before

him had stridden into her hall, the lust of acquisition lighting his eyes.

"Nay, lady, he made it clear he would wait for you."

It could have been courtesy that stayed his entry into the hall Henry had gifted him or merely diffidence. Nay, no matter how rich he be, Weregrave was no mean prize. A man might not want her, but Weregrave was any man's gain. Not diffident then, and it was too soon to assign him courtesy. Perhaps he was only cautious—a character trait she could well applaud.

"Lady," Edward said, "he awaits."

Yea, it was so. Her own caution was riding her hard, yet it was far too late for caution. Henry had commanded, the contracts had been signed, all that awaited was the ceremony that would give her another husband.

"I but finish my thread," she said calmly. "I am come." She would not be hurried with her embroidery; Edward knew as much, as did all who dwelled within Weregrave.

She rose, her ladies with her, and preceded Edward out of the solar. Weregrave was large, but perhaps not the most spectacular of her holdings. Soninges, with its massive double curtain wall, had that honor, but Weregrave was her favorite.

It was most unfortunate that her future husband had found her here. She had never been married in Weregrave and had wanted it to remain so. She had thought he would send forth some knight or squire of his to herald his approach; she could have made it plain that she would be found at Cheneteberie or Soninges or even forbidding Aldewurda, but he had given her no warning and now here he was. When he left her life, would the mark of him remain on Weregrave? She prayed not.

The ladies followed her from the solar and into the great hall, high-ceilinged and massive, its walls softened and warmed by tapestries; the single hearth was broad and low and littered with dogs soaking up its heat. The sounds of shuffling feet, the swish of fabric, and the faintest murmur spread out behind her as she passed out of the hall and down the stone stairs to the bailey. Her ladies . . . were they eager to view yet another husband or were they only enjoying a respite from their needlework? No matter. The question of her marriage would be settled quickly and then they could return to the solar and their tapestry. A respite of an hour, if her betrothed lingered.

She had yet to meet a man who lingered when acquiring a wife and a fortune.

Edward's heavy step was at her side, his sword swinging with each stride. He was a good man, solid and reliable. Unmarried, as were most knights. His thoughts he kept to himself, which suited her well. Another husband was surely among them. What words were needed to mark that event?

Weregrave had but the one wall enclosing and protecting the bailey and the tower, which consisted of the undercroft, the hall, the solar, and two chambers on the top floor. Along the east wall was the chapel, along the west wall, the kitchen. The armory hugged the tower and was fully supplied; the knights in arms and the bowmen slept on the floor above, their weapons close to hand. The single gate that allowed entrance into Weregrave was solid oak, braced with iron within and without, and set into a smaller tower: the tower gate. Above the tower gate lived the porter and the armorer and their families. A most congenial place was Weregrave, snug and warm and safe. Not so large as to intimidate, not so small as to disregard.

And within its walls now sat her next husband, close upon the tower gate. He was not alone, and of the men who sat upon their steeds within her holding, she could not distinguish who was to be her next husband and who was merely witness. The squire she discounted, but of the two knights, which was to be hers?

How many times had she found herself staring at a group of men and wondering which was to be her husband within the hour? Which man was to claim her lands and her wealth and her body as his own? It was like a dream that visited again and again; nay, not a dream but a nightmare with no scream to end it and none to hear if she did. Such thoughts helped nothing, and she tossed them from her like offal.

She started down the stair without a hitch in her step, without a frown, without a sigh. She had lived this dream before and knew how fruitless sighs and frowns and hesitations were. Best to begin it so that it would be the sooner over and done.

He had not meant to come. Worse, he had not known Nicolaa would be in residence. A woman in possession of five strong towers had five places to lay her head. It was his own fool judgment that had brought him to her door. There was nothing for her to think but that he had come to claim her.

Today would be his wedding day.

He looked down at himself. He was dirty. He had come from a minor battle—a skirmish, more accurately—just to the west. He had come on impulse and was ill-prepared to marry.

He did not want a wife, even a wife with five towers.

She could not buy his loyalty or his heart with that; by command of the king, he would give his pledge of loyalty to Nicolaa of Cheneteberie. He would obey. But he would keep hold of his heart. Not even the king could command his heart.

So he would marry and become the lord of a vast, rich holding in England, when all he had ever wanted was to fight.

Rowland smiled ruefully to himself. A married man often found himself in more battles than he wished for, depending on his wife's temperament. Of what temper was Nicolaa of Cheneteberie? By the look of her holding, she was no slattern. Rich and prosperous, yea, but beyond that, Weregrave looked well-ordered and well managed. The people were clean, which William had noted straight off, and intent on their duties. In fact, his arrival had not caused the smallest stir of interest.

Suspicion grew like a shadow at dusk. Such was not the norm, not even for a messenger, and he was lord of this place and these people.

Rowland pulled his sword free as the suspicion rooted in his mind; he was ready for battle, his heart and mind at rest as he balanced the steel, searching for his enemy, eager for whatever battle Weregrave had to offer him.

William, at his side, pulled free his own blade. "Where?" he asked, his gray eyes searching the bailey for threat.

"Everywhere," Rowland answered. "Why do they not react? I am lord here. Where is my welcome?"

"Perhaps they only wait for their lady."

"And where is the lady of Weregrave?" Rowland asked. He had come. Where was she that she did not rush to greet him? Had not Cathryn stood waiting when William had come as lord of Greneforde?

A movement at the top of the stair drew their eyes. The flutter of skirts, the movement of hair as it hung down, and they stopped their speculation. Lady Nicolaa had come.

His first thought was that she looked nothing like Lubias, and for that he thanked God. She was cloud-pale and slim, her hair curled and the warm red of sunrise. Nothing like his Lubias.

She paused at the top of the stair, looking down and across the bailey at him, her manner calm and assessing. He sat still and let her look her fill. Strangers they were to each other, yet they would be wed today.

"You had best give her a sign," William said, "else she will not know whom she is to wed. You are not known to her."

Rowland nodded. It was sound counsel. He urged his horse forward a pace or two, his eyes on hers, his helm lifted. He sheathed his sword. The lady had come; the threat had passed. All continued on within the bailey. The armorer beat a sword against the anvil. The servants talked within the kitchen. The men-at-arms looked from the curtain walk out to the horizon.

All was calm within Weregrave, even perfunctory. As was Weregrave's lady.

She came down the stair, her ladies at her back, and stood on the packed earth of the bailey. She was tall for a woman, her features fragile and fine, and she was calm. So exquisitely calm.

"Good morrow, Lord Rowland," she said. "You have arrived in good time. You will want the contracts finalized today, is that not so? When would you like the ceremony performed?"

Her voice was light, almost musical—nothing at all like the husky tones of the woman he loved. Another point on which to thank God for mercy in a most unwelcome circumstance.

He studied her as she stood before him. A fragile maid, but strong, like the finest blade. But perhaps not a maid? She was not nervous—he could see that in her very stance—and she was older than he'd expected. Too old not to have married. A widow then. The idea warmed him toward her; they would have their losses in common, at least.

"Good morrow, Lady Nicolaa," he said, smiling. "I must ask your pardon in coming upon you unheralded. I was in a skirmish to the west and thought to look at Weregrave while near. An impetuous impulse." He smiled, an apologetic smile for coming upon her so suddenly and unexpectedly.

"Would you like the marriage delayed, to await the arrival of family?" she asked.

He had dismounted while she spoke, and her question caused him to swing his head around to look again at her. Perhaps she did not want this marriage any more than he. Did she seek to delay?

"I ask for your sake only. I am well content to have the matter settled today," she said, her expression as conciliatory as her words.

There was nothing of rebellion in her words or in her face, and he found himself warming toward her. Surely such a considerate and dutiful woman would not burden his life overmuch. She would not demand a place in his life that belonged to another.

If he had to take a wife, Nicolaa of Cheneteberie would do very well in the role.

"I am content," he said, facing her. She was tall, but he taller still. "We can say our vows at your pleasure, lady. Nothing binds me. We may proceed."

William and Ulrich dismounted behind him, and their mounts were handed off to a groom for stabling. Ulrich, William's squire, was holding his tongue, which was a mercy unexpected and much approved. 'Twas a tender time, a husband and wife meeting for the first time, and Rowland wanted to find his way gently, without an enthusiastic and talkative squire to manage. William's careful silence he did not question; his friend read his intent better than any other. He would know to watch and wait, allowing Rowland to feel his way forward.

"If you will allow," Rowland said, "I would like to send a messenger to Greneforde, Lord William's holding, so that my belongings may be delivered here."

"Of course," Nicolaa said, her eyes on William. "It shall be done."

Rowland watched her watch William. 'Twas well known William was a handsome man, and he wondered if her heart would catch at the sight of such a renowned knight. But she did not react to William in any way that Rowland could detect. A most calm and self-possessed woman to not at least blink in pleased surprise at having William le Brouillard to feast her eyes upon.

"I know of you, of course," she said, smiling up at William. "You are well received here, Lord William."

"Thank you, Lady Nicolaa," William said with courteous

reserve. "To be well received is all I wish for," he added with a teasing smirk. "And this is my squire, Ulrich."

"Lady Nicolaa." Ulrich bowed, his eyes on the ladies at her back. "I am pleasured to meet the bride of Rowland."

She nodded her welcome and then turned back to Rowland, a small and serene smile upon her lips. "Welcome, all. Weregrave and her people welcome you."

She turned and, by her manner, encouraged them to follow her. If this woman was afraid, she masked it well.

Rowland and William exchanged a look that defied definition and then followed Nicolaa up the stone stairs into the hall, her ladies following silently, as ladies are taught to be yet so seldom are. Ulrich followed the ladies most avidly, his eyes alight at so many comely ladies upon whom to slake his thirst for romance. He would have his hands full if he attempted the lot. Two were of an age beyond the romantic notions of an amorous squire, but the rest were young and unmarried, the two requirements most necessary. Perhaps the only requirements necessary.

"Remember your place, Ulrich," William said softly to his squire. "Better still, remember Rowland's place. We are strangers here. Keep yourself in hand."

"Aye, Lord William," Ulrich said in agreement while his eyes caught and held the eyes of the comely lass with dark hair five steps above him.

Rowland had no mind to keep his attention on the ever-present tussling that made up the bulk of William's conversation with his squire; he had entered the hall of Weregrave.

The hall was long and the ceiling lower than the one at Greneforde; that was what he first noted. The hearth was long and low and centered within the hall. A stairway rose on the left, a sweep of stone that turned with solid grace to the upper floors. And then there were the tapestries. They lined the hall, flat panels of color and form and texture, softening the stone, brightening the gray interior of the hall. He had never seen so many tapestries in one place, and each one expertly executed. Weregrave might be a tower that could withstand siege and war, but it was also a home.

She watched him, and he feared she would think he surveyed her home, to calculate its worth. He would not have her think him so ill-mannered. He smiled in apology.

She did not return the smile.

"The tapestries are quite fine."

"Thank you," she said, eyeing him.

"Yours?" he asked.

She nodded her answer.

"You are gifted with rare talent."

"Thank you," she said again.

A woman of few words and remarkable self-possession. He had known another bride who appeared so to hide a frightened heart and a bruised soul—Lady Cathryn, William's cherished wife. Perhaps Nicolaa sorrowed still for the husband lost to her. It would explain the careful stillness of her.

"Do you have a preference as to where you would like the ceremony performed?" Nicolaa asked.

Rowland paused, considering. If she'd been married before—and he could not doubt that a lady of her age and property had been married before now—then to repeat the bonding ceremony in the chapel might wound her unnecessarily. Let them say the words where it pleased her. His

19

pain he had carried across continents and seas; what mattered the room to him?

"Nay, choose what will please you," he said softly.

Nicolaa smiled slightly and lifted one delicate shoulder in a shrug. "Very well," she said. Was she amused?

With a look and a nod, she sent one of the younger women off across the near-empty hall. Rowland could hear Ulrich sigh in frustrated longing. On the heels of that wordless exclamation came William's grunt of censure.

"You send for your priest?" Rowland said. In this hall of silent gestures and sighs, he would have words to make all clear. He wanted to know Nicolaa, to understand her, the better to meet her needs. He needed more than grunts and shrugs.

"Aye. Father Timothy," she said.

"Is the hour acceptable?" he asked. It was close to None, by the afternoon sun. And he wanted to keep her talking.

"It will be acceptable," she answered. "What we require of him takes but moments."

An observation that bespoke experience, surely. All his senses told him that she had been married before. That knowledge left him feeling . . . nothing.

"Your pardon, lady," William said, inserting himself in their sparse conversation. "I beg an indulgence. Say there is time for a bath for my friend. A man should not stand before God and swear his life to his bride covered in blood and sweat."

"At least the blood is not mine," Rowland said, smiling.

"It will be, for I will bloody you myself if you think to dishonor Lady Nicolaa with the dust of the battlefield," William rejoined.

Rowland grinned and, turning once again to Nicolaa,

said, "If it is no trouble, Lady Nicolaa, a bath for myself and for Lord William? He will not rest, nor be silent, until this act is accomplished."

Nicolaa had listened in silence and her response was the same: silence. She looked dumbstruck.

"You have no knowledge of William le Brouillard?" Rowland asked.

"No knowledge that did not seem more of rumor than of truth," she answered.

Rowland smiled at William, who shrugged. If she had heard of William and his love of the bath, then she had heard of him too. They were ever together, their tales joined as fully as their lives. If William was familiar to her, what had she heard of him? He was suddenly curious what this near-silent woman thought of him.

Had she heard of his battle prowess? Did she know that he had never been defeated? Such knowledge would give her heart ease, no matter the strength of her tower. But more, did she know of Lubias? She must; there were few souls in all Christendom who did not know that tale. What did she see when she looked at him, knowing his heart was claimed by another?

Yet, in fact, it mattered not at all. Nicolaa would be wife to him, but she would not be Lubias. There was none like Lubias.

"We will delay then," Nicolaa asked, "until you are refreshed."

"If it will not trouble you," Rowland replied.

"I am not troubled," she said.

"By delay?" he asked against his will. What thoughts passed behind her serene expression? He could not read her. Yet. Her eyes were as deep and still as the blue autumn sky.

She looked to him then, her eyes to his. So blue they were; such eyes should be always merry, shining with joy, and hers were . . . still. Guarded. Wary.

"I am not troubled. By anything, Lord Rowland," she said, looking up into his eyes.

It was then that Weregrave's priest appeared, the damsel at his heels. Father Timothy was a young priest, with less than two score years on this earth, and he had a look of strength about him. Such could sometimes be said of a priest, but not often. His hair was tawny, as was his skin, his eyes the gray of heavy cloud; there was a beauty to him that even his robes could not diminish, and an intensity that bespoke more than godly fervor.

But perhaps he was reading too much in just a glance. When he felt William go still beside him, he allowed the impression to stand. If he and William both felt that the priest was something more than prayerful, then he would not discount his impression. Never had the two of them been wrong. The fact that they were still living in a world bloody and battle-eager bore witness to the accuracy of their judgment.

"Father Timothy," Nicolaa introduced, "Weregrave's priest and mine."

"Lord Rowland." The priest bowed slightly, his eyes assessing.

"Father Timothy," Rowland answered, not bowing. He did not understand the impulse that kept him from that small observance of humility, but he gave in to it. His instincts he trusted more than civility. "Would you introduce your ladies, Nicolaa, that all may be named within this house?"

"As you wish," she said evenly. "My mother's mother, Lady Jeanne," she said with a wave of her hand toward the eldest of the women in her circle. She was gray-haired and blue-eyed, her fingers twisted with age, as was the top of her back. Yet she looked none the worse for it and was smiling almost playfully at him.

"My mother's sister, Lady Agnes," Nicolaa continued. Her hair had once been red, dimmed now by wide bands of silver, and she shared the same slim carriage as her niece.

Lady Ermengarde, a distant cousin, was followed by Lady Blanche, a widow, Lady Perette, petite and pretty, and finally Lady Beatrice, barely past her girlhood and with a tumble of pale blond hair.

Casting a glance at Ulrich, Rowland thought he looked ready to burst with joy at so many comely women. The women were far more subdued, with the blatant exception of Lady Jeanne. He could not see any resemblance between Nicolaa and her grandmother, though perhaps truer comparisons would come in time.

"My friend," he introduced, though he was certain it was not necessary, "Lord William le Brouillard of Greneforde, and his squire, Ulrich."

Ulrich bowed deeply and smiled his largest and most encouraging smile. Two of the ladies noted it and returned his look. Unfortunately for Ulrich, one of the ladies was Lady Jeanne.

"Baths are required," Nicolaa said, and a servant rushed off to whisper to another servant, and then a stream of men went outside.

It was all she said, but Rowland was certain that he and

William would have hot water within the hour. She was very efficient, his bride, and ran an exemplary household. The knowledge brought him neither joy nor sorrow. He would not be here long enough to enjoy the efficiency of her household; the king would call him away soon enough.

With a slight movement of her hand and a nod, she summoned the bailiff, a ruddy man of good size by the name of Edward. With a smile, she made it plain that Rowland was to follow Edward. He did so. Such smiling efficiency almost compelled obedience. He did want a bath, after all. Or at least, William did. For himself, he would do whatever was necessary to bring honor to the vows he was about to take.

As they ascended the curving stair, William at his back, he turned to look down into the hall. What compelled him to turn, he could not say, unless it might be the intensity of her stare. For, in looking down, he found her staring up at him, her eyes clear blue in the cream white of her face, her expression unreadable. Meeting his eyes, she spoke a whispered word to the women around her and they all, with only the brush of fabric to mark the movement, surrounded her so that only the top of her red head was visible to him. That and Father Timothy, looking up at him from the bottom of the stair, his stare as blunt as the smack of a sword.

Nothing was said in the presence of Edward, but Rowland could feel William's amusement leaking out of him like red drops of wine from a cracked jug. William found amusement in unlikely places. As did Rowland. Usually.

"Did you mark how the Lady Blanche smiled at me?" Ulrich said in a rush of enthusiasm. "And Lady Perette, is she not the most comely of women? Her black curls are deep enough to drown in, are they not?"

"Enough, boy," William said sternly. Only his eyes revealed his humor. "Have you no breeding at all? Does a knight of chivalry discuss a lady's . . . attributes, and with a man of her house to bear witness? Shame, boy. Render your apologies now."

"Your pardon," Ulrich said, his eyes wide with the shame of public rebuke. "Your most undeserved pardon, I beseech you. I am shamed that my tongue rules my head, and my heart the most willing witness to my shame. I was overcome. I have no defense beyond the beauty of the ladies of this house and my own weakness against it. Can you forgive, Edward?"

They were in the chamber assigned to them. It was large enough for the bed and the ewer and little else, but it did have a wind hole, and the wind hole looked out over the wall to the distant western wood. The sky was studded with clouds the color of metal, the air freshened by a wind that came from the north.

"I can and I do," Edward said bluntly, little amused by Ulrich and his protestations of innocence. Perhaps also little interested. "Your chamber," he announced needlessly. "Your bath will be up anon, Lord William. Lord Rowland, yours will await you in the lord's chamber." With a nod, he was gone.

"A well-run holding," William said, laying off his helm and tossing Ulrich his mufflers.

"Yea, and a woman of strict composure," Rowland said, leaning against the doorway and the curtain that sheltered it, "as you found your bride. Her manner is all they share, I fear."

"Fear not, Rowland. She looks to make a man a fine wife."

"She looks of an age to have been a wife already."

"What matter?" William said, letting Ulrich help him with his chain mail. "Surely you do not begrudge her that?"

"Nay," Rowland answered, crossing his arms over his chest. "It is only . . . where stands her heart?"

Yet, in truth, he spoke of his own heart, given to Lubias and ne'er retrieved, even from her grave.

Chapter Three

She watched him ascend the stair, entering more deeply into Weregrave with each step, trying to learn something of the man from his willingness to delay the ceremony. Perhaps his actions revealed arrogance that Weregrave could not be taken from him; perhaps courtesy to her needs; perhaps only that he was easily led by his friend, William le Brouillard.

Perhaps nothing at all.

When he had turned upon the stair, his eyes instantly going to hers, studying her, she had covered herself with her women, rejecting his assessment. She could feel the intensity of his gaze. She knew what was said of Rowland the Dark; he was a man who saw into shadows and found shape and form where other men saw only darkness. An unhappy trait for a husband to possess. She knew that he was trying to lay her bare, to understand her as a man would want to understand the woman he was to manage. She refused him the opportunity. She would not willingly allow him to study her. Unfair it might be, but life was seldom, if ever, fair.

The women retreated to the sanctity of the solar, which abutted the hall, separated by only a wall, but a wall that etiquette demanded be barred to men. Within the solar, she was safe from husbands.

And priests. Father Timothy would await her in the chapel, in prayerful meditation. She would occupy herself with her embroidery until her next husband had bathed away the dirt of battle. As if it mattered.

"He is most courteous, is he not?" Perette gushed, her black curls quivering. "Very handsome, too, did you not observe, Nicolaa?"

Nicolaa smiled her response and picked up her needle, threading it with blue.

"He looked a fit man for any woman," Jeanne said, avoiding her place at the embroidery. "You will enjoy yourself with this one, granddaughter, or you're not fit to share my blood." She laughed at that and did not seem to care that no one joined in the laughter. It might have been that none dared.

"Hush, Mother," Agnes said, always quick to defend Nicolaa. "Can you not keep still? It is not your wedding day and it is not you who will soon . . . that is, it will soon . . ."

"Aye." Jeanne laughed. "Soon and soon enough for that man. Have yourself a merry time of it, Nicolaa, and spare not a thought to your grayed grandmother who must do with thin strands of thread when a well-favored man grows hard and long within the walls of Weregrave."

"Keep still, Mother! Can you not keep to your embroidery?"

"My needlework," she grumbled. "Little point there is in endless toil—which is ruining my eyes, I can tell you—with no heirs to gift the goods to."

"Rowland or William—or even Ulrich, for that matter—looks fit enough to make any woman a mother," Blanche said. Blanche, a childless widow, was wont to make such remarks. Nicolaa had learned to let them pass.

"By Saint Winifred, hear yourself, Blanche," Ermengarde said. "How coarse you have become."

"I am not being coarse," Blanche said loftily. "I am merely being observant."

"Such cannot be observed," Nicolaa said softly, her eyes on her needlework, "and it matters not how fit Rowland the Dark appears to be. I am barren. 'Tis a fact well known."

"Think you he knows it?" Beatrice asked.

"If he knew, he would not be here," Nicolaa answered calmly, hoping it was the truth.

"She has had a husband before me, and I would know her history, yet to ask directly might offend," Rowland said.

"It is you who usually ferrets out such things, yet there is no way for you to hide here, not when you are lord of this holding. And I cannot," William said.

"Nay, you have not the skill for hiding in the shadows, listening to whispers," Rowland agreed.

Both heads turned to Ulrich.

"I will do it!" Ulrich said, his voice as joyful and determined as the look in his shining blue eyes.

"Aye, but *can* you?" William said, smiling.

29

"I can," he vowed, striving for seriousness. "Let me prove myself. I will succeed."

"You must tread softly, giving no offense," Rowland said.

"I will. I can. I did the same service in Greneforde when first we did land there, did I not?"

"Aye, yet you found out nothing needful."

"Yet I did not offend!"

"Aye, 'tis true." William said.

The decision was Rowland's and he made it. Ulrich must be used. He was willing, he had some skill, and he was the only one of them able to do it. Many battles had been fought and won with just such a list of qualifications.

"Go, then," Rowland said.

The squire was gone before any more instruction could be given, which was likely his intent.

"He will go first to that comely lass with the black hair," William said. "Perette."

"Aye." Rowland nodded ruefully.

It was not to be. There was not a woman to be found. Each one, whether aged or comely, was sequestered within the solar, a place no man dared enter unless expressly invited. It was a setback.

Ulrich had not yet found the opportunity to charm any of the women into issuing such an invitation. Given time, he would. He had all the optimism of a young man who had not yet failed in matters of romance.

With a lopsided smile and a shrug of his wide shoulders, Ulrich departed the tower, searching for a fellow squire on whom to pour friendship and gossip and learn of the history of Weregrave in return. He would be subtle—had he not vowed to be?—and he would be quick. Perhaps if he had found a maid he would have tarried a bit, but what pleasure in tarrying with a man?

It took less time than he would have supposed to pry out the secrets of Weregrave, but only because there were no secrets. Nay, all knew. It was only Rowland who was in ignorance as to the history of his bride and Ulrich commanded himself not to shake with outrage at King Henry's gift. Rowland, after all his suffering, deserved better.

Ulrich raced up the tower stair. Rowland met him at the door to William's chamber and faced him squarely. Rowland's expression was open and calm. That such news must be vomited out on such a man . . . Ulrich fought his anger. Rowland had bathed and dressed, to add honor to his vows of fidelity and constancy. Rowland deserved so much better than what Weregrave offered him.

"Tell me of her husband," he said.

Ulrich swallowed hard and tried to keep his voice from shaking. "Which one, Lord Rowland? Of which husband would you have me speak?"

"How, boy, what say you?" William asked.

"Tell me what you learned," Rowland said very softly.

"Of husbands, Lady Nicolaa has had four."

"Four! Is she four times a widow?" William asked.

"Nay, not ever a widow."

"Repudiated?" Rowland asked. What was so wrong with her that she had been rejected four times? He had seen no flaw.

"Nay, not repudiated," Ulrich said. "Though it is said her last husband was mouthing the words. Nay, king, overlord, and bishop have invalidated each marriage for one reason or another, leaving her husbands free to marry again."

Claudia Dain

"And did they?" Rowland asked.

"Aye, each one, and in untimely haste. Each man taking a bride of greater worth or greater favor. Leaving no child behind."

He had heard of it. He had seen it once or twice in his life. A marriage invalidated for the thinnest of reasons or the weightiest. In one instance, a husband and wife found to be within the sixth degree of consanguinity after fifteen years of marriage. The wife had finished her days in a convent. The husband had died with a sixteen-year-old bride of considerable worth in his bed. And how had King Henry II come by his wife, Eleanor, she who had jumped from the bed of the King of France to climb in with Henry of England, dragging her Aquitaine riches along with her? Aye, it was done, though it was never well done.

"No child?" William said, his anger growing with his concern. "She has never quickened with child, even to produce it stillborn?"

"Nay, there has been no child, living or dead," Ulrich said.

This was the worst of it. A woman who could not produce a child left her line without an heir; all that had been achieved in this life was lost without a blood heir to carry the name and the legacy of a man into the future.

"You must not do this, Rowland," William said. "I know your heart softens for her even now for what she has faced, but you cannot chain yourself to a woman who is barren. Your future will be as barren as she is."

But what of Nicolaa? Four times cast off and each time by a husband who had sworn to stand by her. How bruised her heart must be to have been so used. That explained the stillness of her; she held herself in the stiff quiet of

32

great pain, her body braced for the next buffeting at the hands of her next husband. It was as he had known. She was fearful—if not trembling in fear then frigid with the unending shock of it. How great was her need of a man who would stand true to her.

Had she loved any of her husbands? Had they left her for no reason but greater profit with another wife? He would not do the same to her.

Let her be barren. It did not matter to him. His future had died with Lubias.

He would remain with Nicolaa.

Chapter Four

Father Timothy was on his knees in prayer when he sensed the arrival of Nicolaa. He could feel her. After a moment, he heard the rustle of her skirts, and those of the ladies who ever surrounded her. The gentle tap of feminine feet. The smell of lavender that suffused her clothing.

He finished his prayer, struggling toward sanctity. He rose and turned to face her. She was composed. Calm. Beautiful.

He choked the thought. He was her priest. He could not see her beauty. Her soul was all he was permitted to see.

She was about to be married. Again. He was the servant of God required to perform the deed. It would be his first, though not hers. He had prayed to be spared from ever having to speak the holy words of joining over Nicolaa, and four times his prayer had been heard. She had been married, but not by him. He had reached the end of God's indulgence, it seemed, and must now do the thing he most dreaded.

If Nicolaa felt any dread over her next husband, she hid it well. Her composure broke his heart. A soul should feel *something* upon getting married, but Nicolaa did not. 'Twas just another task to her and one that occupied less of her thoughts than her latest embroidery. 'Twas not what God had intended for marriage, but Nicolaa was the last person to know that truth.

"I am here, Father. It seems we two are the only ones ready for this marriage," she said, standing near him at the altar.

"I know well the blessing I must speak over you, Nicolaa, but are you not . . . hesitant to say these binding vows yet again?"

"Binding?" She smiled. "If I thought they were truly binding, perhaps I would have the wit to be hesitant. But I am not."

"They are binding, in God's sight."

"In God's, but not in man's," she said with a touch of sarcasm. It was the only emotion she allowed herself. "I am wed, again and again, to man, not God. I will be wed again, even today. I do as I am commanded. My service to my king is pure. The results I leave to God."

"That is all any of us can do."

"Aye, Father, and you do good service this day. Do not think otherwise."

He had not yet absorbed that she was comforting him on the cusp of her fifth marriage when Rowland and his men entered the chapel. All went quiet. The women ceased their excited whisperings. Nicolaa turned to face her

35

Claudia Dain

next husband, her manner calm and her face composed, in all ways a wife most willing.

Timothy studied the man striding into the chapel and was discomfitted that he could not quite put a name to the type of man Rowland the Dark seemed to be. He was an obvious warrior—his carriage, his form, his manner all declared what he was—yet he had a quiet and almost gentle demeanor. That boded well if it were true. But no man came by Nicolaa of Cheneteberie by gentleness. She was the gift awarded for battle prowess or political shrewdness. All of her previous husbands had won the gift of her. Rowland was no different from the other men who'd laid claim to her. He was a man of arms.

Father Timothy left off studying this latest husband and summoned the clerk who would record the contract. The only hope left for Nicolaa would be if Rowland's portion of wealth were not equal to Nicolaa's; only then would the marriage not take place, even though Henry II himself had decreed the match. By law, their portions must be equal. This Rowland the Dark did not look a wealthy man, coming as he did without retinue and dressed as a hard-fighting knight, not a land-rich lord. Would that Nicolaa be spared another marriage; it was his most fervent and most oftspoken prayer.

Nicolaa stated her worth without emotion, listing her five towers with neither pride nor engaging humility. Four times previous she had done so. What need for false modesty now?

Father Timothy watched Rowland's face as her worth was listed. He did not seem surprised; he must have well known the worth of his bride. Why marry her else?

Her worth recorded by the clerk, all eyes turned to Rowland. How would his worth compare to hers?

"To this marriage I bring Albret in Angouleme supporting thirty-eight knights, and the tower Berlai in Limoges on the Vienne River holding thirty-one knights."

The clerk gasped.

Father Timothy refrained, but it was an effort.

Such wealth was rare. To be in possession of one tower was to hold power, and one tower could support ten knights, if the land was rich and the villeins productive. Nicolaa held five walled towers and was a woman of rare worth, though her towers were spread wide. Did Nicolaa support even fifty knights in her five towers? He did not know for certain. But if Rowland the Dark spoke true, he far surpassed Nicolaa in wealth. And he had spoken true, for no man or woman would lie regarding the marriage contracts. 'Twas an unthinkable act.

Yet would the contract be valid if Rowland so outpaced Nicolaa in riches?

Timothy looked at Nicolaa and could see that she was as surprised as he by this accounting. Did she see, as he did, that Rowland's very wealth might free her from the marriage?

"Our portions are not matched, Lord Rowland," she said. "The contract—"

"I will gift my holding on the Vienne to the church if that will ease you, Nicolaa. In truth, I do not know how my holdings fare, I have been so long from Aquitaine. You could well outpace me. Will you take the chance?"

She studied him, and Father Timothy could read the speculation and the hesitation in her eyes. She had never had a husband come to the marriage contract with so much land wealth. Yet he had come, by Henry's command. She would not willingly defy the king, not over so small a thing as a husband. All this he could read in her and he knew what her answer would be before she opened her mouth to agree.

"Aye, I will," she said. "Proceed, Father, if you would."

With no impediment, the marriage ritual must be performed. He had as little choice as Nicolaa, and responded with far less grace. He had far less practice.

Reluctantly, he said the words to join them, the words coming out of him like drops of blood, his voice crushed and strained and laden with emotion. In all the chapel he was the only one still searching for a way of escape for Nicolaa. Nicolaa, he knew, was resigned to being married yet again.

With a bruised heart he did his duty to God. 'Twas no duty to Nicolaa; that he knew well.

The words flowed over her, hardly noticed. For the man at her side, sweet-smelling from his bath, his clothing brushed and well-ordered, she spared hardly a glance. She had noted his presence when he entered the chapel and that was all.

She had found it easier if she kept her eyes lowered and her remarks brief while learning the nature of her next husband. If he chose to think her biddable, so much the better. It would make all so much more pleasant if he thought so. After all, after a few beddings, he would be away about the business of managing a large estate and fighting for his overlord. In this husband's case, with vast lands in Aquitaine and with Henry as his immediate overlord, he would be gone very soon and for long periods.

In fact, in a few days she might never see him again.

The Willing Wife

The words from Father Timothy filled the chapel, sonorous and rich and heavy with meaning. For all but her. Her thoughts drifted to blend with the Latin and the sanctified air of the chapel.

He had been willing to give up a holding for her. Why?

It was not the way of men to give up a prize so highly valued and so dearly held. Did he even know of her marital history? Why would a man of such worth, a man in the prime days of his earthly life, accept without comment or question a woman who was clearly barren? Perhaps he did not know. Perhaps if he were told, he would reject the marriage. King Henry would not fault him.

She would be free, if he would only object before the vows had been spoken between them.

"I must beg a halt, Father," she said. She turned to Rowland and, keeping her eyes lowered in feminine modesty, said, "I would not have you enter into this marriage without full knowledge of—"

"I know all I need to know, Nicolaa," he said, cutting her off. "It matters not. Be content, as am I."

She looked up at him and his dark eyes held hers. Aye, she could see that he knew. Small wonder when none of it was secret. He knew she was barren and he did not care. He still wanted to marry her.

This she could understand. He was interested in the land, not in her. If he could only outlive her, then all would be his. Or perhaps he only waited, content to keep her until he could make a better, more profitable match.

She had tried, but freedom was not to be had by Nicolaa this day. Nay, it was to be another wedding day. The ceremony proceeded and she let her mind wander. Her body was present and that was enough to see the deed done.

How different she had been on the occasion of her first wedding. She had been full of raw hope and fanciful illusions; she had been so young. She had been woefully unprepared for what was to come.

She was well prepared now.

The rise and fall of his chest was just visible out of the corner of her eye. He was a tall man; though she was tall for a woman, he topped her by almost a head. She supposed that would please him. It would be well were he pleased. She had learned that much and more in her dealings with husbands.

With a whisper, the ceremony ended. They were joined. Rowland accepted the kiss of peace from Father Timothy, and a chill kiss it was, and then turned to confer the kiss upon her. She lifted her face and waited patiently, a small smile of willing compliance on her lips.

He kissed her. His breath was sweet and his scent pleasing, no doubt a result of the bath. It was a simple kiss, nothing more. Her heart did not flutter against her ribs. Her breath did not catch to press against her throat. It was a wedding kiss, a simple thing to mark a pledge. A light and meaningless kiss to mark a vow of equal weight. Nay, she was not moved.

It was done. She was married. Again.

"Would you eat, my lord?" she asked. Hard from battle and now wed; he had had a full day. Let him eat of Weregrave's table; he had paid well for the privilege.

"Food was brought while I bathed," he answered. "I can wait until the evening meal."

It said something of his passions, perhaps, that he could

hold his hungers in check. The meal delivered to him would not have been substantial.

The men at his back, William and Ulrich, were somber in their congratulations, as were her women. It was a reaction she could well understand. What joy upon a marriage?

"You will want to inspect Weregrave then," she said. It was the prescribed order of events. "I will have Edward escort you."

"I would prefer the lady of Weregrave to escort me through her domain, if she would," Rowland said.

He was courteous and mild, he had called Weregrave *her* domain and he had gently asked for her company. She knew enough of men not to weigh any initial discourse between them too heavily; still, courtesy was more pleasant than a blow.

"Of course," she said, urging herself to smile up at him. "Shall we begin here and progress outward to the curtain wall or would you prefer to study Weregrave's battlements?"

"Follow your own will and wish; I will happily follow where you lead, but to begin here seems the most convenient."

As well as the most logical, but if he would play at chivalry, she would join him. 'Twas not an unpleasant game if one understood that there was no truth in it. She nodded her acceptance of his speech.

"Will you join us, Lord William?" she asked.

"I would not intrude upon a couple so newly wedded," he said. "Go your way and give no thought to me. Ulrich and I will find our own amusements."

At that, Blanche sighed loudly enough to draw a few eyes in her direction, Ulrich's one such pair. He looked at her with a merry amusement, and she did not dissuade him. Nicolaa watched without the slightest trace of amusement and looked at William. William returned her look; he also was not amused by his squire's raw eagerness.

"Ladies," Agnes said briskly, "if you will come with me to the solar, we will continue what we have begun."

"Ulrich, come with me to the town," William said, his eyes the color of steel and his voice just as hard. "I must have clothes for my stay in Weregrave. I cannot live for even an hour longer in my battle gear."

In moments, the ladies were separated from Ulrich, their eyes watching him as he followed Lord William out into the bailey. Jeanne, Agnes, and Ermengarde looked after William, for he was a man to make a woman turn her head, married or no.

Father Timothy watched Nicolaa until her very stillness encouraged him to return to the nave and to his prayers.

Rowland and Nicolaa stood in the portal of the chapel and stared out into the ward. They were alone. It had taken some effort, but they were alone. She did not care if he was alone with her or not; she only wanted Ulrich away from her women.

"He is newly a man and full of the joy of it," Rowland said.

Startled, Nicolaa gazed up at Rowland, her husband of minutes. Had he read her so easily, then? Of more import, had she offended him?

He did not look offended.

"You wanted to see Weregrave?" she asked, refusing to discuss Ulrich's joy of manhood. Well she knew where such "joy" ended. It brought a woman no joy; of that she was certain.

42

"Aye," he said, letting her lead him.

They walked along the edge of the ward, following the wall to the kitchen and brewhouse. "Weregrave was here a hundred years ago, it is said, home to a Saxon lord, killed when William the Bastard came," she said. "A Saxon daughter he left behind to be found by a Norman knight."

"Did he marry her?"

"Marry her?" she said comically. "He made her his woman. Had five children off her before he cast her adrift. She ended her days in a convent, and quite happily, the tale goes. Nay, he married a fine Norman heiress and had four children living of her."

"What happened to the Saxon children she birthed?"

"Edward is one of hers; his grandfather was her son. Gone now, but proud of her, in his way. I remember him," she said softly. "There was a man."

"So you are of the Norman wife."

She looked up at him as they passed the brewhouse. "Yea, I came by Weregrave within the law." None could question her right to Weregrave.

" 'Tis a fine holding," he said. "Weregrave shows your care, lady."

She knew he was only trying to be pleasant. She knew that he was only making conversation as they walked the perimeter of Weregrave's wall. She knew that she should not be irritated, yet she was. He was being so careful of her, as if she would shatter with a nudge. Could he not see that the world could tumble at her feet and she would still be standing?

"The laundry was rebuilt ten years ago and enlarged," she said, continuing with the supposed purpose of this jaunt.

"It is a fine laundry," he said.

He seemed wary of her mood. A wary husband was not to be desired. Taking a breath to calm herself, she chided herself for behaving foolishly.

Another marriage, another man; it would be quickly past. There was nothing to be upset about. She did not want war between them and could almost sense the same desire in him. However brief the joining of their lives and fortunes, she yearned for calm and order and peace. With this man, such might be possible. She knew enough of him from the tales told by troubadours that he was not known for his rage or his pride. This was a tender beginning, something upon which to build a marriage of distant harmony.

"Weregrave passed through the males of the family until it came to me. I am my father's only living child."

He said nothing. Perhaps he feared her temper. A foolish thought: no man feared anything a woman could do.

"Taceham is older still. They say a Roman villa once stood upon that ground. I once found broken tiles there when I was young, blue and green and white."

"Did you keep them?"

"Keep them? Nay, they were broken and of no value."

"Not even for their beauty? Rome had skill in such things."

"They were broken," she said again.

He looked down at her; she could feel his eyes on her face, but she would not return the look. Why did he want to talk of broken tiles?

"Some things are valued only for their beauty, Nicolaa, not their function."

"Strange words for a man," she said. "What beauty can there be without use?"

He smiled and she could see the beauty of him in that instant. A tremor of response tickled her heart, and she felt her own tentative smile twitch in answer.

"What use a smile or a laugh," he said softly, "yet what greater beauty? You have a beautiful smile, Nicolaa; do not hoard it."

"When there is cause, I smile," she said, wondering what cause she had now to smile, yet smiling all the same. "I do not hoard what can be freely given."

"Then my task is to give you cause. Willing duty it will be to receive the gift of such rare beauty," he said. "I will give you cause to smile upon the hour. It is a self-appointed challenge; I will not disappoint."

Yea, the tales of him rang truer with each word. A man of rare heart and gallant spirit. A rare man to so gently urge a wife to smile and then to praise her for such a simple gift.

When had Philibert ever spoken thus to her? How long had she bled inside from lack of all the words he would not say? He had been her first and he had taught her much of men, yet none of her husbands had shown such care in winning a smile from her.

A smile he could have, freely given, but not her trust. He could not win her trust with a single well-turned phrase. There were lessons that could never be forgotten. She would not trust again, no matter the beguiling beauty of his smile.

"Taceham is not far from here and has rich fields. The crops are reliable and the villeins healthy. Taceham puts out twelve casks of wine in a year," she said, ending all talk of smiles.

"That season is hard upon us," he said.

45

It was true. The grapes were tread by Michaelmas, and they were hard upon that celebration. Would he be her husband still next Michaelmas?

"Soninges is the most formidable; it has a double curtain wall and a water moat. My grandfather, Lady Jeanne's husband, built Soninges on land given him by the king."

"How many knights does she hold?"

Another pass at chivalry. He already knew the answer. He would not have come to her, accepted her as his bride, did he not know to the bale and barrel the extent of her wealth.

Still, he was well mannered and listened without interruption. Rowland the Quiet they could have named him. Nicolaa of the Many Husbands they could have named her.

This Rowland at her side, the fifth and latest, would not be her last. If only time would hasten, leaving her quickly old and past all expectation of childbearing, then she would be free of husbands. At last. But she was years and years away from that sanctuary.

She stopped at the base of the stair that led to the top of the curtain wall. "Climb, Lord Rowland, and survey your land, if it please you," she said.

Why would it not please him? Did not all men ache and kill to be lord of such a place? Yet he was lord in Aquitaine, Queen Eleanor's domain; perhaps Weregrave did not compare favorably. He had been silent, so very silent during her recitation of her worth in land and people and things.

He studied her, seeming to want to pry the very whispers from her heart. She stared back at him, willing herself to stillness and silence, leaving him empty of understanding. He had intruded into her life; he would not be invited into her thoughts.

"There is no need," he said. "You have shown me Weregrave very well, Lady Nicolaa. Rarely have I seen a holding so prosperously well managed. There is a beauty to the place that speaks of devotion and care. You are to be complimented, lady."

He said it well, the compliments coming naturally, fluidly, and without a thread of artifice. Yet how did his holdings in Aquitaine compare? He spoke not of them. Did he think Weregrave small when measured against his estate on the Vienne?

He had said nothing like it. His words on Weregrave had been fair and full of praise.

And she believed not a word of them.

He was too . . . careful . . . in his language. His words too precise and too kind. No man could be both kind and sincere.

They stood against the stone mass of the curtain wall, the afternoon sun sliding against their skin, and stared at each other. She said nothing. She studied him as he had been studying her for the last hour.

It was bold, what she did, and she knew better than to display boldness with a man, especially be that man a husband. Yet she could not, would not, look away. As he did not.

Dark, he was that, his eyes black and soft and solemn. His skin was the color of autumn grass; he would not show a blush. His mouth was full, almost soft. For all the soft mildness of his features, there was nothing soft about the man. He had a scar across his nose, thin and old, and another on his right cheek. What other scars he had were hidden, but she knew he had them. He looked what he was—a warrior.

She knew the look of warriors, for none else could claim Weregrave . . . or Nicolaa.

She saw no offense in his gaze as they stared into each other's eyes. He allowed her to look as he himself was looking. Perhaps a fair man then? Nay, 'twas too soon for such a hope. If a man was fair in his dealings, he kept such practice in the company of men. No woman would be granted such consideration. Another lesson she would not forget, no matter the soft entreaty of his eyes. To forget all the lessons of her many marriages would leave her vulnerable; she knew too much of husbands to allow the weakness of vulnerability. She would not be the girl she had been upon her first wedding day. That girl was lost, buried in time and distance, unmourned. She was stronger now, strong enough to smile at a chivalrous man while keeping close hold of her heart.

"I will deal gently, Nicolaa," he said, his voice as soft as carded wool.

The words, the words of promise, whispered against the tattered edge of her soul. What a promise it was, to be treated gently. Had she said she would not succumb to a single well-turned phrase or the beauty of a gentle smile? The lost girl she had been cried out in her far-off corner for it to be so. With a phrase, he had resurrected her, she who had been dead and unlamented for so many years. To trust, to believe that a promise would be kept, a vow honored. How sweet a temptation. How tempting to believe.

"Allow yourself to trust me," he said, taking her hand in his, his touch solid and substantial, giving weight to his soft command. "I will not betray."

"I do not know you," she said, suddenly wanting to know him better, taking a single, treacherous step toward belief.

"I am your husband and your lord," he said. "I am worthy of your trust, lady."

Ah, a husband, and he thought that answered all. The fragile web of yearning desire was broken at the word and she smiled at its destruction. How easily he had almost ensnared her. His words were soft, but his intent was as rough as all the rest. There was no soft, sweet temptation with a man; they were all hard-edged and cold, their own will and wish the only voice that moved them. He would not tempt her again. He must not, though he had proved himself to be very adept at tempting.

She looked away from him, away across the wide bailey, seeking refuge from his eyes. What had he seen in her? Whatever it was, it was too much. He would be gone in days, out of her life as swiftly as he had entered it. Warriors did not hide behind curtain walls.

The bailey of Weregrave was home to her, its people under her care. Arnulf the sweeper worked with his broom to keep the bailey free of debris, hobbling on his shortened leg as he did so. John, head groom, checked the stalls for cleanliness, his hands soft and sliding on the flanks of the mounts. Each archer, knight, cook, weaver, spinner was known to her. The ewerer, butler, pantler, boitlier, steward, and clerk was each a trusted ally in her campaign to win a victory over harsh winds, rotten crops, flux, and sodden fields. Weregrave was her battlefield: Weregrave and Taceham and Cheneteberie and Aldewurda and Soninges. All she had and all she could pour her life into. What did a warrior understand of that?

It was home, the warm familiarity of people who did not leave, the comfort of productive routine.

He would be gone. She had only to wait.

The porter's cry rang against the stones, cutting through her thoughts, calling the approach of a knight, his squire at his back.

Her eyes went again to the man who was her husband. He was not alarmed, and his calm soothed her. A name was called from without. It was not a name known to her, but to her husband it was a name familiar.

"Richard of Warefeld and Dornei," he said, smiling down at her. He smiled overmuch, this husband of hers. "A friend. You will like him."

She would like him? Of what consequence whether she either liked or disliked him? Weregrave was his now, for as long as he would remain. He did not need to ask her leave to open the gates, even if it be to grant entrance to the Antichrist himself.

The gate was opened at his word, and Richard of Warefeld and Dornei entered, his squire behind him.

He was a tall man, as all her husband's cohorts seemed to be, and dark of hair. He had a length and spareness to his frame that gave him an appearance of almost grace in his movements. His helm was off so she could see his face: a handsome man with deep blue eyes and an austere manner, though he greeted her husband warmly enough.

"The king expected you back 'ere now and sent me to aid you, should you have need," Richard said. "The day is waning but, God willing, the fighting has not."

"I expected to be back, but King Henry can find no fault with my delay. I have taken Lady Nicolaa in marriage, as was his will," Rowland said.

"Lady," Richard said, inclining his head to her. "Blessed be the day that finds a man so willingly wed."

Did he jest?

She could not discern, yet it struck her as humorous. And was his squire not wide-eyed at the day's events: fighting in the morning, married at noonday? Not a one of them had expected it.

"Thank you, Lord Richard," she said.

"My squire, Edmund," he introduced.

"Edmund," she said. What else was there to say?

More, according to the fighting men.

"Henry will not have expected this," Richard said. "He sent me to find you, to bring all within his camp tonight. The fighting will continue tomorrow."

"Aye, I did expect it," Rowland said.

"But it is your wedding night," Edmund said.

"It is that," Rowland said.

"Henry will not expect you to rush back to him upon hearing such news," Richard said.

"Nay, I would say that he would not. This marriage will please him."

That each man kept his eyes carefully from her was absurdly ridiculous. Did they not think she understood the ramifications of the wedding night? Did they think to spare her embarrassment?

She could not quite decide if she thought them sweet or simple.

"Edmund, ride back with one of Weregrave's household knights and explain the delay to the king. Ask his pardon most cordially. I will return to him tomorrow," Rowland said.

Nicolaa felt herself smile. Only one night and he would be gone from her. It was as she had known.

Chapter Five

The ladies of the solar all found it quite exciting that another man had made his way into the midst of them, particularly when his squire, Edmund, returned. Between Edmund and Ulrich, Perette was happily engaged. In speculation and dreaming only; Nicolaa would allow nothing else and, indeed, frowned upon even that.

They were back in the solar with the embroidery, heads bent, hands busy, all calm. Except that Nicolaa could feel the tension surrounding her. Perette and Beatrice were murmuring, Blanche was whispering, and her grandmother answered with a mingled snort and chuckle. It was because of the men. Men always brought tension, like clouds brought rain. It was inevitable. They could not help it, she supposed.

But she did not have to like it.

"I would like to be finished with this section by Candlemas," she said into the tittering of female voices.

The ladies bent their heads lower. Beatrice compressed her lips in concentration and . . . remorse? She was not certain, but the enveloping quiet was a blessing, so she left it at that.

It would be better still when her new husband left Weregrave, taking his friends with him. It required only the bedding to see him gone.

She was ready for him. He had only to crook his finger.

Rowland, William, and Richard were in the sheltered quiet of the armory. It was a shadowed place, where the sounds of bailey and town were muffled by stone and steel. The armory of Weregrave was in good supply: swords, shields, lances, perhaps low on maces, but all in all, an impressive display. It gave a man a fine feeling to be surrounded by so many sound weapons.

"A fine holding, Rowland," Richard said. "You are content?"

They each knew well enough that he would never have married unless compelled by the king, but from obedience could come contentment of a sort.

"She is a fine wife," William added.

"Aye," Rowland said, "but . . ."

They waited in silence for him to continue.

Rowland would continue; he needed the counsel of well-married men of honor. What they said here would pass no farther.

"When I talked with her earlier," Rowland continued, "I was struck by her fear."

"Her fear?" Richard asked.

"It seemed to rise out of her very skin," Rowland said.

53

"Odd," William said.

"It is," Rowland agreed. None doubted his assessment; this he knew.

"She is much married," William said, "so well prepared in her role as wife."

"She is no virgin," Richard said, "so the fundamentals of the marriage bed can have no fear for her."

"She has married a man more than equal to her in worth and reputation, which should bring her joy," Rowland said unemotionally.

Nay, they could find no just cause for her fear.

"Yet a woman is often fearful by nature," William offered, "and always bewildering to the order that rules a man's thoughts."

"Yea, but she requires gentleness and understanding," Richard said. "Her cavorting emotions must be ruled by masculine reason."

True. All true.

"Yet I only have one night with her before I must return to Henry," Rowland said.

"An unfortunate circumstance," William said. "The first night with a nervous bride is rarely successful."

The three looked at each other briefly and then to the floor of the armory; the details would never be shared, but both William and Richard bore silent witness to the frustrations of the bridal night with a fearful bride.

"More nights, hours and days in succession, would serve you both better," Richard said, fingering a lance, not looking at Rowland directly.

"Her fears will ease as you make your place at her side," William said.

And in her bed. The words circled within him; the image

of Nicolaa naked and prone, her white legs open beneath him, twirled his thoughts, blurring the vision of his purpose, tangling the fulfillment of his marital vow to Nicolaa with the soft memory of his beloved Lubias.

The memory of Lubias and the joyful abandon of their wedding night he pushed from his thoughts to reside safely in his heart. How best to serve Nicolaa was what must occupy his mind now.

She had found herself possessed of many husbands. Perhaps too many. She was afraid, but he would show her she had nothing to fear from him. The worst of her fears would be of the bedding. No matter how many men had been Lord of Weregrave before him, a woman of gentle nature would not welcome a stranger, though the church named him husband, into her bed without some qualms.

He would soothe her. He would deal softly and he would be quick. She would want it so. There would be none of the playfulness of his first time with Lubias—he would not give that to her—but he would give her gentleness.

Even Lubias would want him to give her that.

"You have never seen such riches of beauty," Ulrich said as he and Edmund slouched by the stable wall. The air was soft with rain and the flies driven to ground. The grooms were talking amongst themselves. Ulrich and Edmund had as much privacy as a holding full of a hundred people could offer.

"Tell me," Edmund said, his eyes eager.

"The youngest is Beatrice, with hair as bright as sunlight, her eyes the blue of a shallow sea—"

"I have never seen a shallow sea," Edmund interrupted.

"Blue, her eyes are light blue," Ulrich said. He hated

being interrupted when the chivalric mood was upon him.

"Beatrice is tall and slender, like willow branches in the wind, and just as quickly moved as a willow in the wind, for she is shy of men."

"I think I could manage a shy damsel," Edmund said with some eagerness. He was new to the game of courtly love and would feel more confident with such a girl.

"And then there is Perette," Ulrich said enthusiastically. "Black curls tumbling like soft, plump kittens down her back. Her eyes as tilted and green as any cat's, shining with play."

"Like a cat," Edmund said, his mind tumbling with the possibilities.

"Blanche," Ulrich said softly, his lips curving upward in a smile.

"Blanche? What of Blanche?"

"Blanche is possessed of black hair and black eyes and skin as white as milk. Blanche is a widow," he said meaningfully.

"Ahh, a widow," Edmund said, nodding sagely. He may have been inexperienced in the dalliances between men and women, but he knew about widows.

"Ermengarde . . ." Ulrich said with some hesitation. "Ermengarde is lovely, but she is haughty. I do not think that Ermengarde will—"

"What is lovely about her?" Edmund would not be put off so easily as that.

"Hair the color of the richest earth, curling softly, shining," Ulrich said. "And eyes the color of waxed oak. Slender as a sapling, yet stiff as the oldest grandfather of the wood; not for you, Edmund. Mayhap not even for me," he said.

"Are there others? You mentioned six."

"Aye, six, but two of them old, mothers long past, their hair grayed and their skin loose upon their frames. One of them, Lady Jeanne, is Lady Nicolaa's grandmother. The other, Lady Agnes, is her aunt."

"Four then."

"Four," Ulrich said. They, neither one of them, had ever had so many as four damsels upon which to feast their eyes. "You choose first."

It was a gift most gracious, a sporting handicap that Edmund accepted in goodwill. Ulrich could successfully woo a hag of seventy; Edmund was new to the game of love and still testing his skill.

"I would see them first. Where are they?"

"The Lady Nicolaa keeps her ladies close about her. She is no Lady Isabel, who, until recent times, performed her duties with a loose and casual hand. But at the meal, they will all be in the hall. Judge for yourself if my words of praise are false."

Edmund did not doubt, but he would see for himself before committing to acts of love. He would not wait long. It was time for supper now.

The hall was filling with people: knights, bowmen, servants, grooms, bailiff, clerk, steward, reeve, falconer, spinner, weaver, pantler, butler, boitlier. The vast and noisy throng was eager to begin the meal that marked the end of the day. Nicolaa was there, as were her ladies.

Rowland entered, the men he marked his friends at his back. The chief men of Weregrave he had met and measured and found fit. All was well in Weregrave.

The wind entered with them, a warm wind for autumn,

wet with the taste of rain, blowing through their hair and through their cloaks, heralding their arrival into the hall of Weregrave. They were a troop of men, the smell of weather and steel and damp wool upon them, and they faced the ladies of Weregrave, who stood at the high table.

The women turned, Nicolaa first among them, to mark the entry of the men. Their clothing was bright in the dimly lit hall. The tapestries that fluttered about them, colorful and fine, moved in the wind and caught the warm light of the massive fire in the hearth and of the iron candlesticks that stood tall upon the high table.

Fragile, the women looked, and Rowland felt the flush of protective instinct rush through his blood. It was the mark of his manhood, this desire to protect the women before his eyes, nothing more. Nicolaa, her spine as straight as a pike and her gaze level and composed, looked as little in need of protection as a fellow warrior. But he knew better.

She needed him. It was the only reason he had agreed to the marriage, so certain was he of her need for a man of honor who would deal gently with her. He was such a man. He would fulfill all her needs, protecting her from the storms of the world, staying at her side though she be bare of life and child. Such a woman, the image of pale fragility, bruised by past husbands and their careless ways, would find rest for her soul in him. There was honor in such a match. He would be the husband Nicolaa of Cheneteberie deserved.

He moved into the hall, as did the men with him. The tables were laid and the offering was heavier than usual. Nicolaa was the one to thank for the inclusion of meat into this light meal; he and his comrades had missed the heavy midday meal and she had made up the lack. It was a kind act, yet he did not think she did it out of kindness. Kindness seemed too soft an emotion to attribute to her; she was all diligence and resolve. Rare traits in a woman, yet welcome.

He watched her as he walked across the hall, his footsteps loud to his own ears; he watched her with her ladies and her priest surrounding her. A most proper lady. A most experienced wife.

"She keeps herself well armored, your lady wife," William said at his side.

It was a truth. Nicolaa was fairly surrounded, and it did not appear by chance. The thought burst upon him suddenly and he did not question its truth: Nicolaa was a woman who left nothing to chance. For a woman who had been so often wed, he could well understand her need for stability and serenity.

He would do naught to challenge her world; let her build her banks against the floods of change. She deserved what peace she could find, as did all of God's creations.

"Let her have her armor of women's skirts," Rowland said softly to his friend. "She has had little enough protection against the world."

"With four husbands before you, I would say she has not been little protected," said William.

"Four husbands when one is the Lord's design," Richard said. Richard, formerly a Benedictine and now a husband of six months, was continually preoccupied with the Lord's design. There were worse preoccupations for a man to have.

"Aye," Rowland agreed, "but she has only the one now. Let her find her rest in that."

Silence greeted his statement, agreeable silence. They understood his motive and did not fault him.

He would not love her—nay, Lubias held that place—but he would stand by her. He would not run as the others before him had done. All who stood with him and who knew anything of him, knew that he would not relinquish Lubias from his heart. But he would also not relinquish Nicolaa from his hand. She had been sorely used, cast about and cast down; he would hold her fast.

Father Timothy, also a man, understood the look of Rowland, this latest husband of Nicolaa's. It was the look of a man digging in his heels and tightening his grip. He looked determined to keep Nicolaa, as others had not yet done.

Yet a man might think anything, plan anything, on his wedding day.

The stark reality of a nonvirgin bride could dash his resolve, as could the monthly disappointment of a wife who could not produce an heir. Resolve meant nothing unless tested against reality.

What priest, sworn to a life of celibacy, did not understand that basic truth? How much more a priest who saw the loveliness of his noble charge and could touch her only with his prayers? Aye, he understood well how hard a battle it was to hold on to resolve when cold and disappointing reality battered against a man's dreams. Perhaps only Nicolaa understood the battle better.

She watched him enter, bringing the smell of the wind with him. A warrior surrounded by warriors, that was what she saw. He was a darker, firmer shadow within the shadows of the hall, the darkness of him spreading out so that she felt it as a touch when he walked toward her.

Aye, she watched him, knowing he was studying her.

Watched him speak softly with his fellow knights, felt their eyes upon her, knowing that she was the subject of their discourse.

She watched the light flicker to life in his dark eyes and watched the mien of resolve drop down over his features as completely as a steel visor.

She understood him. She understood that he was determined to have her and that he meant to keep her. In this moment he meant it.

It did not signify.

Men had their many moods, as certain and as fluctuating as the phases of the moon. Now he was resolute. In a month he would be restless. In a sixmonth, he would rage against his fate. In a twelvemonth, he would seek release from the bonds that held him.

If he was resolute, he would last a twelvemonth.

Her second husband, Hugh, had barely lasted a season.

So Rowland the Dark was resolute. Let him enjoy it while it lasted. Such things were important to a man. It would please him to think of himself so. It would please her if he did his thinking far from her. Which he would. Tomorrow he was gone, back to the king; then they would both be pleased.

Such small moments of mutual pleasure, founded in absence, were all that marriage could give, no matter how resolute a man was that it should be otherwise.

With much more jostling for place and position than was customary, everyone was seated. Ulrich and Edmund, guests and therefore not required to serve at table, elbowed places for themselves below the salt, as did Blanche, Perette, and Beatrice. Nicolaa watched them with a wary eye; those two squires looked too bold for ease, and the ladies too eager for boldness. Yea, it would be better for all when Rowland and his band of warrior brothers left on the morrow. Surely they would all be happier with some war to occupy them.

At the high table she sat with Father Timothy, William, Richard, Jeanne, Agnes, Ermengarde, and her chief knight, Walter. Oh, and her husband, Rowland. Let it not be said that she had forgotten her latest husband. Father Timothy was stiff with suppressed resentment on one side of her, and Rowland, tense with manly resolve, was on the other.

Nicolaa got the wine to her lips just in time to cover a snort of amusement. It was small wonder she had a fragile appetite with the parade of husbands she was made to endure. The bedding tonight should begin to cure some of Rowland's stern resolve. She had found that a man usually could find no rest until he had bedded the woman to whom he had set his hand, if not his heart.

His heart? Nicolaa set the wine cup away from her. She had consumed too much wine if she thought men had hearts to give. She knew better, had learned better with each successive husband. Men had no hearts, no love for any beyond themselves and worldly gain. What the eye wanted, the hand grabbed, but there was nothing in it of hearts. She had learned not to confuse action with emotion.

Yea, the bedding tonight, and then by dawn he would be on his way, away from Nicolaa and Weregrave and her orderly life. In a few hours, twelve at most, he would return to his life and she to hers.

With renewed appetite, Nicolaa began to eat.

The Willing Wife

"Nay, take your portion, Lady Blanche. I will suffice on what remains, only touch it with your hand and it will be rich enough indeed," Ulrich said, pushing the trencher toward her.

"Touch the food I will not eat? Nay, my manners are not so poor as that," Blanche said.

"Then merely breathe upon it and I will be drunk on that alone."

"I do not want you drunk," she said, smiling at him.

Ulrich smiled in return. "But you do want me? Fair words, indeed. I am drunk, lady, and at your mercy. Deal gently."

Her black eyes danced with a flirtatious light. "Gently is my way, but mercy? I do not know if it is in me to grant you mercy."

"Whatever is in you, I will take."

"Take?"

"Only what you will freely give, Lady Blanche. I take nothing by force."

"Yet you speak of taking," she said, turning from him, the dark fall of her hair a shield against his eyes. "You are bold."

"Not bold, only . . . drunk," he said to her back, his smile as constant as his flirtations.

Edmund was not having as vivid an encounter with Perette, but Perette was younger, had never been married, and so she found his halting style more a match for her own skill.

"I never thought to behold such beauty when I armed Lord Richard this morn. This has been a rare day for me, meeting you," Edmund said.

63

She smiled brightly and sipped her wine. That single attempt at courtly phrasing had gone well. He was learning how to tickle a woman's ear with praise and courtly banter. It was well he learned; he would be a poor knight without the skill of courtly love.

Perette ran a hand over her hair, arranging it to fall in ordered chaos down her back.

"Your hair," Edmund said softly, watching her, "is like . . . tumbles like . . . tumbles down your back like rats. I mean cats!"

"Rats?" she said, turning sharply toward him.

"Cats. Cats," he said emphatically. "Your hair tumbles around like cats."

"My hair tumbles around like cats?" She ran both hands over her hair, pulling it in and pushing it down. "That sounds . . . ill-kempt."

"Nay! It is not." He lowered his eyes to his lap. "I am not very adept at courtly phrases."

It was a most solemn, most sweet apology.

Perette smiled up at him and said, "Nor am I."

With her smile, his own smile grew, and they sipped their wine.

Beatrice felt distinctly uncomfortable.

Ulrich, ever attuned to the feminine, was aware of this. For such a lovely lady to be ignored was beyond gauche. Blanche was wonderful, tempting, experienced, but Beatrice was a woman, and no woman would ever be slighted while Ulrich was alive to prevent it.

"Do you have enough wine, Lady Beatrice? Shall I call for more?"

"I am content," she said softly.

"Content?" he said. "I would have you more than content. Shall I not try for fulfilled? I would not do less than my duty to you. Mayhap you would even find yourself satisfied, if we do not allow ourselves to be satisfied with mere contentment."

"Mayhap even sated?" Edmund said, understanding the game and joining in.

"Aye, sated is better yet, and within my power," Ulrich said.

"I am content," Beatrice repeated. "I want no more wine."

"Ah, she speaks of the wine," he said, winking at Edmund.

"And were you not speaking of the wine?" Perette said.

Ulrich looked again at Beatrice. Her head was bowed, her shoulders hunched, her lip chewed between her teeth; she did not play at courtly love, and he would not harm her with an errant phrase.

"Aye, of the wine," he said, ending his game of meanings and countermeanings. "Be content, Lady Beatrice."

"I *am* content," she said.

"Aye, she should be content," Blanche said, "with a betrothed such as hers. Rich as the king, from all they say."

"A rich betrothed? That is a fine contentment," Ulrich said, helping to ease things with Beatrice. "When do you wed?"

"When I am determined ready by Nicolaa," she said, her fair cheeks pink with embarrassment.

"Most proper," Edmund said officially. He had his own betrothal to think of; it was unwise to take a wife unready. His own bride was but ten; it would be years yet before the final vows of marriage would bind them.

"Most wise," Ulrich said, nodding. "And you, Lady Blanche? Are you betrothed?"

"Nay, I am widowed. And childless. Not much worse can befall a woman."

"She can marry again," Ulrich said.

"Only if her family arranges it, and mine has not."

"A most felling loss for the man who has lost the chance of you, Lady Blanche," Ulrich said quietly, his voice for once stripped of all flirtation. It was a terrible fate, to be forgotten by family and to face the future childless.

"I think Lady Nicolaa would not think it was a loss, to be deprived of a husband," Perette said.

"Nay, she would not," Blanche said, happy to turn the conversation away from herself and her troubles. "Nicolaa has had a surfeit of husbands."

"But only one now," Edmund said.

"Oh, assuredly, only one now. One at a time, in keeping with church doctrine," Blanche said. "But so many. Even one at a time, the numbers add up."

"It is not very romantic," Perette said.

"If it is a tale of romance you yearn for, I have one that will make you weep," Ulrich said, setting down his goblet of wine.

"Tell it!" Perette said, leaning forward across the table.

"It begins with war, as must be so, since all tales of men must have a war to mark them. A mighty holy war with the most righteous of goals: to win back the land of Christ from the Saracen. To walk in the Way of the Cross, to walk the long miles to our savior's land, to hold that holy ground for Christendom, this is what our knight had sworn to do. He would go alone, with only his squire to ride with him, as is right on a holy quest for a holy cause, yet this man did not go alone."

Ulrich paused. The women were rapt, their goblets forgotten, the din of the hall a muted echo.

"He did not go alone; nay, he could not."

"Why not?" Perette said.

"Could he leave his love?"

The sighs of the women stirred the air, a romantic response to a romantic tale.

"Nay," he said. "She would not be left. He urged her to stay in safety. He commanded her to stay behind and keep his holding secure. But she would not be left. She would go with her lord to the far, hot sands of Damascus. She would not leave him and she would not be left."

The flames of the fire twisted red and gold and blue, yellow sparks shooting upward into the chill air of the hall. The candles on the table mimicked their larger brothers in flame, flickering softly, golden, a gentle spike of gold in the growing dark of an autumn dusk. The sands of Damascus seemed suddenly close. The heart of a woman in love closer still.

"And so they went together, down the length of France to Verdun and on to the Rhine and the Danube and even far-off Vienna. At his side she rode and at his side he kept her, the lady who held his heart. With his sword ready he rode, knowing that death could await at every turn of the road, for how many return from following the Way? Few. Too few," he said, his voice hushed.

Their eyes were glowing with candlelight, their breathing shallow and quick as they awaited the heart-wrenching romance of the tale. For they all knew that a true romance required loss.

"Far from Damascus, far from those pale sands, far from the battle that had called him, death found the pair. He fought and fell, a simple fall that would not have harmed him, yet to see her love so . . . it could not be borne. To his aid she came, striking the attacking knight on the helm with her bare hands. What could she have done?" Ulrich asked gently. "Still, she would fight for him and with him. He was her life. As she was his."

A log popped in the hearth, yet none who heard Ulrich's voice moved. His voice and his tale were stronger than any fiery explosion.

"At a blow, she was felled, a lady in silks upon the cobbles of a distant town with a foreign name, blood flowing out as her knight killed his foe with her name on his lips. Blood on the cobbles, on his hands, on her white limbs; he lifted her up and carried her away. Carried her, his arms strong about her. Carried her until they were clear of the town. Carried her—carried her without falter, without stumble, without thought. Carried her, her black hair trailing down, entangled in his mail, wrapped around his sword hilt."

Ulrich stared into the flame of the candle, his blue eyes dark, his mouth stilled. The silence grew long and heavy and cold, the flames no match for the silence of abrupt stillness.

"And?" Perette asked softly.

"And . . . so ended the life of Lubias, though her legend lives on in the man who carries her still, though the miles be many since she was struck down."

"Who was the knight?" Beatrice asked.

Ulrich looked at her and smiled. "Why, 'twas her husband. He sits within this hall even now. Rowland, he is

68

called. Rowland the Dark, for the black grief that enshrouds him."

At the revelation, they all looked at the man who had lived such a love. It was a great tale of romantic, chivalric love, even if the woman was his wife. 'Twas most uncommon to hear of such a thing, and they could but stare at the dark and wounded man in the midst of them.

Chapter Six

The meal was concluded in relative peace, though she could not quite ignore the husband at her side; still, she did well. She had managed to consume a fair portion, and that was quite an accomplishment for a bride only hours from her nuptial bed.

As a body the hall emptied, and they made their way across the bailey to the chapel for the evening mass. It had begun to rain, gentle drops from an ashen sky, warmer than the air and pleasant on the skin. A warm and gentle rain that had more of summer in it than autumn.

They filed into the chapel, her husband at her side, their place at the front, closest to the nave. The stone rose bone white in the dim light, the altar candles pulsing softly in the cool air. She loved the mass. The Latin was soothing and constant in a way that only God could be; it was a melody sent to God, the words His own, yet played upon their souls.

She was calm, which was surely rare in a bride of hours.

She had been a bride time upon time; all nervousness had been shattered long ago.

After the mass, when their prayers were still within the stone, having not quite reached heaven's gate, she turned to her husband.

"Please entertain yourself by your hearth and in your hall until you have need of me. I will pass the hour in working upon my embroidery. I await your call."

Put thus, how else could he answer? He nodded, perhaps stunned at her polite dismissal of him, but he accepted it. She had known he would; he was a calm, thoughtful sort of warrior. She had anticipated his reaction correctly. Nicolaa smiled in pleasure. It was always gratifying to understand something of a husband's nature. And be able to use it to advantage.

She walked across the bailey without him, her ladies about her. It was not yet dark and the rain had stopped; it was not even such a rain as to leave mud for her to manage. Well, she had managed a husband; that would have to satisfy.

With diligence, they would finish a section of the tapestry that evening. A worthy goal. As they made their way to the tower and the solar, she could hear the sighs of the younger women and even caught Perette casting backward glances toward the men who stood in the portal of the chapel. Yea, they needed to work more diligently on the tapestry.

The quiet of the solar awaited them, and Nicolaa happily led the way.

Rowland watched her walk away from him, her every step revealing her eagerness to be gone. She avoided him at every turn.

It was an uneasy beginning to a marriage.

"She runs back to her embroidery," he said to the men surrounding him, watching the ladies step gently across the damp bailey.

"She is not idle," Richard said. He clearly meant it as a compliment.

"She said all you need do is call," William said.

Rowland grunted. "She did not say it cheerfully."

"She is a bride this very day," William said.

Rowland allowed the explanation to soothe him. Mayhap it was fear and not lack of interest he saw in her.

"And I am gone again tomorrow," Rowland said. It did not sit well to bed her and leave her. Nay, what woman would welcome that? "Things have proceeded too fast."

"Too fast? You have been betrothed by the king's word for a season," William said. "How too fast?"

"I do not know her. She does not know me," he said, walking across the bailey to the armory. To be among arms when talking of this would feel better than standing in the chapel portal. Richard and William followed, William waving Edmund and Ulrich off when they made to follow. This was not a conversation for untutored boys.

"The bedding is the place for knowing," William said.

"The bedding can wait."

"Wait for how long?" William said.

"Until I can spend uninterrupted time with her. This is

too rushed, like a storm wave on harbor rocks, unwelcome and touched with violence. I would not have it so with her. Let it be gentle, like the changing of the tide. I would not be a storm in her life," Rowland said.

"To leave a marriage unconsummated is to risk annulment," Richard said. His own consummation had been delayed by a day, and he knew well the possibility of annulment.

"I will not seek it," Rowland said.

"But what of her?" Richard said.

"A woman with four marriages behind her will not be eager to end her fifth," Rowland said. "I am gone from here at the dawn. What beginning is that?"

"It is a beginning, at least," William said. "A solid beginning without the possibility of dispute."

"There will be no dispute," Rowland said.

He was as sure of that as of the sun coming with the day; he would not disavow her. He would not abandon her.

That he was not speaking for her or her intentions did not occur to him. But it did occur to both Richard and William, recently wed and recently familiar with the unpredictability of a woman's will.

"At least consider it," William said. "Let her behavior in the bedchamber guide you. If she quails, then follow your course, but if she welcomes you, then—"

"Accept her welcome?" Rowland said. "Aye, I will consider it."

William, and Richard beside him, shared a look of quiet relief. Rowland's judgments were infallible. If Nicolaa accepted him into her bed, then Rowland would lay her down upon it and take her as wife. If not . . . William still thought the wisest course was to complete the bedding, sealing the vows.

And for all Rowland's talk of Nicolaa, he could not help wondering if devotion to Lubias had more to do with this course of willful abstinence than tenderness for Nicolaa.

Their hands were busy, but their mouths were equally busy. Nicolaa was less than pleased, but she had given up trying to stop them. They were too excited by the men in their midst, especially her grandmother, Jeanne. One would think that at her age, the sight of a comely warrior would not set her atwitter. Twittering was the only word for what they were all doing.

"And then he told us a tale—" Blanche began.

"Oh, such a tale of love you have never heard," Perette interrupted, her green eyes dancing in romantic joy.

"A tale of a knight and his lady walking in the Way of the Cross to distant Damascus," Blanche said, her needle still as her tongue took over.

"Aye, such a love they shared that they would not be parted, not even by holy battle."

"Or unholy distance."

"Side by side they were, across France to Verdun, passing the Rhine and the Danube, coming even to the grandeur of Vienna."

"Her life in his hands and in his keeping, as she kept his heart within hers. A rare love they shared, the talk of countries, the beginning of legend."

"Attacked, he was, and she feared for him, and so rushed to his defense, her pale and naked hands bloodied on the attacker's helm."

"And the attacker turned, striking her a mortal blow,

her blood running out and down, encompassing all, covering her knight with the red of her blood as completely as her love enclosed his heart."

"Dead was the errant knight who stole his love. He killed him swift and sure, and then this knight, this stalwart and noble knight, carried his love, his life, his heart, from the streets. Carried her away . . ."

"Her dark hair tangling in his mail and on his sword hilt, yet still he carried her. Carried her . . . and so he carries her still, in his heart and in his memory."

"Never to be free of her, though he would be the last to wish it."

"A most stirring tale," Agnes said.

"Wait, the best is yet to come," Perette said. "Who do you think is this noble knight who carries the memory of such a love through every day and every hour?"

In that moment, she knew. She had been drawn into the tale against her will and been firmly trapped by its romance. A tale most stirring, yea, and quite hard to credit as fact. Yet she knew who the knight was. A tremor around her heart announced it.

"Who?" asked Ermengarde.

"Rowland," Perette said with a victorious grin. Victorious? Why victorious? What had she won but a pretty tale that struck close to home?

Very close to home.

Oh, Nicolaa could well believe that Rowland had defended his wife, killing her attacker. What man would not? Was not his honor bound up in his wife, and would his honor not be enhanced by such a deed of righteous vengeance? It was that he still carried her memory that astounded.

Did any of her husbands remember her?

* * *

The time for the bedding had come.

Even another log on the fire had not provided enough light to work by. The dark pressed against her, muting the colors and the threads until only the shining needle was sharp and clear. With a sigh, Nicolaa set aside her embroidery and rose to leave.

"He'll make you sigh again, that dark one," Jeanne said, her smile ribald. "If he does not, then he is no man as I make him to be. Or you are no woman."

"Hush, Mother," Agnes said. "Is there not enough for Nicolaa to manage this night without your snappish tongue in the bargain?"

Jeanne only laughed her reply.

"Enjoy yourself," Blanche said.

"Bring back details," Jeanne said. "I must work from memory now and could use some help there."

"Yea, your memory of Gerard must still be fresh," Ermengarde said sourly to Nicolaa, "and who could forget Macair? Yea, tell us of your fifth husband's prowess, Nicolaa, while I have had none and we are of an age."

"I would have gladly given you two or three of mine, Ermengarde," Nicolaa said, halting at the door. "Would you have wanted Philibert? His hands were rather cold and his temper uncertain, but he was ever eager in the bed. Too eager, too quick." The ladies laughed in cruel delight and Nicolaa laughed with them; it was all past now. "Or perhaps you would have liked Gerard? A fine man, when he could be found."

"When he could be found?" Beatrice said.

"A little . . . small, you see. His mightiest sword was the one he carried in his scabbard," she said.

Beatrice blushed while the others laughed again, Nicolaa with them. And why not? It was ironic, was it not, to have had so many husbands when other women had had none?

She watched them laugh, delaying her journey to the bedchamber and her latest husband. Only Jeanne and Agnes had been with her for all of them. Ermengarde had come between Hugh and Macair, husbands two and three. Blanche had come to her during Macair, and Perette and Beatrice within weeks of each other just before Gerard, her last husband. She had been without a husband for almost a year; this was King Henry's first match for her.

It would not be his last. She had too many childbearing years ahead of her and too much land bequeathed to her to be forgotten on the marriage lists. How many years more—five? ten?—before she was cast aside as too old, too barren?

How many husbands more?

Beatrice rose and came to stand beside her, a companion of rare heart to walk with her on her journey to the bed and to the husband who awaited her there. Nicolaa slid an arm around the girl's slender waist and held her close. A sweet and gentle girl, more child than woman still, though her courses had come upon her nearly a year ago.

"Will you be well, Nicolaa?" Beatrice asked.

"I am always well," Nicolaa answered, giving the girl a squeeze of assurance. "It is only a bedding. I am not afraid."

"Are you not?"

They left the solar and crossed the wide expanse of the hall; Rowland was not in the hall, and Nicolaa smiled her pleasure. What a fine hall it was without a husband to clutter it.

"And why should I be?" she asked with a broad smile

meant to bolster the girl. "Is he not only a man, and what can a man do but poke and prod with his stick? Shall I be afeared of a soft and fleshy stick the size of my hand? How can that harm me? Nay, I am not afraid of what a man brings to the marriage bed. Nor am I in awe, though that is what they wish of a woman, so I may pretend to give him the response he thinks is due his sex."

"And is there no pleasure, no pain in the conjugal bed? For that is what is whispered," Beatrice said, her face against Nicolaa's neck.

"Listen not to whispers. Listen to me and what I boldly say for any woman to hear."

"I am listening, Nicolaa, to your bold talk," Blanche said.

"Listen well, then," she said to them all. "A man brings only himself to the nuptial bed, and what is that? A body, skin, hair, teeth. What is to fear in that? He is only a man, as God created him, to be sure, but nothing to be feared."

"And what of pleasure, girl—have you not yet found the pleasure in a man's bed?" Jeanne asked.

"Oh, yea, there is pleasure in a man's bed," Nicolaa said. "For the man. He grunts his release, thinking you are pleasured by his pleasure. Let him think so. It is an easy thing to please a man."

"Is there not more to it than that?" Perette said.

"More? What more?" Nicolaa said as they all entered the bedchamber. "He is pleasured. He is nothing to fear if he is given his way in all things, and what he wants most is a wife who is willing upon his bed. Be willing. Be a willing wife and you will have managed him, your course clear and trouble-free throughout your days with him."

"And your nights," Blanche said.

"Days or nights, nights and days," Nicolaa said as they

helped her free of her bliaut. "However long he lingers in your life. A man is nothing to fear."

They disrobed her, checked the fire, lit the tapers on the wall, turned down the bedding; in short, they made all ready for the arrival of her husband. It took only moments before she was naked and in bed, the blankets pulled to her waist.

"Ermengarde," she said from the bed, "you may tell Rowland I am ready and await his coming."

Ermengarde would give him exactly the type of short and angry invitation to her bed that Nicolaa would like to give herself, but would not. She sat quietly, sipping wine from a jeweled goblet, her ladies also quiet now in anticipation.

For herself, she felt only eagerness.

Eagerness to get it over and done.

Eagerness to have him one hour nearer to leaving.

Eagerness to have Weregrave once again to herself.

Pray God and Saint Winifred that Ermengarde had no trouble finding him. Let him vault the stairs and plunge into her bed and into her. She was that eager to get her duty to him done.

Ermengarde had some trouble finding him, which was puzzling. Nicolaa's other husbands had been waiting at the bottom of the stair for word or signal that she was ready. Macair had carried her up the stairs himself, waiting for no word from anyone. That had been a sight—Nicolaa's red hair hanging down over her face, a twisted tangle, her slender feet bumping an erection that could be seen from any point in the sheltered hall. It had been a winter wedding, and Nicolaa had explained away his exuberance by citing the weather. The snow had been deep; he was bursting with the inactivity. Other than that, the incident had not been mentioned. Having come to know Macair, Ermengarde did not believe his exuberance had anything to do with the weather.

Now this one, this Rowland the Dark, seemed to be suffering from a lack of exuberance. So much the better for Nicolaa.

Ermengarde searched the hall and had to cross the bailey in what was now a hard and steady rain to reach the chapel, where he was not to be found. Smothering curses about men who could not find their way to their own beds, she ordered two grooms and a cook's helper to find the man. Nicolaa's husbands were never long-lasting, but this one had flown before he had even taken roost. Ermengarde was on her soggy way back to the hall when a shout from one of the boys stopped her. She turned, and from the wet black of an autumn night, Rowland and his friends came into view.

They came from beyond the wall. What they had been doing out there she did not know or care, but this man had business to attend in Nicolaa's bed tonight. Tomorrow was time enough to wander.

She waited in the rain for him and could not help a gasp of feminine awareness as he appeared more fully out of the gloom. He was a rare-looking man, dark and mysterious, and if the tale told of him was true, then he was capable of great passion and even greater devotion. It was enough to make a woman catch her breath, and she did. But then her anger swept all else away, for why should Nicolaa have all the men the world had to offer? Especially a man who could love with such poetic gallantry?

"Nicolaa awaits," she said, her tones clipped and her brow lowered. "Would one of your men like to accompany you?"

"Accompany me?" he repeated dully.

Ermengarde sighed heavily, this time in exasperation. He might be a fine-looking warrior possessed of a rare talent for love, but he was not exceptionally quick-witted.

"Lord William is a known friend," she said. "You might prefer him. He would make a reliable witness."

Witness? Why would he need a witness? He had no answer, and he did not think this woman would tolerate another question. Ermengarde seemed short-tempered. Rowland wordlessly invited William to accompany him as he entered the hall and made his way up the stairs. Richard and the squires remained in the hall, the fire a welcome friend on such a damp night.

The bedchamber was on the top floor, and as they wound their way up the narrow stair, Ermengarde began speaking.

"As Nicolaa is no longer a virgin," she said, "some outside verification is needed."

Verification?

They were at the doorway to the chamber; Rowland could see the ladies assembled, the warm glow of flame, the muted colors of their multiple bliauts, the long and ribboned tresses of their hair. Of Nicolaa he could see nothing.

"Witnesses will provide that verification," Ermengarde continued.

They entered the room and he could see Nicolaa in her bed, her red hair hanging over her naked breasts, sitting up in bed, awaiting him most . . . casually? Could she truly be as calm and unconcerned as she appeared in the flickering light, her hair reflecting and intensifying the red of the flames?

William, after one shocked look into the room, stayed in the portal and kept his eyes averted. The ladies, with the exception of Agnes, filed out of the room upon his arrival. Apparently only one witness was required from each "side."

He could not stop staring at her. She was pale and slender, her hair a coil of fiery red and burning gold, her eyes as dark and as blue as the heart of flame; her breasts were small and round and gleaming white against the red drape of her hair.

His loins were stirred by the sight of her, but not his heart. He thanked God and Saint John Climacus for both reactions. He could not perform his duty to Nicolaa, God, and king without some stirring for Nicolaa.

Aye, his loins were stirred by her, but not his heart. Never his heart.

Lubias's dark beauty overwhelmed Nicolaa's bright looks. Lubias, with him always, stayed quietly in the corners of his thoughts. He would be able to perform. He was confident of it. But with witnesses?

Was Nicolaa as self-possessed as all that?

"The need for witnesses is unclear to me," he said, watching her face as she answered him.

"Then I will explain," she said. "As I am long past being a virgin, there can be no proof of blood that consummation has taken place. Witnesses will simply verify that the marriage vows have been made complete."

And so they would copulate with a woman of hers and a man of his looking on? Could any woman be so cold?

Was this the fear he had sensed in her, this knowledge that their joining would be a public occasion? A woman of noble birth would well fear such. Could she have come to such reasoning on her own, this need for other tongues than their own to swear that the marriage was lawful?

Nay, 'twas not possible. No woman would have come to such a conclusion on her own.

In that instant, he felt his heart melt just a bit for what Nicolaa had been made to endure. Which of her previous husbands was responsible for this travesty?

"I require no witness," he said softly. "Do you?"

Nicolaa looked into his black eyes, soft and deep in the unsteady light of the shadowed room, studying him. A gentle man, yea—it was in his face and in his eyes; compassion flowed out of him like water from a brook. He met her look with suppressed intensity and held himself stone-still while she gazed into his eyes.

He spoke to her with his eyes and with his manner and with his choice of words. He told her that she had naught to fear from him. He told her that he would not lie about her willingness or the hardness of his cock. If he lay between her legs, he would stand by the deed. He wanted her to trust him on this, and, against experience, against wisdom, against suspicion, she was stirred by the look in his dark eyes. He wanted her trust, yet he would not demand it. Such a gentle entreaty moved her far more than was wise. Yet . . .

"I do not," she said, breaking the look, giving him this small measure of trust before he could ask for more. Before she gave him more. He was a man who stirred her more than was safe; a gentle man, yea, but such men had their own weapons, and she was just learning the feel of his. His greatest weapon was the steady entreaty of his eyes. Such dark eyes—she could fall into them and never be found again. A most dangerous weapon.

Without words, she motioned Agnes out of the room; William escorted her down the stair, and Nicolaa was left alone with her husband.

Rowland closed the door with a muffled thud and turned again to face her. The firelight flickered tenderly over her naked body, her skin the soft white of pearl, her hair twists of red that mimicked flame.

Yea, she was beautiful. His eyes could dispassionately deem it so, his heart remaining untouched.

Yet he could not help feeling sorrow for her, this many-times bride who sat so rigidly and with such stern composure on yet another bridal bed with still another man. It was much to ask of a woman, to yield so often and to so many.

He could not ask it of her, not while they were yet strangers. The bridal bed could wait. He would give Nicolaa time to know him before he touched her. He would give her time, and gladly.

No matter that he had promised to take her if he found her willing. No matter that the marriage would not be lawful until he had taken her. This was the right way, to walk gently into her life and into her bed. A tightness in his chest eased at the decision. He had chosen the right course; he was certain of it.

He walked more fully into the room and she watched him in silence, waiting. He could see the pulse beat at her throat and at her breast, rapid but not racing.

She knew what was to come, what was expected of her and of him. She knew each moment, each touch, each breath of a wedding night. She knew, and was prepared to lay herself down again with the stranger in her bedchamber.

He would not come to her as a stranger, though he was hard and throbbing at the sight of her. An old enemy, this passion; he killed it with a name. Lubias.

"You did not know that you would be a bride this day," he said. He stood with his back to the fire, the heat causing the wet wool of his tunic to steam.

"I did not, yet I knew you would come," she said, watching him still.

"Yea, it had been arranged, all arranged for us, had it not?"

"As it always is," she said, pulling a black wolf pelt across her shoulders, shielding herself from the chill and from his eyes. He did not begrudge her the fur. He only wished it were a bigger pelt. Her skin shone white against the black fur, her hair a beacon in the dim and shifting light. Aye, he wished she would cover herself.

"Aye," he said, juggling thoughts of Lubias and of Nicolaa, Nicolaa, so patiently waiting for him to claim her on her bridal bed. She deserved better than a stranger between her thighs.

And Lubias stood between them.

"Neither of us, I would wager," he said, "at the dawning of the day, thought that by sunset we should be wed."

Nicolaa had no answer to that. She only stared at him, waiting, watching.

"Let us take the time to find our natural rhythm with each other," he said.

A raising of a single brow into an arch of . . . humor? shock? . . . was her only response.

Rowland hurried on. "Our tempers and our moods should be matched," he clarified. "Our thoughts, our plans, learned and discussed before we attempt the greater intimacy of the bridal bed."

It was then that she knew how he would leave her.

Chapter Seven

The marriage would be annulled for nonconsummation.

Nicolaa pulled the pelt tighter around her, distantly aware that the fur felt wonderful against her chilled skin. Annulled for nonconsummation; she had never before had a marriage dissolved for that reason. Oh, the ways a man could find to leave his wife; would that a wife could find even one path of escape.

She watched him, Rowland the Dark who had extensive lands in Aquitaine. He was young, titled, a favorite of the king, and, perhaps, virile. As to virile, she would apparently not be able to answer that question tonight, but such a man would want heirs. Yea, any man would want heirs to carry on his legacy, build upon his wealth, add renown to his name.

She could give no man heirs.

She could give her body, but she could not give life.

Before her stood a man who would not take one without the other.

Was it an honorable act and was he an honorable man? She neither knew nor cared. What cared she for a man's honor? A man's honor served men, not women.

So he spoke of knowing her better. What did that mean, as a practical matter?

"Where would you start, my lord?" she asked.

"What?" he said, seeming startled.

Nicolaa smiled and tried to appear demure instead of smug. He was a man: all action and little thought. Or rather be it said, all ambition and no heart. But she was not dismayed that this new husband of hers had proved himself to be so firmly a man. He proved his sex; she could not fault him.

"Would you speak?" she said. "Tell me of your life, for I can promise my own tale would well prepare you for sleep. Shall I dress? Would you remain here or would the hall better suit your desire for . . . intimacy?"

After a moment of stillborn shock, he spoke. "Let us remain here, and as to your dress, I leave it for you to decide."

So he would have them remain here, without witnesses. None would know that the marriage had not been consummated, not yet. She did not understand his game, but she knew well the outcome. She would not long be married to Rowland the Dark.

"Then I will dress," she said.

She slipped out of the high bed, her bare feet cold on the wide-planked floor. Her nakedness was blatant in the shadowed room; this she knew, and half wondered if he would change his mind about the type of intimacy he sought with her tonight.

Her bliaut hung on a peg set into the stone wall, and she slipped it over her head quickly, eager to be covered, uncomfortably aware that he had a fine view of her backside. Yea, she pulled it on quickly—and found her hand twisted within the sleeve. The more she pushed, the tighter the tangle. She was trapped, with her body bared from the waist down.

If he did not change his mind about consummating the marriage, he would be a very odd sort of warrior.

She felt his nearness as vividly as she felt the chill on her exposed flesh. She stopped struggling and was appalled by the pounding of her heart. There could be no room for fear or trepidation in her; she had done this too many times, her body bared to a stranger's touch and a stranger's eyes and a stranger's whim. She knew she had no choice but to submit to whatever this man, this husband, did. She knew well her place in the divine order of the world and its heavens.

She slowed her breathing by conscious will. And waited.

A hand upon her arm, a twist of fabric, and all fell free. The fabric closed about her like armor, shielding her.

A quick intake of breath, a sign of her relief, and then her eyes darted upward to his. His eyes were black, his lashes so thick and long as to be tangled at the tips. His scars were gentle in this light, mere traces, cobweb thin and silver-white against the brown of his skin. A warrior's face, yet . . . gentle. Gentle? Nay, 'twas too soon to know his character.

Time would prove what he was.

She could almost learn to hope for gentleness. Gentleness was a ghost, ethereal, ungrasped. The hand on her arm was a warrior's hand, the scars a warrior's scars. The muscles that thickened his shoulders and neck and wrist were those of a warrior's battle-hardened body. He was hard, beaten.

Nay, not beaten. Whence came these strange thoughts? *From somewhere behind his eyes.*

He had such beautiful eyes, so dark and . . . shuttered. He was hiding something behind those carefully blank eyes, some knowledge, some secret.

It did not matter. He would be gone, a memory, before long.

He looked down at his hand upon her arm and she looked down as well, to see what he saw. A brown hand upon the white of a woolen bliaut. His hand was large against her arm, threatening. He loosed his hand from her and still she watched that hand. Watched as it hovered, trembling, near her breast. Watched as it moved toward her body. She held herself still, but for the pounding of her heart. He was near and he was going to touch her. He had the right, aye, but more, she found she wanted it. Wanted his touch, wanted to know the heat of this man who wore his devotion to his wife like a shield, bright and impenetrable. What would it be like to be possessed by such a man, even for an instant? Even for the space of a single touch?

His hand, so large, so dark, touched her breast with the lightest of caresses. She did not move. She did not look up to see his face. She only watched his hand as it molded itself to the small softness of her breast. Her heart pounded, rattling against her chest, and she made herself breathe against the heat of his hand.

The Willing Wife

With a softly voiced moan, some name, some word, he closed the distance between them and lifted her face for a kiss. It should have been a gentle kiss. It should have been nothing more ardent than the kiss of peace he had bestowed upon her mere hours ago. Yet it was nothing like. She fell into the kiss with all the startled abandon of a chick falling in first flight. And she flew.

Her arms wrapped around him, holding fast and hard to the heat of him, he who could stay true to the memory of a woman when all other men could not hold to the hand of a wife. She held him, pressing into him, wanting the feel of him to push into her very bones, forming itself to her, never leaving her.

Never leaving her.

He pressed into her, into her soft and soaring heat, as if he would never leave her. He did not want to leave her, not even for the space of a breath. She was light and slight and burning with sudden passion, and she had caught him up with her, taking him away from the firm ground of Lubias and his devotion to her. It could not be. He could not leave Lubias in the space of a single, yearning kiss.

But he could not yet leave her, this Nicolaa who wrapped herself around him, reaching into his heart with every breath into his mouth and every stroke of her tongue. She was fire, soaring and bright, flying into the dark sky, and he could only find the will to follow her, flying blind and lost, tumbling with every beat of his heart away from Lubias.

It could not be. He was more a man than that. No mere kiss would turn him from his vow of honor to his beloved Lubias. No matter the yearning heat of this woman's hands in his hair and on his neck. Lubias would not be sold for so paltry a price as a single, mistaken kiss.

He pushed her from his arms and made himself take a step back from her. She swayed and blinked eyes dark with rising passion. Even now she called to him, her fiery hair twining toward him, seeking to entangle him. With a rumbled cough, he clasped his hands behind his back and turned from her.

She took a full, soft breath, crossed her arms over her breasts in cautious patience, and waited.

"My lord? You would speak with me?" she asked when the silence between them had grown overlong.

He jerked and turned to face her, and she could read the shadow images of guilt on his face. Guilt? When she was the one who had thrown the lessons of a decade to the floor with a simple touch upon her breast? Let them both forget what had transpired, then. It caused them both nothing but ill feeling. He did not want her; he had made that plain. His shoving her from him had spoken more loudly than any words of wanting to see her smile. He had his plan—to annul. He would not risk it for a single tumble with a woman with common experience of tumbling.

"Weregrave is a fine holding," he said, his voice slightly husky. He had said as much before. It did not make for interesting conversation.

"Thank you," she said, keeping her arms crossed against him.

"Does it compare well with your other holdings?"

He would talk of her worth now, when his lips were still moist with the legacy of her kiss? Now, when he had thrown her from him like a shattered lance, splintered and raw with the breaking? Aye, he would speak of her wealth, for what else mattered? Not a kiss, not a touch, not the trammeling of her torn dignity. Nicolaa of Cheneteberie was only land and tower and rents. She had nothing to give him beyond her earthly wealth. He wanted nothing else. She would give him nothing else.

"By what means would you have me make the comparison?" she asked. "By size, Taceham is the smallest, but Taceham is the most productive when compared size to size. By might, Soninges is the greatest, but by familial tenderness, Cheneteberie is the most important. For myself, Weregrave has always been my favorite for the people and the roll of the landscape. For formidability, Aldewurda must rank the highest, for her dark walls and cliffs. How would you then have me compare them, my lord? And how would you rank your estates in Aquitaine to those newly acquired in England?"

"I do not wish to talk about Aquitaine," he said, trying for calm in the face of her heat. "How old were you, Nicolaa, when you first wed?"

"I was fourteen, but I do not want to talk about my marriages," she said in kind. "How long have you been from Aquitaine?"

"I have nothing to say about Aquitaine. How long did your first marriage last?"

"Two years, but why did you leave the Aquitaine?"

"To walk in the Way of the Cross," he answered, his eyes not nearly as soft with tenderness and compassion as they had been earlier. In fact, he did not look compassionate in the least.

"And did you travel alone?" she asked.

The silence that followed that question was occupied solely by their hard stares. They had been engaged in battle, a battle of questions, and they were both equally aware of it.

"You know the answer to that," Rowland said with an effort at gentleness.

"And you know the answers to all that you have asked of me," she said.

He took a breath and lowered his gaze, turning from her to walk to the taper and back. When he was near the door, he leaned against it, arms crossed, his expression calm.

"I only wanted to talk," he said.

"Then talk of your own past, not of mine," she said, and then she took a calming breath of her own, trying to match him in reasonableness. "Or talk not of the past. Tomorrow is all that matters."

He stayed on his side of the room, the bed between them.

"Tomorrow I leave."

"Yea, I know it," she said.

"And care not," he said with a wry smile. "Or perhaps anticipate it greatly?"

"I know well where your duty lies," she said. She held herself very still; he could not know the workings of her mind so well, not after spending so little time with her.

"To the king," he said.

"Aye, to the king."

"And your duty, Nicolaa? Where does your duty lie?"

"Here, in Weregrave, waiting," she said. Waiting had become an acquired skill. She was quite adept at it now.

Chapter Eight

He left the hour after dawn, his men with him. She had risen with him, a dutiful wife, slept chastely beside him during the night, knelt beside him at the mass, waved him off as he rode through Weregrave's gates.

Now she was through with him.

A most pleasant marriage, and the shortest.

She was completely certain the two facts were connected.

She would have made haste to depart Weregrave for Soninges to avoid his return to her side for as long as possible, a method she had perfected in her marriage to Hugh, if she had not been completely certain he would never return to her.

He was back within the week.

She knew she had seen secrets in his eyes. There was nothing more annoying than an unpredictable husband, unless it was one who was constantly underfoot. Worse still, he had brought guests.

"Oh, look, he has brought guests," Perette said, her voice joyous with anticipation.

They stood in the bailey, the hall a stalwart and familiar weight at their backs. The wind was mild, the sky heavy with low cloud, the promise of rain in the air—an autumn day like any other. Except that it had brought her fifth husband back to her.

As before, he had come after the meal had been served, eaten, and cleared. Nicolaa sighed in suppressed irritation; another break in her ordered and calm routine, and Rowland was again responsible for it. It was a husband's way, she knew, to create household disturbance. Worse, they never did seem to realize it.

"He's brought a woman with him," Jeanne said, her tone somewhat sharp. Did she suspect that he had brought his mistress into Weregrave? It was possible, but Nicolaa did not think it in this husband to be so blatantly unfaithful.

"Lord William is missing," Blanche said. Lord William was a man to miss, and Blanche the woman to most note it.

"I wonder who she is?" Perette said. "Her hair is wondrous dark, is it not?"

Yea, wondrous dark and heavily waved, unlike Nicolaa's own tight red curls. What man would not prefer the deep riches of black when faced with harsh red hair?

They rode into the bailey, and Rowland dismounted without a word of welcome or of cheer. She did not expect such from him in any regard. Richard was with him, as was Edmund, yet no word was spoken. Only the woman seemed eager to be at Weregrave.

She sat her horse well, with delicate precision, her hands

calm and capable upon the reins of her mount. Her skin was white and without blemish; Nicolaa thought of the three freckles upon her right hand and the two upon her left and crossed her hands against the sight, left hand over right. A lovely woman of bright countenance, small in stature and in form, with a graceful tilt to her head. A beauty by any measure.

If she was Rowland's mistress, he had fine taste in the women of his choosing.

Leaving his horse with a groom, Rowland walked toward her, and she met his eyes as he came. If he thought to shame her, he was going to find himself mistaken. Let him bring his woman. She could bear it and more.

He came to her, his walk loose and easy, his expression well matched to his gait. He was a tall man, and powerful, with the easy strength and stamina of a wolf loping along the edges of the wood. He had the gaze of a wolf as well, eyes that missed nothing and surveyed all with quiet intensity. He looked a man who killed without hesitation and with no small measure of joy. Aye, a predator. She would share her bed with a predator. Her blood grew sluggish in her veins, yet still it flowed, giving her life. She would survive even a dark predator in her life. He would not defeat her.

Eyes of blackest brown studied her and she met his look, her regard as calm and composed as a woman in repose upon her bed. He would find no weakness in her; this she knew. Any pain she felt at his bringing of another woman into her domain he would never see. He was no one who could hurt her; he was only a husband, and this husband had made his will clear. He did not want her. He did not want a wife, though it was in him to want a woman. Aye, she understood that well enough after their single, searing kiss. He might want a woman, but he did not want her. It suited her well, as she did not want him.

He stopped before her. She did not move.

He did not speak. Neither did she.

An odd reunion with no greeting or comment to mark it.

"You did not think I would return so soon," he said after a silence awkwardly protracted.

"Not at all," she said, telling the literal truth, yet knowing how he would misread the words. A husband was a simple thing to manage.

"Not so soon or not at all?" he asked, his mouth curving up into the merest of smiles.

Her expression froze upon her face. She could feel the shock rising within her. A perceptive man? Could there be aught worse in the world than a perceptive husband?

Aye. One who was annoyingly underfoot.

"I did not think that even you, a known lover of battle, would have run out of wars," she said, her own smile in place.

"Having gained a wife, I must learn to be more selective," he said.

"If you think to compliment me, you have missed the mark," she said softly.

"You did not think I would return?" he asked, stepping nearer to her so that she felt a catch in her breath. "I will always return to you, Nicolaa. Have I not taken a vow before God? Where else would I go?"

"You are a warrior first, husband," she said. "Are there not battles in Wales to occupy you?" She would not mention the dark woman at his back; she would not think of how he could occupy himself with her for hour upon hour with only the fire and their passion to light them.

"There will always be battles, Nicolaa, and I must do as God made me and fight where and when He wills. But when the fighting is over, it is to you that I will come. I can do no other."

Aye, for now and for his duty. But his heart . . . his heart lay not with her.

His heart? What foolishness he caused to rise up in her. He had no heart beyond the function of his will and his way. There was no place for a woman in a man's dark and ambitious heart.

Turning to her guests, she said, "Welcome again to Weregrave. But I see that the company has shifted. You have lost a knight and squire and gained a lady of rare beauty."

"My wife, Isabel, Lady Nicolaa," Richard said as Isabel came forward and kissed Nicolaa on both cheeks. A wife for Richard. Nicolaa took an inward breath and felt her spine relax. An explanation in keeping with what she knew of her husband. 'Twas no mistress he had brought to stand beside her.

"She would not remain behind in Dornei when she learned of Rowland's marriage," Richard added with something of a glower. As his wife ignored his look, Nicolaa did as well.

"You know very well I would not stay behind those walls when Rowland's bride awaited me," Isabel said. "Even Rowland knows me well enough to have made that prediction; is that not so, Lord Rowland?"

Rowland smiled and tipped his head at her. "I know that you will go where you will go, and that none but the bravest would seek to hinder you."

"Or the most stubborn," Isabel said with a smile, looking at Richard.

Richard frowned severely at his wife, who responded by grinning broadly. Nicolaa did not know Richard well enough to say if he was either brave or stubborn, but he was easily named a most indulgent husband. Nicolaa silently wished Isabel joy in this, no doubt her first, marriage. She prayed that all Isabel's subsequent husbands treated her so fondly.

"Yet where are Lord William and his amorous squire?" she asked. She, as well as all the world, knew that Rowland and William were rarely separated.

"Gone to Greneforde," Rowland answered, removing his helm and mufflers. His hair was sweat-damp and curled about his ears. He had the look of a warrior and it moved her not at all. "He will arrive later with his wife, Lady Cathryn. She will want to wish us joy on our nuptials."

Such fuss over a wedding she could hardly credit, but she held her tongue. The flush of first marriage was upon them all; a fifth marriage was little cause for remark.

Nicolaa shook off her thoughts and made the introductions between the ladies of her house and Lady Isabel. Her ladies came eagerly forward, happy at the prospect of a new voice among them. Who could tell what information Isabel would bring? Who could know what tales she had within her to tell? A fresh, feminine voice would always be welcome among them.

"I am so pleased to be here, Lady Nicolaa," Isabel said. "To see Rowland wed is a gift few expected to see in this life. For you both, I am filled with joy. For each of you, my prayers of thanksgiving will ascend."

The Willing Wife

"Thank you," Nicolaa said. A warm response for so simple a thing as a marriage, but then Isabel was young.

They left the men behind and, as a body, walked across the bailey. The weather was lowering, the sky the color of pearl, misty and damp. The tower rose before them, indistinct in the cool fog, coloring all it touched the soft silver-gray of newly forged steel. It would be an early dusk. The sun, even now, could do no more than light the mist to gray. As darkness fell, all would soften swiftly to impenetrable black. An early dusk and a husband to share the night with. Nicolaa sighed lightly and led her guest to the room Isabel and her husband would occupy.

As they skirted the edge of the hall, Isabel said, "What a wonderful hall, Lady Nicolaa. So spacious and so serene. Your tapestries are the stuff of legend."

"Thank you," Nicolaa said again. Could she think of no more gracious response? She could not. Her hall was lovely, her tapestries impressive. What more was required of her by courtesy and hospitality than a heartfelt thank-you?

The ladies talked among themselves as they climbed the tower stair, Isabel's voice the most vibrant, the most enthusiastic. Perhaps a trifle too loud? Well, she *was* young.

Nicolaa led the way into the small chamber that would house Isabel and her husband. It was a fine chamber, the mortar tight and the stones well set; the wind hole faced the west and the river that bordered Weregrave. The land between tower and river had been cleared, but the land beyond the river was deep woodland, shadowy and mysterious in the mist. The river wound black and turbulent in the sunless sky, glimmering only when wounded by submerged rock.

Isabel's satchel was placed on the bed, a sturdy bed with a red woolen blanket and a fox fur coverlet. All was well within the chamber; there was no reason to stay. She had no great curiosity to hear whatever Isabel might say. When her marriage to Rowland ended, her connection to his friends would end with it. That was a truth she had learned well. Better to keep herself to herself, her heart and her privacy guarded against random and fleeting intimacies. With a soft farewell, Nicolaa turned to go, taking her ladies with her. Let Isabel have her privacy for the moment. Only Blanche was left behind to help her settle in and to answer any questions Isabel might have.

But Isabel had no questions; she had only tales to tell and an eagerness to tell them.

"You are newly married?" Blanche asked.

"It shows, I know, but I wager that I will look as proud and as pleased in a decade as I do today," Isabel said.

"If true, it is a rare gift," Blanche said, sitting on the edge of the bed, smoothing the thick fox with her fingers.

"It is true," Isabel said, sitting on the opposite side of the bed, drawing her knees up under her skirts. "And it is a rare gift, but such is Richard to me. A gift most precious, most desired. To be his wife was my earnest and hopeless prayer."

"Can any prayer be hopeless?"

"Nay, you will not hear so from me, for God and Saint Stephen gave me Richard. For all my life I wanted him, and now I have him," she said, her hazel eyes glittering with humor and joy.

"You have a tale in you," Blanche said with a smile. "Tell it."

Isabel needed no more prompting than that to speak of Richard. "I first knew Richard in our fostering. He was a likely lad even then, and he passed by the awkwardness of youth with a bare glance to mark his passing. Tall and dark, solemn and devout, he undertook his knight's training with single-minded joy. I watched him. Oh, it sounds mild," she said, "but I *watched* him. He could not lift his sword but I was there to smile and clap my pleasure at his prowess. He knew—how could he not?—that I was enamored of him, but I was betrothed to his brother, eldest son to only daughter. Our houses were linked, yet he and I were as far apart as two souls can be."

"And his brother?"

"Dead, it did befall, and then the second in line of that house died within the month, and there it came to be that Richard, novice monk at the abbey of Saint Stephen and Saint Paul, was given to me. The contracts were preserved and Richard wed Isabel."

"A novice monk?"

"Aye," Isabel said, nodding. "Bishop, overlord, and king agreed that the match between our houses must be met. And so it was. Joyously for me, who was given what I wanted most and yet knew could never be."

"And your Richard, was he content to leave the abbey, he who had trained as a knight?"

"Better be it said that he was dutiful, but he is content now." Isabel grinned, the face of a woman fully and confidently in love. A rare sight upon a woman's face.

"A novice monk," Blanche said softly, playing with the fur. "And how is it to be married to a monk?"

Isabel laughed. "He is no monk."

103

Blanche laughed with her, the sound sweetening the cold stone of the chamber.

"Now, a tale for a tale. What tale is in you, Lady Blanche?" Isabel asked.

"Not such a tale as yours, I fear," she said. "Only of a damsel and a betrothal. No monk to spice up the stew."

"Tell it," Isabel said, smiling, leaning on her elbow, her eyes showing her eagerness.

"I was fearful to be wed, yet ready to be wed," Blanche said. "The betrothal was sound, our portions well matched, my betrothed of a good age to take a wife. I of a good age to be a wife."

Blanche was silent after that, plucking at the fur, her brow thoughtful.

"And?" Isabel prompted gently.

"And after four years of marriage, my husband died of a tooth gone foul."

"I am sorry."

"As I," Blanche said. "In our four years, we shared a bed for eight months altogether."

It was the way of things. A man, a fighting man, was needed elsewhere, wherever the king called. There had been many years of war, and King Stephen had called upon his followers often.

"I have been a widow for two years now and would marry again," Blanche said, lifting her eyes to Isabel's. "My family has made no arrangements for a betrothal. It is feared I am barren. I am certain I am not."

Isabel met her look, the knowledge of what was being shared and the sympathy of one woman to another passing freely between them.

The Willing Wife

"You did not achieve your pleasure?" Isabel asked.

"Nay, I did not. By God's own design there can be no child without it. With another man . . . I think I could . . ."

"It is the man who makes the difference, I am convinced," Isabel said. Could she have achieved her pleasure with any other but Richard? She could not. And without the release of her seed, no child could come. "You wish to marry?"

"Aye, I do wish it," Blanche said almost on a whisper.

"I will help," Isabel said. "At the very least, Rowland is a favorite of the king and could put your name forward. For myself, I have found prayer to be the surest course, but we must pursue all courses to betrothal. We will see you married."

"It would be nigh to blasphemy to pray for a husband in Nicolaa's house when she is so unwillingly awash in them," Blanche said with a wry chuckle.

"How say you?" Isabel said, sitting up sharply on the bed.

Blanche slid off the bed, silently cursing her loose tongue. Her own secrets she might tell, but of Nicolaa's grief she could not speak.

"Idle words that betray my own fear of never again making a match," Blanche said, straightening the bedding, turning from Isabel.

"Did you not say that Nicolaa was unwillingly wed?"

Blanche locked her lips against her wayward tongue and stared at Isabel, willing an end to this conversation.

Isabel nodded, accepting that this was a tale she would not be told. "I believe that Nicolaa, with Rowland as her husband, cannot fail to thrive."

Holding her tongue against speaking her thoughts, Blanche walked away from Isabel. She held her tongue, but

105

the thought would not die: Nicolaa would always thrive, but it was not because of her husbands, but rather, in spite of them.

Rowland did not expect to find Nicolaa in their bedchamber, yet she entered just after him. He had thought to disrobe and to wash the grime from his face and hands before facing her again, and now she stood before him, servants lugging water for a bath right behind her.

"You are too aware of the company I keep," he said with a smile of greeting, "but it is William who requires a daily bath, not I."

The men halted in their pouring of the water into the standing tub near the fire, looking to him and to Nicolaa, waiting for word as to the destination of the water. It had taken long to heat; it must be used quickly or 'twould cool.

"You have been many days gone," she said. "I thought it would please you, but it can easily be taken to our guests."

"Nay, you thought well. I could use a dousing," he said, not wanting to turn aside this unexpected gift of hers, wanting to welcome her in any way he could. "Will you stay?"

"I will stay and assist, if you wish," she said calmly.

The water was poured in at once by two servants, eager to be about their errand. There was more water yet waiting in the kitchens. This Rowland knew, yet Nicolaa and her calm regard dominated his eyes and his thoughts.

She did all calmly and with the quiet intent to please him. Worthy traits in a wife, yet he could not be at ease around her. He distrusted the image of her. Rowland had learned long ago to trust his impressions, knowing the instinct at the heart of them to be true and pure. He could not ignore them now. He did not fear betrayal or harm from her—nay, not that—yet he knew that the woman he saw was a façade hiding the woman beneath. His pricking of her composure when last they were alone had been unintentional yet instructive. She had a hurt that went deep.

He would heal her.

'Twould give some purpose to this mock marriage. At least he could give Nicolaa a safe and secure place in a world that had treated her coldly. A man could do no less for a woman in need, and Nicolaa of Cheneteberie seemed to be in need most deep.

Yet here she was, calmly preparing to disrobe him and bathe him, a husband who was still strange to her. Except for that one sordid, stolen kiss a week past. He had not meant to touch her. He had seen her nudity, her pearly skin, her small breasts puckered against the chill of the room, and he had thought only to hide all that from his eyes. He had wanted her covered, aye; he had helped her to cover herself against him. Yet when he had been close, when he had smelled the scent of her hair and seen the dark and vivid blue of her eyes through the spikes of her light lashes, when he had seen the pulse of her heart in her slender throat, he had been touched.

Touched? He had been burned. He was still red and blistered from that burning, his guilt at his betrayal of Lubias the surest means of dousing that fire. He was cool now. He could be in the same room with Nicolaa, even to the taking of a bath, and not fear that he would stumble into the fire again. Nay, Lubias he held in a firm grip, his touch upon her memory warm and safe. He had only to find a way to soothe Nicolaa and any fear she felt for the stranger in her room. Even now he could feel her fear, leashed tight, yet panting for release all the same. A simple solution: let her bathe him now. 'Twould be a simple way to get past the awkwardness when neither party was much ripe for touching.

"Thank you," he said, decided. "Have you the strength to assist with the mail? You have the appearance of fragility."

"Appearance only," she said, standing on the stool to reach above his head. "There is little I cannot do. Or have not done."

"I well believe it," he said, his voice muffled as the mail was lifted from him. "You are strong," he said when the mail shirt had been removed. She dropped it to the ground with a huff of breath. The quilted wool of his gambeson was more damp than dry; he pulled it off himself, his muscles stretching as he pulled it over his head. Bare to the waist, he stood next to the tub and looked at her.

She matched him look for look, without a tremor; with her fair coloring he would have seen the slightest blush. Her skin stayed white.

"What else do you appear that you are not?" he said softly, studying her.

"I cannot answer as to how I appear to you. I only know what I am."

"And what are you?" he asked.

"Married."

She did not say it gladly. He could hardly fault her.

"As am I," he said with a soft smile. "We have that in common at least."

"And more besides," she said as he sat to remove his braes.

Nicolaa knelt before him and helped him with his shoes, her head bent to her self-appointed task.

Her hair was curly to the root and darker there, a bright auburn when paired against the sharp yellow-orange of the tips. Nothing like Lubias's hair.

"We are the holders of great estates," she said, continuing their conversation of similarities.

He would join her; it was a conversation that would help to bind them, he thought.

"We answer to the same king," he said.

"We marry at his will."

"We fight at his command."

"We travel when he calls."

She had removed his shoes and sat smiling up at him, her smile a gentle one and full of humor. He returned the smile. Their camaraderie was shared and easy, a welcome change.

He stood and, still smiling, she slid his braes down his legs without hesitation or shyness. Well, she had known four husbands before him. What did he expect? Virginal agitation? Maidenly blushes? Nay, he had not had such even from Lubias; he did not want it from Nicolaa. Keeping his smile in place, he stepped into the tub.

"Is there any portion of your life that is not first touched by King Henry?" he asked, enjoying the heat of the water after hours spent in the damp chill of an autumn day. Perhaps William's devotion to the bath was understandable, after all. He would think of battle and William and Lubias. He would not think of red hair and white skin and blue eyes. He would not think of her touch upon his skin. He would not think of that.

Nicolaa soaped his shoulders vigorously, and he could

not help sighing in pleasure. The soap had no scent; good Weregrave soap, not the scented stuff William collected.

"There is my embroidery," she said, her mouth just above his right ear, urging an unwilling shiver from him. He shook off the sensation and thought about her words.

Her embroidery. She would treasure it, the hours spent on her embroidery, this one piece of her life not controlled by king and the duties of her station.

"A most beautiful . . . freedom," he said softly, yet she reacted hard, like the strike of mace against shield. She stared into his eyes, her eyes so wide and unshuttered that for just a moment he saw . . . fear? anger? . . . and then she dipped her head and attacked his body with the soap.

"And where do you find your freedom, my lord?" she asked as she scrubbed, the sleeve of her gown wet through. "Nay, do not answer. I know."

"I do not seek freedom—"

"Aye, you do, and find it, in short measure. In battle."

She sat back on her heels, setting the soap on the hearth, studying him, her look now confident and . . . victorious.

In battle, she said, and she had the meat of it well in her teeth. The sounds, cries, blows of battle. The grunting, the sweat, the thud of horses, and ring of steel. The blood. The pain. Death riding so hard upon him that he could feel alive for just an instant, instead of this half twilight he lived in without Lubias. The world had gone dark without Lubias to light it. He was nearly blind without her.

Yet even in the half dark that had been his world for year upon year, he could see the bright light of Nicolaa in the darkness, like a single candle in a raging storm. Her sharp beauty pursued him even now as he thought of corpses and souls on their way to purgatory; even now she pushed Lubias from him with a careless hand and left him bare and wanting, his rising need more damning than any unconfessed sin. He was losing, he who never knew loss or defeat. He was losing his battle to not feel the lure of Nicolaa, to not feel at all.

He would never say even half as much to Nicolaa.

"What is it like? In battle?" she asked quietly.

Severed arms, headless corpses, broken bones smeared with bright blood, mud, and torn grass. The images burst upon his mind, pushing aside the image of Lubias until he grasped with empty fingers and found Nicolaa, but his tongue said, only, "Noisy. It is loud."

He ducked his face into the water to rinse himself, avoiding her, if the truth be told. He commanded his body to obedience, and, warrior-strong, his body obeyed. He would not foul Lubias with unholy desire for another woman. He had only one wife and her name was Lubias. Nicolaa he would help, as God had intended, but Lubias was his flesh and his bone. He would not cut her from him. When he opened his eyes, Nicolaa waited with the cloth to dry him.

There was nothing seductive about her touching of him. She wiped him, her hands skimming over his skin. If she noted the length of his limbs or the bulge of his muscles, she did not let it slow her in her task. She attended to the matter at hand and dried him thoroughly. That she was close to him, that he could feel a strand or two of her hair on his belly as she bent to his legs, that she smelled of lavender and applewood when she stood against him to dry his chest, that she did not flinch in shyness when she looked into his eyes; all this he ignored. He did not want to seduce Nicolaa. She did not appear to desire seduction.

Another false impression that had no foundation in truth? He did not know. Yet.

"Embroidery is very quiet," she said when he was dry. "We differ in that, at least."

"We differ in more than that," he said, standing naked before her.

What was it about her that pricked him? He did not know. He knew only that as he sought for peace between them and understanding, she stood ever a pace off, out of reach. Untouched by his desire to help her. Untouched by his desire. Amused by him. She had such a look about her, her eyes upturned with a sardonic and knowing glint, her finely drawn mouth shadowed with the memory of a smirk. He had come to save her by his constancy and she was amused by him.

She stood so now, the damp linen in her pale hands, her long hair a twirling tumble of red down her back, her eyes the fierce and steady blue of a distant sky. Slender, tall, her curves long and fine, she stared at him, her eyes not leaving his face. What did she see? He was Rowland the Dark of Aquitaine; women all across the continent sighed at the whisper of his name. His devotion to Lubias was inviolate, but still the women came, wanting to see the man who had loved so well, wanting to win the heart of the man who would not be won. He knew it was so. He had been told countless times by countless lovely mouths just how desirable he was. How unattainable. And now he was here, with Nicolaa of Cheneteberie. She had attained what fivescore women had not. How did she see him? Did she know the gift she had been given? Did she tremble in thankfulness or fear? She had had four husbands before him; how did the man before her eyes seem to her?

He knew how she seemed to him.

She was the tallest, most narrow taper topped by the brightest flame: fiery red and hot blue atop the purest beeswax candle. Slender, breakable, aye, but untouchable for the flame that defined her.

The beauty of her features, the delicacy of her brow, the soft brown of her lashes tipped in lightest gold, the gentle bow of her pale lips, the tiny tip of her flawless nose, these he would not name, for they did not compare to Lubias and her heartier, darker beauty. Lubias was the measure of all women, and Nicolaa was in no way like his Lubias. But Lubias was shadow, and Nicolaa, with her impossibly blue eyes, was before him, real and warm and within reach. Lubias held his heart, but Nicolaa was just a step away.

He felt himself rise in response to Nicolaa and her steady stare. That blue-eyed stare, as steady as the purest candle on the most still of nights. What did she see?

She saw him rising toward her, steady and firm as granite.

She did not turn or blush, not her; she merely kept staring into his eyes and folded the linen sheet in her hands, her manner casual, her tongue still, and her eyes unmoving.

She did not care. She did not care that he rose to her in rejection of Lubias.

With his next breath, he sank and shriveled, his shame and her disregard the quickest route to normalcy. Decency. Constancy.

"I suppose so," she said to his comment. His own irritation rose up hard and overtook him.

"You have had four husbands before me and I only one wife," he said, showing her the depth of their difference.

He was accusing her and he did not know why. She was

113

not at fault for having had four husbands and now five. She had had no word in the decisions. Yet his anger could not be denied.

Nicolaa looked at him defiantly, a small smile on her lips, the linen folded across her arms. "Yea, I have had four husbands. Four men have come before you, my lord," she said, and he heard the taunt in the words. Four husbands had known her, touched her, possessed her. She wanted him to know it and to remember it. "Yet we have both been married before; we do share that. We know what is expected of us and do as our king requires, though the kings come and go."

He could feel her answering anger, a hot pulse, though kept within the narrow bounds of candle flame. He could not fault her and would not. He had pricked her and could not even to himself explain his reasoning. He knew only that he did not want either her anger or his own. Anger was too hot an emotion, and he wanted only cool cordiality between them. He wanted to give her peace in an unpeaceful world; that would be his service to her. And if she softened at his gift, if she melted under his care and found herself half in love with the husband God had chosen for her, then he would not object. His own heart belonged to Lubias, but Nicolaa's heart . . . her heart should be given to her husband, as was right. He was Rowland the Dark and he would win her heart. Yea, he would be content with nothing less. She would know how great a gift she had been given, and her heart would rise up in thanks for the day Rowland had joined his life to hers.

It would not be an easy battle, for she guarded her heart almost as fiercely as he guarded his. Yet she was a woman; her very nature would compel her to submit to him. He was man and had no thought of losing this battle. He, who had won heart upon heart with no effort, would not lose when he was so determined to win. And was he not of Aquitaine, and had he not been born with words of gentle wooing on his tongue? Four husbands she had known, yet none like him, no matter the sharpness of her scorn.

"You are right," he said. "We have much in common."

She had told him much, though it was raw knowledge that he had no wish to swallow. She did not want to be married to him any more than he wanted to be married to her.

He had not thought she would not want him; never in his thoughts of Nicolaa had he thought that. Well, that would change. It was well within his power to teach her to want him.

Nicolaa brushed the moment aside as easily as she set aside the linen.

"Do you require aid in dressing?"

She said it simply, without shyness or sulkiness. Why did he feel that she would rather be anywhere but in his company?

"Nay, I am sufficient to the task," he said, and then he smiled. He had come because she needed him, whether she knew it or not. He would teach her to know it. He had come to teach her much.

She smiled in return, a cold and contained smile.

"Until the meal, then," she said, and departed.

He stood and watched the movement of the dark curtain that shielded the door; it swung gently to mark her passing for a moment or two and then was still. He knew where she would spend the hours before the meal—in the solar with her embroidery and her shield of women. Finding freedom where she could.

Chapter Nine

They had been an hour at the fine demands of needlework. Isabel felt it was time enough to move on to other pursuits. Something that would take them out-of-doors. Something that would take them closer to the men. Where were the men? More specifically, where was Richard? He was not chained to the end of a needle and thread, that was certain.

"You have tangled your thread," Perette said with a smile. "Again."

"I have," Isabel said, fingering the thread, working loose the knot. Working a tangle was more enjoyable than sewing; she was thankful for even that small respite. And it showed.

"You do not engage in the pastime of embroidery at Dornei?" Blanche asked.

"Nay, not often." Not at all, but she could not say that so boldly; Nicolaa clearly enjoyed it and was skilled at it.

She would not belittle Rowland's bride even by chance.

"Small wonder," Jeanne said, looking at the mess that entangled her fingers. "You have better things to do with your eyes and with your hands with Richard as husband, do you not?"

Isabel laughed and gave up her fight with the thread. "I am a bride of mere months, do not forget. I choose his company over an embroidery needle with regularity."

"As well you should," Jeanne said on a laugh. "A virile man, if ever there was. Why shut yourself up with your needle when a lusty husband is within reach?"

"Mother," Agnes said in censure.

"Nay, she is right," Isabel said with an answering laugh. "I would spend my days—and my nights—with Richard. You must remember how it is to be newly wed?"

"Aye, I have not forgotten the joys a man can bring to a woman," Jeanne said. "My man was in his prime when Henry the first was on the throne. Good times, they were, with few battles to cloud the days. Still, he would go off and fight his fights, and I did not begrudge him his entertainments. A man must have his play. But when he came back"—Jeanne smiled and shook her head—"he found me waiting and willing to meet his lustiness. Nine children I had of him, only two living still. All gone from me now," she said, her eyes misty, "but it was a good life and he was a good man, and if God wants to leave me with only daughters, then God will enjoy His jest if I cannot."

"Thank you, Mother," Agnes said stiffly.

Jeanne patted her arm and said, "I mean no harm, girl, but a woman likes to leave a man on this earth behind her, to mark her place in it."

"The blessing of children is always welcome," Isabel said

into the general air of discomfort Jeanne's words had wrought.

"Aye, that is so," Agnes said. "Two born dead I have endured. Both boys. If there is a jest in that, I fail to see it."

"God will have His way," Nicolaa said, calming them all. "We cannot see His ways, as they are above our own, but do not tell me He laughs when children die. That is not His way from all we have been shown of His divine nature."

"True," Agnes said. "But I would have liked to have a child to hold and then to hold me when my days grew short and my hair gray."

"Humph, I would like to have a man to hold and a man to hold me as my hair goes silver," Jeanne said. "Is that not so, Isabel?"

"If the man be Richard, I could ask for nothing more," she said, "but can you not find another match? Cannot you all?" She looked at the circle of women. It was true that Jeanne was aged and gray, but Agnes might find a man looking for a wife, and the younger women were all of a ready age to make marriages. How that they were all clustered in the shadowed solar of Weregrave?

"I would be betrothed," Perette said, "but my father keeps negotiating for a better alliance. I wait patiently, but the wait grows long."

"A marriage can grow longer," Nicolaa said, her eyes on her thread and the movement of her hand. "Be patient still."

"I have no need for patience," Blanche said, "for no contract is being negotiated for me."

"Nor for me," Ermengarde said, "but I will not marry

beneath my station just for the sake of marrying."

Isabel then understood that Ermengarde's dowry was smaller than her pride and her place in the world. But why that should be so when Nicolaa had the means to gift her with wealth to match her ambitions, she did not understand.

"I am too old for marriages," Agnes said.

Isabel disbelieved her. Men were many and women few who were free to marry. A match could be arranged, if any made the effort.

"What of you, Beatrice?" Isabel asked. "You must have a betrothal contract?"

"Aye, I do," Beatrice said, keeping her eyes on her work, as did Nicolaa. "I but await my readiness to take on the obligations of a vast holding."

"You are wise to wait," Isabel said with a smile. "I was not ready and my holding suffered for it until I grew to the task. But for you all who are without betrothals, surely that can be remedied, and I will happily assist in that task."

"Thank you, but that is not necessary," Nicolaa said sharply, her head rising from her needlework, her blue eyes staring into Isabel's. "All is well in Weregrave. We are content."

Isabel had overstepped, that was clear, and she would take not one step farther, not today. For Perette and Beatrice, both betrothed, or nearly so, she would say nothing more to hurry them on the path to full marriage; she who had delayed her own arranged marriage to Richard's brother for as long as she dared could do naught else. For the others, she wished them well, but she could not imagine a celibate life attached to an embroidery needle a life

119

well lived. Still, Nicolaa was firm, and this was Nicolaa's domain. Isabel would hold her tongue.

Yet it was as clear as a cloudless night that Nicolaa was not happy with Rowland as husband. This she could not understand. Rowland was so deserving of joy and had been so cruelly robbed of it. Could Nicolaa not see that this was her chance to step into the hole left by Lubias? It was a role a willing wife would cherish.

Still, she held her tongue and labored on in her embroidery, the sounds of men in the bailey taunting her. How much longer would they stay within? The day was waning, the light failing, and she had spent most of the day indoors. She felt throttled.

A tale would pass the time. Aye, a tale to make them weep and to make Nicolaa understand the heart of the man now mated with her. Isabel smiled and laid down her needle.

"Would you hear a tale?" she said.

"Yea, tell us a tale," Perette said, slowing her stitches, her eyes twinkling in eagerness. Even Beatrice raised her head.

"Such a tale is rarely told," Isabel began, "because such men are rarely made. A man after God's own heart, such as David of the Israelites was in his day, so this man is today. This man Rowland d'Albret, Rowland the Dark, Rowland the Broken."

"Broken?" Ermengarde asked, her needle stilled.

"Broken, his heart and his spirit, though not his strength," Isabel said. "Broken for love of a woman."

"Aye, Lubias," Perette said.

"Lubias, you have said it," Isabel said. "Lubias, his bride. She loved him with a pure love, and, as is true of such love, he loved her in return. How could he resist? Though do not think that he did try. They had known each other long, betrothed from childhood, their fathers fast and true friends who wanted a fast and true love for their children. And so it was. Fast and true and long they loved. When they married, it was the culmination of a dream, and the dream was sweeter for its being real."

"What did she look like?" Blanche asked, her needle forgotten on the cloth.

"As dark as he, she was, her hair black and thick and shining, her eyes brown and deep with love, her bosom full and heavy, her brow arched, her foot small. A rare beauty out of Aquitaine, her mother distant kin to Queen Eleanor. She was raised in that court and learned the ways of women and of men. She was an accomplished lady of rare heart, her courage a match for the man who loved her. Courage she had aplenty, for is it not an act of courage to follow in the Way of the Cross when the Lord calls His servants to defend the land of His birth? Rowland would go, though he did not want to leave her. He was torn between his love for righteous war and his love for her; he could not choose and so she took the choice from him, following his path, ever at his side as he made his way south and east. As he made his way to the Holy Land of our Lord."

"And there she died," Beatrice said.

"Aye, she died, her body broken and blooded, her soul free, yet . . ."

"Yet?" asked Beatrice, her blue eyes unblinking.

"Yet though her soul ascended in God's perfect timing, yet her heart remains. Rowland carries her with him, their love as pure and as fast and as true as from the first. She lives, in her way, because he breathes life into her. She has not died because he holds her fast, her memory alive in him. Her love for him and his for her anchors her in this place. Lubias lives because Rowland will not let her go. It is a love beyond time and beyond death."

The silence held as long as their motionlessness; even Nicolaa had been caught by the tale. A log fell in the hearth, and the enchantment of legendary love that had fallen upon them all was broken.

"I do not believe it," Jeanne said. "I do not believe a man can be any more constant than the flopping of his cock." She laughed and shook her head at them all. "They cannot help being what they are."

"But what of Rowland?" Ermengarde said. "This is a tale oft told and well believed."

"Oft told and well believed are not the same," Jeanne said.

"If it were not true, all would know it soon enough," Blanche said.

"You have only to look into his dark eyes to see the truth of the tale," Perette said.

Perette was young and excessively romantic, but even Nicolaa found herself wondering, Could it be so? Could a man truly love beyond the bounds of his own self-interest? Could a man love at all?

She had once believed it to be so. When she was as young and untried as Beatrice, she had believed in love. Fed on tales not too different from this one, she had yearned for such a love to sweep her soul to heaven's gate. She had yearned, and then she had learned. Philibert, her first, had taught her the first of many lessons in how a man was fashioned, how differently God had rendered his parts, both external and internal. A man did not want the things a woman wanted; his paths to achieving his ends were not the paths a woman trod in this brief and earthly life.

And was Rowland not a man? Oh, aye, he was, and she could not forget it. Nay, and she would not. No matter the fineness of his form or the soft winsomeness of his smile or the tender passion of his kiss. It was nothing on which to dwell. All men kissed. All men rose in passion when the mood was upon them. All men were battle-hardened and -scarred to show their mettle. All men. He was as all men. He was no different.

He could not be different. She would not tumble into the false belief that he was different, despite the telling of a tale of pure and everlasting love for Lubias. But what a tale. What a tale of love it was.

Could it be true? Could a man—could Rowland—love?

Dusk was hours hence, the sky steely and heavy, the air sharp with the cold scent of water when Rowland and Richard, Edmund at their heels, rode through the gates of Weregrave. They were out to hunt stag, though Rowland's alternate purpose was to learn the lay of his land.

Father Timothy watched them leave, his robes flapping, the stone of the chapel a mighty weight at his back; all the power and authority of the church of God was in his manner. He nodded his farewell to them, and Rowland responded in kind. There was more to this priest than he yet knew, and Rowland was determined to learn more.

That he was tied in some way to Nicolaa he could feel, if not see. There was more to the man than his flapping robes. Of Nicolaa he had no doubts. She was not a woman to skulk and hide, and he did not think it in her to soil her soul by intruding between a man and his vows. Nay, what he sensed was all from the priest. Rowland could feel the surge of protectiveness rise in him. Nicolaa would not battle Father Timothy and his wayward desires alone.

They left the gray walls of Weregrave behind for the golden fields and yellow leaves of autumn. The wind snapped freely once they had escaped the confines of Weregrave's walls.

"I see in Father Timothy," Richard said softly, gently, "something I recognize. Something that should give you pause."

Rowland looked ahead, seeing the river sweeping through the brush, golden and russet and swaying in the brisk breeze. He would not compare the sight to Nicolaa's hair; such was the action of a lover. He was no lover. He had known no woman since Lubias, and so he had wanted it to remain. But a man must bed his wife or the marriage could be invalidated. Did Nicolaa think even now that he was plotting his way out of the marriage? Did she care?

She cared, though her manner denied it. No woman could be so used and not care.

Four men before him, she had said, and husbands all. All still living, having gotten out and gone their way with only priest, bishop, and king to shrug away their passing. Leaving Nicolaa ready for a new man, another husband, her property a compelling lure.

Even for a priest.

Softly, so that Edmund could not hear, Rowland said, "He desires her."

Richard cast him a hard glance. "Perhaps. I am not certain."

"I am," Rowland said, cutting him off, though his voice

was still soft. "I do not doubt her chastity. She would not stumble into that; her will is too strong to fall prey to unlawful passion. If Father Timothy yearns, he yearns alone. She is a woman to love, if a man be free to love."

But Father Timothy was not free; his life had been given to Christ. As for Rowland, he had given his life to Lubias long ago. He was not free; all the world knew that. He was not free, but he was a man worthy of her love and regard, though he could not return it. All the world knew that as well.

They returned to Weregrave just before dusk, the pack-horse laden with a prime stag of eleven points. The sun was not setting, not in this leaden sky, but the light was slowly fading from pearl to gray to black without even the stars to mark the coming of the night. Into the dusk rode William, with Cathryn at his side, Ulrich at his back. They met at the gate, each party seeking entrance to Weregrave before the black of full night fell upon them. It was a welcome meeting.

"You knew I would come," Cathryn said to him, her smile soft.

"It was only whether William would let you that was in question," Rowland answered with his own smile.

"There was no question as to that. What Cathryn asks, she receives, if it be in my power. And so I am in thrall to her. A sorry end to a brave beginning as a knight of some renown," William said, helping his wife to dismount.

"Perhaps you can find contentment in your renown as my thrall?" Cathryn said. "But we have not gathered to discuss you, William, much as that must dismay you. It is Rowland who has all my regard. How fare you with your new wife, Rowland?"

Of all, save William, Cathryn understood best what this marriage must mean to him. If she was concerned for him it was because her heart outsized the distant moon; she would worry, and he would not have it. Cathryn had borne too many worries in her life; let her be free of worry for Rowland.

"I am content," he said. "Nicolaa is a fine wife, a careful and diligent manager. See you Weregrave? This is her doing, her husbandry; any man would find her a most blessed gift. As do I."

Cathryn's brown eyes showed her surprise at his answer, but she said only, "A most fine holding, Rowland. May you be well blessed in Nicolaa."

Could it be that Rowland might come to love again? She prayed so. Rowland had carried the weight of his Lubias long enough; it was time to set her down so that they both could find rest.

The gates of Weregrave opened to them, and they entered, night falling behind them like the drawing of a curtain against a draft. Without a word from Rowland to direct his actions, a groom ran up the stair to the tower, and within moments the ladies of Weregrave spilled out to meet her. The lady of Weregrave was simple to identify. Tall and slender, her hair a torrent of red, her eyes the fierce blue of the sea, she offered Cathryn a warm and solemn welcome. A woman of self-reliance and of carefully managed strength was Cathryn's first impression, and she prayed it was true; she would need strength and independence to be married to Rowland, as he had so little to give a woman.

"Cathryn, I knew you would not be kept away from such

a joyous occasion," Isabel said, hugging her and kissing both cheeks.

"He did not even attempt to dissuade me," Cathryn said with a grin. And then to Lady Nicolaa, "It has been months since we have seen each other, if you will excuse our excess."

"It is hardly excess to show joy at reunion," Nicolaa said. "You are welcome here, Lady Cathryn. Your husband shares a bond with mine that is well known and oft told; I hope we may be friends as well."

"I am certain we will," Cathryn said, wanting it to be so.

The sky wept rain upon them, a slow and light soaking that merged with the growing darkness. With laughs and cries, the ladies hurried to the stair that would lead them to the protection of the hall. Isabel was the last of their number to ascend; Richard, at her back, whispered something to his wife, who grinned and ran up the last few steps eagerly enough. Cathryn did not think it was the rain that prompted her.

When all were inside, William came up to Cathryn, his eyes asking the question to which they both wanted an answer. She looked up into his beautiful face and smiled, shrugging her own indecision. They would say nothing, the chance of being overheard in the crowd of the hall too great, but their desire was the same: for Rowland to be content.

The hall spread upward and outward before her: a rich hall, with tapestries of amazing design and complexity, a surfeit of servants, an abundance of food, and a warmth that spoke well of the woman who made this tower her home. Of envy, Cathyrn felt none. She felt only joy that

Nicolaa had found safety in this world; it was a rare gift and always to be treasured, no matter where it was found, no matter how long it lasted.

They were seated and at their meal with an efficiency that also spoke well of Nicolaa. The meal was light, as was customary, though fine. The wine was sweet and clear, the cheese fresh and smooth, the bread warm and fragrant. Nicolaa had even arranged for apple tarts, a wonderful repast to end a chilly autumn day. The light was gone, the rain stealing away its last remnants. The air blew in from the wind holes cold and wet; the torches flickered delicately against the stone, the strong colors of the tapestries illuminated. The hall was crowded with tapestries, each one an intricate piece of exquisite needlework.

"I am in awe of your skill, Lady Nicolaa," Cathryn said, wiping her fingertips on the cloth, her meal finished. "I have never seen such tapestries, nor so many, and each so fine."

"I compliment you on your perseverance," Isabel said. "So many hours it must have taken."

Cathryn smiled and sipped her wine. All knew of Isabel's dislike of any indoor activity.

"Thank you," Nicolaa said, "but I can accept credit for neither skill nor perseverance. Needlework is a gift I give daily to myself."

"Aye," said Rowland at her side. "Lady Nicolaa is able to fully lose herself in her occupation."

With the slightest stiffening of her neck, Nicolaa said, "I would not say I lose myself, but rather find purpose in the hours spent with my needle and thread."

"To find and fulfill one's purpose is the greatest joy this

earthly life has to offer," Richard said, endorsing Nicolaa's statement.

"If that be so, I would hear of your life's purpose, husband," said Isabel. "Think carefully before you answer," she said with a glint in her hazel eyes and a sharp smile on her lips.

Richard smiled back, his smile wolfish and hard. "None know my purpose better than you, Isabel. Do not say you have forgotten so soon."

Isabel was kept from answering, which was certainly a blessing, by the interruption of Father Timothy.

"Our place and our purpose are set by God in divine order most perfect. This talk of finding one's purpose rubs wrongwise against the truth. To each man his station: king, bishop, priest, baron, knight. Each man's duty is clear from the moment of his birth."

He spoke the truth and it was a truth all knew well. Into the divine order of the world each man was born with a part he must play. The world was perfectly ordered, reflecting the order of heaven itself; to crash in rebellion against God's design was to rebel against God Himself. Only the damned followed such a path.

Into the stiffness of that remark, William asked, "Were you born in the abbey then, Father?"

"Nay, but I was given to the church as a child. I remember no other life. Nor do I long for such," Father Timothy said, his gray eyes solemn.

"You are twice blessed, Father," Nicolaa said, "in both knowing your path and finding it so readily to hand."

Rowland could sense Nicolaa's anger. He only waited to determine the cause. It was more than Father Timothy's heavy-handed entry into a jovial, if meaningless, conversation.

"You did not mention a woman's place in your celestial list of divine order," she continued, looking the priest full in the face. Father Timothy flushed slightly, but held her gaze. Rowland watched in fascination, learning more about Nicolaa with every word she uttered. "Will you not make your list complete, Father? What should be my purpose on this earth?"

Father Timothy looked as though he wanted to swallow his own rash tongue. He did not wish to say the words every one of them knew to be truth. The biblical mandate was clear, the church's position firm.

The agony of love in the priest's eyes was clear as he said, "If not to give your life in service to Christ—"

"Which I have not," she interrupted.

"Then to marry and produce children," he finished softly.

The hall trembled quietly at the words, Nicolaa's anger and frustration as palpable as the tapestries surrounding her.

"And failing that?" she said. "Will God forgive a life without purpose?"

Father Timothy could only stare at her, his pain at wounding her measurable.

"God judges the heart, Nicolaa," Rowland said, laying his hand on hers. "You have done all that has been asked of you."

Sliding her hand from beneath his, rejecting his comfort, she said lightly, "And produced tapestries."

"I would that I could work thread so fine," Cathryn said, compassion pouring out from her like water.

"I would that work of such beauty would miraculously

appear on the walls of Dornei," said Isabel. "I do not even dare to risk the prayer that I be given such skill for fear that God would attend my prayer and thereby require me to actually sew."

The hall broke into laughter, which Rowland knew had been her intent. Between Cathryn and Isabel, they had managed to turn the talk again to lighter concerns than a woman's inability to produce a child from her womb. Father Timothy let the conversation go its course, clearly sorrowful that his words had led to Nicolaa's pain.

Rowland had learned much of Nicolaa in that exchange. She held her hurt deep, yet it bit hard for all that. More, he had seen the sharp edge of her tongue and was not displeased by it. That she could fight and hold her place against the clumsy wounding of a tempted priest was all to the good. The careful and shrewd management of her holding now came into clearer light. No soft and mild woman could hold her possessions in so firm and solid a grasp. Nay, it would take the force of fire and the strength of stone to hold Weregrave and Cheneteberie and all the rest. Nicolaa had all of that, and he found the qualities pleasing, even admirable. Surely it was nothing more than admiration he felt when he watched her smile at Cathryn, her pale cheeks glowing in the firelight like precious pearl. Rowland cleared his throat and swallowed deeply of his wine, taking his eyes from her with the action. She was a wife he could leave for the duration of a war and know that all would be well on his return. A man could ask for naught else.

The meal proceeded pleasantly enough, Nicolaa's women mixing happily with Isabel and Cathryn, the sound of feminine voices strong in the hall. A strange occurrence in England, but one that put him in mind of Aquitaine, where intercourse between men and women of noble rank was considered the highest art. Queen Eleanor had been the most ardent patron of chivalry. Nicolaa had arranged something similar in her own domain. She had created a hall of women.

Once the meal was finished, the folk of Weregrave settled on benches around mugs of ale for an evening of games and storytelling while Nicolaa led Isabel around her hall, encouraging her to choose one of the many tapestries for her own. It was a generous gift, for a single tapestry took years to plan and complete; it was obvious that Nicolaa came from a line of talented women who had spent their time with a needle productively, for no woman of Nicolaa's years could have produced so many. Isabel appeared, even from across the room, to be shocked at the suggested gift, yet Nicolaa was insistent, persistent, persuasive. Even from his chair at the high table, Rowland could see Isabel wavering, her desire battling with her good manners. Nicolaa was strong, stronger than even Isabel perhaps; Nicolaa would have her way in this.

Rowland smiled quietly and looked up at the tapestries, wondering which one Isabel would choose. It was then that he saw what he had not before seen. The tapestries were all of women. No images of battle or crusade or knight were portrayed there in them. There were women in the wood. Women at the hearth. Women weaving flower garlands. Women at prayer.

A hall of women.

Four husbands before him and not a man to be seen in the work of her mind and heart and hands. She had given them no place, for they had not stayed.

Rowland watched her as she walked the hall, pointing

to her treasure, determined to give one to Isabel. He watched her, his sorrow at the life she had been forced to live more than a match for Father Timothy's. But all that was changed now, since he had come into her life. He would not leave, and she would find the rest she so deserved. All she had to do was give him her heart.

The prayers of vespers washed over her skin and through her soul like a fragrant breeze, warm and welcome. In her prayers, she could almost forget she had a husband at her side. In her prayers, she could almost ignore the pained expression in Father Timothy's eyes. Almost, she could forget.

At the conclusion of the mass, Father Timothy beckoned her to him. Rowland watched with something like suspicion clouding his eyes and then left them slowly, his steps marking his exit with biblical foreboding. Nicolaa sighed. Husbands had the strange ability to complicate the most simple things. She but stayed to talk with her priest and his; what harm in that?

Father Timothy, his gray eyes clouded with intensity, approached her, and she smiled at his coming. He was her priest. He knew all the secrets of her life, making them not secrets at all. He was her link to God. If he was also a man in the prime of his manhood, if he was fair to the eye, if he was gifted with a form that would serve any knight, she did not let such observations mark her thoughts. He was her priest. It was all he could be. It was all she needed him to be.

"Yea, Father, what would you have of me?" she asked, smiling.

"I did not intend to harm you with my words, Nicolaa. Never would I harm you," he said.

"I am not harmed," she said. "Be at peace, Father Timothy, as I am."

"You will forgive me, then? I did not think where my words would lead. I did not intend to remind you—"

"You cannot remind me of what I cannot forget," she said. "All is well with my soul. Truly."

"And with your heart, Nicolaa? How fares your heart?"

He looked into her eyes, his own eyes searching for a hurt he could heal. He looked in vain. She had no hurt, or none that a priest could reach.

"My heart is my own and I keep it very well," she said, turning from him to face the altar. "You know that."

"I have prayed nightly, hourly, to find a way to release you from this marriage. You deserve better and so much more, Nicolaa. You deserve to be loved . . ."

He had come up behind her, his words brushing against her hair, the warmth of his body a presence she could feel even in the cold stone of the chapel.

"I am loved," she said. "Does God not love His children, and am I not a child of God? So, I am loved. 'Tis enough for me. More than enough."

She took a step away from him and then turned to face him. His torment was obvious and she felt the shame of his struggle like a blow.

"I want only to help you," he said, honoring the distance she had put between them.

"You are a good priest," she said, reminding him.

"Am I? I had no choice in my vocation. All choice was taken from me long ago."

"Yet are we not all called to walk the path the Lord of hosts has set for us? We each walk the path He chooses, Father. The only question is, how well will we walk it?"

"I would not choose to stumble," he said.

"Nor would I," she said. "Let us walk our paths as well as we may. If you would aid me, I would treasure your encouragement as I walk the path of yet another husband. I need my priest to uphold me in my journey."

"If you need your priest," he said, smiling against the single tear that hovered at the corner of one eye, "then I am most contentedly your priest. I would only be what you need me to be."

"Thank you, Father," she said softly.

After vespers, Nicolaa disappeared again to the confines of her solar, taking the women with her. Isabel, surprising no one at all, dawdled within the hall, making straight for Rowland once the women were sheltered behind the wall of the solar.

She was in a fury, that much was clear before she even opened her mouth. When she did open her mouth, her words were worse than anything he could have imagined.

"Bed your wife," she said in a hiss.

Rowland could only stare at her.

"Why do you believe I have not?"

"Are there secrets in any holding, Rowland? Naturally I know. Nicolaa told Lady Jeanne, though I think anyone could read it on her face. She has not known your touch."

The feel of her breast beneath his hand and her mouth hot under his burst into his memory like flame, a flame he kept cold and small by well-practiced will alone.

"I wait only out of kindness," he said.

"Being made to wait for consummation of vows is no kindness and, in fact, is the worst sort of torture a man

135

could devise—and only a man would be devious enough
to think of it," she said.

She came ridiculously close to shaking a finger in his
face. It was only the solemn voice of Nicolaa, calling her
to the solar, that ended what was the most embarrassing
moment he could remember. He had no wish to discuss his
conjugal relations with Isabel.

He was standing beneath the tapestry of the women in
the wood, studying the shading of the leaves, which appeared especially realistic in the shadowed light of the hall,
when Richard came to stand at his side. Rowland relaxed.
But he was not yet safe.

"Do not make the same mistake I did," Richard said, his
blue eyes troubled, "though it appears to be too late for
that counsel. The wedding night has passed and Nicolaa
has yet to know your touch. The church is clear, Rowland.
You are bound to perform your husbandly duty to your wife
upon the marriage bed."

When Rowland could only stare, Richard offered encouragement. "God will sustain you if your own will fails."

Again, he had no words for such unexpected and unwelcome counsel. When had his conjugal performance become a matter for public debate? It was when two kitchen
wenches looked pointedly in his direction, their brows lowered in scorn, their voices hushed in whispers, their heads
wagging in what could only be disgust, that Rowland felt
the hard pinch of honest frustration. Did they know nothing of him at all?

Did none understand that he abstained out of compassion for Nicolaa?

As to that, how had they learned the outcome of his
wedding night?

With a manly nod of masculine understanding, Richard left him. Before Rowland could breathe a sigh of exasperation, William was at his side. With William there would be no censure. William understood all and trusted the heart and the mind of Rowland; it was always so.

Yet not in this.

"However honorable your purpose, you must bed Nicolaa," William said softly.

"I will," Rowland said; they were the only words he could seem to choke out.

"Aye, but you have not. Can you find nothing in her to inspire carnal desire?"

Rowland swallowed and looked at the floor. The rushes were tightly woven and clean, as he should have expected with Nicolaa in charge of them.

"I believe I will be able to perform," he said reasonably. He could not stop the image of himself after the bath, his member hard and ready.

"Is she that fearful?" William asked. "She seems a woman of rare self-possession."

Fearful? Nicolaa seemed neither hot with agitation nor cold with fear. Nay, since that one wild kiss, she'd exhibited no interest at all. For all that everyone else was pushing him to her bed, she was not. If he never went near her, she would not take it as an insult. And if he tumbled her in the stable, she would likely shrug and lift her skirts obligingly.

"Nay, I do not think her fearful, but neither is she eager," he said.

William smiled and then winked, the moment rich with the flavor of male camaraderie. " 'Tis you who must teach her to be eager."

Aye, but did he want an eager wife?

Chapter Ten

Isabel sat ripping out all her stitches while the ladies continued with their embroidery, the talk among them more robust than was customary. Nicolaa could not maintain the quiet she so well loved with guests among them. Etiquette demanded that she provide them with conversation. Unfortunately, they seemed to want to talk of only one thing.

"I am quite certain that Rowland knows who might be available for marriage. He is well traveled, knows almost everyone, and is even a favorite of the queen, and she does know *everyone*. An arrangement could be made within the year, with some effort. Shall we try?" Isabel asked.

"Some of the ladies have arrangements in place," Nicolaa said. "And we must keep to our embroidery. This section should have been finished last week."

"We can talk and sew both, Nicolaa," Cathryn said as she took a stitch, proving her point. "It is so very sad that arrangements have not been made for Ermengarde and Blanche."

"And what of Agnes?" Isabel said. "You would like to marry again, would you not, Agnes?"

Hesitating, Agnes looked at Nicolaa before answering. "I have thought of it once or twice."

"Of course you have," Isabel said. "What woman does not want to marry? We shall see it done, between us. A heartfelt prayer would not be amiss; I found that method to work most quickly, though I caution you to pray with care. A misspoken name and you might find yourself married to Gilles, a young and pimply squire of Dornei."

Nicolaa did not join in the general laughter that flowed from this remark. Isabel would not be stopped, it seemed, from interfering. Nicolaa decided to take it in good humor. Let her plot and plan; nothing could or would be done on her whim.

What was more alarming was the excitement Isabel's talk of marriage birthed. Some of the ladies actually spoke as if they wanted to marry. Young Perette sounded eager for the vows that would begin her married life. If this proceeded, even Beatrice might be tempted to give up her chaste and serene life for the role of wife. Nicolaa cast Beatrice a sidelong glance. Was that not a half smile and a blush staining her childlike face? This talk must end.

The growing heaviness of the night was her excuse; the wet darkness seen through the wind hole seemed to crush the very flames of the fire in the solar.

"It is too dark to continue," she said, stilling her needle. "Let us withdraw."

Of them all, Isabel was the most overjoyed, and Nicolaa

found not the heart to be offended. Clearly Isabel had no talent for needlework.

They stored their thread and their precious needles and rose as a body. As one, they left the solar and reentered the hall, which was bright with firelight and candlelight and murky with wood smoke and men's voices. At the sight of them, Isabel burst into a radiant smile, so glad was she to be in the same room with Richard again. Nicolaa noted her smile, understood the cause, and wondered if she had ever been so young, and if any of her many husbands had ever made her so wish to smile.

She had no memory of anything like the joy Isabel found in her husband's company, but then, she had taken control of her memories, sorting and discarding, long ago.

"Good night to you all," Nicolaa said. "Until the morrow mass."

Good night? Isabel watched with an open mouth as Nicolaa and her ladies walked through the hall—Blanche casting a lingering look upon Ulrich—and up the curved stone stair. If Blanche was inclined to linger, she was made to forgo her inclination; Nicolaa walked at the rear of the party, directing the stragglers to their beds.

Cathryn looked as shocked as Isabel felt. There was only one explanation for such behavior, and they both hurried to Rowland to tender that explanation.

The men had turned as the women entered the shadowed vastness of the hall, each of them glad for their coming. They were, to a man, men who appreciated the sight and sound of women, and Nicolaa's fascination with the diversions of the solar only made them the hungrier for feminine company. For did a man not crave what was difficult to find and hard to hold? So it was with Nicolaa and her women; ever they whispered away from masculine congress, their skirts brushing over the rushes, their hair dangling down their backs, their eyes averted. Ulrich, by the look of him and the sounds of agony he made in the back of his throat, was near to bursting for want of feminine association. Well, no man had expired from lack of women, though most men had felt they would.

The ladies passed by them, Nicolaa urging them through the hall, her eyes about her business and most definitely averted from Rowland's. Rowland was not surprised. Nor was he offended. Skittering glances were not her way; if she wanted to look at him, then she would look. Coldly, directly, unapologetically, she would look. She did not look now. Nay, now she marched her ladies through the hall and up the curving stair. With obvious reluctance, she let Isabel and Cathryn escape her, to slide their eager way back into the center of the hall. It would take more than civility to keep Isabel from Richard, more than a frown to keep Cathryn from William.

Rowland watched all, studying Nicolaa as he was wont to do, but he found nothing new in her actions, no new paths into her thoughts. She did as she always did: avoided him when she could, faced him politely and distantly when she could not.

Isabel and Cathryn positioned themselves before him.

"Ulrich, why do you not . . ." Cathryn made a fluttering motion with her hands.

"Yea, and Edmund as well," Isabel said. "I would speak with Lord Rowland, and what I would say, it is not necessary for you to hear."

Ulrich, his shock and hurt mirrored imperfectly in Edmund's face, sniffed his offense and left them, Edmund at

141

his side. They carried themselves off with all the stiff pride of squires moments away from becoming knights, when no one would be able to push them off like so much dusty baggage.

"The ladies are to bed," Isabel said when Ulrich and Edmund were out of hearing.

"All to bed, and at Nicolaa's urging," Cathryn said. "She was quite eager that we leave the solar and make to our beds."

"Aye, and why is this something that the boys could not be privy to?" William asked.

"Why, can you not see it?" Isabel said to the three men standing before her. By their look, it appeared they did not. By her look, she thought them dull.

"It must mean that Nicolaa is ready for her husband to join her," Cathryn said.

"Why else to bed, without game or song to enliven the long evening?" Isabel said.

"She did seem most eager for the day to end and even now must be waiting . . . for you, Rowland," Cathryn said.

To that, the men had nothing to say. It was Rowland's place to speak, yet he held his tongue. They seemed to think it obvious that Nicolaa wanted him in her bed, but it was not so obvious to him. If they saw eagerness, he saw resolve. Could a woman read a woman more clearly than a man? Perhaps.

Eager or not, he would bed her, if only to give her heart ease that he would not seek an annulment. A woman so used, so misused, would think nothing else. Let her know that he would not abandon her. God willing, he would be her last husband. And if he had his way, he would be the husband she most cherished.

The Willing Wife

* * *

Nicolaa, alone in her chamber, lit the taper near the door. The room brightened to a soft and warm glow. Slowly she disrobed, slipping the woolen bliaut from her skin and hanging it on the peg. Would he bed her tonight? Would he bed her at all? It did not seem likely; still, she must make herself ready for him, should he decide to grab hold of what God had placed in his hand. For herself, she could lay hold of nothing, not even the dreams of her youth, when she had believed that marriage was her divine duty and that she would therefore be divinely content. She was not content. She was resolved. It was not a bad exchange, as to that. She had no regrets. Though sometime she was beset by the ghostly echoes of dreams long past.

She heard the echoes tonight, now, with a new husband within the walls and her nakedness her only defense.

Rowland the Dark. The name—the man—of legend. His love was a light that shone across continents and seas, turning hearts to water with the tale. Even her heart felt less than stalwart now. If he had loved his Lubias, if he had truly loved his wife, could he love again? Could he love another wife in another land with another name? Could he love . . . her?

She was Beatrice again: young and hopeful, that girl who believed that marriage was the answer to all troubles, all dreams. She had barely survived as that girl, in that place of dreams. There was no rest for her in that place; she would not go back.

Still . . . Rowland was . . . different. He was gentle and kind and constant, or he claimed to be. Certainly he had been so with Lubias and was still. It was enough to make her ponder. And dream.

Dreaming was dangerous. Dreaming carried her to places that did not exist, with people born only of wishes and longings. She had learned so well the pain of dreaming, and so she no longer dreamed. She lived in a world she understood and that she could control, safe within the solar with her tapestry taking shape in her hands, all within the bounds of her control. She could not control a dream.

Lifting the lid of her trunk, she went carefully to the bottom and pulled free the cloth that rested there. Her tapestry. The tapestry she did not work in the solar, but only alone. Her private, secret tapestry. Her dream tapestry, if she would name it aright. It was small, barely two hands wide, and tall, the stitches finer than any she had ever done. When had she begun it? In her first marriage with Philibert? Or had it been in her tumultous marriage to Hugh? The men were gone, only names now, but the tapestry remained. She fingered it, her touch light on the web of fabric and color.

The design was of a man.

He stood firmly on the ground, his destrier at his side, on a wide plain. Far behind him was a river, and beyond the river a wood gone half-bare with autumn. He appeared in the harvest season, a season of plenty; that was how she had depicted him. He was tall, the trappings of his knighthood indistinct and plain. His helm was off and she had picked out the outline of his hair and the barest beginnings of his face. He was not known to her, except in her dreaming, yet he was as real to her as the thread that made him. He had no face, but he had form. He was as real as a dream.

He was the knight she yearned to find in the secrets of her dreaming. He would put her needs above his own. He would listen to her counsel. He would fight when the need was upon him, and he would win. He would love her. He would purely love her.

Climbing into bed, shivering in her nakedness, she pulled free her thread and began to sew. The knight of her tapestry would be given black hair. Yea, black hair seemed to be the right color for a dream.

How it had been accomplished, none would say, but Perette, with a halting Beatrice at her side, had made her escape from Nicolaa. Ulrich and Edmund, keen to such moments, had found them almost immediately. All were most content at the result. All, perhaps, except Beatrice.

"It is early yet to be abed," Ulrich said to Perette's profile. "Yet late for my heart, Perette. You have stolen it, and now you must have a care or I will not survive this theft."

"I have stolen your heart? Can such a thing happen when I did not will it? For, willfully, I stole nothing," she said.

"Yet willfully it is gone from me to dwell in your bosom, next to your own heart, their beating a single pulse of love," he said.

"Then I did not steal it."

"Aye, you did, with my first sight of your tumbling hair and kitten's eyes; you must not run from your responsibility in this, Perette. You are a thief. No man can stand untouched by you. And am I not a man?" he asked, stepping closer to her.

She backed up a step and felt the stable wall behind her. A solid wall when all around her swam the sweet words of a squire adept at wooing. She could drown in such words.

Beatrice, at her side, did not enjoy the wash of Ulrich's words and seemed little prepared to learn the skill. Edmund, his own skills in want of practice, tried to ease her into the game of courtly love.

"Aye, you are a man," Perette said with a smile. "I know the look and sound of one, though I am young."

"You should know the sound and look of a man," Ulrich said, "for your beauty and your sweetness call to a man like the hunter's horn, teasing the blood to quicken, urging him on to conquest."

"Conquest?" Beatrice said, her blue eyes troubled. "What talk of conquest? Are we not betrothed? Is this not a gentle meeting?"

"It is a conquest," Edmund said to her, trying to find his way into her heart. "How can it be else with such eyes as yours, gentle Beatrice? Does the blue sea not defeat the shore with every rising of the tide?"

"I know not what you mean to say," Beatrice said.

"Your eyes are as blue as the sea," Perette translated for her. "He is defeated by your look; you have won him."

"Aye, and, as the shore, I do not protest," Edmund said. In truth, he was becoming more adept at love with every encounter. 'Twas fine sport.

"I do protest," Beatrice said, shifting her body away from Edmund's, trying to take Perette with her. "This talk is not proper. We should not have come. There can be nothing of conquest here, not even the talking of it."

"You have conquered Edmund," Ulrich said to her, his tone chiding. "Can you not grant him grace with a soft word and a kind look? Will you be a churlish lady and deny him any reward for his devotion? Love is indeed cruel for you to be so heartless, Beatrice."

" 'Twas not my intent," she said, her eyes full of sudden tears. With mumbled words of sorrow and regret, she left them in the stable, gone in the time it takes for a heart to break.

"I did not intend for her to . . . take my words so hard," Ulrich said, stricken to the core that he had caused a lady grief. "She has a soft and gentle heart, broken by my heavy and careless tongue."

"You have not played it well with Beatrice," Edmund said. "Never have I seen you stumble, yet this is a mighty fall, Ulrich. What were you about?"

"Take it not so hard upon yourself," Perette said, standing upright from the worn wood at her back. The game was done. "She has a mild temperament and has been much cautioned by Lady Nicolaa about the ways of men."

"I will find her. I will beg her forgiveness," Ulrich said. "I would never cause her one moment of pain; she must understand this of me. I would not wound her for anything."

They were out of the stable, Ulrich already disappearing into the dark of the bailey.

"If you came upon her now, she might fling herself off the battlements in shame and fear," Perette said. "Let it wait. Tender your apologies when she is calmed and her tears a remnant. I will comfort her tonight."

"You are certain?" Ulrich said. "I would not be thought cruel by her, or by you, Perette. It was never my intent."

"I know," she said, smiling up at him. "Let it rest for now. Good night. Until the morrow mass."

They watched her go, trailing distantly behind her like two beaten hounds. A most unwelcome end to such a shining beginning.

* * *

Rowland, acting on the faint belief that women might see the heart of another woman more easily than a man, made his way to the lord's bedchamber. Nicolaa was within. She was prepared for bed. But she was not alone.

Beatrice, crying brokenly into her lap, was with her on the lord's bed.

"My lord, I am engaged," Nicolaa said.

"I see. How may I help?" he said.

Beatrice continued her weeping into the fur on Nicolaa's lap.

"You could leave," Nicolaa said with raised brows.

"I would rather stay."

"Then I suppose you will stay," she said. With those words, she bent her red head to the tossed golden strands of the girl and ignored him. "Cry your fill and then hear me, Beatrice. All will be well."

"All will be well," Rowland repeated. "Tell me what has befallen and I will set all to right. Who has hurt you?"

He was ignored by them both.

Nicolaa ran her hands through Beatrice's long, smooth hair, her movements slow and easy and rhythmic. She rocked the girl lightly, her body moving gently back and forth, her voice low and soft.

"Ulrich meant nothing. Edmund is no one to fear. You have nothing to fear from them." Beatrice's cries melted to hiccups. Her face she kept buried in the fur and in the shelter of Nicolaa's warmth. "The very best thing to do is to avoid them. If that fails, ignore their attempts to disturb you."

Beatrice lifted her face, red with splotches, and stared up at Nicolaa. Nicolaa smoothed her hair back and smiled down into the pale little face.

"You must understand, Beatrice, that men are different from women and are known to show their regard for a woman by using violence and intimidation. It is their way. Unpleasant, but unsurprising."

Such counsel Rowland could not let stand, not even though he was being ignored. And he was being ignored. A fly buzzing in the corner would have been more welcome in that chamber than he was.

"Beatrice," he said softly, stepping closer to the bed, "has either Ulrich or Edmund harmed you?"

"Can you not see?" Nicolaa said. "Do you think she cries for her own amusement?"

It was now Rowland who ignored Nicolaa. And he could see that she did not like it.

"Beatrice," he said again, lifting the girl's small white face with his hand, forcing her to meet his eyes. "I cannot believe two such lovesick boys would seek to harm you."

"If you would not believe, then why should she try to dissuade you?" Nicolaa said sharply.

"I will believe whatever you tell me, Beatrice," he said, sensing that this assurance would be a major point with Nicolaa. He would that he could use this moment to lead her into trusting him. Such was the way to begin to win a wife.

"Speak, Beatrice," Nicolaa said, "so that we may find the depths of Lord Rowland's belief in the word of a woman against a squire." She studied him as she said it.

It did not come quickly; nay, Beatrice shook with emotion and flushed with shame before she found the words to begin her tale. Rowland did not hurry her. He waited calmly for her to find her way to the story.

"We, Perette and I, met them in the stables. We did not

149

plan to meet, yet it was no accident when we did."

"I comprehend," he said on a smile.

"The talk was . . . warm, familiar. There was talk of . . . the word conquest was used. I am betrothed. Perette is nigh upon her contract. There can be no conquest. I said as much. And was rebuked for being cruel. Churlish."

"Nay, there can be no conquest, unless it be the conquest of hearts?" he said. "I fear you do not know your own value, Beatrice, but Edmund and Ulrich both see it. You are a beautiful young woman, gentle and pious, just the sort to incite a man's admiration. Edmund is new to the demands of courtly love, Ulrich his eager tutor; you bruised their pride by your restraint. That is all."

Beatrice took a deep breath and disentangled herself from Nicolaa, her eyes clear and settled, as her emotions seemed to be. Nicolaa watched her, and ran a hand over Beatrice's smooth cheek.

"It has been a worthy lesson for Beatrice," Nicolaa said, looking up at Rowland, "to so early learn that a man's sharp words and heavy-handed rebuke spring from bruised pride. For male extremes, there is always an excuse."

With a movement of her hand, she encouraged Beatrice to leave the chamber, which the girl willingly did. When they were alone, Nicolaa stared up at Rowland, her face composed and her eyes mocking.

"You took my words hard," he said.

"Their meaning was hard. You laid the blame for Ulrich's words at Beatrice's feet."

"Nay, I sought only to give meaning to his intent."

"His intent was to scold Beatrice into behaving as he wanted. No explanation as to his intent was necessary. He is being well trained as a warrior."

"You put too much weight upon this thing. It was a flirtation taking a wrong turn."

"Ah, thank you for dismissing my concern and my anger. All will be well with me now you have ordered my thinking."

She blocked his attempts at peacemaking at every turn. He could not find his way with her, for she would not be found. She was well armed against his arguments and his charm; a woman who had sparred with many husbands was not going to fall easily into trust. And without trust, there was no path to love. He wanted both from her. He was due both from her. How to get them? How to win a battle of hearts with a woman who kept hers well guarded?

Laying down his arms and showing her that he was not an enemy to be bested was a start. A direct assault on Nicolaa was unlikely to succeed. He had won many battles with an unexpected blow. Such would be his method with Nicolaa. He must find a way to bring her ease; then her heart would be vulnerable for the taking. Aye, that was the way.

Rowland sighed and then smiled at her. She would be contrary, even to not returning his smile. She scowled in the face of his attempt. Well, he had not expected her to fall into trust with a single smile.

"You have studied me well enough to know that my response to you will ever be mild. You are very brave when there is no price to pay for a sharp tongue and a contentious spirit."

"Should a woman be made to pay a price for speaking her mind? What price will Ulrich pay for speaking his to Beatrice?"

"Ulrich will pay, that I promise you, and he himself will

151

devise the recompense. But as to you, Nicolaa, speak your mind; you will not be censured by me. Only sheath your knife."

He said it with a smile, watching her for her response. The only sign of her struggle to defeat her anger and move beyond it was a slight turbulence in the blue of her eyes, like the tumbling of surf upon the sand. With a quick grin, she regained herself. He could not help admiring her self-possession.

With a wry grin, she said, "It is sheathed. You are now safe."

"Thank you, lady," he said, bowing. It struck him then how like a warrior she was. She fought hard and she fought to win, yet when the fight was done, it was done. She did not sulk, nor did she cajole. A rare woman, she was, worthy of love, worthy of devotion. Yet he could be only her husband.

Straightening, they stared at each other. She was naked, her body covered by her hair and the blanket; she had been awaiting him, as Cathryn and Isabel had assured him. But how to bed her now? Their argument had not paved the way for consummation.

Nicolaa, four times experienced at conjugal nights, solved the matter.

"Did you think to consummate the marriage tonight?"

"I have been much advised that we should," he answered.

It was a cold answer, but he could not think of any other that would be as true. In his dealings with her, he would show her that he would be true. She had had enough of false and brief husbands. Let her find what rest and truth she could in him.

Nicolaa had only to toss her hair back over her shoulders to reveal her breasts and her readiness to him. He had only to undress himself. It was a far longer process.

His gambeson came off slowly, his fingers reluctant and clumsy. Yet he could not blame his fingers; it was his memories that slowed him, his heart that faltered. Lubias was with him.

Praise God and the saints that their wedding night had been nothing like this.

Lubias had come to him joyfully, her joy open and trusting, her heart engaged fully with him. They had run to the chamber like puppies, tripping up the stairs, laughing in their eagerness, innocent of anything but their own joy. Such joy they had found.

He had known her from childhood. He had watched her breasts grow full and heavy, a promise of life to the children they would have. He had learned the meaning in her eyes, how anger drew her dark brows down, how delight made her shine, how worry clouded the dark depths of her. He had learned her and he had loved her. A shared love had been their earthly gift, until God had robbed him of his joy.

He was disrobed. He had managed it. With thoughts only of Lubias, he had managed it.

He turned and found Nicolaa out of bed, standing on her side of it, the fire warming her back. She was as slender as a blade, her curves as long as a Saracen scimitar. Her breasts were small, yet so was her waist. She was narrow at hip, rib, and thigh. Her thick and wildly curling hair was the most abundant thing about her. Or perhaps the blueness of her eyes in the milk-white fragility of her face. Yet there was nothing fragile about the look in her eyes. She burned him with her look: banked fire, hot resolve, all held within her blue-eyed stare.

Even with Lubias in firm possession of his heart, he felt himself rise in readiness.

She held his gaze, her eyes shifting down quickly to note his arousal, and then she said, "Do you find fault with me?"

There was such vulnerability in the words. "Nay, I do not," he answered her. Not at all, not in any way, he wanted to say. But for all her straightforward talk and the quiet fire in her eyes, she held herself aloof. He did not say more. Would she be aloof in the matter of her bedding? Would she find any joy in their coupling? Would he?

"Shall we then begin?" she asked, holding his gaze.

He could not find voice to answer her; to give his assent would be to take his first, hard step away from his vow of constancy to Lubias. He could not say the word, yet he could not take his eyes from her as she lifted the blankets and slid into bed. Her skin gleamed white like new snow on sunlit fields. Her hair glowed red even in the dim light of the firelit room, and the hair that sheathed her womanhood seemed a darker red stain between her thighs.

She laid herself down on the bed and dragged up the blanket, watching him with her wide and vivid eyes, holding herself as still as a doe in the field, wary of the man who stood so close upon her. Wary, that was what she seemed to him, yet she was all calm looks and steady breath. She did not seem afeared. Nay, all the fear in the room had its source in him.

He wanted her. He was hard with just the scent of her in the room, the tangle of her hair curling upon his heart as surely as any trap. He wanted her body, that was all. He needed to plunge into her, to seal their vows, to give her ease and comfort. Aye, it was for her that he rose hard and pulsing. It was for her, not for himself. Lubias had all of him. What he gave, what he was required to give to Nicolaa, was the function of his body, not his soul. Not his heart.

With his purpose clear, he slipped into bed beside her. The scent of her rose from the linen like a cloud of costly Damascus perfume. He held himself still against the onslaught of desire, held himself away from her on his back, his hands clenched into fists against his hips. He would not turn to her until he could get the scent of her out of his head. He would not touch her until . . . until . . . Saint John Climacus, how was he to touch her without staining the memory of Lubias?

He turned to look at her in profile and she smiled softly at his look, awaiting his touch with wary submission. How was he to bed a woman, even be she a wife, with so little common ground between them? He was not a man to tumble with a stranger, no matter the needs that assaulted a man in his prime. He had not dallied easily in his youth, before Lubias; he was far less inclined to plunge without caution now.

"We are strangers still, Nicolaa," he said softly, giving her a way of escape from this path of rude and hurried intimacy, even as his manhood throbbed the lie with every beat of his heart. He wanted her, even though they were strangers. He had never known such desire, and it shamed him. He could not remember such aching need with Lubias in his bed.

"Let us consummate this marriage and you will know me well enough," she said.

"You are ready for that intimacy?" he asked, staring hard into her eyes.

"Do I not appear ready? I am no virgin, Rowland. I am not afeared," she said.

And he believed her. With a jolt, he understood that he wanted to believe her. Perhaps this was the first sign of her trust in him. Why should she be fearful, after all? She was no virgin. She was his wife. She was the wife of Rowland the Dark. Many women since Lubias had striven for that place. He was not a man who sought the attention of women—nay, not as William had done in his day—yet he was a man who had had his share of women trailing after him, like hounds on the scent. Aye, he understood his worth. He knew his appeal.

As he knew hers.

He reached out a slow hand and touched her hair at the brow. So soft and tightly coiled it was, so hot and bright and yet so cool to his hand. She smiled, encouraging him, giving him the gift of her willingness, silently asking that he take her, laying herself out for him and holding nothing back. Nothing. How long had it been since he had had a woman give herself so sweetly into his care? How long since he had touched a woman?

As long ago as Lubias.

Even with the name of Lubias in his thoughts, he could not keep his hands from Nicolaa. His fingertips skimmed down her face, touching her lips, her throat, her breast. . . . She rose against his hand and moaned, giving him the gift of her desire and her willingness, though she barely knew him. Yet did she not know him well enough? He was Rowland; the tales of him were well known. She knew him. She knew enough to give herself to him, her husband, her lord. Aye, she gave, and what she would give, he would take. He could not stand against such eagerness. He threw aside the will to try. Lubias would understand. He had to walk this path. This was ordained. He had no choice. He had to possess Nicolaa.

It was no thought, but instinct and need that made him kiss her. He tasted her lightly, slowly breathing into her mouth, coming upon her gently and softly, falling into the scent of her. With a breath she answered him, her arms wrapping around his neck, pulling him down and into her, urging him onward, rubbing herself against him, caressing the ends of his hair. Aye, she was not afeared. She was a woman in need and he would meet that need. It was his calling and he would not turn from it. It would be wrong to try.

She tasted like apples and honey and over all the scent of lavender. He breathed her scent and bathed in her heat. He was starving for this, and he had not known he even hungered. With every touch, every breath, he knew how great was his need for this, for her. He could not eat of her fast enough. He trailed his mouth along her throat and across the ridge of her collarbone. She was slender and soft, hot and cool beneath his mouth. Her heart pounded beneath her breast and he wanted to taste her there, at the source of her life. He licked her throbbing nipple and she arched her back, thrusting her breast into his open mouth, gasping her longing, her need, her passion. She gripped his head and held him there, with his mouth on her, licking her, tasting her, the hard pebble of her desire rising to fill his mouth with sweet passion.

He wanted her. She wanted him. It was all. There was room for naught else. Not even Lubias.

Claudia Dain

He suckled her and, with his hand, he plucked her other nipple and was rewarded with her moan of pleasure and the thrashing of her body in his hands. She wanted him. The knowledge made him shake with need, and he surged upward and found her mouth again, hot and open under his assault, her breasts hot and hard under his hands, her hands holding him to her with the steely grip of a warrior. Or of a woman deep and lost in passion. Such was Nicolaa.

He wanted her. He would have her. She was his for the taking.

How long? How long had it been since a woman, a wife, had opened to him, wanting him? Needing him?

He had to have her, take her, mark her. He would. Now.

His knee he wedged between her thighs, and he felt her slowly soften against him. She wanted him, but this was new. He was new to her. He would be gentle. He would not force himself too quickly, though the need that raged beneath his skin was howling with all the fierce hunger of winter wolves. He chained the beast to his will and gave her gentle encouragement instead. He kissed her, soft and long, deep and hot. He kissed her and widened the gap between her soft, white thighs, making a place for himself. Urging her to give herself to him. Urging her to trust.

She breathed out her willingness on a sigh of air and held herself wide under his hand.

Gently he trailed his fingers down her body, down the slope of her breast, past the rise of rib and the flat fall of belly to the soft mound of hip and thigh. Down to the center of her heat and passion and womanhood. Down to the place where he would take her, marking her as his, claiming her and putting his scent upon her and within her. He touched her and she groaned at the touch, her

158

torso thrashing in the teeth of passion, her eyes closed against the sensation.

She groaned again and he felt an answering growl rise from deep in his throat. His hand between the soft vulnerability of her legs, his mouth upon her breast, the beat of her heart strong and hot beneath his tongue. He had her. He had her in his hand and in his mouth and he would take her. He would take her now. She was ready.

He pressed his hand against her womanhood, cupping her, feeling the shape and heat of her, wanting to bathe in the scent of her. He touched her in her most vulnerable, most womanly spot. She had no defense against such an assault. She gave herself willingly; aye, nothing less than willing was Nicolaa.

The thought, the words, filled his mouth with cold ash as he touched the entrance to her body. Lifting his mouth from hers, he spoke past the pain of her betrayal.

"You are as dry as bleached bone."

He had spoken, challenging her conclusion that he preferred silence to talkative coupling. She looked into his eyes, black even at this slight distance. He looked . . . angry. What was it he had said? She was dry? If that detail was pertinent, she failed to grasp why.

By the light of fire and taper, Rowland's eyes looked black as night, velvet soft and deep. Hugh of Foix, her second husband, had had eyes of cool gray, though his manner had not matched. Macair of the Haye's eyes had been the amber brown of ale, and Gerard's eyes the silvered green of thyme, Philibert's wondrous blue. And now black. Perhaps, if she lived long enough, she would see every shade and color in God's creation. How many husbands would that be?

Rowland was studying her and she returned his look, her expression purposely expectant. There were so many false starts with this man. Could he not simply finish what he had begun?

His first kiss had been so delicate, like no kiss Macair had ever given, surely. She had closed her eyes and breathed into it, wrapping her arms delicately around his neck, matching his mood. How long since her last kiss? How long since she had felt the flutterings of desire in her empty womb? It did not bear thinking on. She had a role to play: that of a willing, eager wife. She played it well. She had played this role so many times. Time upon time. If this man was more gentle, more tender than most, it was only a small and momentary gift. There was no room to dream of more, not in this bed; this bed was all of duty.

"Why did you moan?" he asked.

"Why?"

She had moaned and thrashed her head, knowing it would please him. A man liked to think he could bring a woman to such a state. Macair had particularly liked it. Once she had tossed her head so violently that a single strand of hair had been thrown into her eye. To reach up and carefully dislodge it would have ruined the moment, and so she had tried to thrash it out again. Macair had been quite impressed with himself that night. She had been more careful in her head thrashing ever since. Groaning was safer.

"You are not . . . ready. You led me to believe otherwise."

"I *am* ready."

"Nay, you are not." He sat up and away from her.

Nicolaa sighed and closed her eyes. They were apparently not going to consummate this marriage anytime soon.

"Are *you* not ready?" she asked.

He was as large and brown as a loaf; he could give only one answer.

"Aye, I am," he said solemnly, "but only because I believed you . . . wanted me."

She snorted at that, sharing the jest with him. What man required a woman's willingness to see his needs met? He was supposed to believe himself deeply desirable, and it was her duty to give him that impression. There was no more to copulation than that.

"Again I ask, why did you moan when I fondled you?" he asked.

"Did it not please you?"

"Naturally it pleased me."

He sounded a bit angry. She would have to cut down on her moaning as well as her thrashing. This husband seemed to prefer a less enthusiastic bed partner.

"Then why are you displeased now?" she said.

"Because you are dry!" he said sharply.

Nicolaa took a calming breath and said reasonably, "If you would only proceed, things will . . . moisten . . . nicely."

He frowned. "Are you saying this is normal for you?"

"Of course it is normal." He was a most unusual man; perhaps he lacked the usual experience in these matters. Was her marriage to be annulled because her husband was shy in his duties? "Do you not understand the way of things between a man and a woman?"

"*What?*"

"I know that your wife has been dead many years now,

161

and if in being constant to her memory, you have forgotten—"

"I certainly know what to do with a woman! My concern, and it is concern and not ineptitude, is that you do not understand what is supposed to happen between a woman and a man."

"I know very well what happens. I have had a wealth of experience," she said, sitting up and pulling the blanket up to her chest.

"Oh, aye," he snapped, "you are well tutored in false grunts and moans, but I think not in passion."

The insult bit against her pride in a part well played, and she replied in kind.

"Macair never voiced a complaint," she said with a hard grin.

"From what I have heard of Macair, he was not overmuch concerned with speech. His animal appetites consumed him fully."

"At least he had appetites," she said. "At least they could be satisfied."

He got off the bed and turned to retrieve his clothing from the floor. He had slovenly habits, too, on top of all else.

She got out of bed, not willing to be the only naked person in the room. Her clothing was hanging on the peg, where it was supposed to be, and she yanked her shift over her head.

"Satisfied? I think Macair could have satisfied his appetites with his own hand. What need had he for a wife? Do not think that you satisfied him. A woman of such coldness, such calculation, could not long please a man."

She whirled as if struck, which indeed she had been. "At least I am *capable* of copulation!"

They stared into each other's faces, breathing hard and loud in the silence of the room. She had pushed him too far with that last, and they both knew it. A wife could not say such without reprisal. With each breath, they strove for calm. This anger would serve nothing. She had a husband. She wanted a peaceful existence with him. All else was wasted emotion and energy. She waited, watching him to see what action he would take. He could well beat her. He had cause.

"I do not seek an argument," she said, trying to ease the tension between them.

"Nor I," he said.

It was a good, firm step toward peace.

"My only thought was to please you," she said.

He knew that for a lie. She had been occupied by many thoughts, none of them of him, else why would she have remained unmoved by him? He knew the path to a woman's pleasure, and he could read the signs of success. But not with Nicolaa. She had been tutored by other husbands to deceive.

"If you would please me, do not deceive me," he said.

Deceive him? Nay, she had not, yet she did not want another argument when the last one was still breathing out its dying breath. Never had she had such open discourse with a husband, and it was not a pleasant experience. She had only to mind her tongue and her manner and all would be well between them. For as long as he stayed. She could meet whatever expectation he had of a wife, for a time. She could do anything for the scant weeks he would be part of her life. If this one wanted an honest wife, she could learn to give him what he wanted.

"It has never been my intent to deceive you," she said.

163

His look said that he did not entirely believe her. Yet he did not look angry. It was a start.

"Truly," she said.

"Then tell me what you were thinking when I touched you," he said, crossing his arms and leaning against the stone of the portal.

An easy answer sprang up. "I was thinking of . . ." *You*, she almost said. Was that not what he wanted to hear? But she could see by his look that he was expecting that answer and was already disapproving it. Nicolaa sighed. If he wanted the truth to be content, then she would give him the truth. "I was thinking of what color to paint the ceiling."

She did not tell him she had been thinking of other husbands. No man wanted that much truth.

He looked little enough pleased to hear about the ceiling.

"And what color did you decide?" he asked eventually.

Hesitating only slightly, she answered, "Red."

Clearing his throat and looking thoughtfully up at the ceiling, he said, "I like red."

Did she care that he liked red? Nay, she did not. It was her home and the ceiling would be red long after he was gone. She did not need his counsel nor his approval. She most certainly did not need his permission. But she did not want another argument and so she held her tongue.

"What are you thinking now?" he asked, unfolding his arms.

Since the blunt truth had been demanded she answered him most readily.

"That we are not to consummate our marriage tonight, are we?"

·

Chapter Eleven

They did not consummate the marriage. He could not, not with all that had gone before. She had been contemplating paint colors? Rowland ground his teeth until they squeaked. He had much to do before she was ready for the bond of consummation.

That he had felt the lick of passion while she had felt nothing was a sharp blow. He had stroked her smooth body and tasted of her, the scent of lavender tainting every breath he breathed; he had risen hard and aching and he had strained against her every moan and sigh, holding back because he wanted her ready and unafraid when he took her. Unafraid? She had been bored. Every moan a lie. Every touch, every caress, every kiss the tutored willingness of a whore.

He had misread her. He, who heard every whisper and who could read the meaning in a sigh, had misread Nicolaa. That was a truth that burned as hot as her false passion under his hands and his mouth. He had not seen her deception. He had tumbled in passion alone.

It could not be so. It *would* not be so.

He had not wished for this marriage. He had not wanted a wife. He had not wanted her. Yet he had her now, his life was joined to hers, and he would possess her. More, she would come to want his possession. He would accept no other truth. He would tolerate no other path. He was Rowland the Dark; many women had wanted him. He was a man of whom legends were whispered; Nicolaa, with her false moans, would learn to call herself blessed to be his wife. She would. He knew how to win a woman's heart. Was he not from the Aquitaine? Was he not well tutored in the chivalric art of courtly love?

He knew exactly how to break past each and every defense she had against him. He would woo her with soft words, gentle speech, heartfelt praise, a tender touch. Aye, more of touching did she need, the tenderness of sweet affection. All women turned toward the warmth of affection and appreciation. He would give her that until she lay panting, spent, every weapon with which she surrounded her heart cast from her willingly. Aye, then she would be willing, as a woman should be.

Aye, he would win her, breaking past all the defenses of her heart. It would be so. He would not share his life with a woman of such cold detachment. He would make her yearn for him, for his touch, for his very presence in her life.

He had spent most of the night watching the flames die in the fire in the hall. Lubias had seemed very far away in that midnight hall colored with another woman's tapestries. He had resented Nicolaa for an hour, looking at the shadowed tapestries and seeing Nicolaa's curling red hair and slender white body in his mind when all he wanted to see was the beloved form of his dark Lubias. In time she had come and driven his new bride away. It was then that he had relaxed and been able to contemplate the problem of Nicolaa.

It went beyond the bedding. It went to the very pattern of her life. She had no need for a husband, though she had had four, and very little tolerance for one. He was not a man to be disregarded, and he had no inclination to accustom himself to the idea. Changes must be made. He was more than prepared to make them.

She had come down in good time for the mass, stood beside him in the chapel, smiled politely as they broke their fast, and then retired to the sanctuary of the solar, surrounded by her ladies, as was usual. All very pleasant, very distant, very cold. They were two fellow travelers on pilgrimage, that was all. He would make no progress with Nicolaa until he had rid her of her armor of women; this he now understood. How to do it?

He had walked out of Weregrave this morn, leaving Nicolaa to her stitchery, walking to find his purpose in this forced marriage. That he was simultaneously learning the length and breadth of Weregrave he counted only gain. It was a fine morning; the rain had been driven off by a cold, steady wind out of the west; the sky was free of cloud, the sun high and bright. Weregrave rose behind him, gray and solid, a niche of safety in a hostile world. Nicolaa and her many husbands had kept well her place in the world. Weregrave reaped a good harvest, the town was thriving, the villeins were many. Henry was well seated upon his throne, order restored after years of civil war between Stephen and Maud. None would push Henry off the throne of England. All was well.

There would not be many battles left in England, which was a pity.

He strode the land, his head up, his brow furrowed, as was his way when looking for a diverting battle. What battle could Weregrave offer him? How to battle a cadre of women to reach the heart of Nicolaa? How else to save her but to heal her heart?

Her heart was torn and bloody, a ragged remnant of the whole heart a woman should give to a man, her lack of passion only one sign among many that she was not as a woman should be. God had not designed a woman to be so cold, so hard. 'Twas against nature and divine will. A wife was to yearn for her husband's touch; had not God told Eve it must and would be so? And so it must be. Nicolaa's heart must be healed, her passions restored. Yet how to accomplish it?

The sound of a horse, a single horse and rider, broke into his thoughts. He was not alarmed, though he was afoot. He knew the sound of that rider and turned to see William bearing down upon him. He understood the man's mood by a single look and was not happy that their moods were not better matched. He would find no lightness of spirit until the dark problem of Nicolaa had been laid to rest.

"A fine day for a walk. It must be, for a knight to go about without his steed," William said by way of greeting.

"A fine day. Let us leave it at that," Rowland said.

"I will leave nothing. What is not fine? Have you not a

fine and prosperous holding and a beautiful and capable wife? Be cheered, Rowland."

Rowland kept walking. William, with a slight frown, dismounted and walked beside him, his horse following heavily behind them, a most unusual chaperon.

"You did not bed her," William said, striking and hitting the mark with one shot.

"I did not bed her," Rowland said without elaborating. The matter of the paint would never be mentioned by him. Some things did not bear repeating, even to William.

William kept his eyes on the horizon. "You surprise me."

"It was a bit of a surprise to me, as well."

"If you find her that unattractive, you should consider getting the marriage annulled. To be saddled with a wife who cannot produce an heir is bad enough; to be wed to a woman who can give you no pleasure is beyond what God or king can ask of a man."

"I will not seek an annulment," Rowland said flatly, kicking a stone out of the path at his feet. It careened into a swath of drying autumn grass with a satisfying crackle.

"None would fault you. The marriage is but days old. Surely the sooner you act—"

"I will not have this marriage annulled. I would not hurt Nicolaa in such a way."

"How is this hurtful to Nicolaa?" William asked in exaggerated innocence. "You hardly know each other. She seems well equipped to wave good-bye to another husband and occupy herself most happily at her embroidery until another comes through the gate. Or is it that you think she cares for you? If so, if her regard has grown so deep and so fast, then I can understand your refusal to consider a way out of the marriage."

The only response Rowland could find to such observations was to grunt and lengthen his stride.

William matched his stride and said, "Or is it that you have grown to care for her? I can well see it. She is a lovely lady, soft-tongued and well mannered. And accomplished. The price of her tapestries alone could keep a man in steel for all his days."

"I will not discuss this, William. I am not going to slither my way out of this marriage, no matter her manner or her riches."

"Well, if your mind is set, I will say no more," William said, his mouth twitching against a smile. "I was only trying to help."

Rowland was kept from having to form an answer by the arrival of Richard. He, too, dismounted to walk with them, his mount taking the opportunity to lift its tail and relieve itself. The smell of pungent manure rose to taint the autumn air. The men kept walking, as accustomed to the smell of manure as to the smells of blood and sweat.

"I am glad I found you, though the ride was pleasant. It is good land you have found here, Rowland. Weregrave is most fine," Richard said.

"Aye. It is," he answered.

"Isabel is anxious to speak with you," Richard said. "Indeed, she sent me off with a most desperate look. If she finds you, then she will escape the confines of the solar and the prick of the needle, though there is more on her mind than that. She wants you to arrange for the ladies to be married off. She thinks they are eager for husbands of their own."

"Are not all women eager for husbands of their own?" William said, looking askance at Rowland.

Aye, if not all, then most. Isabel had the right of it. Women of a certain age were meant to be married. The way to battle a cadre of women was to marry them off. Rowland grinned and lifted his face to the sky, sighing deeply. Nicolaa would no longer have her shield of skirts.

Blanche escaped the solar by pleading a need for the garderobe. With a squint of disapproval, Nicolaa let her go. Perette cast her an envious look as she left, as did Isabel, who was sucking a bloody finger. Blanche left the solar with a smile of victory and came across Ulrich and Edmund loitering in the hall just outside the solar wall. They greeted her with smiles of eagerness.

"You have flown the nest, lady," Ulrich said, coming toward her.

"I have flown straight into the hunter's net, it seems," she said.

"We will not harm you, gentle dove, nor eat you, nor cage you. Only let us . . . stroke your feathers," Ulrich said.

Blanche smiled. "When boys talk of stroking, then must a woman fly."

"I am no boy, lady," Ulrich protested. "I have reached my manhood fully."

"A man does not need to proclaim the existence of his manhood. It is apparent for all to see."

Edmund smiled at the turn in the conversation, glad he was well out of it. It was beyond his skill at courtship, but he was learning. It was true what they said of widows, judging by Lady Blanche.

"Look again, lady, and see my manhood," Ulrich said, coming ever nearer.

"I have looked. Do not all boys have hanging about

171

them some sign of the manhood they will one day achieve?" she asked, moving away from him even as her eyes urged him onward.

"Ah, but lady, my manhood does not hang. Not when a lady of your beauty and charm stands so near," Ulrich said, grinning at the wicked turn of their conversation.

"You flatter me," she said, returning his grin.

"I speak only the truth. If you doubt, I would allow you to stroke me and test the truth of my manhood yourself."

At that, Blanche burst out laughing and gave Ulrich her hand to kiss. He took it most gallantly, his kiss most chivalrous, his eyes gleaming.

She had forgotten the thrills to be found in dealing with men. What would it be like to marry again? Listening to Isabel had opened the door of speculation and possibility. That, and seeing how happy in marriage were both Isabel and Cathryn. It was possible to find happiness in marriage, even contentment; with only Nicolaa's marriages before her eyes, she had forgotten that truth.

"How long have you been a widow, Lady Agnes?" Isabel asked, pulling at a knot in her stitch.

Nicolaa would not allow herself the sigh she longed to voice. Back again to talk of marriages. Isabel seemed to have only one song and was determined to sing it relentlessly.

"Past ten years now," Agnes answered.

"Closer to twelve," her mother said.

"Aye, you are right. It was at Martinmas, now I recall it," Agnes said.

"Were you married long?" Cathryn asked.

"More than twenty years," she answered. "I was just into my time when the vows were exchanged."

"Yet ready, for all your youth," Jeanne said. "Your father would not have sent you off unless your body was ready for a man."

"I will not argue it," Agnes said easily. "I was ready. I wanted to be a wife. I yearned for children."

"You were plumped within the year," Jeanne said.

Agnes smiled and put down her needle. "Aye, and grinning through all. I was ne'er sick, not once. My body loved that child from the moment he was planted within me. I wanted him with all my strength."

The talk faltered, for all knew that Agnes had no living children, but it was Agnes herself who continued the tale, talking freely of something that she spoke of seldom.

"He came early. Early and hard. Ranulf was gone on some task for the old Henry, this one's grandsire; he was always off and about, valuable to the king and valued by him. A fine man with a stalwart reputation. A fine man," she said softly. "It was Candlemas, cold and dark; the sun had not shone for weeks. No child should be be born in winter. I pushed him out against my will, but he would come." She looked down at the tapestry lying beneath her hands. "He came. Dead. My first child, my lord's son, dead in my arms. He never drew a single breath on this earth. He's held his place in heaven now for thirty years."

None drew thread through cloth. None moved and none spoke. What worse could befall a woman than never to hold her living child?

"A bad time," Jeanne said.

"It was," Agnes said, taking a deep breath. "But I was plumped again soon enough. Ranulf claimed it was God's will and no fault of mine that his heir lay dead in the chapel. He never blamed me, and for that alone I would have loved him. This child was due midsummer; I was certain all was well and all would be well. I was sick from noon to dusk every day, so different from the first. I thought, Oh, this one will hold; this one will thrive. I was round and full when the pains began. Good, strong pains they were, your mother at my side, Nicolaa, praying for me and the babe. It was a good birth. I knew what I was about, this second time through, and the babe came easily. Dead, like his brother. The cord was wrapped around his throat. He lived long enough to die in his birthing."

"How horrible," Perette said.

"Aye, horrible," Agnes said hollowly.

"It happens," Jeanne said. "There is naught that can be done."

"Yet it is never easy," Cathryn said. She sat next to Agnes and took the older woman's hand in hers. It was a simple thing, to hold a hand, yet a wondrous kind thing as well. Agnes smiled and shook off her melancholy.

"All long ago," Agnes said. "My Ranulf dead now with them. A good man. He ever and only treated me well. I have only good memories of him. Without his arms about me, I do not know how I would have stood against the loss of two babes conceived only to die."

"He was a good man," Jeanne said, changing the tone, if not the direction of the conversation. "Your father was well pleased with him, I know. A fine-looking man, too, was he not, Agnes? We managed that well for you, did we not?"

"Oh, Mother," Agnes said, chuckling against her will

and her nature. "You are ever on the scent of a fine-looking man. There was more to him than that."

"Oh, aye, there should be more, but it does not hurt that he pleased the eye, does it?" Jeanne said. "Admit it once, ere you stand before God's throne. Did he not please you?"

"He pleased me," Agnes said with a gentle laugh, tucking her head against the answering female laughter.

Nicolaa did not laugh. That her aunt had married Ranulf in her youth she had known. That her aunt had suffered two stillbirths she had known. That Agnes had loved her husband and been gently loved by him she had not known.

"That is as it should be," Jeanne said, "for I would not have it that any child of mine be less contented in her marriage than I was."

"How long were you married?" Isabel asked, her needle abandoned.

"Five and thirty years, short a month," Jeanne said with some pride. It was a goodly distance for a marriage to have traveled. "A good match, it was, too. My father was most pleased. It netted us Aldewurda, which would be any man's pride. That Roger came with it was my pride."

"Was he handsome?" Beatrice asked.

"To my eyes, he was," Jeanne said. "Red-haired, green-eyed, as big as a siege tower and as unyielding." She grinned. "I found my pleasure of him."

"How old were you?" Beatrice asked.

"Old enough to want him," Jeanne said. "Younger than you are now, but times were different then and women were made women younger than today. I can only tell you I was ready, and never regretted an hour in his arms. Children he gave me by the armful; that was his greatest gift to me."

This story she had heard time upon time, yet the mood of the room was one of wistful longing and romance; even young Beatrice was asking questions Nicolaa would prefer she did not ask.

"But tell me of your man and how you came by him, Isabel, for the talk is that he was recently a Benedictine," Jeanne commanded.

"The talk . . ." Isabel said, pausing dramatically, "is true." And she smiled to show her victory over the Benedictine order.

" 'Tis no small thing to steal a man out of the Benedictine brotherhood," Ermengarde said.

"With prayer, all things are possible," Isabel said.

"Did you pray him out, then?" Jeanne said.

"Tell the tale from the start," Cathryn said. "It is better than spitting out parts when the whole is so remarkable."

"You are right. It is a remarkable tale and I will tell you the best of it." Isabel leaned forward over the tapestry, the firelight and the bright sunlight from the wind hole lighting her eyes to clearest hazel. Like precious glass her eyes were, revealing all within her heart. That she loved her husband was blindingly clear. "I loved him from childhood. We were fostered together, and ever and always my eye went to Richard. He was the most beautiful, the most noble of men. Any task, any skill to which he set his hand, he excelled at. It was a waking dream to watch him train in his warrior skills, and how I did watch."

"Yet were you not betrothed?" Perette asked.

"Oh, aye, and to his eldest brother," Isabel said. "It was shameful of me, I do know it, but my heart can bear no shame where Richard is concerned. With a prayer, a childish prayer of heartfelt longing, I prayed for Richard to be my husband. At the word," she said solemnly, "at the very word, I received the news that my betrothed was dead and that my contract had been arranged upon Richard."

"A miracle," Beatrice said.

"It was," Isabel said. "God answered my selfish prayer. By my words, I killed a man. Two men, for the middle brother died as well, to be certain that Richard would be all-encompassed."

"Encompassed?" Perette asked.

"Yea, for did Richard want a wife? Nay, he wanted to live out his life as a Benedictine, serving God in that holy way. Think you he wanted me? Nay, he did not. And so my prayer was answered, but my heart could only grieve at what I had accomplished. Two men dead and a husband, a most unwilling husband, in my bed. Nay, listen to this part of my tale with great attention: do not pray with selfish motive lest your prayer be answered and you are made to live with the result."

"Yet all is well now," Perette said.

"Aye, for God is most merciful and Richard most forgiving," Isabel said. "He has left the Benedictines behind him, longing for that life not at all. The secret of my tale is this: Richard has loved me as long as I have loved him. A love requited, most deeply requited, is my daily portion. I am most content," she said, and it showed.

"All can see the depth of your contentment," Jeanne said.

"That is good, for I would not hide it," Isabel said with a laugh. "Now ask for Cathryn's tale of love, for it will warm your souls."

All eyes turned to Cathryn, who sat quietly between Agnes and Ermengarde. She looked reluctant to speak, for which Nicolaa could only commend her. All this talk of love and marriage was most disturbing. It could only feed unrealistic dreams within the heart, dreams better left unspoken and unrecognized.

"It is only a tale of a marriage arranged by a king. Who among us has not the same tale within her?" Cathryn said.

Well said, Nicolaa thought. Cathryn of Greneforde was a woman not given to frivolous dreaming nor of making much of very little. An arranged marriage—for what other kind was there?—was all that a woman could expect. Love was the theme of troubadors and legends; it was not the stuff of every day, not even with Rowland the Dark as husband.

"Not all women find themselves married to William le Brouillard," Jeanne said.

"Nay, that is true," Cathryn said, a smile growing on her face. She was transformed into radiance by that smile. "The king chose well. I, too, am most content."

"You look it," Jeanne said.

" 'Tis my husband's wish that I do so, as well as proclaim my well-being with devoted regularity," she said, her smile growing. "I find it most amusing to tickle his ear. Or not. As the mood moves me."

"You are devilish, lady," Agnes said.

"When the results are so sweet, I cannot find the will to repent," she said with a playful shrug.

"I am most eager for sweet results," Perette said with a heavy sigh. "I declare myself ready for a husband, if only my father would decide who it is to be."

Nicolaa tamped down her alarm at this unsolicited statement. Surely it was only the result of the present mood of the room. Perette was too young to marry.

"It cannot be long now," Isabel said, completely contradicting Nicolaa's thoughts. "And is your betrothal set, Beatrice? Your time is also close."

"Beatrice's betrothed," Nicolaa answered stiffly, "is a man older than her father, who has had six wives under him. That he delays in snatching up Beatrice is only cause for rejoicing."

The romantic mood of the solar grew instantly sober, and the conversation faltered to a halt. Nicolaa could not have been more pleased.

"I would like to make a gift to you, a delayed wedding gift, if you choose to think it so," Nicolaa said. "Cathryn, Isabel, I give you each a tapestry. For Cathryn the woodland tapestry, and for Isabel the prayer tapestry. Please take these gifts with my heartfelt wishes for your continued contentment."

"Nay, it is too fine a gift to bestow upon a near stranger," Cathryn said.

"Please tell me you did not listen to my talk of wanting a finished tapestry," Isabel said. "I spoke in jest. I did not want you to think—"

"I thought nothing," Nicolaa said. "You are guests, welcome guests. Our husbands share a bond, is that not so? I think Rowland would be most pleased to find that I have given you each what is only of my bounty."

"You seek to please him with this gift?" Cathryn asked.

"If it pleases you to think so, then I do this to please him," Nicolaa said. "I give you only out of my abundance. I am rich in tapestries. My mother, Lady Agnes, the ladies of my family back as far as words can tell, have created more tapestries than we need. I have only time to create more."

Day upon day, hour upon hour. She had time.

The talk of the tapestries and of husbands ended with the arrival of Father Timothy into the solar. Nicolaa had no choice but to grant him entrance; he was her priest, after all.

"Your husband has returned," he said, "and would see you."

He did not say it joyfully. She did not hear it joyfully. Still, it was a small request, and she had no reason to deny him.

Rowland, bred in Aquitaine, would no more think of entering the solar, the exclusive domain of women, than he would of hearing confession. 'Twas not his place to do either. Nor would she invite him in. The solar was hers, the sole place where she could withdraw without fear of husbandly interference. So she would go out to meet him.

She rose to her feet and was beaten to the door by both Isabel and Cathryn, eager, no doubt, to reunite with their husbands, if the tales of love they told could be believed. In fact, as she stood, all the ladies rushed to the doorway, eager to be free of the solar and out amongst the men, fleeing the sanctuary she had created for them. She was left alone with only Father Timothy at her side.

"This marriage," he said haltingly, "does it sit well with you?"

"I am content, Father. Have no care for me. I know my duty and will perform it diligently. Is that not what God requires?"

"God also would give you the desires of your heart," he said, searching her profile. She felt his look like a touch and moved away from him to the door.

"I am content. My most pressing desire is to finish this

tapestry. I think it will be my finest yet," she said.

"You are skilled, Nicolaa," he said, moving with her.

"Perhaps. What I am certain of is that I am diligent. One stitch after another, Father. It is as simple as a single stitch. It is the key to surviving this life, I think. One stitch upon another; let God manage the design."

He smiled. She returned his smile. He understood her meaning. She was a lady of the land; he was a priest bound to God. Let them each find what rest they could in that, step by step, stitch by stitch. A life was built on such small acts of seeming unimportance. Only God could see the significance of the whole as He directed their paths to His own glory.

"Tell me, Father," she said, ending the moment, "how does Etienne progress on the panel he is fashioning for the chapel?"

"He fares well. His talent is genuine, his touch light as goose down. It will be a fine addition to the chapel."

He continued on, accepting her change of topic gracefully, as she knew he would. She had told him what he needed to know as her priest: she was faring well in her marriage. He need not worry about her. That her marriage was unconsummated was not something he needed to know at present; all would know if Rowland sought an annulment. She was not as certain now that he would. He had seemed, if not eager, then determined enough to consummate last night. Until the matter of her dryness. She still found his remark inexplicable. Why had he been angry? Had she not been willing, supine, available to his every touch? Yea, she had. It was her duty to be so, and she knew well her duty in matters conjugal.

Yet . . . yet she knew that he had touched her with more

than his hands and his mouth. He had touched upon the edges of her dream with his gentle passion. She had not expected that he would strive so to bring her to her pleasure. How odd that a man should take the time for that. If not for the memories of other men, other hands, other mouths upon her body, she might have faltered and fallen into passion and wanting. She could not. She would not. She knew better than to fall with only the promise of a man's arms to catch her. She knew better than to trust anything a man might say or do. Even if that man be Rowland the Dark.

The solar behind them, Nicolaa and Father Timothy entered the hall. At sight of her, Blanche and Ulrich broke apart somewhat guiltily, which caused Isabel to smile and shake her head. Nicolaa could see no cause for amusement. Better for all concerned if Blanche stayed in the safety of the solar.

Isabel stood in front of Rowland, Richard and William cast about him like casually thrown dice. Her head back and her manner ardent, Isabel spoke to Rowland. He looked down at her, his manner somber, and nodded. In agreement? In understanding? The distance was too great to discern. Richard spoke sharply to his wife, a rebuke of sorts, which she answered quickly. Then she smiled, a blinding grin that drew an unwilling smile from her serious husband.

Rowland looked at her then, his own countenance serious, his eyes scanning the hall. The ladies were all about him: Blanche with her amorous squire in a corner, Ermengarde at the fire, Agnes at the doorway to the stair, Jeanne in a chair by the fire, Perette and Beatrice edging closer to Edmund, who stood behind his lord, Richard. On Rowland's face was a strange look, full of intensity and purpose. It was never well when a man had such a look. It meant he had decided something, and what a man decided to do was usually troublesome for a woman. What was his intent?

She would find out. It was time for the midday meal, the largest of the day. It was a lengthy meal, and she sat next to her husband, with William seated on Rowland's right. She would have more than enough time to determine what thoughts lurked behind her husband's dark eyes.

The blessing was spoken, the bread broken, and then she spoke.

"What was it you wanted to discuss with me?"

Rowland took a long swallow of wine before answering. She waited patiently and sipped her own wine. She would be pleasant in all things; that was the way to manage a husband.

"I am going to begin discussions to arrange marriages for the unpledged ladies," he said. She dripped wine onto her bodice, having forgotten to swallow. "And I want to move matters forward on the betrothals of the two younger girls, Perette and Beatrice. They are ready for marriage now."

He had spoken softly, yet the words rang within her loud and harsh. There had been a note of finality beneath the softness of his voice. He meant to do it. She looked down absently at the stain on her bodice; there was a fine line of dark red drops on her pale yellow bliaut. It was ruined. And Rowland had ruined it.

He was going to arrange marriages? This was completely beyond her experience. Her other husbands had left in her care the managing of the betrothal contracts, or lack thereof. Rowland was completely overstepping his bounds, though she knew what he was suggesting was legal. Nay, he had not suggested. He had declared. It was within his legal rights to do so, but it was *wrong*.

An angry retort was on her lips, pushing, rushing to get past as sloppily and as urgently as the wine had. She could just refuse. She would refuse him. Her ladies would stay with her, in safety and comfort. He could not force them out.

But he could.

Nay, she could not refuse, but could she softly reason him away from his declaration?

"All is well in Weregrave," she said. "The ladies are content."

"Are they?" he asked, his look amused. "Shall we ask them?"

After the tales they had heard today of love and marriage and children, nay, she did not think it was the time to ask if they would like to marry. But she would not retreat so early from this assault. When attacked, she would hold her position, bluffing her way to success.

"Ask them if you will," she said, hoping he would do no such thing. "They have been content for year upon year, safe, loved, protected. What more could they want or need?"

He took a bite of his fish before answering. "It is said in Aquitaine that the greatest gift is to love, not to be loved. To risk all for the chance to love . . . is that not a risk worth taking?"

"I thought we were speaking of marriage, not of love," she said, setting aside her knife, her appetite flown.

"But will they find love outside of marriage? The church frowns upon such, Nicolaa," he said, smiling.

He had the most irritating sense of humor. She supposed

that was another trait acquired in Aquitaine.

"The church understands well the nature and source of love," she said. "It is to be found within God's bosom, is it not? God is the author of perfect love, sacrificial love. What would a man know of that?"

"Yet Jesus Christ was man and God in perfect harmony, and did He not give His life in sacrifice? I think a man may know the pain and joy of love very well, Nicolaa."

"If the man be Christ, I will and can believe it," she said, staring into his eyes, defying his charm and the unspoken promise of love he held out to her. "I will not believe it else."

He smiled and reached out a hand to touch the red drops that stained her bodice, one by one. His finger brushed against her chest, skimming the gentle rise of her breast. "Yet a man sheds his blood for the woman of his heart, does he not, Nicolaa? Would I not let myself be bled for you, drop upon drop, to see you safe from all the harms the world deals out?"

"For the woman of his heart?" she said, surprised at the pain and tenderness his words evoked. "Does a man then have a heart? Christ's heart was pierced upon His cross. What man can say the same?"

"I can," he said, his dark eyes hot and soft, intent upon her face, his hand rising to her chin to hold her softly.

He could, if she believed in the tale of Lubias. He could, if she believed that he walked the earth empty of love because Lubias had flown to heaven with his heart. He could—he could claim a broken and bleeding heart, given to the woman of his . . . dreams. Aye, his dreams. He could claim such, and if she believed, then he would have won his point. But she did not believe. A man could not love.

She would not believe he could for if it be so, then why had no man ever loved her?

"You have a scattering of golden freckles on your nose," he said, smiling, breaking the darkness of their conversation, forcing them into the light. "And one on the edge of your mouth, just here," he said, touching the corner of her mouth with his fingertip. "Like stars they are, like the shimmering of pearl in the night, like the sparkle of snow in the sun. Glimmering, fetching." He smiled. "Beautiful."

She ignored him. She ignored his words and his touch and the skittering of feeling that sparked along her spine and in the pit of her belly. Yea, she ignored him and his words; he wanted to have his way in the matter of the marriages. That explained his use of courtly love. They were embattled; he only used the weapons he thought would win his cause. She was not so foolish a woman as to fall for such a simple ruse.

"When do you plan to begin?" she said, ignoring his attempts at humor and chivalry.

"Immediately," he said, without even the courtesy of pausing to pretend to consider. He dropped his hand and sat back in his chair, his attempts at wooing over.

"Perette is very young and Beatrice younger still," she said. "Delay will only benefit them."

"Are they younger than when you first wed?"

"You know my age when first I said the vows."

"And it went badly for you. But do not think that all women suffer the same, Nicolaa. A woman needs a husband. A woman must and should be wed."

"Not at such an age," she said softly.

"Aye, at just such an age," he said.

He would do it. He was determined. Further argument

would only reveal the direction of her thoughts and the state of her mind. She would do neither. He would be going back to one battle or another soon and then she would end all talk of marriages and contracts and alliances. She had only to wait. He was determined, but she was patient.

"I will return," he said. "I will always return."

She turned to face him, her eyes wide with shock at the accuracy of his strike into her plans. His dark eyes stared into hers, black and impenetrable and unblinking. He would be back. He believed it; she could see the belief in his eyes.

But the marriage between them had not been consummated. It could be annulled before he next returned. He might never return.

She let the thought rise up in her eyes, giving him the chance to read her, testing his skill.

"I will not seek an annulment," he said softly, his dark eyes moist. "I will not leave you. I will convince you of that, Nicolaa, as well as teach you the joys of the marriage bed. There is so much I want to show you. So many ways for a man to bring a woman to her pleasure. It will take a lifetime to teach you all I know of pleasure. I will not ever seek an annulment from you. Put it from your thoughts. Cast it from your heart."

She turned from him, hiding her eyes and shielding her face with the barrier of her hair. These words, these Aquitaine words that framed a promise she could never again believe, tore at her defenses. He was a very adept warrior to understand her, his foe, so quickly and so well. Yet she was as experienced with men as he claimed to be with women. He would not win a point from her so easily. Nay, he would not, though the test she had devised had not given her the answer she sought. He was too adept at reading her thoughts. Such skill in a man was never good for a woman. Even more reason to wish him gone, and quickly. It was early autumn, the season of battles and hunts. The king would need him soon enough. He would leave and she would rule her own house. There would be no marriages that she could prevent. The only woman she could not seem to save from the rigors of marriage was herself. But she would save the others.

"Will you not?" she said to him. "You have grounds for annulment."

"But not for long," he said, laying his hand atop hers.

His hands were rough, scarred, brown. His left thumb was bruised at the base, and the veins were thick upon the backs of his palms. Warrior's hands.

That hand rose to touch her face, his fingertips gentle on her chin, drawing her face to meet his, urging her eyes to read the message in his own. He wanted her to read him and the look in his dark eyes. He wanted her to read him as he had read her. She did not want to know him so intimately as to know his thoughts. She did not want the intrusion of such intimacy. Her heart fluttered all the same at the intent behind his words and the velvety intensity of his black eyes.

He meant to consummate the marriage. It was a promise.

"You say that with great certainty. I am not so certain," she said, mocking him.

She had insulted him, to put it gently, yet she understood him well enough to know that he would not strike her. She did not have that to fear from him, at least. He was a mild man. Yea, he was mild, but she did not expect his response.

Rowland laughed.

Worse, William laughed.

That, she had not intended. She had not intended to shame him before his friend. That far she would push no man, no matter the purity of her cause. She had shamed him, yet he did not act shamed.

"Your lady wife doubts your abilities," William said. "You have much work ahead of you."

"It will not be work," Rowland said lightly, touching her hand again, showing no displeasure.

An odd sort of warrior, this husband.

"You have left her in doubt. 'Twas unkind of you," William said, winking at her.

"It was. I will mend my ways and then all doubts will be cast off. I take full responsibility."

"As well you should. 'Tis the man's province to convince his wife of his prowess."

"Aye, as we all have heard," Rowland said, grinning. "Let us hear no more of that for now, William; I would protect Nicolaa from your coarse ways."

"I? Coarse? Never," he said. "I only—"

"William, you do not help," Cathryn said.

At her words, William stopped. Nicolaa could only smile her thanks. Her smile faltered at Rowland's next whispered words.

"You *can* be certain, Nicolaa. Our marriage will be consummated."

Because he had said it in front of William, making it

something of a point of honor, she was convinced that he was certain he would perform. She, however, was not certain. How many tries did a man require to penetrate his willing wife?

Chapter Twelve

As the tables were being cleared away, the company of the hall broke into smaller groups. Blanche made her hurried way over to Nicolaa, her look uncharacteristically animated.

"Nicolaa," she said, her black eyes shining, "what can be done to see me married again?"

"What can be done?" Nicolaa repeated blankly.

"Aye, what can be done? My uncle has forgotten me; that seems obvious. Can we not remind him that I am of marriageable age with a dowry that would suit many men?"

"You want to marry," Nicolaa said. The words were strange, but how much stranger the desire that prompted them.

"Of course she wants to marry," Jeanne said, joining them. "What woman would not?"

Nicolaa only stared at her grandmother, giving her answer with a look.

"Blanche is a young woman, ripe with life," Jeanne said. "It is natural for her to want to marry, to have a man of her own, to have children."

"Without a sizable dowry, she can have none," Nicolaa said. "And her dowry is small."

"Still, there must be men who would find my dowry sufficient. I am not Ermengarde. I would rather marry a man equal to my worth than hug my pride to my chest night upon night."

"And what of your uncle?" Nicolaa said. "He is not eager to make a match for you."

Blanche lost some of her ardor at that blunt reality until Isabel said, "There are more marriageable men than women in the world, Blanche; you will have your pick from many, not from few. And I have been talking to Richard, who is cousin to your uncle by some distant connection; he should be able to prod your uncle into making a proper match for you. All should fall together nicely," Isabel said, smiling confidently.

Nicolaa could hardly wait for the day when Isabel and her single topic of conversation were safely back behind the walls of Dornei.

"Do you truly want to marry?" she asked Blanche again. "You have been married; you know what it is."

"Aye, I know what it is to be married. I know what it is to be unmarried. I choose to marry," Blanche said.

That was all and more than Isabel needed to hear; she twined arms with Blanche and they strode across the hall together to find Richard. Nicolaa could only watch, her mouth unhinged.

"You have let slip what few wits you had at your baptism, Nicolaa," Jeanne said, "to believe that any woman would prefer a life without a man to life with one."

"I have experienced life both without and with. I prefer without," Nicolaa said.

"More fool you," Jeanne said. "I have lived both ways as well and would much prefer living again with Roger than this dim life I live now. And you cannot tell me that you do not have your own fond memories of your time with the men who have spoken vows with you. You have had your fun, with Macair most assuredly, if you were honest enough to admit it. There was a man to make a woman smile away the day."

"I have no wish to smile away the day."

"Another foolish wish. What better way to spend the day than in dreaming of the night? Is this the face you put before Rowland? Have you scared him from your bed?"

"I have not," Nicolaa said.

"Nay, I know you are not so foolish. As to that, what sort of man would refuse the gift of a willing woman? Whatever odd views you hold about marriage, I know you well enough to know that you would not deny your husband that most basic of needs. What is wrong with Rowland, then?"

"There is nothing wrong with Rowland," she said, completely shocked by her impulsive defense of him. "He is a gentle man, thoughtful of my needs, concerned that I be comfortable in his company before attempting consummation."

"Humph," Jeanne said. "There are better, quicker ways to learn a woman."

"Would you have me argue the point when he sees this as a gift of considerate restraint?"

"Nay, you have it aright. Let him follow his course. But it is a strange one," Jeanne said, shaking her gray head.

There was no arguing that. What was wrong with Rowland that he could not seem to bed his wife?

"She thinks something is wrong with you," William said.

Rowland shrugged. "That shows the depth of her mistreatment. I only endeavor to bring her to arousal. She knows not the state."

Never had they spoken so openly, and never had William seen greater need for honesty. None of what Rowland said would ever pass his lips, not even to Cathryn; this was the talk of men closer than brothers.

William understood that Rowland was trying to heal Nicolaa's hurts.

Yet how much of Rowland's reluctance to join with her was traceable to Lubias? Rowland had been celibate many years, nourishing the memory of Lubias, polishing their love. What place did a living wife have in that shrine?

He could not broach the subject with Rowland, that he knew. None dared pry the memory of Lubias from his grasp; Rowland had made that clear from the beginning. Did Nicolaa know as much? It might help her in this new marriage to know the depth of love Rowland was capable of.

It would be a blessing most profound if Rowland could find peace with his new wife. Love might never be possible, not with his heart so fully engaged with Lubias. But there were other gifts in marriage: peace and harmony and joined purpose in this life.

But first, he would have to consummate the marriage.

*   *   *

The orchard was deserted, the trees waiting patiently for their winter pruning, their branches reaching for the high stone walls and the freedom of the field. But they were rooted firmly in Weregrave soil. They would go nowhere. Even their high-flung branches would be cut back in the dark of deep winter, stunted to make them produce. For all of that, the trees of the orchard did not look saddened; they only looked well tended.

Perette and Blanche walked beneath them. Perette longed to climb her favorite tree, but held herself in check. She did not want to look childish in case Ulrich or Edmund was watching.

"I heard them at table," Beatrice said. "The marriage is not consummated."

"You must have misheard," Perette said. "That cannot be right. Rowland is most handsome. Nicolaa is no tender virgin. It cannot be right."

"I heard them," Beatrice said.

"Do you think they are too old for such urges to be strong?" Perette asked, tossing back her curling hair.

The urges were most strong upon her, and stronger still with the arrival of Ulrich and Edmund. She could not quite decide which she preferred. Ulrich was very handsome, his blue eyes winning and his shoulders impressive, but it was his manner of speech that most beguiled her. Edmund had a fine look and a good seat, and he had the advantage, at least with Perette, of being as unskilled in the courtly arts as she. They were well matched in that. Still, Ulrich could turn her head with a single well-phrased compliment, and there was no denying the pleasure of such chivalry.

"Nay, I think that urge stays long upon a man, at least

the priests tell us so," Beatrice said. "I think it is that Nicolaa is afraid of such intimacy with a stranger."

"He is her husband and lord!" Perette said, shocked. "No stranger come sneaking between the sheets."

"A stranger a week past. A husband of two nights," Beatrice said.

Beatrice did not think that lack of interest was the source of the delayed consummation. She remembered too well meeting with her betrothed not six months past; he had seemed most interested, and he was fully fifty years in age. But she would not say such to Perette. Perette liked all men and was too eager for her own marriage to feel anything approaching fear. Besides, Ulrich and Edmund were upon them, closing the distance to the orchard. It was not proper to discuss such things as consummation—

"Why does Lord Rowland not consummate his marriage to Lady Nicolaa?" Perette asked the very moment the two were within hearing distance.

Beatrice sighed heavily and closed her eyes in embarrassment.

Edmund cleared his throat awkwardly in answer and cast his eyes sidelong at Ulrich. Ulrich was to answer for them both, and he was ready for the task. He answered as if all mankind, himself foremost, had been insulted.

"Lord Rowland is a worthy knight," Ulrich said. "All he does, or does not do, is out of honor and tenderness for his wife."

"He honors her by not possessing her body? I pray now that the Lord spare me from such an honorable husband," Perette said.

"You would do well indeed to have such a husband as Lord Rowland."

"How would I know I have him, then, if he dare not enter the marriage bed?" Perette said, her eyes showing her amusement.

Ulrich grinned. "Oh, a lady such as you would know when a man of worth is within her grasp."

"Not if I cannot lay hand to him. You do give my sex too much credit if you think us capable of that."

"Can an honorable knight give a lady too much credit? Is that not the very source of courtly love?"

"Do we speak then of courtly love? I thought the topic was marital love. But I think Nicolaa better served by courtly love, for on marital love, she has a tenuous grasp. Or be it better said that Lord Rowland's grasp is tenuous."

"Nay, he is tender only. His grasp on Nicolaa will withstand all."

"Yet he hesitates to touch her," she said.

"Tenderness is the most powerful touch, is that not so?" he asked, moving to stand next to her.

"My own husband shall instruct me as to that, and with a firmer hand that Rowland seems to possess."

"You do not doubt him," Ulrich said on a laugh.

"Doubt him? Not at all. He cannot lay hold of his wife. Nay, I do not doubt. He has proven himself well enough in that."

For herself, Beatrice had passed beyond embarrassment to mortification. After a quick glance at Edmund, she judged he felt the same. This talk was no fine thing to bandy in the damp air of an autumn afternoon. Even the branches of the trees seemed to twist upon themselves in shame.

"You do not know him," Ulrich said. "There is no knight more courteous or gentle in his dealings with women than

Rowland d'Albret. He will lay Lady Nicolaa down on the marriage bed and see his duty done upon his wife."

"The best time for seeing marital duty done is upon the wedding night, and that night is long past," Perette said.

"Not so long past for Rowland, for he is longer yet," Ulrich said, grinning.

"Can any man be so long as to stretch more than one night?"

"Aye," Ulrich said. "Ask your lady in a week. If she can speak beyond her smiles, she will answer you."

"A week? Must she wait another week for him to find his way into her bed? He may find himself without a wife if she be made to wait so long upon a hesitant husband."

"He waits for her," Ulrich declared.

"He waits for naught. She is before him; let him come." Ulrich laughed and elbowed Edmund at the word.

"You understand little of these things," he said, chuckling.

"I understand enough to know that Nicolaa is not breached and Rowland is the cause. Or lacks the cause, since he tarries when any man would rush—"

"Aye," he cut in, his voice rising to match hers, "any man, yet Rowland is not any man—"

"Aye," Perette said hotly, "mayhap he is no man at all!"

"Enough!" Edmund said, ending the riposte. What had started as play had ended in anger. "No one speaks ill of Rowland nor of Nicolaa; none here would think it. You played at words and they sliced you. Leave off."

Ulrich smiled and dropped to his knee at Perette's feet. "I ask your pardon. My tongue ran off with me."

"Only because I urged you on," Perette said. "Let us pardon each other. I would not speak ill of Nicolaa's husband, a man so honored by all who know him."

"Well spoken, Perette," Edmund said, smiling at her.

Well spoken, yea, but still they wondered as they left the grove: when would the marriage be consummated?

"I do not know when he plans to consummate the marriage. I only know that for reasons of his own, he has not," Richard said.

"Whatever his reasons, he is wrong," said Isabel as they walked through the town. "To delay consummation is the worst sort of torture, for Nicolaa, if not for himself."

She spoke from experience; this they both knew. Richard had delayed the consummation of their marriage by one night, for what he considered very good reasons at the time. No doubt Rowland did the same. And no doubt Isabel was right; it was a mistake. A mistake of two nights. Double the damage to an unsteady relationship, if damage could be figured in such a way.

"I have no power to force him to bed his wife," Richard said, frowning. "He will do what he thinks best, as must we all."

"I think what is best is for me to talk to him, if you will not."

"If that is a threat to force me to action, it is ill-judged."

"Better ill-judged action than none at all!"

"You will *not* interfere in this, Isabel. What happens in their marriage is between them and God."

"I am concerned only with what is *not* happening."

"I will not bandy words and meanings with you. You will not speak of this to him," he said, his voice grim.

"You are determined to stop me? Very well," she said, smiling, goading him. "I invite you to try."

"If you would get yourself another husband, now is the time to try," Jeanne said.

"I am too old," Agnes said, looking into the fire.

"Ridiculous." Jeanne snorted. "I had your brother when I was older than you, and you have a fine, fat manor to sweeten the pot."

"What of Nicolaa?" Agnes asked, looking at her mother.

"Nicolaa has a fine husband who shows no signs of leaving her, though he be slow to perform his manly function. Any man who will stay with a woman without the bedding of her is a man who will stay. Nicolaa will be fine, though it is clear she does not yet know it. Nicolaa's life is her own. Look to yourself. Would you remain a chaste widow when there is a man to be had?"

Her mother spoke the truth, as was her way, though sometimes the truth rubbed hard. Nicolaa would be well. Her lot in life was no different from many another woman's.

When Agnes hesitated, Jeanne said, "I taught you better, girl, unless you would prefer the cloister with its routine of silence, prayer, and fasting? For mark me, this husband is not one to let Nicolaa turn his holding into a mock convent, as the others have done. Nay, he begins even now to shove us out the gate and into the care of waiting husbands. He may even find one for me. And I'd take him, without hesitation. Better to die in a strong man's embrace than smothered by all these skirts. So I ask you again. Will you marry?"

Agnes looked into her mother's eyes and gave the only answer she could give.

She gave the only answer she could give with those black eyes staring down at her.

"Yea, I would marry. The right man."

Rowland smiled down at her. "I would not have you marry the wrong one."

Ermengarde was a little taken aback by the sweet beauty of his smile. What was wrong with Nicolaa that she could not draw this man into her bed?

"With my paltry dowry, most men are the wrong man," she said.

It was her cross to bear in this life, that her position was so much more substantial than her dowry. Yet if she had no lands and rents to bring to a marriage, what man worthy of her could even ask? None could or should marry a woman with so little in material wealth to bring to the marriage contract. So she was unmarried. She would not marry beneath her status, no matter how her brother railed. She would have gone into the convent long before now, but she lacked even the sum to see herself well situated in a worthy convent. The best convents did not take paupers.

"What do you bring?" Rowland asked, going to the heart of her dilemma. She appreciated his directness. It was a relief to be able to discuss her situation openly.

"I have a manor, Migeham, but it has been ill-managed. The profits from it are very low. It is quite pretty, but what man cares for pretty when there are no profits?"

"Only the wrong man cares only for profits," Rowland said. "But how if I add to your dowry? I have much land in Aquitaine; would a gift of twenty acres and a small manor add to your worth sufficiently to net you the husband a woman of your merit deserves?"

Twenty acres in Aquitaine? It was a rare gift, and it left her speechless. With her manor and twenty acres of desirable Aquitaine land, she could have any husband she would want.

Raising her head and looking up into his dark eyes, Ermengarde said, "I thank you. I will agree to consider a possible betrothal."

Rowland smiled and bowed before her. "That is all I ask. That you consider."

"All I ask is that you consider," Father Timothy said.

He and Nicolaa were kneeling side by side in the chapel, the cold stone under her knees keeping her firmly rooted in reality. She needed such rooting. His suggestion was astounding. As astounding as the parting of the Red Sea or the turning of water into wine in that long-ago wedding, against the natural order of the natural world.

She could have the marriage annulled. *She* could end this marriage. She could be free of husbands, at least for a time, until another husband was found for her. Until another man was rewarded for good service and given Nicolaa and all her earthly possessions into his use. Unless she gave all to the church first, beggaring herself, and retreated to the feminine confines of the cloister.

Then she could be free of husbands at last.

She took a slow breath, steadying herself at the heady freedom of the thought. She sensed that Father Timothy had his own reasons for suggesting such a course. He would rise in esteem and power for arranging such a spectacular donation to church lands and coffers. He would possibly remain as her priest, the lone man allowed access to her. She understood men well enough to know that some dark purpose of his own might be fulfilled in such an arrangement. Yet, for all that he was a priest, he was also a man, and she knew how to deal with men. Also, he was not a bad man, nor a bad priest; he was only tempted, and who among them had not been tempted by one thing or another?

For herself, it was freedom from the rule of men that tempted her.

The marriage had not been consummated. The marriage would remain unconsummated until Rowland deemed her ready for his possession. She would never be ready for that. Another man thrusting and grunting between her legs, taking physical possession of her, was nothing she yearned for.

To have the marriage annulled, to cast off a husband as she had been cast off so many times, held a mesmerizing appeal. To give her legacy to the church, to cast away all the wealth her ancestors had striven to gain, was the single catching point. Yet, without a child, had all not been cast away already? What truly did she have to lose? Except Rowland. Nay, except a husband.

Nicolaa smiled and bowed her head before the altar of Christ.

"I will consider it," she said softly.

"It is in consideration of you that he hesitates," Isabel said.

Nicolaa had somehow gained a companion as she left the chapel. She increased the length of her stride, but Isabel had a quick step and would not be left behind.

"He does not know me. I do not think that consideration of me is foremost in his thoughts," Nicolaa said.

"He is your husband—"

"He is a stranger and I have been given to him as wife," Nicolaa said. Let Isabel attach no romantic notions to the marriage, as was her tendency.

The comment at least made Isabel pause, which was something.

"It was not so for you and your husband," Nicolaa added.

"Nay, it was not. We knew each other long ere we wed," Isabel admitted.

"And cared for each other as well?" Nicolaa prodded. "You have the look of ease, of comfort with each other, and the manner, too. There is none of that in my bond with Rowland."

Bond. They had no bond beyond the marriage contract, and that could be dissolved. She knew better than anyone how readily it could be dissolved.

"You put it most simply," Isabel said. "I can assure you that there was nothing simple about it. I have no wish to dishonor my husband, but he was not eager to marry. In fact, he was violently opposed to the idea."

"Violently?"

"Violently, but in that he misjudged. I am not afraid of him," Isabel said, smiling softly.

Nicolaa chuckled at the woman's confidence and silently wished her the joy of first marriage, when a woman could still believe in such a thing as love. It was a sweet time in a woman's life and too quickly over, yet she could not wish such fantasy back upon herself. Reality might be cold, but the footing was firm; she knew what was possible and what was not. She did not yearn for more. She would not go back to the girl she had been.

"I wish you the joy of that. It is not pleasant to fear a husband," Nicolaa said.

"You need not fear Rowland," Isabel said, misunderstanding her meaning. "Do not misjudge him. He is a man made to love."

"Hmmm," Nicolaa said, her expression amused.

"Truly," Isabel insisted. "You know of his Lubias."

"Yea, you yourself told the tale very well. And . . . I had heard something of this great love before, perhaps three winters ago. This is a well-known tale, is it not?"

"A tale, yea, it is that, but William has known Rowland long, and the truth of this tale of love is deeper than the telling. Lubias died before Rowland reached Damascus, yet he went on, his thirst for death as great as his love for her. He almost died, there beneath the hot walls of Damascus, but for William riding to save him, his own life at risk. They have been together ever since, yet not even William can come closer to Rowland than the living memory he carries of his Lubias."

"The friendship between Rowland and William is as familiar as Rowland's grief for his wife."

"Yet is it not more than grief? Is it not love, a love that could not die, though she did? She died long years ago now, yet still he loves. No other woman has come to him since Lubias left his arms. No other. Until you, Nicolaa."

But he had not come to her, had he? Was his devotion to Lubias the thing that kept him from her bed, rather than the consideration for her that he claimed? It was odd to attribute such devotion to a man, but it was a more likely reason for his hesitation than any other he had offered.

Could Rowland have truly loved Lubias? Was any man capable of such devotion? It was something to ponder.

They had almost reached the hall, and still Isabel kept talking of Rowland and his attributes. Could any man hold so many honors without bursting? Rowland, according to Isabel, could.

"Never would he abandon his vow to you, Nicolaa, no matter what the cause." It was then that Nicolaa knew Isabel was aware the marriage had not been consummated. And if Isabel knew then all did.

Nicolaa could only smile her delight. She would have no shortage of witnesses in ecclesiastical court as to the state of her marriage. Was there anyone within Were-grave's walls who did not know?

Chapter Thirteen

"Was that the reason for William's jest? I heard only pieces of words strung loosely. I did not know," Cathryn said.

"How could you not? All know of it," Isabel answered. "But I have talked with Nicolaa, assuring her of the depth of Rowland's heart; he is capable of such great love. I think I eased her."

"You spoke with her about his great love? About Lubias?" Cathryn asked.

"Aye," Isabel said.

They sat within the chamber Isabel and Cathryn now shared, the men having been relegated to the floor of the hall. They were alone and assured of privacy, as the tower was nearly empty this time of day. The day was bright and mild, the sun full and warm, the earth drying fast. It was a good day to be out-of-doors, yet they sat within, talking of men and marriage and the depth of a man's love.

"In that, I think, you have stumbled, Isabel," Cathryn said, rising to her feet and crossing the room to the wind hole. The breeze blew against her face, bringing to her senses the rich smells of earth and grass.

"Nay, I did not," Isabel said, sitting with her back against the wall. "I showed by my words what Rowland brings to this marriage: love, devotion, commitment, fidelity. He is a man of great honor and deserves the joy of marriage again. He will love her well."

"He will love who well?" Cathryn asked, turning to face Isabel. "There is only one woman in Rowland's heart, and you convinced Nicolaa of that truth."

"Nay, I meant only to show her—"

"You showed her only that Rowland loved another and will never stop loving her. How would you have liked to hear of Richard's undying devotion to another woman?"

Isabel turned white, and then the flush of emotion rose up her throat to stain her cheeks. "I meant only for her to see his constancy."

"To another."

At that, Isabel was silent.

A misstep, yea, surely it was. Yet Rowland had not breached his wife, and that was a misstep of greater import. Did he hesitate out of concern for Nicolaa? Certainly, he was capable of such consideration in not wanting to rush his new wife into the marriage bed, but what was truer was that he was even more determined not to shove Lubias out of it. Rowland would not give Lubias up. He had made that abundantly clear. What room then for Nicolaa?

Also, why was he not more determined to solidify his claim on Nicolaa and Weregrave? William had shown no such hesitancy in claiming either Greneforde or Cathryn, and his urgency had told its own tale of his desire for both wife and holding. Rowland's delay spoke loudly of his lack of interest in both, no matter his words of constancy. Nicolaa, wife to four husbands, would understand this. Men shouted with their actions what their words only whispered. Rowland, with every act, shouted that he valued Nicolaa not at all.

Nicolaa seemed not to care.

Cathryn had cajoled her away from the solar, empty but for shy Beatrice, by asking for a tour of the holding. There was little to see. Did her own holding of Greneforde not look the same? Still, she had much to say to Nicolaa, and this was as ready an excuse for them to be alone as any.

"A fine holding," Cathyrn said. "You came through the time of King Stephen well."

"A hard time, but over now," Nicolaa said. "How did Greneforde fare?"

"Let me say only that it was a hard time," Cathryn said, ducking her head to avoid Nicolaa's gaze.

Nicolaa did not pursue the topic, yet she laid a gentle hand upon Cathryn's arm and stroked her briefly. Cathryn smiled her response and they left off talking of past wars and hungry winters.

Weregrave might have come through the civil wars that raged all over England, but Nicolaa was a woman much abused nonetheless. Cathryn knew the signs of a woman's torment and ached to see them so clearly in Nicolaa. She had been sorely abused; not physically, but her very soul had been torn so that it lay in tatters within her, and Nicolaa knew not that she was even wounded.

"Times will be better now, with Rowland as lord here," Cathryn said.

"That is good," Nicolaa said breezily. "Times can always be better, no matter how fine they are now."

"Have you had fine times here?"

"Weregrave is favored by me," Nicolaa said as they walked toward the orchard.

"And you are favored to have it," Cathryn said, "as well as favored to have Rowland to husband."

Nicolaa nodded pleasantly, if distantly. Without any great interest, she asked, "You have known him long?"

"Almost a year now, but he and my lord are close."

"Yea, all the world knows of the bond between Rowland and William," Nicolaa said. "As well as knowing about the bond of love that binds Rowland to Lubias."

"That love was real," Cathryn said, pushing it into the past, where it must stay.

"Was it?" Nicolaa kept her eyes on the branches of the orchard, keeping her eyes away from Cathryn's. "I must confess that I have never heard of such devotion shown by a husband for his wife. To his sword, yea, but not to his wife," she added with a smile.

Cathryn remembered well when she first heard the tale; she, too, had wondered if such love could ever be for her. But why would a wife want to hear of her husband's love for another woman? Would she not believe that he would never love her with the same devotion? Yet Nicolaa did seem to want to talk of Lubias.

"He did love her, by all accounts and by every tale told, yet . . . despite all loving, Lubias is dead. Her earthly life is done and Rowland's must go on. Weregrave is his future," Cathryn said, unable to say more to a woman she hardly knew. Nicolaa was his future and his present; where else for Lubias but in the past of memory? She could hold no place here on earth. Unless it be in Rowland's heart. Aye, that was the problem.

The clank of steel drew their eyes from the sculpted branches of the orchard, and they turned together, knowing what the sound portended. Across the ward was the training ground, and there Rowland and William attacked each other joyfully, as men were wont to do.

Cathryn was drawn to the sight of William like a hawk to the falconer's hand, and Nicolaa walked with her, easy in her role as hostess. It was very clear to Nicolaa that Cathryn was in love with her husband. And that her husband was in love with her, or as much as any man could be. It did not hurt that with Cathryn had come Greneforde and Blythe Tower. Take away her holding and then see how long he tarried at her side; that would tell the tale. Nicolaa's own husbands had been nice enough—until a marriageable daughter with a richer holding than hers had been dangled before them. They had, each one, found cause to leave her fast enough at that. She prayed that Cathryn of Greneforde never had to find out how true her husband's devotion was.

Her prayer sent skyward, Nicolaa turned to watch the men at their practice. That her eyes strayed and stayed on Rowland she did not give too much import. He was a fine swordsman. His body was strong, agile, quick, his size a match for William's, their height similar and their reach equal. Yet Rowland fought with a feral grace that caught and held the eye, his movements smooth and deadly, his very eyes lit with joy at each blow. All men loved to fight, yet he seemed to find the very air of battle sweet. He was a warrior and, by the look of him, a splendid one. Henry would likely gift him another wife and tower before he was through, and then she would be waiting for husband number six. Unless she was in a cloister, the bride of Christ. The thought was sweet and tempting; how that her priest was the bearer of this fruit? That bore a sharper look, yet the idea was still sweet within the chambers of her heart: to be free of husbands, even this husband.

Her eyes were again on Rowland, studying his technique, nothing more. She was a woman with much property in a warrior's world; she was well schooled in the arts of war, and she had learned early how to judge a man's prowess. Rowland was formidable. He did not tire. His left arm was as strong and controlled as his right; that talent was rare and must have saved his life many a time. He was dark and quiet and compelling, difficult to turn from, though she felt she should try. He was intense, his attention never faltering, his eye never straying from his foe, his foot sure and his hand steady. With just such intensity he mourned a wife dead so many years. Could it be so? Could a man feel anything more deeply than his own honor and renown?

The question rang in her thoughts, repeating and repeating, with no answer she could find. The men soon stopped their battle and gave their weapons to Ulrich. Rowland needed a squire.

She did not know where the thought came from; it was not her responsibility to arrange for such a thing. She threw the wifely thought away and stroked her hip, wiping her hand clean of the thought. It was none of her concern. Just as it was none of his concern when and whom the girls would marry.

So with that thought, the image of his battle grace and

prowess was blown from her mind, to be replaced with the hard knowledge that Rowland was stepping into her life with all the grace of a battle ram and with as little regard to the destruction he caused. Nay, that was wrong. He wanted to destroy her carefully ordered life; he wanted the women under her care married and gone. It was with that thought that she faced him, the light of battle in her eyes as it had just been in his.

Rowland understood well the look of her.

He was a warrior. He knew the gleam of challenge and of bloodlust when he faced it. He faced it now in the blue eyes of his wife.

He did not want to battle her.

He had felt her watching him as he fought William, and the feeling had been sweet. That had been a surprise, a guilty pleasure. It had been years since a woman's attention had been directed at him in any way beyond the sexual, and even that sort of regard had waned as his fidelity to Lubias had become known. He had welcomed the world's knowing. It had made for fewer awkward moments. He was known as a man who could love with the sweet voice of poetry, the perfect knight who lived out the chivalric ideal; Queen Eleanor had named him so, and her words had carried across continents. So he had been pursued by ladies of many courts and many halls; young and less than young, beauteous and virtuous, shy and bold, all had come to see the man who loved Lubias. All had tried to win his heart. All had failed. Once in Normandy, a woman had awaited him in a wood covered in only a blue cloak. Even with her clothes on he would have been able to read the desire in her dark blue eyes. He read no such need in Nicolaa, either in bed or out of it.

213

Which should please him, except that he must and would bed her. The idea of consummating their marriage aroused neither fear nor anticipation in her; whether and when they consummated seemed a matter of flat indifference. Worse, he had misread her. Again and again that realization stung like a hundred bees against his knowledge of himself. How had he seen fear in her? There was no fear in Nicolaa; there was sometimes anger, always caution, but he could detect no fear. Not now. Not after last night and her calm contemplation of paint colors. Was she even now beginning to melt beneath the heat of his ardent wooing? He could not see it. He could not see that he was making any progress against the chill of her regard, yet he was a warrior to the heart; he would not run from this battle to win her. He would do all within his skill to win her heart, no matter how firm her defense against him. What could she do but relent? Was she not a woman, and did not all women yearn for the promise of love and safety? Yet how often had he noted that Nicolaa was like no woman of his knowing?

He had no answers. He had only Nicolaa and her hard blue eyes. She was angry. He must begin to soften her eyes or there would be no softening of her body; that he knew well enough.

"You watched me," William said to Cathryn, his silver eyes glowing, "and I stumbled. You must take the blame, Cathryn. I cannot best Rowland when you distract me."

"I think that you stumbled before I left the orchard," Cathryn said. "I will not be blamed for your . . . inadequacies . . . as a knight."

"Inadequacies? You insult me?" he said, his brows raised in shock.

"Rowland did not stumble, and his wife watched him," Cathryn said.

"I did not stumble *because* Nicolaa watched me. I could feel her regard, even from the orchard, and I would not show myself as anything less than the perfect knight for her," Rowland said.

"And what is it that defines the perfect knight?" Nicolaa asked, showing the blade of her tongue, though her tone was soft.

"Honor," said Rowland.

"Fidelity," answered William.

"Compassion," said Cathryn when Nicolaa looked at her. "What say you, Nicolaa? What is it that a knight must possess to be perfect?"

"I do not know what would make a perfect knight. I cannot think what attribute would encompass all."

"Perhaps constancy?" Rowland said, looking deeply into her eyes.

"Constancy is a fine trait. Rare. Precious," she answered, lifting her head to match his look.

"Aye, it is," Rowland agreed, studying her. "Yet I possess it in great measure. Say that constancy is what you most desire and I will be content, lady. I would only please you."

"Constancy is fine, most fine, and very rare in a man, yet is a dog not constant? I would think that a knight of valor must needs be more than constant," Nicolaa said, fighting against his charm the only way she knew how.

Cathryn laughed softly and said, "Well said, Nicolaa. A man must be more than constant. Do not settle for less than his all if he means to woo you."

"A hard wooing if constancy is insufficient," William said. "I do not envy you this battle, Rowland. You stand alone against your wife, as is a husband's lot. I think she is a match for you. You will not be offended if I wager in her favor?"

"Offended?" Rowland said with a smile, looking at Nicolaa but answering William. "Nay, for I know how well you love to win. But who shall wager against you? Will any man stand against Nicolaa?"

"Will any man stand with her? That is more clearly the question," Nicolaa said, drawn into this jesting against the wisdom of experience. This parley would not serve her heart, yet when had she last been so merry with a man? When she sought to strike against his pride, he answered with a smile and softness. A most strange warrior, truly, was Rowland the Dark.

"A man? Aye, a man would stand with Nicolaa," Rowland said. "It is only boys who strut like men and then run when the dice fall against them."

"Would you make all men boys then?" Nicolaa asked.

"All men are boys," Cathryn said, "if you watch them at their play."

"Nay, this I must protest," William said. "I am no boy, yet I will have my play. It is the playing out of manly pursuits that points most truly to my manhood."

"Ah, and again we come to William's manhood," Cathryn said, grinning at her husband.

"Can I be faulted if the conversation turns ever to me?" William said, grinning back at his wife and then at them all.

"Nay, you cannot. All the world knows this to be so," Nicolaa said, smiling at William. "You are a man about whom many speculate, but never on the subject of your manhood."

"Ah, I am relieved, lady," William said.

"So, then, Nicolaa," Rowland said. "You admit to listening to tales of men in your hall of women. What tales, then, have you heard of me?"

He was more serious than comical in his request, and she saw the true heart of his question in his dark eyes. "Only tales of constancy, husband, which should please you," she answered, trying for lightness.

"Only constancy? I will admit, I had hoped for more," Rowland said. "Perhaps I can convince you that there is more to me than constancy, and then you will be able to spin your own tales of Rowland. I would give you all you ask, Nicolaa. What tale will be told by your lips? What is it you want from me if constancy will not suffice? Ask, only ask, and I shall give it unto you."

Nay, she would not answer that. That was striking too deep into her dreams, coming close upon her heart. She would not even play at a response. She did not dare.

"I do not look for tales. I have little use for them," she said, looking at his throat and no higher. She did not want to meet his eyes. "If you will excuse me. I must away." With a small smile she withdrew, ending the conversation, ending the camaraderie he had been trying to build. "I have much to do," she said as she walked away. "Enjoy the day."

She was in the shadow of the tower when Cathryn spoke, certain of not being overheard.

"Forgive me, Rowland, for my frankness, but I must speak. By delaying consummation, you are succeeding well with Nicolaa if your desire is to reject her. Show her you care enough to keep her. Do the one thing necessary to seal the vow you have spoken before God."

" 'Tis good advice, Rowland," William said softly. "Pray,

heed it. She bleeds from your neglect. The drops follow her steps even now."

Rowland watched Nicolaa disappear up the stone stair into the tower, her red hair a glowing beacon lifted by the wind to move softly in the air of a day going quickly gray. Tall she stood, slowly she moved, as graceful and indomitable as a torch on a high cliff.

"She needs you, Rowland," Cathryn said, her voice rich with compassion and pity.

It was a truth. She did need him. He had only to convince her of it to be content.

All she wanted was for her life to be the way it had been, orderly and predictable, without a husband under her every step. If only he and his friends would leave, all would be well again. All would be normal, calm, safe.

The late-afternoon sun was in battle with the sky; the clouds massed gray and purple, hovering in the west, planning their assault on the westward-moving sun. There was no escape for the sun, for west it must go. Nicolaa sighed. It would be another night of rain. The ward would be deep in mud again; the night would fall early. Husbands enjoyed early nightfalls. Wives did not.

The tables were being laid for supper while her ladies stood in agitated excitement by the hearth. Nicolaa swallowed her sigh of irritation that they were not where they should be—namely, in the solar working on the tapestry— but talking frivolously by the hearth. Had she not just given two precious tapestries away? She must be about the finishing of a new one.

As she approached them, she heard their whisperings. It was as she had feared: the talk was all of marriage.

"He said he would gift me twenty acres of land in Aquitaine to build my dowry," Ermengarde said, her brown eyes sparkling with happiness for once. It completely transformed her. She looked lovely in the firelight. Of course, twenty acres in Aquitaine would give anyone a glow of loveliness.

"That will certainly help," Blanche said. "I hope to be married by Twelfth Night."

"Truly?" Perette said. "To whom?"

"I do not know, but there must be someone out there who is looking for a bride."

"If that is true, then I will find a man of my own," Jeanne said. "I will not be left by the hearth while all others run to the marriage bed and a pair of hairy arms to warm them. I will not face another winter with my daughter as my bedmate."

"Perhaps I will marry by Twelfth Night too," Beatrice said, her blue eyes glowing with the wish.

"You will *not* marry by Twelfth Night," Nicolaa said, shoved past all endurance by this endless talk of marriage. "That I can promise you. You think that marriage will please you?" she said in a snarl, her eyes the bright blue of a hot fire. "You think that a pair of hairy arms are all that a woman requires? You are wrong. You are all wrong." She was enraged, her terror and her anger flowing out from her like a hot wind. Never, in all the years of her married life, had she lost control of her temper. She had lost it now. This foolish talk of marriage must and would stop. "A man is more than bones and flesh and hair. A man is pride and strength, all used for his own gain and naught for you, his wife, his possession. You are nothing in his thoughts. A fly in his life, a body in his bed, a foul canker when he would be rid of you, that is what a woman is to a man. I will not hurry you to that. I will not allow you to run to that."

They were stunned into silence. She had never spoken so, never been so bold. The servants stood at their places, their faces frozen. She did not care. These women, these foolish, romantic women, would not be destroyed while she breathed to save them.

Of them all, only her grandmother was untouched by her fury. Nay, she had not marked Jeanne. Jeanne laughed. Nicolaa turned to face her, their eyes, matched but for their years, locked in battle.

"Why would you consider marriage when all your needs are met here? What can a man give you that I cannot give you twice over and with more peace?" Nicolaa asked. She truly did not know. Jeanne had always and ever been beyond her comprehension.

"Why? Because I like men. I would not mind having another one before I die," Jeanne said with a crooked smile.

Nay, that could not be so. No woman would answer so. Everything was off balance, and it was Rowland who had made it so. Rowland must go. Order must be returned, and so Rowland must go, taking his talk of husbands with him. Taking his talk of constancy and of giving her her heart's desire off to a place where she could not hear such deceitful, tempting words. She had no desires a man could meet. That had ended long ago. She would not return to the desolation of disappointment.

"You like men," Nicolaa said to her grandmother. "That is very generous of you. The question to be answered, however, is whether men like women. I have seen nothing to show me that they do."

With that she turned and made for the chapel and Father Timothy.

Chapter Fourteen

"Make the arrangements," Nicolaa said. "I want an annulment."

Father Timothy's eyes glowed at the news. He clasped her hands in his and smiled his approval. He was too joyous. He was a good man, but she would prefer an old, stooped priest to hear her confession once she was in the cloister. She might even make that a stipulation in her contract. For wealth such as hers, the church should be able to supply her with a priest to her liking.

She excused herself quickly, her heart and mind at ease. Nay, she was in joyous flight. She had not felt this free in ten years, since her first marriage. And this . . . this marriage was to be her last. Her joy was a ribald thing, pounding within her heart and quickening her breath. Oh, there was such joy to be had in ridding oneself of a husband. Had this been what her husbands felt in ridding themselves of her? No wonder they had done it; such joy was beyond the reach of repentance.

She hurried to the hall and was the last one to enter it. Rowland was at his place and stood, awaiting her, making her feel even tardier than she was. A husband was a most worrisome thing. How lovely to have the means to be rid of one. The last one. The last husband: what a wonderful phrase. She could hardly contain her smile when she looked at him, and then she did not try. It was her hall, and she could smile as she would; let him make of it what he might. She could hardly wait to be rid of him and his searching eyes. Let him study another woman, trying to read her heart and her thoughts. She rejected such intrusion. She rejected him.

As she sat at his side, he whispered, "I have arranged for a larger meal than is usual, Nicolaa; our guests leave at the dawn, and I would give them hearty sustenance before their ride."

Wonderful news, to be sure, and surprising. Guests rarely stayed for less than a week, as distances were great and travel difficult. Still, if they would leave, she would not bar the gates against their going. It was another firm step on the path to normalcy, and she could only welcome it.

"Will you be leaving as well?" she asked, washing her hands before the first course.

"Not yet," he said on a smile.

Dropping her head to wipe her hands on the cloth, she murmured to herself, "Too bad." She was certain he had not heard her, and it was the last thing she said to him for the remainder of the meal. Her conversational skills were all directed at Cathryn and Isabel. That Rowland did not demand entrance into their conversation caused her only joy and no surprise. Had she not noted that he was perceptive for a man? That he understood he was not welcome in their discourse was not cause for comment or praise.

She was chewing on a tender piece of spiced rabbit when Ulrich came from down the winding stair carrying a lute under his arm. The talk all around her quieted; indeed, the entire hall grew more hushed with every step he took. Nicolaa could feel her brow furrow and tried to force herself to relax. He was a troublesome man, always sniffing about the women of her home, smiling away his offenses as if that were all that was required to make all right again. What was he about now?

Ulrich came to a stop in the center of the hall, the tables arrayed before him, the door to the ward at his back. The firelight touched him but lightly, but the high wind holes let the sun shine down its rays to illuminate his form. His eyes shone blue and his profile cut a clear line in the soft light. He looked well pleased and at ease, yet solemn as well. When did Ulrich ever wear a solemn face? At no time that she could recall. Her brows lowered again in suspicion.

With a bow, he raised the lute and began to play.

His touch was light, the tune sweet; she had heard worse in her time. It was when he opened his mouth to sing that all began to unravel.

He sang of Beatrice. He sang of himself. He sang of his sorrow and his pain that he had caused her woe by his ungallant behavior. He sang his apology, begging forgiveness with a smile and a gleaming eye. He sang out his sins and smiled when he named them, asking Beatrice to forgive his clumsiness, blaming his faults on his eagerness to please her.

223

The hall smiled in return, urging him on, pleased with his offering, counting it the finest example of courtly love. All smiled. All except Nicolaa, who shook in her fury. And Beatrice, who hung her head in mortification.

Did that matter to him? Nay, not at all. He sang and he sang, and when he finished, he was met with riotous approval from all within Weregrave. All save Weregrave's lady. All eyes were on Beatrice, eager to hear her courtly response. Did not custom demand that she give a gracious and lengthy reply to such an effort on her behalf? Yet it was not in Beatrice to banter privately; could she do better in so public a forum? Nay, and so she was left with all she had to give in her limited arsenal of feminine weapons. She blushed. She stammered. She whispered out her acceptance of his apology.

Ulrich, his grin widening at his victory over Beatrice, bowed and left the hall, taking his weapon, the lute, with him. All sighed to watch him go, this gallant man in the full prime of his manhood, his tongue ever overflowing with sweet words. Sweet words, aye—sweet to his own ears.

"Why are you troubled?" Rowland said softly, his words heard by none but her.

"Why? Can you not see what he has done?" she said in a hiss.

"What has he done, Nicolaa?" he asked, his eyes intent upon her face.

She turned to face him and said, "He has done what all men do," she said sharply. "He has turned the occasion of his seeking forgiveness into a moment to glorify himself. What was there for Beatrice in that display?"

"He has sought forgiveness of her and it has been given.

What harm in that? I do not see his actions as you do," he said.

"I am hardly surprised by that," she said, throwing down the remnants of her rabbit. She was past eating now.

"Explain your anger to me. I would understand you, if I may," he said, catching hold of her hand and holding her gently.

His gentleness was wasted on her, yet she did not pull herself away from him. Let him touch her if he thought it would help his cause. She knew better. She was hardened against his touches; he would not win her with a caress on the back of her hand. Nay, she was made of sterner stuff.

"I do not know how to explain to you what is as clear to me as bright sunlight. How is it that you cannot understand that what he did was for himself and not for her? How was she served by that display of male pride?"

"Male pride? He hurt her in private, yet made his apology public. There is little of male pride in that."

"Aye, he made his apology public, which only serves him. Can you not see that?" she asked.

"Nay, I cannot."

"Say instead, 'would not,' 'will not,' 'do not,' but do not say 'cannot.' It is too plain, too clear."

"You wanted him to make amends to her," he said stiffly. "That he has done, done well, and done publicly. I cannot see how he could do more for what began as a misstep in flirtation."

Of course he could not. He was a man; he would see what served his own pride and honor. He had not the eyes to see what served a shy girl.

"What of Beatrice? What of her needs and what would

225

best serve her? Look you, does she look well pleased by this display?"

"She looks . . . modest," he said. "A most proper countenance for a girl of her years. What else should she display but modesty at an apology so gallantly delivered?"

"Modest? She is red with embarrassment, husband. You do not understand women as well as you think, though perhaps the women of the Aquitaine are of a different breed than the women of Britain. I tell you, this apology served no one but Ulrich."

"I have eyes, Nicolaa," Rowland said, leaning toward her, pulling her hand down beneath the linen, where he held her hard and fast. "I know what I see. I see a woman who cannot be pleased by a man, no matter the honor of his cause or the purity of his heart—"

"The purity of his heart? Now I say that you truly are blind."

"Nay, not blind," he said in a soft growl, "for I see you very well, Nicolaa. You need a man to teach you what a man is, not these boys who have played in your bed and in your life."

"Have we not agreed that all men are boys?" she said in a hiss, looking hard into his eyes, accepting the challenge he offered.

"Nay, not agreed, not on that," he said. "I am a man. I have it in me to teach you what it is to be a woman."

"I know very well what it is to be a woman," she said, pulling her hand from beneath his, lifting her arm, and pulling back the tight sleeve of her bliaut. "It is to be bruised on a man's whim," she said, showing him the marks he had left on her arm. "It is to be used to salve a man's endless pride. It is to be the step on which he builds his honor."

"It is to be cherished," he said, taking her wrist in his hand. He lifted her wrist to his mouth and kissed her on the purple mark he had caused. "It is to be protected." He kissed her again, slowly, his mouth lingering on her skin. "Forgive me, Nicolaa. I have no wish to hurt you."

"Nay," she said, her eyes misting at the tenderness of his kiss, "you have no wish to hurt me. And yet you do." *And yet you will.*

Nicolaa ended the argument between them, an argument he had insisted upon, by the turning of her head. It was not worth the effort to try to make a man understand what was important to a woman, especially with a man who was about to leave her life for good. Smiling, she spoke warmly to Father Timothy and then excused herself and made for the solar, Perette at her side. The other women stayed behind in the hall, with the men. Beatrice, she noted, held her head still lowered in embarassment, fighting for composure. She would not want to move from her place until the shame aroused by Ulrich's apology had passed.

It was with cold delight that Nicolaa planned for Rowland's eviction from her life.

Ulrich, his precious lute safely wrapped and stored away, returned to the hall with a buoyant step. He was greeted with smiles and jests, which he happily returned, yet he did not linger, but made his way to Rowland, who still sat in his place at the high table.

"How was it received with the Lady Nicolaa?" he asked Rowland. "I could see that she did not smile."

"Do not let your thoughts tarry on Nicolaa," Rowland

227

said. "Your apology was well and truly done. All the women of Henry's domain will be demanding an apology from you by this standard you have set. You will start a fashion for offense that must and can be mended only by a musical and lyrical apology."

"Think you that Beatrice liked it well?" Ulrich asked.

"Did she not accept, her head lowered and her cheek flushed in the way of a woman well pleased?" Rowland responded.

"Aye, she did," Ulrich said, smiling. He turned then to find Blanche, who was easily found.

Rowland watched him go with a smile on his lips, yet his smile was not for Ulrich but for himself. The self-possession for which Nicolaa was known was fading by the hour, and he suspected that he was the cause. He was unrepentantly pleased that he could get any response from her. It was progress, though anger was not the emotion he would choose to prepare her for consummation. Still, it was proof that his plan to get rid of the excess women of the holding was a good one. At least Nicolaa was noticing him now.

In pursuit of that plan he had suggested that William and Richard leave, taking their wives and their squires with them. To reach Nicolaa, he had to strip her of all defenses, even the defense of other people. Let her find herself alone with him; then he would find a way into her heart and her life.

He sighed in satisfaction. He would prove to Nicolaa that she could trust him. She would then be able to relax and enjoy consummation, which was only as God intended, and they would live out their lives in harmony. He would battle for the king. She would manage the estates and turn out tapestries. A fine life, and one that would soothe her troubled heart. Lubias would approve.

It was when Jeanne beckoned him from the doorway to the ward that his plans began to shatter.

Beatrice sat with her eyes lowered until the heat in her cheeks had cooled. The sounds of the hall swirled all about her, and she welcomed the din, for it allowed her to hide. When her heart had stopped pounding and her flush had receded, she raised her face and, eventually, even her eyes. No one was looking at her. It was a relief. She gradually relaxed her posture into an easy position and let her eyes wander over the people in the hall; at the end of one table, where the light was murky with smoke and shadow, Ulrich sat close upon Blanche.

Too close. For a man who had sung his apology to her with such fervor, he seemed to have discarded all thought of her as easily as he had rid himself of his lute. Nicolaa's words on the nature of men tossed in her mind like dice in a cup, the pattern of the numbers and the words taking shape.

He did not care for her. He did not care if he had offended her and he did not care if she was soothed by his apology. He cared only about his own reputation and his own amusement; all else, Beatrice herself, was dung to be scraped from his boot upon the nearest rock.

In that moment, when the dice stilled and revealed their faces, she decided that she did not like Ulrich. She had been unwillingly charmed by him. She had been made uncomfortable by his words more than once. She had thought him dangerous and impulsive and quicker with his tongue than with his head, but she had never disliked him. She disliked him now. She also concluded that Nicolaa was among the wisest of women for understanding men so well. In that moment, she resolved to be more like Nicolaa.

She stood, and Ulrich's eyes shifted to her at once. She supposed the fairness of her hair made him look; people were wont to comment on its pale color. It was certain he had not looked because of *her*. Stiffening her neck, she returned the look. He whispered something to Blanche, who laughed, all the while Ulrich stared at her. It was almost a certainty that he did not care for Blanche, not if he could look at her as he was while talking to Blanche, his hand upon hers. That he was so free with his touches and not only his words told the tale of Ulrich very well.

Slowly she walked through the hall, never taking her eyes from him. He could not seem to take his eyes from her either. With a smile, a kiss on the hand, and a bow, he disengaged himself from Blanche and paralleled Beatrice's walk out of the hall, his steps twice the length of hers. She knew that his rapid approach spoke not of earnestness, but only of anatomy. His stride was long; it was only logical that his approach would be quick.

She had reached the curving stair when he caught up with her. The light was very dim, the sounds of the hall muffled by stone and a distance that seemed great because of the wood smoke clouding the room. He stopped her by touching of her hand, and she turned to face him, withdrawing her hand. He was too quick to touch. It told much that he could not keep his hands where they belonged— at the ends of his own arms and nowhere else.

"You have forgiven me, Beatrice?" he said, his tone urgent. Urgent? How, when he had been trading smiles with

Blanche not a moment past? "I would do nothing to harm you."

"You have not the ability to harm me, Ulrich," she said, enjoying the hardening of her heart. She would not drop her eyes in shame and humiliation again, not from anything *he* could think to say. "I do forgive you, if you care."

"If I care?" he asked, his blue eyes wide. "I have only care, Beatrice. I would bring you only smiles; it is my sorrow that I caused you distress."

"Aye, your sorrow," she said with as much bite as she could manage. What would Nicolaa say? "Your sorrow lasts as long as it suits your purpose, I think. You do not have the heart to sorrow truly."

He looked dismayed at her response. *Wonderful.* Let him find out what it was to be caught in a net of conversation that moved constantly out of reach and out of control.

"Nay, you do not know me—"

"I know you as well as I would like. In fact, I know you too well for my liking," she said. That had sounded right; Nicolaa would deliver just such a charge and she would not blush. Beatrice breathed deeply, holding her blush at bay.

Ulrich seemed to be stripped of words. He stood staring into her eyes, looking for a way around her rebuke, and finding none.

"You have not forgiven me," he said. "I have wounded you too deeply and too sharply."

"I am not wounded," she said. "It is only that I have no liking for a man who talks so coarsely of others and their bed habits. I have no liking for a man who touches all women as though they were dogs at his heel. I have no liking for—"

231

"I hear you well, Beatrice," he said, laying a hand upon her arm, despite her words. It was as Nicolaa said; men heard what suited them and tossed all else to the wind. "I have forgotten your age and inexperience in my admiration of your beauty and your gentleness. You are right. I spoke unwisely in your hearing. You are too young for such words and for any actions of mine. This remorse I feel most deeply, you can be assured."

"I am very well assured that you feel nothing unless it promotes your own honor," she said loudly. Did the sounds of the hall behind them quiet? She was too angry to note any but the man who stood before her and the hot flush of her own skin.

"My honor is sacred to me; I would do nothing to tarnish it. Including offending a girl too young to know when she is being flattered and admired," he said, keeping his voice low.

"How that you are the one to decide if I am being flattered? How not my own counsel on the matter? It is not admiration to talk of conquest and the pleasures of the marriage bed with a woman betrothed to another."

"It is only the game of courtly love."

"As you play it. Did it ne'er cross your thoughts that you play it badly?" she said in a hiss. Her voice sounded loud to her own ears, and she could feel her ears turning red with heat.

"You are young—"

"I am betrothed. I am not so young as to not understand that my heart and my life are bound to another. You think me young because I honor that contract? I think you dishonorable to ignore it at your whim."

Ulrich straightened himself up and stood closer to her,

pulling her arm to his chest and whispering harshly, "You speak in anger and in hurt. I would never foul the contract of a betrothal by word or action. Never would I do anything to soil my honor."

His words rang loud and she could not think why. Then she turned from him and looked around his shoulder to the hall behind. All was quiet. None spoke. All eyes and ears were turned to them, the focal point of interest in the hall of Weregrave. Beatrice felt her blush heat her face to the edge of her hair and she cast her head down in shame.

"Release me," she whispered. "All eyes are upon us."

Ulrich did not turn around, but slowly lowered her arm, loosening his grip. "Leave the hall. I will deal with what my words have sparked."

She looked up at him then, a quick look, and was caught by what she saw. He did not tease or flatter or flirt. Nay, he looked at her most solemnly, giving her a way of escape, promising to stand and face the fire of public humiliation alone.

"Go," he said, his body a shield against curious eyes.

She turned and went, her feet soft and silent as she stumbled hurriedly down the wooden stair.

She heard the pounding of his step before the door flew back to punch the stone wall of the solar. A chunk of wood flew off to skid across the wooden floor until it bumped into her foot and twirled to a stop.

She mangled a stitch.

Rowland charged into the room, his fury a fire that blazed out of his very pores. A small corner of her mind dispassionately noted that she had not thought him capable of such excess, and then even that small voice was silenced as she stared into his rage.

"*You* were going to seek an annulment?"

"I am," she answered, rising to her feet. "I have the grounds."

"Not for long," he said in a growl, coming toward her. He looked every inch a predator and she responded instinctively; she backed away from him, fully aware that Perette was wide-eyed.

"Why should you care?" she said. "Do not tell me you did not think of it."

"I *did not* think of it! I never planned to annul our marriage."

He kept coming toward her and she kept backing away. It was an empty exercise. Had she not already determined that he was not a violent man? But she had never expected this display.

"Then why did you not consummate our marriage?"

She held a hand out to him, stiff-armed, as if that would stop him. There was nothing gentle about him now.

"I was waiting for you to be ready!" he shouted. A vein in his forehead was pulsing angrily.

He sought to blame her? He would not lay this at her feet. She had done her part and more. "Not ready? Naked and with my legs open is as ready as I know how to be!"

"I take you at your word, lady," he said. He was upon her then, and she quickly found herself thrown upon his shoulder, the blood rushing to her head. "I would take you here, if not for this innocent."

"What restraint," she snapped through the blanket of her hair.

"Aye, remarkable restraint."

"This is just what Macair did when he first—"

"I am *not* Macair, nor any of the others you carry with you like beads on a rosary. I am Rowland d'Albret of Aquitaine. You will kindly remember that as I shove my way into your dry sheath."

They were out of the solar, her sanctuary, through the hall, and climbing the narrow stair to the lord's chamber before she could form an answer. The stair was too small a space for an audience, the curving stone wall blocking all eyes; yet, though no eyes watched, she could feel the unnatural stillness of a hundred pairs of ears listening. The loss of decorum and dignity unleashed a rage within her to match his own, the difference being that hers was justified. She had finally found a way out of her endless marriages, finally stumbled upon some measure of power because he had inexplicably refused to consummate the marriage. She was not going to lie docilely beneath him, while, to sate dominating male arrogance and hurt pride, he stole her power away from her.

She knew just how to stop him. He wanted truth from her? Well, he would get it.

Rowland slammed open the door to the lord's chamber. She was certain that the crack was heard in the kitchens. A long step and she was thrown onto the bed.

The gentle warrior had vanished; an enraged husband looked down at her.

"Take off your bliaut or lift your skirts. I care not which," he said, his voice cold as wintry steel while his eyes still burned.

"Nor do I," she said, sliding off the high bed to stand on the floor, facing him, "but this bliaut is a favorite of mine and I would not see it ripped." She untied her laces and eased herself out of her dress. "I have had more bliauts ripped by a husband's overeager hands, or perhaps merely his haste, than I can tell. But let me try anyway," she said. She slid out of her bliaut and hung it carefully on the peg. "It will not surprise you to know that Macair ripped no less than six of my bliauts from my body. I would have willingly disrobed, or just lifted my skirts, as you so gallantly suggest, but he seemed to find some perverse pleasure in ripping my clothing."

"I do not want to hear—"

"Oh, but you do, for did you not want to know my thoughts? Was it not you who said that the way to please you was to tell you the truth? I have truth to spare, husband."

She stood in her linen shift, Rowland in his leggings, his torso bare. To take her now would be an easy matter, done in moments, but she held him at bay with words: stones of truth.

He walked toward her, around the high bed, his face revealing the anger in his heart.

"Take off your shift," he said in a growl.

"Why? You have seen my body. It did not cause you to lust. But Hugh, he was a man who liked to look and look again. I saved the coin for cloth when he was my husband, for he kept me more naked than clothed. I have been ever thankful that he was gone before winter, else I should have frozen hard."

He stood before her, his body throwing heat that she felt in pulsing waves. She had not moved. She would not move. Let *him* run. He could do nothing that had not been done to her a thousand times, and with that knowledge she would bleed him white.

"Enough!" he said in a snarl, grabbing her arms, pulling her against him. He was hard against her, his manhood high and hot. He had wanted her ready? What deceit ruled a man. She had never shown herself less willing, yet he was hard as stone.

"Enough? Nay, not enough, for I have had four husbands before you, and you have not begun to learn of their various ways."

His hand was on her scalp, his fingers threading through her hair, and then his mouth covered hers, stopping her words, stopping her breath, trying to push the memory of any other man from her thoughts. No man had the strength for that. Her memories had a ten-year hold, while this husband had barely touched upon her life.

No man could drive from her what had already been. Her memories were as solid as the tapestries she worked. He could not kiss them away.

He attacked her, a man's choice, his hands hard upon her and his mouth harder still. The violence of him, he whom she had thought so gentle and so strange, surprised her for an instant, and then surprise was gone. He was as all men: his need was hard upon him, his pride had been pricked, he would do anything to have his way. He would not be thwarted, not by a woman, and he would use his body to see his will done. His passion came out of him like blows against her, hot and dulled, yet blows nonetheless. He sought to fire her, this she could feel, yet all she had for him was cold resolve. Let him beat against that.

His mouth left hers and at once she began to speak. Her words were her best weapon and she did not hesitate.

"Gerard was a man who liked to have me where he would, in stable or field, once behind the kitchen. I think the need came upon him suddenly, without prediction, and he could but follow. He had many of my women, in all my many halls. What could he do but find the nearest maid and slake himself upon her? You are like that, I think. The need comes upon you hard. You have no will to stop."

He pulled back and stared at her, his eyes alight with dark sparks of rage or of lust; she did not care which. He had his hands in her shift, two fists ready to tear and rend what she had not removed. He looked a wild beast, and so she had named him.

"I will not stop, Nicolaa; you have that aright," he said, his voice as hard as his cock.

With the next breath, her shift was ripped down the middle, baring her to him.

He stared at her breasts as if he had not seen them just hours ago. Deceitful man; she was not charmed by his fascination. Nor was she afeared.

"Nay, for what man will stop when his cock rises, shouting for release? No man that I have ever known."

"You have known too many men and have too many words to tell of them."

"I have not words enough to tell of all the many things men have done to me."

He kissed her then, sensing her intent to speak and speak again of the men who had consumed the very essence of her life. His kiss was softer than before, more beguiling, more persuasive. He wanted her willing—that she could believe of him—but he had not the words nor the means to persuade her. She would not lie quiet while he took what she would never give.

She wrenched her mouth away and said, "I thought you gentle, yet there is more of Philibert in you than I believed.

He was all haste, all hurry, and quickly done when his need was met."

He looked, raised his fist to strike her, and ground out between clenched teeth, "Close your mouth, Nicolaa. No more of this."

She recoiled slightly from the expected blow, and then made herself stand firm.

"You have surprised me, husband, for I had judged you a gentle man. Yet you would not be the first to hit me. There is no virgin ground here, husband. Many and many have plowed this field before you."

His fist he lowered at her taunt, but he grabbed her hands in one of his and forced her to the floor. She had but moments now to turn him from this path. Her only goal was to prod him hard enough to make him turn from her and annul the marriage himself. Every word she spoke was to remind him that he was shadowed by other men who had come before him.

Even with her hands above her head, her back upon the cold floor, she could sense his desperation not to hurt her. In that, she had read him true; he was not a man who reveled in violence or in force. He would prefer her willing. But he would have her anyway.

He spoke above her, his eyes consuming his face in their intensity. "Your heart is crowded with memories of past husbands. I only want you free of that."

Oh, yea, he would want her free of that, of the memories of other men, of the knowledge of their touch upon her body and her life. She held fast to her memories; they had taught her much of the world, and she would not go back to the credulous girl she had been.

"There is only one husband I want to be free of," she said, her eyes boring into his.

"You shall never be free of me, Nicolaa," he said. He was at her, his cock pressing against her, pushing for entrance. Her hands were going numb. But not her tongue.

"You think you are any different?" she said, her voice hoarse with anger and defeat. "You think this has not been done to me before? Even in taking me unwillingly, others have been before you."

"Stop, Nicolaa!" he cried, the vein in his forehead jumping. "A man kills for less cause."

"Aye, a man does. To protect his name and his honor," she said in a snarl, twisting beneath him.

He was pushing into her. She clenched against him, from her jaw to her ankles, tight against his sanctified invasion.

"Open for me, Nicolaa. I do not want to hurt you," he said, his voice hard and soft at once.

A tear slipped from beneath her lids and she said, "But you do not truly care if I am willing or no, as long as your honor and your will are satisfied."

"It wounds my honor to hurt you," he said under his breath.

"Not enough to stop," she whispered hoarsely.

He stopped his pressing into her and immediately lost ground within her body because she was so resolutely pushing him out.

"Why?" he asked.

"You take from me the one thing I want," she said, looking up at him. "Freedom."

Freedom from him. There was no other freedom to be had in annulment. The word punctured him.

He could not give her freedom. He would never give her that.

"I will stay," he promised. "I will not leave you as the others have done."

She laughed, the sound high and shrill, and closed her eyes against the sight of him. "Are you a gift of such rare price? *I do not want you.* I have had enough husbands."

That she put him in with the rest of them, those men who had so little honor as to leave a wife for a greater purse elsewhere, that she could not see the difference in him, left him bleeding from a thousand pricks. She was so wounded, she could not see how desperately she needed him. His constancy would heal her. He would not let her go.

"Argue your case with king or bishop, Nicolaa, for you have been given me. I take you now as wife."

With one solid push, he was inside her. A harsh gasp from her marked his entry. She was tight and dry, a sharp cushion for his fall into her. With a sigh he escaped her. But the marriage had been consummated. There would be no annulment.

Chapter Fifteen

The night dragged slowly. They lay side by side in the lord's bed, breathing in awkward rhythm, not touching. The pattern of clouds in the night sky, the hushed beat of an owl gliding past, the shrill scream of a mouse caught and held, colored the space they shared.

They said nothing. The silence was neither peaceful nor hostile. It was simply exhausted.

She should have known. Her mistake had been in not waiting until he had gone before proceeding with the annulment. He would not have bedded her; he had made that obvious. He would leave; he was a warrior and a husband. Two irrefutable reasons to leave. Her mistake had been in trying to wrest the reins of power from him. His rigid sense of honor would not allow a woman to claim nonconsummation against him. His pride had been threatened and he had attacked. She understood exactly what had happened.

She was more married than she had been yesterday.

She shifted her body on the mattress, feeling for bruises. Her backside was tender and her right shoulder stiff; there was a throbbing burn between her legs that told her very well that the marriage had been consummated. She had not thought it in him to force her. She could see now that he had wooed her into forgetting what she had learned first of men and knew best: a man took what he wanted. She had ten years' experience to know that for a truth. How had she forgotten it? Rowland, with his dark eyes and ready smile, had urged her to forget.

She closed her eyes against the darkness and rubbed her fingertips firmly across her forehead, pushing in the memory of this night. She would not again forget.

She sighed and felt the hitch in her breath, no doubt caused by a bruise on her ribs. It was not defeat and surely not betrayal that snagged her breath. Nay, not that. Not after so many nights of similar treatment by so many men. She understood that he acted only according to his nature, as the wolf hunted the weak.

She took a full breath, giving air to the fire of her resolve. Nothing had befallen her that she had not met and managed before. She had only to wait for the wolf to leave, sniffing for other prey in other battles. She had only to wait and he would be gone. She knew well how to wait.

"Did I hurt you?"

His voice came from the darkness, low and soft. Aye, now he showed his gentleness; now he had nothing to lose by it.

"Nothing I cannot bear. Nothing I have not borne before," she said. She could hear the defeat in her voice and had not the strength to care.

243

"Do not," he said, his dark voice strained. "Do not walk that path again."

He sounded as defeated as she did herself, which was inexplicable. He had won. She had failed in her methods and in her purpose. She saw no reason to walk the path of past husbands again.

"I will not," she said.

"I did not want it to be . . . that way," he said.

"Did you not? Then we are one in that," she said.

She could believe it. He had wanted her willing, eager for his touch upon her body and her life. A man liked well such moments of victory and power. None knew better than she that a husband and his pride were fed upon the knowledge that his wife turned willingly to his touch. She knew how to be willing. Now that all chance of annulment was past, she would give him her willingness. It was a small thing to give her body, holding mind and heart intact; a small thing, to save her soul, while the body tumbled from man to man, touch to touch.

Silence ruled the room again, and they bowed before it.

The moon moved through the sky, lighting the thickening clouds to shining white. The air thickened as well, the smell of rain building as the moon walked her nightly course. The next day would bring rain.

"I thought that, by delay, I would avoid this," he said after a time, his words rising up to the unpainted ceiling to fall gently back down on her. "I never wanted this for you. For us."

"The marriage has been consummated. I will not dispute it."

"Nor will I. I never would have," he said.

He seemed to feel the weight of failure, and this she

could not understand; he had his plan, she had hers, and he had won. She did not begrudge him either his victory or his method. She only mourned her loss.

"All past now," she said, making peace with what could not be changed.

Their voices were gentle in the silence of heavy night. She could feel his need to speak and felt a matching need rise up in her.

"If I could answer for what others have done, I would," he said. "You have walked a hard path, Nicolaa."

"None can answer for any but themselves, and that is hard enough to do. Think not on any others. You are here; that is all that need occupy us," she said. "All walk a hard path in this life, for by it we are sanctified. Your own path has not been smooth."

"Nay, it has been no harder than any other's," he said.

"Shall we fight over who has made the most difficult journey?" she said, sarcastic laughter buried deep in her voice. "Perhaps we can determine whom God loves most dearly, for are we not taught that God disciplines most rigorously those He loves most passionately? If we can fight about that, we can fight about anything."

She was not angry. He could hear and feel that she was defeated, exhausted, yet not angry, not tearful. A strange sort of woman, beyond his knowledge and new to his experience. Nay, there was no fear in Nicolaa, only the will to fight for what she wanted and the strength to live with what she got. A most strange and unique woman. Rare, perhaps even precious.

The thought smelled of betrayal, and so he pushed it from him, keeping Lubias safe.

"I would not like to fight again with you," he said, his

own voice lightening to match hers. "You are ruthless."

"Thank you," she said, smiling at the dark.

"You take a compliment well," he said. " 'Tis a rare thing."

"I enjoy a compliment. They come rarely. I savor each one for as long as it lasts, which is usually for the space of the breath it took to launch it. Even for the space of a breath, it is a good moment to savor on life's uneven path."

"I will give you compliments with every breath," he said. "You deserve no less."

"You will soon be breathless and then what good will you be to me?" she said, making a jest of his intensity.

"I will stay by you, with breath or without, with child or without. I shall be your last and best husband, Nicolaa. You will suffer no more at uncaring hands linked to unfeeling hearts."

Insight into his heart flashed like lightning against the full moon. "You seek to save me." She laughed then, a hard laugh that rose from memory and experience and knowledge to sweep all the romance of his chivalric vow to a place beyond the unreachable moon. "I do not need saving."

"The world has been a cold, hard place for you, Nicolaa. I would save you from that."

"If I could be saved from husbands, all would be well," she said.

"You have named it. This will I do," he said.

It was a vow, bound by his honor; they both heard the ring of it fill the chamber. They said no more after that. Each lay in the darkness, thinking how little the other understood anything.

*   *   *

246

The moon was long past viewing when Nicolaa finally tumbled into sleep. When he was certain she would not awaken, Rowland rose, lit the taper on the wall, stoked the fire to greater light, and watched her as she slept. Her hair, bright and wild, rose around her face to cushion her cheek as she slept, a single curl hurling itself free of the mass, a coil of red that twined loosely above her throat. Nicolaa slept deeply and silently. To sleep in such peace after what had gone before . . . it told him much of what she had endured in her many marriages. It put him in mind of the heavy sleep a warrior found in between battles; deeply and instantly a man would fall asleep, relaxing into the silence between the screams of war, storing up strength and will for the next encounter with the foe. So Nicolaa slept, preparing to wake and find herself sharing her bed and her life with a husband by her side. Aye, the comparison was apt and horrible.

She did not need saving? He believed her to be both honest and sincere, but she was wrong. He had never known anyone so in need of saving.

She needed him. She needed him to keep her safe from the world, standing as a bulwark against all pain and violence and death. She needed a man who would not leave her. She needed a man who would fight for her. She needed a man who would . . . *love her*. Nay, not that. But he would treat her tenderly; she had never been treated tenderly, and a woman—this woman—needed tenderness. He would heal her with tenderness.

That she needed him was a truth, a truth irrefutable. He would not have married her else. That she could not see her need or how well he would meet it was his pain, a wound in his pride that bled slowly and steadily. How could she not see how deeply she was in need of him and how perfectly he would heal her?

He would never have joined his name to hers if he had not believed she needed him.

She had never been valued for herself alone; all her worth was in her estate. He would show her that he valued her above her holding, which was larger than, yet not as rich as, his holding in Aquitaine. He did not need her for her wealth.

He did not need her at all, he reminded himself. She needed him for what he could bring her. She had known four husbands and they had not given her what she so piteously needed—tenderness, care, protection, security. Four husband, and none had given her what every wife deserved. He would do what they had not. He was the man to illustrate to her and to the world what boys the others had been; careless, thoughtless boys to so use a woman as Nicolaa had been used. He *would* save her from the cycle of marriage upon marriage she had endured.

With such tenderness in his thoughts, he touched her.

Just a single touch, to push an errant strand of hair away from her eyes. She twitched in her sleep, but that was all. On she slept, her breath rising deeply from her chest. She had a hand tangled in her hair, pressed against her brow, the other hand thrown across her breasts; she was curled upon herself in sleep, protecting her head and her heart. She revealed much in her sleep. Seeing her thus, he saw more clearly how carefully willing she was whenever she was awake. When first he had touched her, she had lain quietly, a willing wife accepting her husband's touch. But she had been so still, so guarded, so deliberately willing, with no rest or ease to mark her compliance. Unlike now.

He laid a gentle hand upon her shoulder, a stroke unintended. A caress to soothe and calm. A promise to protect and guard and value. A touch. A gentle touch to wipe away all violence and all strife. She had such need and was so unwilling to accept the gift he offered.

A caress to mark the silky smoothness of her breast, her nipple rising slowly in response. She did not waken. But she did respond.

She murmured and buried her head within her hand, deep in sleep. Unguarded.

He had not been able to arouse her when she had been awake and willing, so secure was she in her armor of false passion. He had not been able to touch her heart when he had forced himself into her, dry and unready, her single tear of defeat her only sign of emotion. Nicolaa was a woman who had endured many hands, many battles played out upon her body. He could not reach her when she was awake and armed. Could he touch her emotions in her sleep, sliding silently around the barriers to her heart?

He knew no other way, and things could not be worse between them than they were.

Before the thought was fully born, he touched her breast, warm and light in his hand. She was small and white, but soft. So soft. Her waist dipped down from ribs he could feel, the cage that guarded her heart, and then up to narrow hips, white in the firelight. She was as luminously white as the moon, her hair the full and twisted red of flame, glimmering red and gold as fire.

Moon and fire, she was; like them, she beckoned yet could not be touched. But he touched her now. And in her sleep, she gave him what she could not when awake. She gave him passion.

She rolled upon her back; he did not coax her—she did it willingly. She lay upon her back, her breasts upthrust, her nipples pink and erect. He stroked her gently, so gently, and she mumbled in her sleep.

He wanted her. God and Saint John Climacus help him; he wanted her. Lubias had flown, every remnant of her pushed from his thoughts by the hand that even now stroked the pearly skin of Nicolaa. Could any woman be so soft? She was like silk, smooth and fine, her slender length splayed out for his eyes and his hands to feast upon.

He was hard against her, his cock pressing, prodding against her hip. He wanted to invade and conquer and possess. He wanted to touch and taste and claim. Her wrists were bruised where he had caught her up and held her down, and he found he wanted even that. He wanted her marked and bruised and branded by his touch, by his very presence in her life. He wanted her, and the force of his wanting shook his heart.

He had to bed her, aye, but he could not want her. He had to save her and he wanted her need in return. But he could not need; he could not want; he could only touch. Touching was all he could give. Touching was all he could let her take.

And so he touched. He touched her at his will, silently calling forth her desire. Lubias was safe within his heart; it was Nicolaa who was at the mercy of his hands. For Nicolaa there would be no mercy, not in this. He wanted her need and he would take it in any way he could.

His hands trailed down her body, lit by firelight, a white glow in the shadows of the chamber. He found her cleft and touched her there, lightly, as lightly as goose down falling to earth. A simple stroking, a gentle meeting of his fingers and her womanhood. He watched her face; she did not waken. He watched her breathing quicken. And he stroked her faster, calling forth her need.

She was wet, her legs pressed against the weight of his hand, her hands sliding down her body. So quickly was she come to her passion. So quickly when her will was not awake to dull the power of his touch.

He watched her. Her mouth opened and she took a hard breath. He touched her breast, thumbing the nipple, and watched her tilt back her head, sucking air, his gaze upon her as hard and unrelenting as his cock. No mercy. No remorse for seducing a woman as she slept in the safety of her bed. He wanted her too much for mercy. He wanted her beyond the reach of remorse. His wanting was a wolf that hungered and howled in the dark. He saw nothing beyond it and prayed even now to be spared the memory of it.

His wanting quickened the beating of his heart. He could not turn from it. He had no thought to try.

She was ready for him as fast as that. He was ready for her. He throbbed; his shaft pulsed painfully, seeking her. Wanting her.

She pressed her hands against the seat of her desire, pressing his hand ever more forcefully against her heat. She was slick and swollen with wanting. Wanting him.

He lifted her hands and his own and watched her eyes flicker behind her blue-veined lids. Her breathing changed. Soon. It was coming upon her, the honest pulse of passion, the driving need that consumed man and woman both.

Pushing open her legs, he lay in the center of her, driving into her heat with a single thrust.

With the thrust, she stirred.

She was tight and wet and hot. A different woman from the sharp welcome of just hours ago. He groaned as she closed around him, his arms holding the weight of his body away from her.

She opened her eyes, blinking, still caught in the throes of sleep. He did not speak. He did not kiss her. He did not put his mouth on her. He only hurried to bring her to her release before she found the will and the means to stop him. She would not take this gift willingly. She would not want to submit so fully to any man, not even a husband. Most especially not a husband.

A woman had to give herself to a man, trusting him, wanting him. This woman trusted no man and would never give anything beyond the outward measure of her duty. She had never given herself. What she would not give, he had taken.

She was on the edge of release; he could feel the tremors within her. She fell sharply into the jolting release of her seed; a contraction, another, and then she awoke. Fully awoke. The pulse of her desire faded in that instant.

He looked down at her, his own seed pouring out of him in that moment in shooting bursts of pleasure. Her eyes were closed and her breathing harsh and heavy in the stillness of the room. He slipped out of her, slick and soft, and lay at her side.

"What have you done?" she said under her breath crossing her arms over her breasts and pressing her legs together, closing the gate when the curtain wall lay in rubble. He had breached her defenses, taking possession of her tower; all need for defense was past.

It was her first; every expectation she had of joining told him that. She did not know other than a dry, hard entry into her. She did not know other than bodily submission while her thoughts flew far and away above the touch of the man in her bed. He had given her pleasure, her first release.

What had he done? Given her what no man before her had done.

What had he done? Shown her what was intended between a man and a woman by divine design.

What had he done? Shared his body and his seed with a woman. A woman not Lubias.

What had he done?

Chapter Sixteen

She could be with child. Even now, life could be beginning inside her. A child to be nurtured and protected while husbands came and went like a pestilence of flies in their season. A child, when the convent beckoned. She could not leave for the peace of the convent, leaving a child behind in the world. She could not do as her own mother had done.

She knew enough of conjugal relations—aye, more than enough—to know that they had each achieved release. It was her first time. It brought her no joy, though the pleasure had been real enough. Saint Winifred, what pleasure. If this was what men could do, small wonder that they boasted.

The pleasure had exploded within her like pine sap on a hot fire, the sparks still careening through her blood and within every breath. She could not think past such a fire.

Her legs twitched and her arms lay heavy and lifeless across her aching breasts. Her whole body was in rebellion to her will. She wanted to reach for him, feeling his length and weight and heat against her; such was the depth of her fall from logic and invulnerability.

She wanted his touch. She wanted to lay her hands on the sculpted muscles of his chest and feel his heartbeat, matching its pace against her own. She wanted his mouth to taste her skin, and she wanted the scent of him in her nostrils and the taste of him in her mouth. She hungered for him with each pulse of passion that rocked against her womb, the distant echoes of the desire that had scorched her at his touch.

She wanted him. She had never wanted a man before. She could not afford to want one now.

Her heart pounded within her breast, matching the throbbing within the heart of her womb. She was wet. This was what he had meant when he had touched her and found her dry. This full and hot wetness was what he had wanted for her.

She did not want it for herself. She could not; the cost was too high.

She thought it had been a dream, the dream she had on occasion when her heart raced and the pounding between her legs pulsed and pulsed until she woke with her hands pressed hard between her legs, pressing that pulse down and away.

It had always frightened her, her body acting without the direction of her will, responding to the touch of the man in her dark and shadowed dreams, flying away from her, shooting upward into some great darkness, pleasure so hard and so high that she feared to break with the falling.

Aye, the dream, when it came, frightened her. But not as much as feeling the pulsating contractions of her release beating against the matching contractions of her husband's. It was with such dual contractions that babes were made. Without her release, a husband could pump his seed into her every day for a year with no result. Without her seed, she would remain as barren as the world saw her. That was what she wanted. How else to work her way off the marriage lists? How else to free herself of husbands?

If she proved herself capable of breeding, the line of potential husbands would stretch to London.

She could be with child. Children were brought forth out of mutual pleasure. Rowland had brought her to her pleasure, the first of her husbands to do so.

Why?

"Why?" she asked softly.

Why? He asked it of himself and could not remember his reasoning. He had had his reasons, reasons more noble than watching a beautiful woman in her sleep. He could not have betrayed Lubias for a mere naked and vulnerable beauty. He could not be a man who took a woman in her sleep because he had no will to stop; he could not have fallen to that. It had been for Nicolaa, aye, for her sake, not his own. He had wanted to show her that she was desirable, valuable for more than her wealth. He had wanted her to know the joy of pleasure in her marriage bed, not the cold willingness of dry submission. He had brought her the knowledge of something more, and in the bringing had given her pleasure. A noble gift done with noble purpose.

"For you," he said, turning to her. "You are more than land and tower, field and town. You are Nicolaa. Not Nicolaa of Weregrave or Nicolaa of Cheneteberie. Just Nicolaa. And that is sufficient for me. There is value enough in that. I do not seek more."

Sweet words. He could feel the struggle within her. She wanted to believe, but could she? She had been measured by her holdings all her life; could one man's whisper to the contrary knock down such a protective fortress as sheltered Nicolaa's heart? He prayed so. He wanted to save her from pain.

"You do not hope for a child? An heir?" she asked.

"Nay, I do not want even the wealth of your womb. Be simply Nicolaa and I will be content."

An honest answer; it passed easily over his tongue. He wanted no child not of Lubias's body.

"Why did you trouble to coax my seed from me if you have no wish for a child?"

She faced the dark ceiling, searching for the flaw in his reasoning. She would find none; he had done all for her. For himself, he wanted nothing.

"Why? When all you have endured is sorrow upon sorrow in your life? Your past husbands have been callous in their treatment of you. A woman deserves the joy of release as much as a man. That this has not been so is—"

"It is nothing. You make too much of small things," she said.

"It is not small to disregard a woman's heart and a woman's need. You have endured much."

"I have endured very little."

"Nay, you have endured much, suffered much, at the hands of ignoble men. I would save you from such a life. I will not give you such a future."

"I do not need another savior," she said, and he could

257

see the smile that turned up her mouth, hear the humor in her voice. Always she searched for a reason to smile. "Jesus Christ is sufficient for my salvation."

"Not a savior then, but a husband," he said, catching hold of her hand and holding her warmth next to his own. "You do need a husband, Nicolaa. For all your marriages, you have yet to find a husband."

The sun was rising, lighting the stone to pale gold. The first birds of the day were chirping their joy at another day dawned. And Nicolaa watched the eyes of the man who lay naked in her bed, a man who claimed to be her first true husband. She could feel the tremors of longing that the thought birthed and struggled to strangle the notion with her next breath. She would not want what she could never have; it was not in her to dream of what was not possible. She knew the world too well to trust the words of a sated husband lying naked in her bed. No matter that he spoke words she had never heard before. No matter that he offered what she had dreamed would be on the advent of her first marriage. She knew the world and men better now.

The question remained: did she want a husband? She knew well enough she did not need one. She could not ever let herself need one. Most especially not Rowland the Dark, who long ago had given his heart to another.

After the mass and the meal, Weregrave's guests gathered to depart. It was raining, a light, misting rain that bothered no one. Such a light and lingering rain did not even turn dirt to mud, but only softened the air and blurred the memory of the sun.

The ladies, Cathryn and Isabel, had their tapestries

rolled against the weather after one final refusal to accept a gift of such worth and Nicolaa's answering final admonition to take the gift in good heart and without regret. It was a gift given freely.

What they gave her in return, she would have been happier without. She was left with a list of potential husbands. Or, it was better said, Rowland had the list; no one seemed to trust her with it. A most uneven exchange.

They all looked so happy with the list, her own ladies happiest of all. Blanche glowed like a young girl, and she was fully Nicolaa's own age, her dark eyes gleaming like onyx at the prospect of another husband. Ermengarde was freed of her scowl, almost unrecognizable now, and quite lovely with her curling hair hanging down like a young damsel's and her haughty demeanor a thing of memory. Even Agnes looked a woman reborn, and she of an age to be well free of the obligation to marry. Beatrice spoke with all about her own betrothal, openly eager for the speaking of the vows. Such innocent ignorance was to be expected of her—she had no real knowledge of men—but for the rest? It went beyond logic and her knowledge of the world. Even a world that had Rowland in it.

One of them had told Rowland of her annulment plans. One of them had betrayed her. She would never know which one; they all now stood so close in purpose and friendship. How her own ladies, her friends and family, had turned from her without even the courtesy of hesitation she did not know. They must have been exceedingly willing to be turned. But turned toward marriage? What could be said to make a woman want to lose her freedom?

Nicolaa watched Rowland saying his farewells to Cathryn and William; Isabel and Richard, along with Edmund, had already departed. It was a warm friendship they all shared. A warm friendship from a warm man. He gave his loyalty and his fidelity well and truly, to both comrade and wife, if the wife be Lubias. For herself? She did not know, though he spoke a fine phrase to tempt a woman to want to be a wife. A rare trait, and pleasing. Aye, he had the ability to please her. An astonishing thought. It was turning into a rather astonishing marriage.

Perhaps because he was an astonishing man? He was a pleasing sort of warrior, well formed and of attractive countenance, his manner mild and his temper rarely beheld. Aye, he was pleasing, with his softly waving black hair and his black, bottomless eyes. That he had taken her unwilling she understood; they had been embattled and he had won. He required no forgiveness for the consummation of their marriage. That game she well understood. The other? She had forgiven him already his assault on her sleeping body, for had his purpose not been to give her a gift of priceless value? So he had claimed, and she could find no other reason for his actions. He had seen her body many times and not been driven wild with lust. She was his wife; he could take her where and when he pleased. That he had coaxed her body to find release she could not hold against him long.

She could be with child. The thought twisted through her. She wanted a child, even if a husband be the price. With this husband, the price could be met. He was better than most husbands, perhaps better than most men.

She was softening toward him; she could feel the softness rising in her like birds taking wing, and could do naught to stop it. It was the beginning of trust, and such weakness should have repelled her.

The Willing Wife

Trusting a man was a dangerous game, and one she had stopped playing years ago. She had been like Beatrice once, eager for a man of her own, eager for the rite of passage into womanhood, eager to manage her own domain. How young she had been. Fed on tales of men and chivalry and romance, she had expected so much more than she got. Philibert had been her first instructor, and she had not forgotten a single lesson. Each marriage, each man, had taught her more. She would not discard a decade of learning because of one man's smile. Nay, she would not. She would not be the child she had been.

He said he wanted her for herself alone. The idea was so foreign as to make even the words sound strange to her ears, like an unknown tongue from far-off lands. To be only Nicolaa. To be wanted for being only Nicolaa.

She could not take her eyes from him, studying him as he helped Cathryn to mount, as he laid a brown hand on William's leg in final farewell. His smile was warm as he waved them off, still warmer as he turned to face her across the bailey. William and Cathryn, Ulrich at their backs, turned and waved to her, and she returned both smiles and waves in kind.

Did it matter who had told Rowland of her plans? The deed was done and her moment past. It did not matter now.

Father Timothy came to stand at her side, his presence warm and familiar. "You will need to stop the annulment. It would no longer be valid," she said, still watching Rowland. He was very beautiful, if a warrior could be beautiful.

"I know," the priest said. "I grieve with you, Nicolaa."

He was aware? Well, she could find reason to smile at that; there were no secrets in any holding. The lives within

261

touched too often. But the priest did seem upset about the consummation of her lawful marriage, and that was a worrisome thought.

Rowland watched her with his dark eyes as he crossed the ward to join her and their priest. Father Timothy stood close by her and did not give ground when Rowland came to her, and that also did not bode well. A priest should not be so bold. Rowland put his arm around her waist and pulled her to his side, pulling her away from Father Timothy very neatly.

"There will be no annulment, Father. It would not be lawful," Rowland said.

"I am aware of that," Father Timothy answered, his eyes as intent upon Rowland as Rowland's were upon him.

"Good," Rowland said, his manner cheerfully combative.

Most awkward. She did not relish having such open problems with her priest.

Father Timothy, his own angry look met in full by the lord of Weregrave's, gave ground and turned back toward the chapel. He looked of a mind to pray Rowland into purgatory this very hour. She could not help being amused, and showed it.

"You seek to save me from my priest?" she asked, nestled within his arms and not finding her position especially irksome.

Rowland grinned and squeezed her waist. "If there is need," he answered.

So he had noted the thread of deeper emotion the priest tried so desperately to pull from him—and blamed neither priest nor wife for the tangle. A gentle husband, and reasonable. Who had ever heard of such a husband? Not she, certainly. He was a welcome change.

"There will not be need," she said, setting the matter to rest.

"Nay?"

"Truly. All is well," she assured him.

"Or well managed. But I am here, should the need arise," he said, keeping his arm about her. Most strange, such open affection. "You have a fine hand for more than thread. Weregrave shows your care. Are your other holdings as fine?"

She stiffened and pulled away from him. Again he would know the sum and substance of her worth? What of his talk this morn as she lay damp and breathless from his attentions? What of "only Nicolaa"?

"Be content, Nicolaa," he said, pulling her back against his side. "I seek only to praise you for your diligent management, nothing more. I am clumsy in complimenting, that is all."

"And I clumsy in receiving them this day," she said, calming herself, choosing to believe him. "Yea, all prosper, and for that I give thanks. What of your lands in Aquitaine?"

"I have been gone many years, since the last call to follow the Way of the Cross. I have not returned in all that time."

She could not grasp hold of the thought and keep it still within her mind. To be so long gone from land and heritage and legacy, from people and place and ties that stretched back over years; how to hold land and people and not dwell there? She was too careful of her holdings to condone such negligence. How well could his holdings have fared without their lord to see and know and act on behalf of all who needed him?

"You must return. Your land needs you, the lord who must protect all who dwell therein. This is not what your father envisioned when he passed his legacy into your hands."

He did not answer her charge of negligence. With his hand on her waist, they walked through the gates of Weregrave, past town and into field. The rain lightened to a mist that sparkled in the morning light, leaving thousands of rainbows in the air to touch their skin. The fields were golden, the sky pearl, the earth beneath their feet soft and brown and rich with promise. A line of geese covered the sky to the east, black and broken by a few lazy birds who lagged behind the leader of their band. Their noise was the call of autumn; each year she waited for them to make their journey and each year she was rewarded. Lammas might mark the beginning of the autumn season, but until geese flew south, it was summer still.

Rowland took her far from Weregrave, into the open fields that surrounded her holding, past them, to the edges of the wood, where the fields were wild with meadow flowers holding high the last blooms of the year. He was silent long, and then he spoke.

"I could not go back," he said. It was all he said, but it told much.

They slowed their walking to an amble and then still more to a shuffle. He took her hand in his rough, callused ones and looked into the dark green of the shadowy wood. He had his sword and his dagger; more, he had his strength and his warrior resolve. She did not fear; none would touch them, neither wolf nor boar nor man. He was a fierce warrior; all the world knew that of Rowland the Dark. Nay, she did not fear any living foe with him at her side. She feared only the name of Lubias.

She was not a woman who let fear rule her. With a breath, she said the name.

"Tell me of her. Tell me of Lubias."

He squeezed her hand and then let her go, turning his face back to the fields and the greater light to be found there. He did not look at her; he looked off, to a place she could not see. He looked to where he could see Lubias.

"She was not like you," he said, and she made herself breathe against that beginning. "She was dark and full, like good wine. Our fathers had arranged the match; she was my betrothed from her cradle days, and we were well content with that. I knew her all my life," he said. His eyes looked off down the well-worn track that marked the way to Weregrave. "I could make her laugh."

"You liked to please her," she said, wanting more than legend for this woman who held her place in history by holding on to Rowland's heart.

"She was easy to please, but, aye, I liked to please her," he said, his eyes focused far off. "It was my need to please her that killed her," he said softly. "I should not have let her come with me. I knew my duty, to fight and fight again, wherever king or pope called. I am a knight. I must fight."

"It is your calling and your duty," she said. There was no choice in that; knights must fight. It was their destiny, decided at birth unless they chose the cowl.

"Aye," he said, "to fight is why I live. But Lubias . . . I could not break her heart by leaving her and so I took her with me. And so I killed her."

"She would not say so," Nicolaa said. If any of her husbands—if this husband—had asked her to follow him to

Byzantium, she would have followed with only the clothes she wore. But she had not been asked. "She would not lay blame at your feet."

"Perhaps not," he said, his gaze lost in the dirt at his feet. The back of his neck was exposed, vulnerable. He looked like a boy in need of a mother; a man in need of a woman. And she was not the woman. "Yet she is gone and I am here. I cannot go back to where she should be and is not, because of my failure. I did not protect her. I did not keep her in safety, as was my duty and my privilege."

The geese were gone, the silence as empty as the sky. Even the mist was gone, fallen to earth. The sun struggled against bands of purple cloud, yellow showing through in long and ragged patches. She could hear the careful snap of deer making their cautious way through the forest at her back, but she could only look at Rowland.

"She was where she wanted to be," she said. "Few women are given that gift. You gave her that."

"I gave her only myself," he said. "We had not been married long. She had no child of me; she had no time to prove herself as the lady of a great holding. She had not even begun her first tapestry," he said, smiling slightly, showing her that he had not forgotten to whom he spoke.

Her first tapestry? Who would care for tapestries when such a man with such a love was before her eyes? Would any woman not have followed such a love as Rowland gave?

"I think she was well content in what you gave and what she had," Nicolaa managed to say over the birth pangs of belief.

Belief. He loved his wife. Beyond grave and shroud, he

loved her. He loved her now, walking in the autumn mist with Nicolaa at his side.

Who would save her from that?

"You are kind, Nicolaa," he said, turning to face her, turning from the wood.

"Nay, I am not kind," she said. "I am a woman. I understand her better than you, perhaps."

"Perhaps," he said, taking her by the hand and leading her toward the path that would take them once again to Weregrave. "Can a woman read the heart of a woman better than a man? I have wondered it. If true, then a man should read a man better than any woman. Shall I tell you how wanting in honor and worth I find the men who have found their way to you, Nicolaa?"

"Nay," she said, shaking her head. "Was it not you who did not wish to tread this path again?" she said, smiling to soften her response. "I know all I need to of past husbands. Can you not say the same?"

"Again I say you are kind, Nicolaa," he said, pulling her into a light embrace as they walked along the path.

The air had warmed, a light caress full of the smells of autumn. The dirt was dry beneath their feet, the grasses along the edge of their way rustling gently, golden and tawny in the sun. They walked together, his arm about her waist, for a time. Slowly, because it was awkward for her not to, she slipped her arm around him. He did not remark upon it and, eventually, her posture relaxed. It was companionable to walk along so. To talk of little things, of nothing, to touch without the need for coupling, to touch, to hold another soul for the clean pleasure of an embrace. She did not know the last time she had been held so. Perhaps she never had.

"You deserved better," he said after a time.

"As did you," she said.

They kept their eyes on the path before them, but he pulled her a little closer to his side and kissed the top of her hair. A light kiss, it should have meant nothing, yet her heart skipped for just an instant. Just an instant, but it changed everything.

In that instant, she yearned to trust.

Chapter Seventeen

They returned to the warmth and smoky heat of the hall, their walk back to the protective walls of Weregrave spent in talking of nothing beyond the change of seasons and the changes in the land since the coming of Henry to the throne of England. Henry was no warrior king, but he had much to do to clean up the ragged disarray left behind by Stephen and Maud; Rowland was glad of that, for it was in battle that he found his joy. Even a small battle could make him smile. It was with a smile that he entered the hall and found the women of Weregrave clustered about the low hearth. At his entry, they smiled and curtsied, their manners as fine as if they stood before Eleanor herself. Rowland had wrought change in Weregrave, that was certain.

He entered into the midst of them, Nicolaa at his side,

and asked the question they each wanted to answer: "Are you willing to be wives?"

"Aye," came a chorus of female voices spoken not in perfect unison, but united.

"Answer for yourself. Think upon your answer," Nicolaa said.

"Aye, you must answer singly and with careful thought. 'Tis not an idle question I ask of you," Rowland said.

"I am, Lord Rowland, most willing," Blanche answered.

"I am, if a husband of worth can be found for me," said Ermengarde.

"I am," said Perette. "I am ready to be a wife."

"I am," said Jeanne, "if a man still living would take a wife of my years. Be he near the grave, I will make him breathe again." She grinned.

"I am," Beatrice said.

"Nay, Beatrice, you are not," Nicolaa said.

Beatrice blushed and then lifted her chin with all the stubbornness of a child. "I *am* ready."

"Let us talk now of those who do not have betrothal contracts signed," Rowland said, letting the dispute with Beatrice wait. "I will talk with the king. For those of you who do not have family to make the arrangements, I will be your voice. There are many men in Henry's lands who yearn for wives; I know many of my acquaintance who might suit. I can make no assurances, but I do not foresee any reason why each one of you should not become a wife."

"If that is what you wish," Nicolaa said, despite the flagrant joy in each woman's face. It was clear they did wish it. They looked as if he had just announced the Second Coming of Christ.

Rowland smiled in the face of her caution and wrapped

his arm around her waist, drawing her close to his side. He was doing that often. She was coming to like the feel of him pressed against her, the solid feel of his arm around her, the easy warmth of his casual embrace. It was affection, she realized, not desire—a warmer, more lingering feeling than desire. She leaned into his embrace against all wisdom. She would fall into the weakness of needing such touches if she did not have more care.

"You do not believe that there can be such a thing as a willing wife," he said, grinning.

Nicolaa looked askance at him, her own smile twitching at the corners of her mouth. Oh, aye, he could afford to be playful; he was getting his way in the matter of the marriages. What man would not grin when he had his way in all things? Still, the betrothals had not been arranged yet, had not even begun to be arranged, and such things took much time. In the matter of Beatrice, who, of them all, was the only one with a firm contract, she would not give way. The girl was too young to marry.

"I believe what I know," she said to Rowland.

"You know only what you have experienced," he said.

"There is no fault in that," she said as the ladies began to disperse. No one was going to the solar, she saw.

"Nay, but I think I can give you experiences that will change your beliefs." His black eyes sparkled softly as his full and lovely mouth smiled his humor. Was he going to kiss her now, in front of all?

She pulled herself out of his arms and moved closer to the fire, an ill-planned retreat. Where could she now run? "That is possible," she said, "but I do not yearn for new experiences."

He moved closer to her, pressing her back against the

heat of the fire, his arms bracketing her body, his hands on the stone of the hearth. She could not run. She did not want to.

Eyes like the night sparkled with humor and passion, showering her with longing. His arms encompassing her whispered the promise of safety. It was a promise she could not believe, though the words were sweet. She did not want to run from him, nay, but she could not believe the offer in his eyes. She could not trust and she would never love, no matter the gentle tenderness of the man before her. No matter the pulse of yearning he had birthed in her.

"That will be the first lesson," he said, his mouth just above hers. He had the most glorious mouth. "To teach you to yearn."

He kissed her lightly, playfully, his mouth just touching, warm and moist and sweet on her lips. A gentle kiss, a tender kiss of affection married to desire. A kiss that was not long. A kiss that was not deep. A kiss that left her yearning.

A kiss that left him smiling.

Worse, she was smiling up at him, her gaze gone soft as a doe's.

"I could do with some of that," Jeanne said, walking by them, shaking her head. "Make the arrangements, if you can, as quickly as you can. I grow older and more desperate by the hour."

Rowland laughed, but Nicolaa could not. Was not desire unnatural at such an age? Could her grandmother have learned to yearn all those years ago, and did the yearning still hound her? Unnatural.

"Beatrice," she called, breaking free of Rowland's arms and his lessons. "Let us speak privately." Rowland did not move. It had been a small hope that he would let them talk in private. Let him listen then; he would not turn her from her purpose. Beatrice was not ready for marriage, and she would make the girl see it. "You are swept away by talk, constant talk, of marriage, but you are not ready. Can you not see that?"

"Nay, I cannot see that," Beatrice said, her pale cheeks flushed with the challenge, her light blue eyes as hard as ice. "I am ready. My betrothal has been long. I have learned all that you have taught me. I wish to speak my vows."

"You are too young to know what you wish and where such wishes will take you," Nicolaa said.

"I am not as young as all that. I am not too young to know my own mind. And my heart. I want to marry."

Beatrice, always so quiet and compliant, was determined to be married. It was as if a marriage fever had swept through Weregrave and consumed them all; and Rowland was the happy carrier of the contagion.

"Are you ready for the responsibilities of running a holding?" Rowland asked Beatrice.

"I am," she said, her high and childish voice a mockery of what she affirmed.

"Are you ready for the physical demands of matrimony?" he asked.

With hardly a blush, she answered, "I am."

"Let your lady and I discuss this together, Beatrice," Rowland said. "You have answered well, doing honor to your family and your house."

Beatrice was gone from them before Nicolaa could say a word to stop her. She would probably have left in any case, Rowland's words being so much more to her liking than

273

Nicolaa's. Which left Nicolaa in a quiet fury, a fury she welcomed, as it drove to ground all tenderness. Rowland showed himself a man in forcing the issue of marriage upon the women in her house. He stood in flagrant opposition to her will and wish, and he cared not. Nay, he stood in all his pride, certain he was right and certain that his will would be done. Nicolaa's will mattered not at all. All softness, all weakness, died within her, and she thanked God for it.

"She is not ready," Nicolaa said, uncaring if Beatrice heard her.

"She has her courses?" Rowland asked bluntly.

"Aye," she said reluctantly.

"You have taught her to manage, to sew, to physick?"

"Aye."

"She is ready," he pronounced.

"Nay, she is *not*."

Rowland considered her, and she met his gaze. "How old were you when you first wed?" he asked.

"Fourteen. Her age. And I was *not* ready."

"But you thought you were," he said with a concilatory smile.

She had thought so. She had been eager. She had hoped for so much and found so little. Would she feel the same if this man before her, this Rowland the Dark, had been her first, her only husband? She knew enough of him to know that Lubias had joined herself to him eagerly. But Jean de Gaugie, to whom Beatrice was pledged, was nothing like Rowland. She would not give Beatrice to him, even if Beatrice herself should demand it.

"Yet I was not. I was wrong. Beatrice is wrong."

"When will she be ready?" he asked.

She kept her silence, but it damned her.

"You believe no woman is ripe for marriage because your husbands, each in his turn, bruised your heart. Marriage need not be so, Nicolaa. Marriage is ordained by God to uplift both husband and wife, a loving bond of commitment, devotion, and service."

"You say what marriage *should* be, not what it is. Not what it would be for Beatrice with Jean de Gaugie."

"You speak from your pain, which I understand, but this is an advantageous marriage. All parties have signed the contracts. She must—she will—be wed."

It had been a quiet sort of battle, this latest between them. She had kept her voice low, she had kept her demeanor calm, and she was still furious. She was tired unto death of Rowland's relentless attempts to woo her while tossing those she was trying to protect into harm's way. She was tired of his smiling arrogance, so certain was he that he knew what was best for them all, and she was tired of his soft-spoken ruthlessness in pursuing his own course. He behaved more like a husband with every breath he drew.

"Beatrice is under my protection, the arrangements for fostering made with me. You have no part in this," she said on a hiss of breath.

"As your husband, I do," he said, his anger rising, though he kept it quiet.

"A fortnight ago you were not my husband."

"How does that signify? We are wedded now. All that passes within Weregrave's wall with Weregrave's people is my concern."

"For a week! For a mere week. What when you are gone

and your pronouncements mere echoes? These women—
this child—will still be wed."

"I will *not* go. I have sworn—"

"Yea, you have sworn," she said, and heard the hard bite
of sarcasm in her voice. She thought it well deserved. "Let
us not tumble into deeper discord by arguing the strength
of a man's vow when honor calls him elsewhere."

Rowland, the vein in his forehead prominent, took a
deep breath. "Fine. Then let us talk instead of Beatrice's
willingness to marry her betrothed. If you care for her, and
I know you do, then listen to her. Trust her. Give her what
she demands."

It was a strong argument, and she had only one truth to
hold against it; she knew more than Beatrice.

"What she demands will destroy her," she said, looking
deeply into the fire and seeing only twitching flame. To
follow Rowland's logic, she should give Beatrice a burning
stick to play with because she had clamored for it.

"Nay, it will not," he said, taking her by the arm and
turning her to face him.

She took a deep breath and tried to compose herself. He
was a man; he believed his mind and will to be ruled by
logic, though she knew well that he was ruled by the clam-
orous voice of pride and not the soft tones of reason. Let
them discuss this logically; she would try that route, giving
him the chance to prove himself to her.

Plainly his tender kisses still held a soft, small place
within her heart; there was no other reason to give a man
so many chances to prove what he was not.

"Do you know Jean de Gaugie? Is his name familiar to
you?"

"Nay," he said easily, "but Beatrice's father must know

the man. He would not arrange a marriage—"

"You know neither her father nor her betrothed, yet you defend them without hesitation," she said, disgusted.

Rowland drew himself up and released his hold on her. "I have been patient, but this dispute is done. These are the facts, Nicolaa. Adjust yourself to them. The women who wish to marry will be married. The women who are betrothed will seal their vows. I am *your* husband unto death; I will not leave you until then. These facts are not, and will never again, be in dispute."

He strode out of the hall looking firm, resolute, warrior-stubborn. He could look as he wished; when he left, she would do as she wished.

It did not take her long to find Beatrice; she was in the kitchens, eating a hunk of barley bread soaked in sweet cream. Beatrice did not want to talk to Nicolaa, but Nicolaa was determined, and Beatrice could only bend before such a will as Nicolaa's.

"You must not rush into what cannot be rushed out of," Nicolaa said. "This is not your time for marriage. Your time will come soon enough. You have another year at best before the vows must be finalized. Take that year for yourself. You will not regret the addition of another year added to your maidenhood."

"I will regret it," she said, a touch of cream still clinging to her upper lip. "I want to be loved; I want to be loved as Lubias was loved, and marriage is the gateway to that love."

Nicolaa sighed. Always it came back to Lubias and the legend of a single, shining love.

"I understand," she said. "I understand the longing for

such a love, but marriage is not the answer."

"It is," she said, her pale eyes shining with certainty, hope, and pure romantic fantasy. "I know it will be so. To hear of such a love as Lubias enjoyed is to know that a man can love with a passion that both heals and destroys. I want such a love. I think that such a love awaits me . . . with Jean."

"Do you?" Nicolaa said, forcing her voice to a hardness she did not feel. "And did devoted love await me in my marriages, even my marriage to Rowland?"

It was a question that gave Beatrice pause.

Jeanne found Rowland just as he was entering the armory, the metal gleaming softly through the open doorway.

"I betrayed my granddaughter's trust in telling you of her planned annulment," she said, her blue eyes sharp and speculative. "I hope you made good use of the information. You made a strong start when you carried her up the stair. You look a man to know how to finish what is well begun."

He could hardly hear her, had hardly felt her hand upon his arm, so angry was he still over the words he had exchanged with Nicolaa. Why did they always have to fight? Had he and Lubias ever clashed so often? He could not remember that they had. He was a calm and reasonable man, so there was no necessity for quarrels. Therefore, it was Nicolaa who was so difficult. Why did she reject his will when all he did was out of concern for her? Why could she not simply trust him? He was worthy of it.

"Why *did* you tell me?" he asked, looking down at her.

"Because the married state is where a woman should reside. She has had five husbands now. Would that the church had sanctioned half as many for me. I have had but one man in my bed my whole long life. With your help, I will get yet another before I die."

Rowland smiled in spite of himself; Jeanne was the exact opposite of Nicolaa in temperament and outlook. It was hard to believe they sprang from the same seed. But perhaps Nicolaa was more like her mother.

"I will help, but I cannot promise more."

"That is all I ask. Just give me the chance," she said.

"You would help me if you could tell me something of Nicolaa's mother. Does she favor her?"

"In looks, nay, except for being as shapeless as a willow branch; her mother, Matilda, is brown-haired and blue-eyed, as I was. In temperament, they are of a single piece of cloth. Ever a sour face was Matilda, always wanting to be at her prayers, and no time but what he begged of her for her man. When he died, off she went to the convent, and there she has been ever since, kneeling and praying away her years. But she is contented in her life, which I am glad of. I would not have any more of my kin run to the convent; I could not stand silent when Nicolaa planned the same for herself."

"How old was Nicolaa when her father died?"

Jeanne thought hard and then said, "I think she was seven, but she may have been older. It was before her breasts sprouted, that is certain. She was away at her fostering when it happened, her life fixed and secure."

There was nothing unusual in Nicolaa's history; she had been fostered and married at the common ages. That her mother had been ensconced in a convent for the past ten or fifteen years was no ordeal, as Nicolaa would have been fostered out at that time in her life anyway. Nay, he could not see that her childhood had been in any way unusual.

"Better to ask me how old I was when my man died, for I was and am too young to be a widow."

"You are not too young to be a widow if your own daughter is widowed as well," Rowland said with a grin.

"I *feel* too young, and that should count for something," she replied. "Tell me now, has my granddaughter been breached?"

"There will be no annulment," he said.

"Good. And have you gotten her with child? Those other fools, for all their efforts, could not seem to manage it. Though Macair—"

"That is in God's hands," he said hurriedly, cutting off mention of the infamous Macair, "for it is He who opens and closes the womb."

Jeanne laughed softly and said, "Only Mary, the blessed mother of God, managed to plump with child without a man. Since then, a man must do his part."

Rowland kept silent, but he could not stop the chuckle that filled his mouth. Jeanne joined him in his quiet laughter and then said, "And now let us discuss the man you have in mind for me."

"Yet he is the man my father chose for me," Beatrice said to Nicolaa. "Certainly he gave a thought to my heart and my future contentment."

Fathers thought only of wealth and honor when parceling out daughters, but Nicolaa would not wound Beatrice by saying so.

"Fathers judge bridegrooms by different standards than a bride," she said instead.

"Yea, higher and surer standards, according to my father. I must obey him. I *wish* to obey him, Nicolaa. I wish to marry." Let Ulrich mock her youth then. She *would* marry; she was ready, and she would prove it.

"I wish to marry. Especially now that Ulrich has departed," Blanche said. "If Rowland can arrange it, I will fly from here happily."

"And what of Nicolaa? Would you leave her here without solace or succor?" Agnes asked.

"Without succor? Have you not studied that husband of hers? Would that I had one such as he to succor me half so well."

"He is only a husband. A woman needs women to build her life upon," Agnes answered.

They were in the solar, but only because Agnes felt they should continue the tapestry. Blanche was there because Ulrich had gone and she needed a way to fill the hours until a husband could be found for her.

"A woman needs children to give warmth and meaning to this life, and for children a woman needs a man. I am ready for a man of my own. And this time, one who knows enough of women to give me my pleasure. 'Tis no fault of mine I am childless; Robert Fitz Hubert could not have brought *himself* to pleasure without a day and a night of constant effort. What chance had I?"

Agnes laughed in red embarrassment to hear such scandal; then she laughed again at the truth of it. "Follow your leanings, then. You are young still and your body plump with youth and life. I am content to stay with Nicolaa."

"Your courses still run hard, Agnes. Let a man plump you with life. Let Rowland see to Nicolaa. He is not a man like her others. Surely you can see that," Blanche said, smoothing her thread.

*   *   *

"Surely you can see that your father has much to gain by this marriage, and so does Jean de Gaugie," Nicolaa said as she and Beatrice left the kitchen.

"That is why it is a good match," Beatrice said.

"Yea, for them, but what of you, Beatrice? My concern is all for you."

"I know," she said softly, "yet you need not worry. I am content. I want to be a wife. And a mother."

Nicolaa looked at her in loving exasperation; only the young could be so confidently content for so little cause. "Aye, as did I. Yet I have been many times a wife and never a mother. Do you think I did not yearn for my belly to swell with life?"

"I did not think . . . What I mean to say is, I did not know you wanted a child, Nicolaa," Beatrice said, her brow furrowed in concern.

"Not want a child? Is there a woman under heaven who does not yearn for a child?" Nicolaa said. "Four husbands, now five, and I have had no child to suckle. Having a man in your bed does not promise the warmth of a child, Beatrice. A husband brings many things into a woman's life, but the least of what he brings is his presence. Think you: I have been married for most of ten years, yet in all that time a husband has been rarely by my side. Philibert was in my bed for less than three months, Hugh even less, and Macair, lusty Macair who poked his stick at me with such joyful abandon, never got me with child. The wife he took after me is childless as well. He is a man who cannot make a child, I think, yet he was my husband given. How if the same befalls you?"

*   *   *

Father Timothy and Rowland found each other at the kennels. That they had been seeking each other out was more than plain and the kennel boy darted out of their company as soon as he took a quick look into each stern face. This was no priest and penitent who stood facing each other, but two angry men.

"All know what befell Nicolaa at your hands last night," Father Timothy said, getting in the first word.

"Aye, the marriage was consummated," Rowland said, standing an arm's length from Weregrave's priest and staring fully into his dark gray eyes.

" 'Twas more than consummation, what you did to her. The skin of her wrists carries the bruises of your tender touch upon her."

"I have committed no sin," Rowland said. "I have done all that was required of me and made Nicolaa my wife."

"Through violence," Timothy gritted out.

"I did what was needful and no more. Has Nicolaa complained?"

"You know her well enough to know that she would voice no complaint, though she had cause enough. She bears all silently, as did Christ upon His crucifixion."

Rowland studied the man, seeing the flame of desire buried within his black robes. He did not doubt Nicolaa; nothing had yet occurred between the two of them, yet this priest was more than priest, and he would not have Nicolaa fouled by this man's desires.

"You care deeply for your flock, and for one lamb in particular," Rowland said. "How stands your own soul?"

"You are not my confessor," Timothy bit out, "but I am yours. Surely you need to confess that your treatment of

Nicolaa has not been marked by loving care and consideration. Do you not have need of me?"

"For my priest, aye, but you talk not as a priest, but as a man. Which are you, Timothy?"

"I am what Nicolaa needs. I am her priest, and I tell you that she has been made to bear much in this world," Timothy said, his eyes stony and hard with righteous resolve. "I will not stand silent while she is made to bear more at your hands."

"I have done nothing beyond what was needful," Rowland repeated, believing it. "I would not and will not harm Nicolaa. I will be her husband. I will seek no escape from this marriage, and I will not stand silent when she talks of being free of me."

The silence birthed by that statement touched Timothy visibly, leaving him flushed. It was then that Rowland knew whose idea it had been to have the marriage annulled. Worse, he could not fault the priest. Had he not made it his life's duty to see Nicolaa well protected and secure? Could he fault the priest for wanting the same for her and doing all within his scope to see it accomplished? Nay, he could not. On the matter of Nicolaa, they were of a mind.

"You are commanded to love her," Timothy said.

"I know the commandments concerning marriage. I am to love; she is to respect. Think you she holds me in respect, Father?" When Father Timothy did not answer, Rowland said, "Nay, she does not, but such will come in time. All will be well with us, given time. And godly counsel. Are you the man for that?"

Let Father Timothy answer as to the condition of his own heart. Which was he to be? Priest or man? If he answered as a man, Rowland would kill him where he stood. Nicolaa would not be fouled by this man and his unholy desires, even though he be a priest. He would dwell in purgatory for a thousand years to save her from Timothy and his spiritual battle against unlawful passion. He would indeed save her from her priest, if need be. Timothy's answer would decide the matter.

Timothy held Rowland's eyes as he answered. "I am her priest, and yours. Let God use me as He will."

"As He uses us all, Father," Rowland said, content that the priest would keep to his place in the divine order of the world. "Let us find what rest we can in that."

Chapter Eighteen

The solar was full of women again, though it had taken some force of will to assemble them. What a joy it would be when Rowland departed for some war or other and she could return to the freedom of comforting routine.

Just when she had gotten the ladies to their tasks, all needles moving rhythmically, all threads untangled and smooth, all whispers hushed, Rowland appeared in the doorway to the solar, without the customary knock, and grinned at them all. The needles stilled and the whispering resumed. Nicolaa sighed and silently prayed for a very small war to give her some peace.

"I am to train. The day is fair and bright."

Why she should be interested in how he spent his day, she did not know, but she answered cordially. "I wish you well then."

The Willing Wife

"I want you to watch me," he said, coming fully into the room.

A giggle came from Perette and a snort of amusement from Jeanne. The silence and comfort of the solar were crumbling rapidly.

"I have tasks and responsibilities of my own to complete," she said, pleasantly.

"And you do them very well," he said, grinning. "I cannot, I fear, do what I must do without the lady of my life watching me, encouraging me to excel. Is it not true that a man, to win the praise of his lady, will do great deeds, accomplish profound acts of bravery and valor? What can I hope to accomplish today with my sword or mace or lance without Nicolaa to watch and sigh over my efforts?"

"Sigh? I will not sigh," she said with a chuckle that slipped past her involuntarily.

"Then I am challenged, lady, for I would and will make you sigh," he said, and with those words, he lifted her in his arms and carried her from the room.

Over his shoulder she could see her ladies arrayed about the tapestry; they looked both starry-eyed and envious. Thus she understood his purpose in covering her with courtly speech.

"You did that to sway them toward marriage," she said as he strode through the hall.

"I did that because I want you to watch me. And if they are swayed . . ." He grinned and twirled her in a circle. She held on to his neck and closed her eyes, her face buried against the hard wall of his chest. She was befuddled and disoriented. Grinning.

"Where did you learn such speech?" she asked, holding back her sighs.

"Did I not say I was from Aquitaine?"

"Then the rumors are true."

"Rumors? Rather call them legends," he said, raising his eyebrows comically.

"Is there more truth in a legend than in a rumor? It must be a very fine distinction."

"There is more to the world than you know from your experience, Nicolaa," he said, his teasing over. Then she did sigh, for she did not relish another lecture on the world and its ways.

"However limited you think my experience, I know it is no measure of courtly love to carry a woman when walking is within her power," she said, striving for lightness, yearning for the tenderness of teasing.

"Even when a man has the power to carry her?" he asked. "I enjoy the feel of you in my arms. Did you know that your scent covers me as fully as any cloak? I could bury my nose in the hollow of your throat and drown in the scent of you."

Her belly tumbled at the words and the dark look of longing in his eyes. These were words that fed the hopeful girl who hid in the shadowed reaches of her heart. That girl, the memory of who she had been, could live on such sweet words. Nicolaa closed her eyes and shut out the words, willing herself to starve. And failing. Every moment with Rowland and his sweet words and gentle ways brought the girl she had been, the girl who believed in love and the promises of marriage, back to vibrant life. She could not live in the world as she knew it with an open and trusting heart. She was as she was because she had learned the art of survival. What Rowland called forth in her would kill her, tearing her soul past all repair. Yet he called; with every look and every tender word he called, and she could not find the will to turn from him. But try she must. She had to save herself.

"I think the truth is that you like to exercise your power. That is the way of a man, even if he be from Aquitaine and knows well the ways of courtly love."

"It is no measure of courtly love to commend a woman for the way she smells, Nicolaa," he said with a grin. "You have reduced me greatly. I am not the man I was to admit to a woman that her scent drives me mad."

"And so you carry me because you are mad? I find I can believe you," she said, smiling, though she knew she should not if she would not encourage him.

"Ah, she believes me," he said, his face to the heavens. "God be praised for each and every miracle. It is a miracle of great import for Nicolaa to believe."

"Aye, it is," she said with a laugh.

"Aye, it is," he said, his eyes serious as he looked at her.

They had walked, or he had walked and she had been carried like a babe, through hall and across bailey to the wall and the armory. No one had stopped to stare at the lord of Weregrave and his lady; they were too well trained to take note of any such thing. Weregrave continued on, no matter the behavior of its current lord and the depth of his madness.

The armory was cool and shadowed after the bright light of the autumn day, and he waited for their eyes to adjust before setting her on her feet. The room held a brightness of its own, with walls deep in gleaming metal, sharp points, and heavy shields. It was a wealth of weapons arrayed before them, as much a part of Weregrave's wealth as her grain and her land, for without weapons and the men to wield them, all would be lost.

"A man's power need not be a bad thing, Nicolaa," Rowland said, a pile of swords at his back. He had shifted the conversation, casting her off balance for just a moment before she righted herself and faced his new assault.

"Not when it is used to further a man's goals; certainly no man would disclaim such a virtue," she said, taking a deep breath and facing him.

"Would you then disdain a man in his entirety?" he asked. "Is there no forgiveness to be found in Nicolaa's heart?"

He had shown her patience and tenderness and gentleness unending. He had seen her need and heard her silent cry for rest and safety. He had done all and more that a man could do, and still she pushed him off and away. She had not changed. She was not healed. She did not trust, not completely. She did not want him. He was Rowland and she did not want him. Not enough. He wanted more from her than this slight softening. He wanted all.

"Do you require forgiveness?" she asked.

"You must answer as to that," he said, keeping his distance. "How long will your heart be hard against me, Nicolaa? What must I do to cleanse you from the wounds others have inflicted upon your soul? I am not as other men."

Nicolaa studied him and heard the hurt his words revealed. He was a darker form in the dark room, his eyes shining in solemnity. He did not touch her. She missed his touch. More, she missed his companionship and the easy ability he had to make her smile. Now, with her words,

she had destroyed their mood of gaiety. Even if he were to
be an infrequent visitor in her life, she had come to want
his smiles and his soft and willing tenderness. She wanted
Rowland. God and Saint Winifred help her, she wanted
him.

"A man must be as God created him; I will not quarrel
it. I am only weary."

"Of husbands," he finished.

She did not answer. She did not want to hurt him, and
he seemed capable of being wounded, which she could not
understand. She knew only that she had the power to hurt
him and that she did not desire it. She was so very weary
of battling him. He wanted so much from her. He wanted
her trust, and in that he wanted too much. She was not a
girl in the flush of hope that marked a first marriage. She
knew too much of marriage and of men to trust, even if
the man be Rowland. Even if she had somehow stumbled
into wanting him. She could not give him more. Was her
wanting, the very weakness of wanting, not enough?

"Let us not quarrel," she said. "Why am I in the armory?
Has Weregrave's armorer not fulfilled his purpose?"

"I find no fault with Weregrave, her armorer, or with
you, Nicolaa. And I would not quarrel, but I would know
your heart."

"I fear my heart is full of quarrels," she said.

She felt the sudden urge to weep and was more alarmed
than she could say. When had she last felt the urge to cry?
Had it not been two or even three husbands ago? When
had a man ever cared what tumult tumbled inside her if
she be but pleasing and docile? A willing wife. Rich lands.
Fecundity. A man's list was short, but weighty. Here stood
a man who voiced no care for other than the state of her

heart. How to answer such a man? She had not the words or the will to tell him that the state of her heart was precarious indeed. With every look, every entreaty to know her, he pushed her toward the last of her defenses. She could not give him more. Yet he demanded more. He wanted all of her. She could not give him all and still be standing when he left.

"Then speak of quarrels; only speak, Nicolaa," he said, his dark eyes soft with tenderness.

She did not know what to say; she had little practice in talking to a man. Talkativeness was not on the list of what a husband required in a wife. If she spoke of the tumult in her heart, she would weep and throw herself into his embrace. She did not dare speak. She held with a trembling hand the last of her resolve. She had no weapon to fight the sweet temptation of his words. He had stripped her bare.

"Why are we in the armory?" she asked again softly, to fill the silence of his command.

"I want you to watch me train. I would have you choose the weapon."

"Why?" she asked, unable to stop the quarrel that was rising within her to overpower her tongue, this new weapon sharp and cold within her grasp. He had revived her will to fight, though he knew it not. She could see the weakness of him suddenly and it fired her strength to fight. She had in her this one last battle to save herself from the grasp of uncaring masculinity, and stood now facing her foe, her husband.

"Why?" he repeated. "It has been many years since a woman watched me train. I find I have a yearning for it."

Yea, it had been many years since Lubias had watched

Rowland practice arms. With Nicolaa as his wife now, he recalled all he had done without and yearned for such again. Through her, he would have his needs met: his needs for a woman to praise him and pet him and pander to his pride. Aye, he would look to Nicolaa to feed his vanity. Yet who was his wife and who his shadow wife, moving along the edges of his thoughts? She knew who stood in shadow and who stood in the light of Rowland's heart. Small wonder she felt the stab of tears.

"Why me? Why not any of the women of the solar?" she asked, her eyes burning with tears unshed.

"What question is that to ask of me? You know the answer," he said.

"Tell me." It was not a command. It was a plea. She searched his dark eyes, almost yearning to find a reason to trust. That was how far he had weakened her, and she trembled at her vulnerability.

If he could only say the words she yearned to hear from him. If he could only open up his heart to let the smallest bit of Nicolaa inside. If only . . . She was the child she had been, wanting "if only" from a man. There was no "if only"; there was simply what was, and she was strong enough to live with that. She had to be. Rowland could not give her what her heart whispered in its longing. He could not give her love.

"You cannot," she finally said. "It would require you to use the word for me you will not use. Wife."

He did not even pause to let her words wound him; he attacked, as any good warrior would.

"There is a word *you* will not use, Nicolaa, and it is my given name. You call me 'husband' and nothing else."

"You *are* my husband."

Claudia Dain

"As have been four others before me. Will you not even attempt to learn my name? Do you expect, no matter what I vow, that I will be gone from you so soon?"

It was as if he had never carried her. It was as if he had not teased her. It was as if nothing of kindness or tenderness had ever passed between them. Because he was a man and he had no use for tenderness now. Because she was his wife and he had no need to be tender to her, not unless it served his purpose. He had wanted to sway her ladies toward marriage, and so he had been tender. Her trembling heart closed against him as neatly as a lake swallowed stone, her tears drying in that instant. He gave her nothing. She needed nothing from him. He was a husband; that was all. It was good that he had so well reminded her. She had nearly forgotten the truth of things.

"I know your name, Rowland the Dark, as a wife should. How neatly you have turned away from my observation. Between us, between your bruised heart and my stony one, there can be only quarrels."

"Even quarrels are better than silence," he said.

The room was full of weapons, sharp, deadly, within easy reach, and he wanted a quarrel.

"You are valiant, husband," she said, smirking. "Any husband of mine I think must needs be." He was not her first husband. He would not be her last husband. And no matter how close he had come to destroying her, she would still be standing when the last husband rode away from her. She would not let him or any man destroy her, not even with tenderness. Not even with the promise of love. She had too many memories, hard memories, to believe in promises.

"I will be your last husband, Nicolaa."

"Yea, so you say," she said dismissively, and turned from him to face the weapons on the wall.

"Why do you doubt me? I am here. I have no quarrel, no complaint with you. Can you not trust?"

The word, the accusation, struck the small hidden wound deep within her that no mending could ever cover and broke all into tangled threads of blood and soul, torn past any repair. Her anger surged upward and she breathed it to life, wielding the weapon of her tongue and the truths she knew would wound him.

"You are here, you say? I *will* quarrel with that. You are on the plains of Aquitaine with Lubias, your heart as surely hers as mine belongs to me and me alone. You are here? Mine? You are hers. Even now, married to me, you are hers."

The darkness of him grew to dominate the shadows and the sleeping violence of the room, matching the size and intensity of her own anger. She was not afraid. He was only a husband. He had wanted to be more; yet in the end, he was only a husband.

If he had loved her, if he had offered her even a sliver of his heart, she would have been lost. But she was not lost. She was found again; all the confusion his tenderness had birthed within her was gone. Dead. She was herself, Nicolaa of the Many Husbands, and she was not afraid. She had left fear behind her long ago to rest with innocence and trust and the belief that a man could love. Oh, aye, Rowland had birthed in her the belief that a man could love. Aye, he had given her that back again. But he could not love her.

He did not love her.

"Do not speak of Lubias," he said in a growl, sounding like a beast of the wood and the darkness.

Nicolaa laughed in the face of his fury. "Nay, I must not even dare speak the name of Rowland's true love, though all else he would have of me. My trust, my body, my lands, my thoughts, my very heart. And in return I have his stoic promise that he will never leave me. Leave me?" She laughed, stinging tears gathering in the corners of her eyes. "You were never here."

Rowland's rage was as black as his name, and it pulsed out toward her from the darkness like a running wolf after a wounded hart. His hands were on her shoulders, his grip bruising, sliding up toward her throat, so white, so slender, so vulnerable. He wanted to rip Lubias's name from her lips, to choke off her words, to stop the truths that struck like lances into putrefying wounds.

"Will you kill me, husband?" she said in a snarl, her eyes as hard and bright as sapphires.

He heard her through his rage, a pulse that demanded satisfaction. His hands were on her throat, brown on white. He had killed with his hands before, time upon time. He knew what to do. He had to get her to stop the poisonous flow of her words. That she had dared to speak of Lubias . . . That she questioned the honor and the sanctity of his vows to her . . . That she sought to tear Lubias from his grasp . . . No one would attempt such and live. . . . No one. Not even Nicolaa. Nicolaa, who had tempted him to tear Lubias from his heart. Nicolaa, who had wound herself around his thoughts until he had begun to think of her as his wife. Wife, when Lubias was the only wife he had ever known or ever wanted to know. Nicolaa had woven herself into the very fabric of his soul, and he wanted nothing more than to rip her out of him, returning to the purity of his devotion to Lubias. He could not want Nicolaa. He could not succumb to the lure of Nicolaa; his very honor demanded that he not.

The heavy point of a blade was at his belly, the point piercing the thick leather of his gambeson.

He did not know whether it was the prick of steel or the cold fury in her eyes that stopped him. But he did stop.

"Or will I kill you?" she said on a growl as fierce as any wolf's. "Either way, I am free of a husband."

He released her and it was like releasing pulsing flame. They stood staring into each other's eyes, their harsh breathing in strange rhythm. She lowered the blade in her hand, but she did not drop it. Even now she did not fear. She had the courage and heart of a warrior, and he knew why. How many husbands had she faced so? How many batterings had she endured? How many forced entries into her hard sheath had she withstood? How many times had Nicolaa stood alone in her own defense because no one else would stand with her?

How many lies had she heard from the lips of the one man sworn to uphold her?

How many lies from him?

He had no thoughts but those, and they tangled with the vision of Nicolaa standing to face him, holding her dagger. She had spoken true; she was not fragile. She could face anything and survive, even a husband's hands around her throat. She was a woman worthy of legend. How that he had not seen that till now?

A squire called from without, calling his name, yet their eyes never left each other.

"Aye," he answered the squire, his voice as hoarse as if hands had been pressed to his own throat.

"King Henry sends for you, Lord Rowland. He travels to Wales at the turning of the day."

"Prepare my horse," he called, trapped by the look of Nicolaa in her unmasked fury. She blazed high and bright, a fire to burn any man. Even a husband.

"Another battle," she said, "and away you ride." Her voice was raw and sharp, as was her meaning. "Perhaps I will find myself a widow. I have not yet been a widow."

How strange it was to fight when the thought of leaving Nicolaa widowed hovered over him like a shadow. The joy he found in fighting leaked out of him like drops of blood, drop by drop, staining all he knew of his life. He did not want to die. Did she truly care so little for him that she could see him dead and feel naught but joy at her brief freedom? Brief, for she would be married again, her name attached to another man's, her people and her life given over to husband number six.

By dying, he would leave her, and he had sworn never to leave her. Had he made the same vow to Lubias? He could not recollect. Now, staring into the fire, all he knew was that he did not want to leave her. Her. Nicolaa. When had her name supplanted Lubias's in his thoughts?

He sat by the fire and stared into it, seeing nothing. Even Lubias kept her distance, and he could not summon the strength to call her to his side. Let her memory rest, he thought; let them both rest. Just for now. He sharpened his blade on a stone, the movements slow and soothing.

Without the joy of battle to sustain him, without the presence of Lubias to comfort him, what was left for him in this life? Take all away, all that had held him up for year upon year, and what was left? A shadow. The shadow of Rowland, his legend, which would fade quickly. Would Nicolaa grieve for him if he did fall in battle? Would Nicolaa remember his name long enough to name him to her next husband in a moment of fiery anger?

Nay, he did not think that Nicolaa had ever shown her anger to her husbands, just as she had never shown her passion. He, of them all, was the single man to know the woman who hid behind the tapestry she was ever weaving. She moved through her life, touching only thread, being touched by no one. A shadow. A careful and wary shadow.

A shadow he had touched. A shadow he had but fleetingly touched. He wanted more from Nicolaa, and more *of* her. Nay, it was simpler yet. He wanted *her*. The thought was a betrayal of all he knew of himself, yet he could not summon the will to feel even shame.

What had he become? Was this the Rowland of legend? Nay, he did not know himself. Nicolaa had remade him, as if he were no more than strands of silk to be woven to her will.

He resheathed his sword and spied a shining gleam of red tangled in the wool of his cloak. He pulled it free and held a strand of Nicolaa's bright hair. The long, curled red hair rose up before his hands, his fingertips holding firmly on to the silk-thin strand. A remnant from a shadow, wrapped around him, red as blood and stronger than war. A single hair of her head and he felt branded by the presence of her.

Lubias was far off. Nicolaa wrapped around his thoughts, around his very soul, like silken cording. How that a woman could so entangle a man?

The strand of hair caught the firelight and was caught by the draft of hot air, twirling in his hand, shining. He could let it go, let it fly to the fire and be consumed in an instant. He could, but he did not. He could not. He wrapped the hair around the hilt of his sword, just above the guard, tangling it to keep it in place. A talisman, to make his arm strong and keep his fighting pure. A talisman to keep Nicolaa from widowhood. A single, shining remnant of a shadow.

Chapter Nineteen

Jean de Gaugic was in Wales, as were all knights who served King Henry. After a week of careful and quiet searching, Rowland found him. Found him and learned to keep company with the man. William, less accommodating, found it hard duty, but side by side they learned the temper and nature of the man who stood in opposition to Nicolaa's will.

Rowland did not like him. He would not turn the point more sharply, but it could fairly be said that he did not like the man. Dislike was not a cause for the breaking of a contract, any contract, and it would not serve in the matter of Beatrice's betrothal. Jean was older than she by many years, but still a sturdy knight. He was clean in his habits, careful in his speech, and skillful in his warfare. Worthy traits, good enough for king or comrade or even wife. What Nicolaa found so hard in the man he could not see. His holdings were prospering, according to all the talk, his squire well trained and orderly. He did not favor wine above clarity. He did not wench more than was seemly. He did not snore through the mass.

Still, Rowland did not like him.

William did not like him.

'Twas a problem.

They shared a fire for a night, the wind hard from the northeast and full of the smell of winter. Wrapped in his cloak, Jean asked of his betrothed.

"She must be pressing against her time," he said. "I saw her within this year and she was close upon it. A lovely lass, white as foam and just as gentle, is she not?" Jean said.

"Foam can be hard when it crashes into rock, smothering a man," William said. "Though it be lovely."

"You say she is hard?"

"He jests," Rowland said, casting William a look that silenced him. "Beatrice is lovely, pale as moonlight and just as soft upon the eye. A gentle lady of tender heart."

"That meets with what her father, Lord Philip, says of her. Lady Nicolaa is training her well, I am told," Jean said.

"Well in the ways of thread and stitch," William said. "If you find use for such, you will find her well prepared. If you look for other skills, you will look hard."

"This is true?" Jean asked Rowland.

"It is true she can turn a stitch and that she spends much time at her embroidery," Rowland said.

He and William were of a mind, as was their way; they did not want to send Jean running to gather Beatrice to his side, yet they also dared not dissemble. Jean had fair claim to Beatrice; they could not, by law, keep her from him. As yet, they had no reason even to think of such a thing—if not for Nicolaa and her objections.

"Well, let her have her stitchery," Jean said, pouring heated wine into his cup. "I want children of her. She can do that well enough with just a prod from me."

He laughed at his jest, less crude than some they had heard around battle fires, but they did not join his laughter. Beatrice was too tender to carry such coarse jesting.

"You have no children?" William asked.

"Aye, I have done my part," Jean said.

He did not make a jest of it, having learned the temper of his fire mates, and swiftly adjusted himself to their temper. Rowland watched how quickly he learned to change his nature to suit his comrades and could not praise him for it. It was not courtesy that ruled Jean; it was expediency.

"My children, those few who are not fostered, need a woman to mother them. Beatrice, her nature told me by her father, seemed ideally suited to the role," he said.

"Aye, she is gentle, but how many children do you claim?" Rowland asked.

"Six, I have: four boys and two girls. All but the youngest three fostered out, their lives set upon the path. They await Beatrice with eager hearts, as do I."

He spoke not one word out of tune, yet the melody was discordant to Rowland's ears. If Nicolaa had told him nothing of this man, would he have found him amiable, a fitting husband for any wife? He was too moved by Nicolaa and her fears.

Yet William distrusted as much as he, and William had no womanish fears to blind him. Yet how to class Nicolaa with womanish fears? A woman fashioned to face anything, even a husband's rage, and her only fear was of mating Beatrice to Jean?

"I think she will love them well," Rowland said.

"You think her ready to wife?" Jean said, his eyes earnest and eager.

Rowland swayed on the edge of a blade. His honor demanded one course; his instincts, guided by Nicolaa, urged him down another path. He could only say the truth and pray to Saint John Climacus that his words would not change the turning of the marital tide that flowed around Jean and Beatrice.

"I think that she will soon be ready."

Jean smiled. "I am gladdened to hear it. I will go to her when this is done. She is at Weregrave, then?"

"Aye, but there is no need for haste," Rowland said.

"It is not haste, but only eagerness you see. I yearn for a wife," Jean said. "They make the nights sweet and long, do they not?"

Rowland and William said nothing, only grunted into their wine. When Jean went off to empty his bladder, William said, "You used to have the gift of silence. The gift for talking around fires does not serve you well."

To that, Rowland merely grunted.

"She is not here," he said.

Rowland sat his horse within Weregrave's bailey and looked down at the priest. Father Timothy did not offer him welcome within his own domain. He was little disposed to tolerate such temper from his priest.

"Where is she?" Rowland asked. "And when did she leave here?"

Father Timothy, his gray eyes as cool as mist, said, "She

left just days after your own departure. She knew you would return here, thinking to find her. She wanted to be well gone."

The words tore what little remained of his restraint. Rowland dismounted and handed off his horse to a groom. He took the priest by the arm and dragged him into the chapel. The good father balked at every step. Well favored and tight with muscle he might be, but he was no warrior and had not been trained as one from birth. Where Rowland wanted him to go, he was forced to go.

Once inside the sanctified gloom of the chapel, Rowland released both the priest and his tongue.

"The battling of your demons is between you and God, but you will not stand between me and my wife. Where is she?"

"Buried, as all the dead must be or else the stench of their decay would foul the very air," Timothy said.

Rowland felt the darkness edging in, clouding his sight and his reason. Buried. Nay, she could not be buried. No such brightness as Nicolaa could be smothered by earth and stone. She could not be beyond his reach, he who had so briefly touched her.

"Where?" he croaked.

"Only Rowland knows where his wife is buried," the priest said, holding his gaze without mercy, his eyes sharp and silver-bright in the gray of the chapel.

"What?" Rowland said, fighting his way out of the darkness.

"Rowland has only one wife, and her name is Lubias," Timothy said. "All know that his heart is bespoken. All know that where Rowland walks, Lubias is at his side, though her grave be far from here in both distance and time."

"I speak of Nicolaa," he said. "Where is Nicolaa? I must find her. She will have need of me. Jean de Gaugie is on his way to claim Beatrice."

"She did have need of you," Father Timothy said, undaunted by Rowland. "Yet you gave all to Lubias."

"Stop speaking of Lubias. None shall speak of her," Rowland said in a growl, an act of memory. Did he not always growl his warning when any man attempted to steal Lubias from his grasp and from his heart? Did he not even now hold to her as the thought that Nicolaa was beyond his reach set his heart to pounding and his ears to ringing? He could not think of any but Nicolaa, but Lubias, ever Lubias, was the name he turned to hear.

"None shall speak of her? Why, all Christendom speaks of her. It is to try to loose your grasp on her, this woman who is dust and worms now, that is forbidden by Rowland. Else all may speak of Lubias and of how Rowland loved her," Timothy said, his hand hard upon Rowland's arm. He did not speak, look, or act as a priest to his charge, but as a man fully angered.

"I come about Nicolaa. Tell me, is she alive or dead? What of Nicolaa? This is naught of Lubias," Rowland said, freeing his arm.

"It is all of Lubias, but it is well you ask of Nicolaa, even late as it is," Timothy said, turning from him and going to stand before the crucifix of Christ. Rowland did not follow, but stood his ground upon the stones of this sanctified place, straining for purchase as his world tilted.

"How is it late?" God above, was she dead? Had Jean come, attacked, harmed her? "Speak, priest, lest I kill you at the altar of Christ, damning my soul past all saving. Speak to me of Nicolaa if you would keep your life."

"I will gladly speak of Nicolaa to you, Rowland the Dark. You were given a gift most rare when Nicolaa was given you," Father Timothy said calmly. "That you lacked the wit to see it was unbearably painful to watch."

"You love her," Rowland said, past all boundaries of rank and station, his hand upon his sword hilt, fingering the guard that shielded his talisman.

Timothy dropped his head and then turned to face Rowland. "I am not free to love her. My life's course was chosen for me long ago, beyond my will or voice to alter it. I am a priest, my devotion chosen for me. But you," he said, his eyes burning like molten metal, "you are free. Oh, you will say in your heart that you are not, that Lubias holds the chains to your heart and your memory and that you cannot, will not, be freed of her. But you lie, and in your lying you wound Nicolaa, and that must not be."

"I will not speak of Lubias with you," he said stiffly. "And I have done nothing to wound Nicolaa."

He said the words and pushed away the memory of her bruises and her blue eyes swimming with tears she would not release. Nay, he would not admit to hurting Nicolaa, but his heart bore witness that he had and beat against his words of protesting innocence.

"Then hear what I will speak of both your wives, for Nicolaa is your wife as truly as Lubias ever was. Lubias is dead, her soul flown, her body decayed, as all things of earth must decay. Would you carry a corpse of a decade around on your back? This you have done, and forced Nicolaa to bear the stench of it. Nicolaa, who is alive and who needs a husband who will see her worth and cherish

307

it." His voice grew hoarse with unshed tears, and he blinked his eyes to clear them. "I am not free to love, yet you are free. Can you not see what she is? Can you not see the brightness of her soul?"

Rowland touched his talisman, his only handhold in a world gone dark and then bright too fast and too hard. Could he not see what she was, this fragile woman who had made herself as hard as steel to survive a brutal and bloody world? Aye, he could see. He saw Nicolaa, the wife he had claimed with his mouth, but not his heart. The woman he had wanted to need him and trust him and want him while giving her none of the same, holding himself aloof with Lubias at his side most cherished. All he had done was for Lubias. Of Nicolaa he asked all and yet gave nothing but the legend of his name. Yet Father Timothy had not finished.

"Nay, you cannot see. Your arrogance and your pride cast all about you in shadow. 'Then I went down to the potter's house, and there he was, making something on the wheel. But the vessel that he was making of clay was spoiled in the hand of the potter; so he remade it into another vessel, as it pleased the potter to make.' Do you heed the words of Jeremiah as he speaks, revealing the heart and mind of God? Are you the potter of the clay that defines a man's life? Aye, to be Rowland d'Albret is to be equal to God, for he will not accept God's design for the pattern of his life. He will cling to Lubias, though she be safe in God's hands. 'On the contrary, who are you, O man, who answers back to God? The thing molded will not say to the molder, "Why did you make me like this," will it?' Will it, Rowland? Is this not what you have done with your life? Have you not questioned God's divine will with every breath?

308

Have you not sinned in holding to a wife who is in God's keeping? We are taught the sin of excessive grief, for it holds the sting of rebellion against God within its cloying sorrow. He is the potter; He will make you and direct your path as it pleases Him. Yet here stands Rowland, in bold rebellion, proud of his sin, throwing Nicolaa from him without thought, without . . . heart," Father Timothy said, his voice breaking.

Rowland knew the verse, from the book of Romans, and yet he had never understood its full meaning. He had no words against the charge, no defense. It was a truth so bright he could not help seeing it, though he would turn, running from such an accusation if he could.

He had stood upon the earth, shaking his fist at heaven and God upon His throne for changing the path and pattern of his life. He had been battling for year upon year, with God Himself for an opponent. With such an adversary, he was destined to fail, an endless fall from which there was no rescue. And in his fall he had crushed Nicolaa. Nicolaa, who stood straight as shining steel in the face of any affliction, any husband. Nicolaa, whom he had vowed to heal. Nicolaa, whose anguished need of him was to be his meat and drink.

What vanity ruled the heart of man. He had come to save her, yet what had been the secret heart of his intent but to destroy her? To take from her all that made her what she was, all she had learned in her many marriages, so that his pride could be polished on her naked need?

Rowland raised his face to the distant ceiling of the chapel, the gloom of stone overriding all but prayer. Yet, within his prayer of forgiveness, all was shining bright. And within the light, he saw.

Lubias had been chained to him by his own hands, for his own purpose. And what of Nicolaa, the bright light of Nicolaa? Did she not bear keeping? He had forced her to stand far down and far off in his devotion to Lubias, she who had been in God's keeping for year upon year. How did that serve Nicolaa?

How did that serve Lubias?

How did that serve Rowland?

It was that question and the answer whispered to him with the intimacy of God's own voice that blinded him fully with the white-hot light of painful truth.

Jean de Gaugie wanted Beatrice. Nicolaa was not going to hand Beatrice over to him. Out of that stalemate the siege of Soninges began.

She had departed Weregrave with her ladies soon after Rowland left for war. If he returned for her, let him hunt her out at Soninges, she had thought. She had not expected to be grateful for his arrival.

It was on the third day of the siege that Rowland came. He came with knights and men from Weregrave and Cheneteberie and Greneforde; the field before Soninges was littered with men and animals and the machines of war. How he had known to bring aid, she did not know, but suddenly Jean de Gaugie was fighting Soninges at his front while Rowland with his allies appeared at the rear. Rowland's arrival was timely; Soninges was strong and double-walled, but de Gaugie was building mangonels with her wood and gathering heavy stones to hurl at the walls. Soninges might fall, but Nicolaa would not relinquish Beatrice.

Now that Rowland was here, would Rowland, who had

so recently felt her steel against his belly, stand by her?

She watched from the wall, hiding behind a thick merlon, careful of the beacon that was her hair; she watched and saw Rowland astride his black horse, tall and immovable in the saddle. She saw him raise his sword and fight the army of de Gaugie. At his back, the knights of her holdings rode, a mass of men and horses that looked as solid as stone from her place on the wall. He battled the army of Jean de Gaugie though he did not support her cause. Nay, he supported her.

There was no other truth to give to what she was watching and she felt the burden of tears press against her chest. She would not cry. There was nothing more to this than battle, and all knew that Rowland lived for battle. This was not of her. He did not do this for her. She clung to that denial while her eyes followed him, his every move, the shining of his heavy blade, the men he struck down into the bloody mud beneath his horse. He was a warrior; his gentleness had been the illusion of dreams.

He was fighting his way to Jean; that she could see from her place on the wall. When he did face him, they exchanged a single blow, and then Rowland lowered his sword. Jean hesitated and then lowered his as well. A truce. A binding truce that would deliver Beatrice, or a temporary truce to allow diplomacy to rule the day? Whatever Rowland had said, his actions showed that he had defended her, despite his own intention that Beatrice marry de Gaugie. His loyalty warmed her as nothing should if she were to keep her heart intact. After their last exchange with her dagger at his belly, she would not have been surprised to find him joining forces in the siege against her.

Rowland approached the gate alone, de Gaugie well to

the back of him. Did he hesitate? Did he wonder if she would pour boiling water down upon his head as he passed through the gates? That would make her a widow soon enough, and she had threatened it. For a woman whose only desire was to keep her husband content until he rid himself of her, she was not doing very well. She did not think Rowland would ever claim contentment at having Nicolaa to wife.

With a word from her the gates were opened, and Rowland entered, alone. She climbed down the stair that led from the curtain walk to the outer ward and walked without hesitation to her husband. Without hesitation—that was putting a dull edge on it; she had all she could do to keep from running to him. When she was near him, her mouth dried up of words and left her with only the bitter taste of her fear.

From beneath his helm, he spoke to her.

"Another fine tower. You could have withstood attack without my help."

She heard his meaning. *You did not need saving.*

"Help is always welcome," she said.

I needed you.

"Is talk of widowhood still on your tongue?" he said, his voice rough beneath the steel.

Do you yearn for freedom, even at the cost of my life?

"Nay," she said. "It was a hasty thought, lost to regret as soon as I spoke it."

Forgive me. As I have forgiven you.

A grunt was his answer, and he lifted the helm from his head. He was thinner, his beard days old, his brow damp. He looked bone-weary, soul-weary, his life a burden he no longer wished to bear. Had she done that to him?

She had told him that her greatest joy would be in freedom from him. She had told him that she held him in small esteem. She had told him that she did not believe his claims of constancy, and more—that she did not care if he was constant.

She had pushed him from her as every man before him had pushed her. She had treated lightly the one man who had sworn to treat her with consideration, and she had neither noted nor cared.

Until now.

He came to her aid because he was her husband, a word that held a wealth of meaning for him. He loved another wife, his first, but she was not wounded, for love had not existed until she had met him. Love was the stuff of troubadours and legends; it was not a thread that would ever touch her life. She had wrapped herself in that belief and found warmth, of a fashion. Until Rowland came. By watching him love Lubias, she had learned to believe in love. 'Twas enough. 'Twould have to be enough.

Could he read her resignation in her eyes? Would he want to? She had no answer. She did not even know if she wanted him to run that far into her thoughts; she knew only that the sight of him pleased her, expanding her heart to press against her will.

"I have my own regrets, regrets that slice as deep as the finest blade," he said.

"I would not wish for any blade to slice you," she said, looking up at him. He looked so weary and so worn, nothing at all like the Rowland of legend who lived for battle. How much truth was there in legend?

"Peace then, wife," he said, and with a smile he added, "I need a bath."

Wife. She looked into his eyes, her breath stopped in shock. Wife. Her heart stopped to match her breath and then hammered a new beginning, hard and loud within her chest. Wife. He had given her much with that one spoken word.

"That is a need most cheerfully met, my lord Rowland," she said. A gift for a gift. She gave it gladly. Rowland. Her husband.

He smiled at her, his face transformed. She smiled, handing him her tenderness.

A new beginning.

"Should a bath be prepared for William?" she asked.

"Nay, for he stays without the walls of Soninges, to keep Jean de Gaugie well mannered."

The peace between them had been so brief; the name of Jean de Gaugie cast the wedge between them again. She looked up at him, her eyes full of questions. He shook his head and dismounted, pulling her to his side as he handed off his horse to a groom. "Show me a tub full of hot water and I will be content. Let us leave all troubles without. Is that not what curtain walls are for? You will assist me?"

"Aye, willingly," she said, smiling again.

"Then I am at heaven's gate," he said.

"Strains of Aquitaine," she teased.

"Nay, only the strings of Rowland's heart."

He had changed. He was still romantic, but more vulnerable. And yet a month and more ago his hands were at her throat. How such a change?

They walked through Soninges side by side, finding contentment in their nearness. Soninges was larger, much larger than Weregrave, and she watched to see what he thought of the holding. Soninges had four towers on her outer wall, the outer bailey filled with kennels, mews, dove-cote, forge, well, fish pond, orchard, and stables. They passed through the inner gate and were within the inner bailey. The great oven and kitchens were here, bakehouse, granary, a walled garden, and a second well. The tower rose three floors and was strengthened by buttresses on each corner. It was fine tower, solid, with a strong door reached by a wooden stair that could be burned if all were taken and only the tower remained unbreached.

They climbed the stair, still silent, and she wondered what he would say, or if he would speak at all. The hall took up the entire first floor, the hearth arched and large against the north wall. The ladies stood before the fire and turned with smiles when they saw who was with her.

Rowland smiled and then said softly to Nicolaa, "Soninges has no solar?"

"Nay." She smiled. "Soninges is more warlike in her aspect, less of comfort."

"You were expecting Jean de Gaugie?"

"Nay—"

"Ah, only a husband," he said.

She looked quickly and saw the humor in his eyes and ducked her head against her answering smile. He understood her too well. It was, perhaps, his gravest fault.

"Lord Rowland, my father has written me," Perette said, her green eyes luminous. "How did you arrange for my father to decide?"

"Lord Rowland," said Agnes, "my heart is full of thanks at your generous spirit. I am most, most willing to meet with Lord Walter. A date has been discussed—"

"And I await your choice for me, Lord Rowland. I am not discouraged at the delay, but can there not be—"

They were interrupted by Nicolaa. "Leave off. Can you not see that my lord Rowland is covered in the dirt and blood of battle? Can you not forget yourselves long enough to give him ease? He has no time for talk of marriage now."

She hurried him up the stair to the lord's chamber, away from the women and their endless talk of marriage. It would be truer said that *she* could not make the time for talk of marriage.

"Soninges is bursting with willing wives, it seems," he said.

She ignored him and his lopsided smile until she had him in the chamber and the door behind them was closed.

"Let us leave all troubles without. Is that not what doors are for?" she said.

"Agreed, wife. All troubles are without. In this chamber, it is only the two of us. Think you even now we have escaped our troubles?"

She could not answer for the arrival of the tub. The men carried all within, tub and water arriving with much bustle and noise. Through all, she stared into the eyes of Rowland and he stared back at her. They searched for peace with an intensity that would have boiled water, yet they were unsure of finding it. This she saw in him and knew he saw the same in her.

When they were alone, the door closed again against the troubles that awaited them without, Rowland said, his voice hushed and intense, "In the courts of Aquitaine I learned many things, many pretty words, but I never learned what to say to a woman after laying violent hands upon her. What words for such an act, Nicolaa? What atonement?"

He had touched her in violence; that was true. He had

316

wanted to kill her for assaulting the memory of his wife and his true love for her. What man had ever felt the memory of love so strongly? When had a man ever loved so true as Rowland loved his Lubias?

He looked at her now, giving her the right to pronounce his penance for doing what was within his right to do. If he beat her, he had the right. If he killed her, he had the right. Neither God nor king would fault him; that was a truth they both knew, and yet he sorrowed for something he had not done. He had not hurt her. Whatever had been in his thoughts, he had not acted. What man could say that? No man that she had ever known.

"You have given me all I require in giving me your sorrow. What words for a wife who draws steel on her husband?" She offered her own sorrow up to him, giving him her guilt in equal measure to his own.

"Words of praise only. If I ever lose myself in such a manner again, draw blood. I will not censure you, even from the grave," he said, laying a hand on her hair, touching her softly.

She smiled, wanting a lighter mood between them. This talk was too much of the heart, and his heart was not hers.

"Let us not talk of graves and blood; you are too fresh away from both. The door is closed upon all that. The water is hot, but not for long. Come, and I will help you with your mail."

"Nay, the water can wait, for I must say more on graves and blood," he said, taking her hands in his, the steam rising at his back.

The lord's chamber of Soninges was small, and she felt suddenly oppressed by stone. Each breath was heavy in her chest. She did not want to talk of graves and blood. There could be no peace in such talk, and that was all she wanted with this man: peace, serenity, friendship. What friendship in graves?

"I went to find you first at Weregrave," he said, "but you had flown from there."

She did not look away from him, but she knew that he saw the truth in her eyes; she had been hiding from him, avoiding him. She saw in him that he did not fault her for her action. She had known, somehow, that he would not.

"I searched for you because I knew that Jean de Gaugie would come, seeking Beatrice, and that you would not relinquish her. I knew because I fought beside him in the hills of Wales just weeks ago." He looked at her, the last of his smiles as far gone from him as the geese of autumn were from the lavender skies of Michaelmas. "We talked of Beatrice. I told him she was ready for marriage."

Nicolaa clasped her hands tightly together and lowered her gaze. So. He had brought the enemy to her gates with his words.

"He left the battle as soon as Henry gave leave, and, understanding something of his temper, I made for Weregrave. I would not have left you to face him alone," he said.

She could feel his eyes on her, but she would not look up to face him. She saw his legs, long and muscled beneath his mail, his spurs muddy, the smell of sweat and dirt strong on him. He would deliver Beatrice to de Gaugie. Nay, he would demand that she do it.

"I found Father Timothy. He met me at the gate, most eager to counsel me," Rowland said. "I had little time to give him, so eager was I to find you, but he would not release me until he had spoken the words God had laid upon his heart."

She did look up at that. What could Father Timothy have had to say to Rowland? Surely nothing of earthly weight when his mind and thoughts were so heavenly directed. Rowland turned away from her and faced the single wind hole set high into the wall; it was too high for her to see out of, but a full-grown knight would have no trouble in letting arrows fly from such a height. Rowland spoke to the air and the clouds that hung there as thick as unwashed wool, yet his words were for her.

"He spoke to me of marriage and of women, which is rich with an odd humor, is it not? He spoke to me, his hand on my arm like to break it if he could, and said the name of Lubias. Lubias. That name I will allow no man to speak—Father Timothy spoke of Lubias and my devotion to her."

Nicolaa stood, stiff with apprehension, her hands clenched white.

"I have wronged you, Nicolaa," he said, his voice heavy as stone. "I have wronged you most grievously. I have kept the image of Lubias so bright, I lost all the world to shadow."

"What did Father Timothy say to you?" she asked, her voice a whisper.

"He said that no man chooses his path, but is set upon it by God, and it is the measure of the man how well he turns his eyes and his strength to the task laid out for him. He praised you most highly, Nicolaa, as a woman who gives all her strength to the course before her, and he is right in that. He has learned from you to walk in the path of duty set for him long ago when he was given as a babe to the church. He praised you, lady, and you deserve each word."

She could only shake her head in silence at such words, so ill-deserved. She had been created to marry and produce children; she did neither well.

"He spoke true, Nicolaa. The echo of your words, your charge that I demanded all of you while giving nothing in return, struck me hard. You spoke true and were right, right about all."

"I do not ask you to abandon your love for Lubias," she said, taking a step toward him, laying down her pride. "To know that a man, that you, are capable of such love is a gift I never thought to see. That such love could be—"

"Nay," he said sharply, his eyes bright with pain, "do not say it, Nicolaa, for my next confession will wound you sharper and deeper still. I loved Lubias; that is true. I mourned her long with a true and honest grief. And that became my downfall."

They stood a pace apart. She wanted to touch him, but was afraid of what she saw in his eyes. Shame. Regret. Fear. What had he to fear?

"I do not understand you," she said softly.

"Do you not?" he answered, his voice a murmur that filled the room with hurt. "You have said it again and again. What does a man value above all else?"

She did not even have to think, the answer was so readily upon her tongue. One thing men prized above all else. One thing drove them. One thing rewarded them. One thing ruled them.

"Honor," she whispered, understanding coming as softly as a winter dawn.

"Honor," he repeated hoarsely. "Do you comprehend the honor that attached to me by mourning Lubias? Rowland the Dark, an ordinary man who loved with an extraordinary devotion. Awe, respect, renown, all attached to me because of Lubias. She made me a legend. How could I let her go?"

"Do not," she said over her rising tears. "Do not say more. I believed." Her eyes were full of tears and accusation. "*I believed.*"

Chapter Twenty

She had believed. She had thought a man could love. She had thought a man could value something more than his honor. She had been a fool, for had she not learned all she needed to know of men? She had, but she had forgotten. Rowland, with his dark eyes and his gentle ways, had urged her to forget. He had made her yearn after all.

Pain wrapped around her as tightly as tangled thread, choking off her air, squeezing her heart to strangled silence. This pain was greater than Philibert's first desertion, deeper than Hugh's first insult, sharper than Macair's first hard and unwelcome entry into her, more bruising than Gerard's first blow. Rowland had surmounted them all, as had been his wish; he had made her believe in love.

It had been a lie.

Love was not real. Love was the promise of heaven and

God eternal. What did man know of love? Nothing. Nothing but the sweet, lying promise of it.

He had made her believe. She was a fool, a romantic fool no more sophisticated than Beatrice. He had made her forget all she knew of men. She had believed a man could love.

She would never forgive him for that.

He reached for her, his eyes dark and deep with pain. Another lie. She slapped his hand away from her; if he touched her now, she would thrust her dagger in his throat.

"Do not," she said under her breath, her voice harsh and guttural. It would be his only warning. She would kill him if he touched her, kill him if he said one word in his defense. He had no defense. Every word, every act, had been a lie.

He could not love.

She would never be loved.

She turned away from him and went to the trunk at the foot of the bed. With a movement so swift he could not think to stop her, she pulled her dream tapestry from the top. Aye, at the top; she had fallen so far in her belief that she had not hidden it, even from herself.

"Look," she said, her voice shaking with suppressed tears. "Look at what I have done, at what you made in me when all had been unmade. It is a dream rendered, a dream touched, a dream . . . broken."

She had finished it. Even after he had laid his hands upon her throat, she had not found the will to turn from the dream of him. Such was the hold he had taken of her heart. The tapestry warrior stood upon the plain, his dark hair waving in an unseen wind, his face the beautiful contours of the man in her chamber, even to the fragile white scars that marked him as a warrior. Even to the dark, compelling beauty of his eyes. It was Rowland. Within and without. Complete. The vision of a dream. The rendering of her heart.

"See? Can you see what I have done? What you have done?" she said, her tears spilling over to line her face with silver scars that shimmered in the stony light. "I believed." She sniffed away the weakness of tears and then smiled into his startled face. "But no more." And with those words, she took her dagger from her waist and ripped the tapestry in two. It did not rend easily, nay, for she had made it strong. But she would not relent; she was stronger than mere thread, and with a stab, a striking blow, she ripped the thing, the dream, the lie, in twain.

"Nicolaa—" he said, his voice choked and dull. He had driven her to this, as he had sworn to do in his arrogance and pride. He had won her heart, aye, and what a winning. Had she wanted him? She had. Had she cast all her defenses from her? She had. But such was the strength of Nicolaa that, even defenseless, her heart bleeding and torn, she still stood and endured, crippled but not defeated. Even now she was not broken. She stood to tell him of his part in the destruction of her dream. She stood and named him the deceiver he was. She stood and ripped the dream he had spun for her, ripped it and threw it from her, still standing. Still surviving. Still Nicolaa.

She was a woman to make a man dream. She was a woman to wrap herself around a man's life and hold him fast. She was a woman to love.

Her face a mask, shutting him out, she let the divided parts of her tapestry fall to the floor, holding his gaze, her armor shining and in place around her bleeding heart.

The ringing of steps running up the stone stairs broke the torture of her thoughts, and then a knock came hard upon the door. A groom burst in without waiting for admittance, so frantic was he to deliver his message.

"My lord, Jean de Gaugie is at the gates, Lord William le Brouillard at his side. He has come to lay out his terms, my lord. You are required."

Nicolaa turned and was out the door and down the steps before Rowland could precede her. She would not leave this in Rowland's hands. She would face Jean and his terms and she would decide what to do. She was surrounded by enemies, Rowland first and closest. Whatever she had believed of him was torn apart beyond repair. He was a man as she knew men to be. With another sniff to banish all moisture, she hurried out of the tower to the inner ward below. She could hear Rowland on her heels, but she would not turn. Never again would she turn to him.

Jean, a knight of his holding, William, and Ulrich stood as far within her domain as the outer bailey. She would not grant them leave to proceed farther into the heart of Soninges and so informed her chief knight, Yves. He hesitated, this knight she had known for a decade, looking to Rowland for leave to obey her command. She drew a hard breath and closed her eyes against the sight; these men, they stood shoulder to shoulder against a woman. A matter of honor for them, she knew. Bile rose to choke her; the taste of a man's honor was bitter to a woman.

"The outer ward only, and that far enough," Rowland said.

Yves nodded his agreement and went forth to make it so.

325

"Stay away from it, Nicolaa," Rowland said as they walked across the wide outer bailey to meet her adversary. "Stay in the tower, safe from all that threatens harm. I will—"

"I have no trust in what you will or will not do," she said. "I will not run from this. I will not run and hide from Jean or from this battle. Let him run from me," she said, her voice tight with rage and betrayal.

"This is the business of men," he said.

"Ah, I know it," she said on a laugh that was heavy with unshed tears. "And for that, I do not trust any of you. Not a one," she said, looking straight into his troubled eyes. "I will hear every word spoken between you."

"You can trust me with Beatrice's welfare," he said, catching hold of her arm, slowing her.

"I can trust you only to follow the path of honor," she said, yanking her arm out of his grasp. "Where Beatrice falls on that path I cannot know, and I am little disposed to risk."

At that he was silent. Before them stood Jean and all who had followed him into Soninges, men all, and angry.

"I have come for my bride," Jean said, outrage pulling hard against the constraints of courtesy. "All is legal; there is nothing untoward in this. I wish you, Lord Rowland, no harm, and I bear you no ill intent. The girl is ready for marriage. I have come for her."

He looked so reasonable, and appeared almost polite in his terms. His manner was that of a most respectable, rational baron come to claim the woman who had been promised him.

She hated him.

"Beatrice is not ready," Nicolaa said, her words falling as heavily as rocks at his feet.

"She is of an age," Jean said, still looking to Rowland.

"I was married at such an age and it was too young," she said.

He looked at her then and smiled. If she had been closer, he might have patted her like a dog. "You came through your marriages very well. It clearly did not harm you to marry in your prime."

"The issue," Rowland said, "is not whether Nicolaa was ready or unready, but whether Beatrice is ready to be a bride."

"Then let us ask Beatrice. I would hear her words on this," Jean said.

"Beatrice is too young to know her mind," Nicolaa snapped.

"If that is so, I have the right to be party to that judgment. I want to see her," Jean said.

Jean was being very reasonable. William was being very quiet, so unlike him. Rowland stood with the other men, one of them. Nicolaa could feel it all moving out of her control, and she fought to keep her breathing calm and even.

Beatrice was eager for marriage. Jean was eager for another bride. Rowland would do whatever satisfied his honor. William would do whatever would honor Rowland. She was the only one who understood that this marriage would destroy Beatrice. She was the only one who put Beatrice before honor.

"Bring Beatrice," Rowland said to Yves, and Yves obeyed him.

Beatrice was brought forth quickly; Nicolaa was certain

she had been in the gate of the inner bailey, breathless for a look at her betrothed. Beatrice came, her blue bliaut fluttering happily about her ankles, her pale blond hair hanging down in a long, fat plait. She was the image that men dreamed of for a bride. Agnes was at her side, stuck like a burr, and equally unmovable. Nicolaa was thankful for that. In Beatrice's present mood, she was capable of flinging her arms around Jean's neck and begging for his possession. Did it not matter to Beatrice that Jean was of an age with Agnes? Apparently it did not.

Beatrice curtsied prettily, her cheeks flushed with excitement.

"My lord, I am glad you have come," she said.

"Are you?" He looked at Nicolaa. She returned his look with blatant animosity. "I am glad I am come, then. Is it not time for us to finalize our betrothal contract? I would like to make you my bride, if you are ready for such."

"I am ready, my lord," she said, ducking her head modestly and then raising it again to look her fill of the man who shaped her girlhood dreams of romantic love.

"You are comely, Beatrice. You make me more eager to claim you than I was, and I was so eager then as to lay siege to this place to have you. Shall this war continue or shall I withdraw?"

"Do not withdraw, my lord, yet do not be warlike on my account. I am ready to be a bride. There need be no war over me," she said, her blue eyes skimming the men who stood in battle gear: William, Jean's knight, Ulrich.

"She is *not* ready," Nicolaa said.

"You seem to be the only one unwilling within these walls," Jean said sharply, his blue eyes gone swiftly cold at such blatant opposition.

It was true; she stood alone, and a woman alone in a world of armed men stood no chance at all. Jean knew that. What had he to fear from her? She stood alone. Ever and always she had stood alone. And never more alone than now, with her broken dreams scattered in her wake, caught within the very hem of her bliaut, tangling with the ragged edges of her heart. She stood alone, Rowland at her side. Alone.

Into the hard silence of Jean's words, Rowland spoke. "I also am unwilling. Allow the girl to mature another six-month. At Hocktide let us meet again—"

"You would have me wait until after Easter for her when Beatrice is willing to be my wife now?" Jean said.

Standing close beside her, Rowland reached out hand and touched the twirling ends of her hair. A bare touch, almost no touch at all, yet Nicolaa felt it, shivering at the contact.

"Willingness is not the same as readiness," Rowland said softly.

Nicolaa could only stand in stillborn shock. How many times had he said the same to her? He had understood this long before she had and he now spoke the same lesson to Jean. She had been sure he would stand with the men, his honor bound by their regard. It was what a man would do. Yet he had not. With that one sentence, he broke from them to stand with her.

Rowland had stood by her; he had not demanded that Beatrice, eager for marriage, be given in marriage. He did not agree with Nicolaa. He thought nothing ill of Jean de Gaugie. Yet he stood by her. Without agreeing with her, he had chosen to stand by her. The warmth of joy jumped through her veins to race with her suspicion. She could not trust. She had sworn she would not. She knew better than to trust, especially this man, who had won her trust too easily and betrayed it with the ease of any husband. Yet he was not any husband. He was Rowland. How far would he go to keep Beatrice from Jean? How far would his honor let him go?

"Willingness is sufficient for me," Jean said, his manners slipping with each moment of delay and opposition. "To be bold in my speaking, the contract is between Lord Philip and me. You have no legal standing here."

"Beatrice is under my protection. I will not relinquish her," Rowland said. "Yet," he added with a curt smile. "I ask you only to wait until she matures."

"She is ripe now," Jean said. Beatrice blushed. Nicolaa was afraid it was in pleasure. "Will the king need hear of this? I will make my case known to him, if I must."

"Do what you must," Rowland said, planting his feet and crossing his arms. He looked as immovable and unafraid as an angel blocking the gates of Eden. "Nicolaa knows Beatrice best, and until Nicolaa tells me Beatrice is ready for marriage, Beatrice will not marry."

"You are known for having an unnatural attachment to your wives," Jean said with a sneer.

"Nay. Not unnatural," Rowland said, pulling Nicolaa against his side in gentle solidarity.

She heard not Jean as she stared up at Rowland. His voice was as even and firm as the plains of Aquitaine, yet he stood in Soninges and spoke of following Nicolaa's will. Nay, it could not be so. He stood before a fellow knight and set his loyalty upon a woman, and that woman not his Lubias. It could not be. She knew so much of men; she knew this could not be. No man would gamble his honor on the word of a woman.

"I will not decamp," Jean said. "I will lay siege to Soninges until I have what is lawfully mine."

"If that is where your honor calls you, then follow it," Rowland said.

"This is a fight you will lose; the king will see to it. You will lose all in defending a betrothed who wants to be a wife," Jean said harshly. Even Beatrice was taken aback by the violence in the man's manner.

"Perhaps," Rowland said easily, his smile relaxed, "but I will lose nothing I value. And I fear no fight."

He would lose nothing of value? His lands here and in Aquitaine. His good name. His standing with the king. His honor. All lost if he fought this fight, refusing to give Beatrice to Jean. All lost because he chose to align himself with his wife's will and deny his own.

He could not love; nay, he could not, and she would never allow herself to believe that again. No matter that he threw down his honor. No matter that he lost his lands and hers. No matter that he did all to save a girl who did not want saving and to stand by a wife who did not want him. She did not. She could not. She would not want him. And love? Had she not already known that love did not exist except in legends?

But she would not let him stand alone as he cast all from him with a smile and a shrug. She would not let him do that. She was a better wife than that.

"My lord is a warrior of some renown," Nicolaa said, her eyes bright with a misty sheen of tears. He would not stand alone before Jean; nay, she would stand beside him. "He is as eager for battle as you are eager to be a husband. Be warned."

Jean was not pleased to heed a warning from the woman who was the source of his troubles. At that, Jean turned and strode through the gates. If he hoped to pass through those gates again, it would be with ram and fire. Before Jean and his knight had made it through, Rowland turned to William.

"Leave this place and return to Greneforde. This is no fight of yours," Rowland said urgently.

William grinned and said, "You are ever greedy with your battles, Rowland; this is one I would share."

"You cannot," Rowland said. "Go to Cathryn; she has more need of you than I."

If Rowland wanted William gone, then she would assist him. His intent was her only map, and she followed it at a run.

"You cannot stay," she said. "We have not enough stores for your men and ours in a siege."

William stared at the two of them and frowned. "What can I do? I cannot leave you alone."

Nicolaa looked at Rowland then, the question in her eyes as clear as starlight. He had done much—much more than she thought it in a man to do. Yet . . . how far would he go in his trust of her? How far would a man walk away from honor?

He answered her with his next words. Though he looked at William, spoke to William, it was to her heart that he whispered.

"Find a way to break the betrothal," he said.

"Nay!" said Beatrice.

"Aye, Beatrice," Rowland said, looking at Nicolaa, his

dark eyes as warm as a summer night. "You must learn to trust Nicolaa, as I do. She would not keep you from Jean without good cause."

How far would a man walk away from his honor? As far as she beckoned.

"I agree," William said, as Rowland's words fell upon her heart like a shower of sparks. "There is something about him that rings false. But I must go now if I am to leave at all." Turning to go, he clasped Rowland's arm and asked, "You are certain?"

"Go," Rowland said in answer, his voice echoed perfectly by his wife's.

"I shall do all in my power to break the betrothal. God keep you," William said.

He clasped Rowland in a sturdy and brief hug of farewell and then, grasping Nicolaa by the shoulders, kissed her full on the mouth.

"You are good for him, and for that alone I will see no harm comes to you," he said softly.

In an instant he was gone from them, Ulrich at his back. Before they were through the gates, Ulrich turned to give them a brisk and jaunty bow. Beatrice waved, her eyes on Ulrich, as his were on her, and then they were gone. The gates closed, locking the world away from them, leaving them in the midst of a siege.

"Are we ready for a siege?" Rowland said, all emotion save urgency drained from his expressive eyes.

"Aye, but—"

"Who is in command? I want to speak with him," he said, turning from her to scan the inner battlements, looking for weakness.

"Yves, but—"

"Send him to me in the armory and send the blacksmith as well, also the steward," he said, his voice fading quickly, as he was already turned from her and striding toward the armory. "And you may as well use the bathwater. I have not the time now."

"But are you not angry?" she shouted, drawing eyes to her.

"Angry?" he said, smiling at her as if she were the town simpleton. "Over a war of my very own?" He looked like a child at play.

"But," she said, looking at him awkwardly, "you do not hold the same beliefs about Jean that I do."

He stood twenty paces off from her and smiled gently. " 'Tis not needful. I have listened. I trust."

When that declaration left her without words, or even breath to speak, he walked the distance between them and kissed her on the mouth. It was a kiss she returned in full measure: her first. A warm kiss, a kiss of trust and respect. A kiss that touched her soul, knitting the torn edges to the center of her heart. She molded herself to him, lips and hips, and wanted more—a first. A kiss of yearning, aye, it was that; but more, it was a kiss of fulfillment. Never had she known that such a kiss could be.

He broke it off before she had found her breath and said, "Have no fear, wife; you are as safe from harm as if encased in angel's wings with both William le Brouillard and Rowland les Oreilles vowing no harm will come to you."

"Les Oreilles? Rowland the Ears?" she asked.

"Aye, my hearing is very sharp," he said, grinning, urging her to remember. "Still, I was pleased when they began calling me 'the Dark.' More romantic and definitely more ominous. Have no fear, wife; all will be well." He tarried no longer with her; he had a war to manage, after all.

All would be well? She did not understand the mind of a man. But she did understand that Rowland had heard every unkind word she had muttered in his hearing. And that she had started a war.

Beatrice, her fair looks gone dark, was not happy to be caught in the midst of a siege with her betrothed. In fact, no one was happy about it, except Rowland. Rowland she had watched from a distance, conferring with Yves and directing the positioning of the bowmen, seeing that all was well ordered within the walls of Soninges. For herself, she had been left to see to the hall, and was arranging all to accept the injured who were certain to come by day's end. As yet, none had been injured. Jean's men were finding their range, their arrows coming erratically through the merlons that protected Soninges. In a few hours, that would change.

The mood of the women of the hall had changed, for the worse. All were disapproving of her and her refusal to allow Jean to have Beatrice, her grandmother most of all. Agnes, as much as she dared in the current climate, was her only supporter.

"Your obstinacy is going to cost lives, Nicolaa," Jeanne said. "Let the girl go to her betrothed. Stop this nonsense now and perhaps the king will not hear of it."

That Beatrice was sheltered under Jeanne's arm, her eyes red with tears, only added to the charge against her.

"Have I said nay to Perette? Let her go to the man her father and Rowland found for her. I will not hinder her. But I will not hand Beatrice over to Jean," Nicolaa said, trying to relax her fingers and smooth her brow. Was the fighting without the walls not enough? Did they have to battle within her own hall?

"I do not know what you will do when Perette's betrothed comes to the gate," Jeanne said. "Anything is possible. Who would have expected you to start a war over a simple betrothal?"

"Mother, that is enough," Agnes said. "Rowland is the one who started the war, and most contented with it he seems to be."

"Oh, a man will start a war on any grounds he can find," Ermengarde said. "It was Nicolaa who stood in the way of the betrothal. All know that."

"I have cause," she said in answer.

"What cause beyond he be a man?" Jeanne said. "That is cause enough for you. How you came to this, with none but good and upright husbands in your bed, is beyond my understanding."

"There is more to a man than what he brings to the bed!" Nicolaa said, losing her temper.

"As to that," Agnes said, "I remember Jean de Gaugie from my betrothal days. He did not have the land wealth to bid for me, yet now he has more than enough for any woman in this room, except Nicolaa."

"And that only proves him admirable. He has made his way very well in this world," Jeanne said, holding Beatrice.

"He has buried as many wives as he has married," Nicolaa said.

"It is God who numbers our days, Nicolaa; why hold that against Jean?" Jeanne answered.

She had no argument her grandmother could not disembowel, so she did not reply. She would not sway Jeanne, and she herself would not be swayed. She was weary of arguing with her grandmother. Her mother's days in the convent must be so peaceful, locked away from Jeanne as she was.

Nicolaa left the hall and went up the stairs to the lord's chamber; a bath would be most refreshing now. She felt the need to wash many worries from her and would pray that the water would do what talking could not. She was right not to give Beatrice to Jean. Marriage was not the answer to a girl's dreams of love. Jean had been married six times, too many times; 'twas unnatural. Yet she had been married five times, and of what was she guilty?

But with Jean it was different.

Different how? Because he was a man?

It was true; she did not trust men. For cause, good cause, yet . . . were all men unworthy of trust? What of Rowland? Aye, what of Rowland?

She quickly disrobed, wanting to leave her thoughts with her woolens on the peg, and climbed into the cool water of the bath. The heat was long since spent. Her hair trailing out upon the floor, she soaped herself quickly, rubbing away thoughts of Rowland. He was himself, unique, incomparable; Jean was nothing like him. Would Jean de Gaugie have gone to war on the word of his wife? Nay. No man would do such, yet Rowland had done. Smiling, at peace with himself and his actions, he had done. Aye, none could be compared to Rowland. None.

Of his lies she did not think, though the dream tapestry still lay upon the floor. He was trying to heal the breach between them, this she knew, yet to start a war on the word of a wife? Nay, his actions spoke of more than a husband seeking to soothe a wife's temper, for what man would invite a siege to that end? He loved battles, aye, but no man would welcome a siege; there was no swordplay in a siege. Had he done it purely for her? To prove some emotion beyond the love he could not feel?

The soap did not work. She could not rid herself of him, not with all the scrubbing of a day.

She rose and dried herself quickly; the air was cool and the day was waning. She had much to do to prepare Soninges for what was to come. First, she must put on fresh clothing. Why, she did not know. She would be tending the wounded, leaning into blood as she sought to stem its flow. She should be putting on her worst and most ancient bliaut, and yet she pulled out a bliaut of pale lavender with an undergown of lightest blue. A most costly garment and nearly new. Rowland had never seen her in it, and Blanche said it suited her coloring beautifully. She slipped it on, not understanding herself. Her hair she let fall to her waist—another poor choice, as it would get in her way when she was busy at her mending of men and flesh. But Rowland would be there, and perhaps she could tempt him into admiring a long fall of red curls.

She shook her head in bewildered disgust and left the room, her new bliaut and falling hair unchanged, and ran into Rowland upon the top of the stair. He was running up, his head down and his smile half-forgotten upon his face, thinking of other, warlike things. But she would run across the outer ward to see even half a smile from him, though she could only half admit it to herself.

"Your pardon, Nicolaa. I did not see you," he said, catching hold of her hand and bringing her back into the room with him. She went, a willing prisoner to his hand and his smile. "I want a quick dunking before the evening begins. They will start the mangonels come dark, their range being almost found. I have not bathed in weeks and would start my war fresh and smooth." He grinned at her, and she answered him with a grin of her own. Of what use to smile? Why, none, yet she did it and felt no regret.

He pulled off his mail, with her ready hands to assist, and then she set about his gambeson. He was disrobed in short time and climbing into the bath.

"Let me send for fresh water. This is cold and spent. I availed myself of it. You should not—"

"I am content. I would not waste the time or effort in heating water except to drop it on de Gaugie's head," he said, smiling.

His smile vanished when his skin was immersed in the water, long cold now. But he shook and made the noises men make when they are happy and hurried, and was soon up and out of the water, the rims of his lips blue with cold. She wrapped him in the drying cloth and rubbed his back with both hands, as happy and as hurried as he had been. He turned within her arms and she found herself with her arms wrapped around him in an unintentional embrace. She looked at his chest, brown and furred, at the old scars he bore so lightly, at the muscle beneath all. He was a man. He was a man to the heart, and, for the first time, it was a man she wanted.

He had given her his trust. She did not deserve it. Had she not drawn a blade against him? Had she not wished for his death? Had she not cast him from her with every breath she took?

Yet now he took her every breath, robbing her of air just by standing near her.

"I do not understand any of this," she said, keeping her eyes lowered.

He touched his fingertips to her hair and stroked her gently.

"Do you not? Let me help you," he said, wrapping the cloth about his hips.

He was lean, his muscles lying flat and hard on his torso, his arms bulging from years of swordplay, his neck thick and strong. He was like a wolf, all muscle and pelt and staring, hungry eyes. He stared at her without blinking, studying her, reading her. Like the wolf, he anticipated her next action, her next thought, and she could only stand and stare back, captured by his stare.

"Do you remember the parable of the pearl?" he asked, his voice soft and deep.

"Nay, but I would hear the tale from you, if you would tell it."

"A man saw a pearl of great price, perfect and luminous, as white as the moon, impossible for him to possess, unless . . ."

"Unless . . ."

"Unless he sold all he owned, every precious thing he carried with him on the earth. Unless he sold all, beggaring himself, he could not have the pearl as his own. He had a choice to make and it was a hard choice, yet he could not be content until he had the pearl, and so he sold all he had: his home, his sword, his shield, his horse, his land, his mail, his all. Even to his very honor. All given. All, Nicolaa, to own the pearl."

"He would come to regret such a bargain," she said, her eyes tearing.

"Never," he said, smiling down at her, holding her in his arms. "It was even required that he give up what he treasured most of all, that which had no price to any but himself. He had to relinquish a memory."

"Nay, it is not part of the price," she said, laying her head upon his chest, hearing the beat of his heart.

"Yea, to own the pearl, all must be given. All sacrificed. And he did so. Willingly, he did so. For he could not . . ." he said softly, his voice breaking. "He could not live without the pearl."

The linen was white against the brown of his skin; he was brown and hard and wounded all over. He was beautiful, his face the most perfect map of perfection she had ever seen.

"I gave you nothing, Nicolaa," he said, his voice a whisper against her hair, "and demanded you give all to me. You wanted your freedom and I wanted my honor. Now I give. I will give all to have you, and whatever you desire, I will give it."

"Even to giving me my freedom?" Now that she did not want it? Now that he had found a way into her heart?

"Nay, wife, that I cannot do. Only—"

"Only?" she whispered.

He took her face in his hands and whispered against her lips, "Let me be your freedom."

He stopped her heart. She gasped her next breath. Her freedom. It could be so. With this man, it could be so. He was a man worthy of legend.

For answer she kissed him, and everything she felt was in the kiss. Joy. Hope. Freedom. Into the kiss, into his open mouth, into the very breath of him, she laughed for pure joy.

He kissed her eyes, her mouth, her throat, her brow, and all the while she laughed, a giggling, girlish laugh that bubbled up from her belly and shook her hands. She hugged him to her, pulling him down on the bed, wanting the feel of his body against hers, wanting the scent of him to mark her . . . wanting him.

"You are awake? You are ready? You are willing?" he asked, nipping at her ear, lifting her skirts.

"Aye, aye, aye to all," she said, running her fingers through his hair. It was as soft as any wolf pelt must be, her wolfish warrior who thought her a pearl worth any price.

"A cause for laughter and rejoicing then, to find Nicolaa awake and ready for a man."

"Not just any man," she said, looking into his eyes. She could drown in such dark eyes and never want for air.

He kissed her hard at that, and she returned it stroke for stroke, his mouth as hot as fire, his hands upon her legs warm yet shaking. He was eager. Yea, as was she.

"I must be quick, wife; there is much I must do," he said against her mouth. His hands were in her skirts.

"Aye, task upon task you have," she said, grinning like a fool just to look at him. "Will you give me a child?"

He grinned as his hands touched her heat, stoking her fire like dry kindling on embers. That quick, she was hot for him. She could not wait. He would not make her wait.

"If God wills, I will give you a child. I will do *my* part."

She laughed again and pulled his hips to hers. He was ready, as she had known he must be. "If you do your part well, then God's part will be easier."

"And what of your part in this creation?"

"Am I not a willing wife, and have I not always been so?"

"Never so willing as now," he said.

With a grunt he was in her, smooth and slick and hard in her. She received him well and truly, her mind on him and him alone, and then not on him at all, but on the bond between them and the joy of union, body, soul, and mind.

"What color will you paint this ceiling, wife?" he whispered hoarsely against her throat, his grinding weight all that kept her on the earth.

"What ceiling?" she said, vaulting with him to heaven's gate, his heartbeat echoing with hers against the white light of the stars.

No words after that, no words and no thoughts, just joy wrapping itself around her like a silk cocoon, precious, warm, and safe. The explosions within her wrapped around him, drawing him in as she released her seed of life. She wrapped her legs around his hips, keeping him in her, reveling in the feel of him inside her. He filled her up. Without him, she would be as empty as a broken husk.

He was out of her in the next instant, when the last of their shared explosions had faded away like sparks in the night air. He reached for his clothes and began to pull them on, his cock still wet with her essence.

"My pardon, Nicolaa, but I must away. There is much awaits me."

He would not look at her, intentionally she sensed, until his sword was on his hips and he was ready to leave her. When he did look, she lay rampant on the bed, her legs splayed and hanging down, her curls still wet with his seed, her eyes so heavy with passion that he looked indistinct to her. Yet on she looked, and encouraged him to look his fill of her.

"Ah, Nicolaa." He groaned softly. "If there ever was a

woman to keep a man in bed when a fine battle is just outside his door . . ."

He leaned down and gave her a hard kiss, a kiss that made her wind her hands into his hair, holding him to her, demanding his heat. Lurching up from her, his voice a muffled groan, he broke away, pulled down her skirts, and was off down the stair.

When the sound of his foot falls was gone and only his scent lingered, she sat up in bed and started the slow process of untangling her hair. 'Twas a fine compliment he had given her, coming as it did from Rowland the Dark. She grinned and finger-combed her hair. High praise, indeed.

Chapter Twenty-one

The attack was focused on the tower near the kennels and the mews; the ground was wetter there, the mortar not as firm. It was a good place to breach. Rowland would have chosen such a spot himself and had seen the weakness of the mortar on his first pass through the confines of Soninges. The mangonels had been positioned in the wood across a wide and muddy stream, opposite the tower. In a day, they had found their range. By nightfall of the first day, the dogs had stopped their howling at the sound of stone hitting the walls behind them. By the second day, they were whining shrilly. By the fourth day, today, they were cowering and off their food. No matter; they would turn right again with silence and with routine. The same could be said of men.

Soninges was being hard hit. At dusk of the second day, Rowland had expressed his sorrow to see one of Nicolaa's fine holdings so damaged. She had brushed off his concern, she who cared so much for her holdings, saying that Beatrice was worth every stone. He had believed her. To risk so much, she must be certain that she did right, though the other women of her tapestry court were losing patience by the hour.

On the sixth day, Beatrice's father, Lord Philip, came to the gates of Soninges, demanding entrance. He came unmailed and unarmed, a white banner flying from the hands of his squire. He was allowed entrance. It would have been unthinkable to refuse him.

He came, a tall man of fair complexion, ruddy now with anger and distress. Rowland met him in the outer ward, well away from the weakened tower. He would not willingly give this potential enemy a view of his weakest point. It was his greatest hope that another man's army would not be added to his list of enemies. Yet though the king himself be added, he would stand by Nicolaa.

Baron Philip sat his horse, looking down at Rowland. Rowland understood the game and did not let the other man's advantage touch him. What mattered where the man sat or if he was looked down upon? They had met to exchange words, not blows.

"You know why I am here," Philip said.

"Your daughter, Beatrice, is fostered here," Rowland said.

He looked behind him quickly; he had demanded that Nicolaa stand well away. She stood where he had left her, by the gate to the inner ward, though he knew no command could change her will. She who would hold a blade on her husband was beyond commands.

"Aye, fostered only. Why this commotion over a simple betrothal that is beyond your bounds? Your fight cannot be backed by law. I demand that you give over Beatrice to me. You have no right to keep her," Philip said.

Philip spoke true. Rowland had no right to keep Beatrice against her will from either her father or her betrothed. To continue to refuse would place him outside all boundaries of honor and chivalry.

The air was dead and cold, the smell of heavy frost hard upon him. He looked back again at Nicolaa standing at the gate; her hair hung down, red and vibrant in the gray day, her bliaut bloody from tending those who had been wounded, her eyes, her very heart, on him. Six had died and ten had been wounded from this lawful siege against a man who kept a daughter and a betrothed against her will.

Nicolaa looked across the hard-packed dirt of the outer ward, awaiting his words. She had a well-learned distaste for marriage. She wanted to protect all women from the state God had designed for them.

In his heart, he did not see the threat of Jean de Gaugie. He could give the girl to her father, who would give her to her betrothed, and all would be well. Another marriage arranged. Another wife, another husband in the world. Had his own marriage been any different?

All this his heart spoke to him, and he could only listen.

But his will, deeper and more constant than the whims of his heart, chose Nicolaa. There could be no other choice. He would rise or fall with her, content wherever they landed. He would not abandon her, and he would prove it to her with every breath of his earthly life. If honor be the price, he would pay it. Worldly honor was a chill companion next to the fire of Nicolaa.

"Yet I will keep her," he said, speaking of Beatrice, though his thoughts were all of Nicolaa.

"By the saints, you will not!" Philip said, pulling a dagger from his sleeve.

Rowland pulled forth his own dagger and met the man, the father defending the rights of his child. He would not kill this father who fought to free his child; that was the charge he laid upon himself.

Philip, angered, less able in the art of hand-to-hand combat, attacked. Rowland, who had fought thus time upon time against foes from the Saracen to the Welsh, had the advantage. He did not use it.

In a pass, he felt the sting of steel on his cheek before the blood rushed up to spill out. At the next strike he struck the dagger from Philip's hand to lie upon the dirt. As the knights of Soninges stood close upon Philip to keep him from laying hands on another weapon in this unlawful fight under the white banner of truce, Nicolaa ran to Rowland's side, her lips white and her blue eyes wide.

"Escort Lord Philip to the gate," Rowland said, watching as the man was led out, his very steps showing his fury at being denied the right to his child. Rowland could not fault him; he had added another enemy to his lengthening list. Let the list run the length of the Vienne; he would not take one step away from Nicolaa.

Nicolaa touched her fingertips to his face; the dagger had laid open his cheek. The sting was raw and throbbing sharply, but her touch was gentle and willing. Her willing touch was worth any wound.

"Why?" she asked.

"Why was I cut?" he said, touching her hair. It looked alive; he could stare at the fiery twists of her hair for a lifetime and not feel he had yet begun to look.

"Nay, nay," she said, her eyes misting over. "You do not even believe what I believe of Jean; I know you do not."

"Ah," he said, looking into her blue eyes. Did she know that he could read her thoughts as easily as if she spoke them? "I stand with you, wife; our causes are one. For you to believe de Gaugie is dangerous is enough for me."

"You are forfeiting all," she said, her hand over his cheek, the blood running down through her fingers.

"Not all," he said, grabbing her around the waist and pulling her close to him. Not nearly all.

"I am not worth such loss," she said, her raised eyes as blue as the great sea that caressed the land of Christ.

"You are worth all. All loss, any gain," he said, his anger flowing out to touch her. "Think you I would not have done the same for Lubias? Think you any man in Christendom does not know it? How can I do less for you, Nicolaa? You are my wife."

"You loved her? Truly?"

She wanted to believe that he had loved another, for only then could she believe that he could love her. Nicolaa, who did not believe a man could love, yearned to believe in him. Against all experience she wanted to believe, and Lubias was the gate to that belief.

What could he tell her but the truth?

"Aye," he said softly, his thoughts wrapped around a memory that was fading by the hour. He let her go; fondly and with tenderness, he let Lubias go. The woman of his future was within his grasp. He was not such a fool as to let Nicolaa go. "That love was real. Believe, Nicolaa."

It was what she needed, to know that a man could love. She had no idea how deeply a man could love. But he would teach her, though the lessons lasted a lifetime. He would teach her.

Nicolaa looked into his eyes, the question there for him to see. Her blue eyes, so dark and deep, said what she was too afraid to speak. It did not matter that she feared, for this was all she feared, all she had ever feared. This was the fear he had sensed in her. This single pulse of fear that she allowed him now to see.

Nicolaa's heart was in her eyes. How had he ever thought her hard to read? Only a blind fool could miss the yearning wish in her eyes.

Do you love me?

"Aye," he said under his breath, kissing her softly on the mouth. "I do love you. More than honor. More than memory. More than life. I love you, Nicolaa," he whispered. "Can you not see it?"

She stared into his eyes, the tears weeping out of her slowly and silently. "I see it," she said, smiling through her tears. "I see it. But how did you know? How could you—"

"I heard you," he said, tenderly kissing the top of her head.

"If you do not say it again, I will stitch you in the design of a flower," she said, hovering over him. "And I will use blue thread. And I will—"

"By the saints, you are ruthless," Rowland said, grinning through her stitchery, his face her tapestry.

"Thank you," she said. "Even a compliment repeated is a compliment cherished. But I do not hear you mouthing the words I want from you. Perette!" she called over her shoulder, "bring me the blue thread."

"I love you!" he said.

She nodded, grinning, and bent again to his face. He lay on one of the tables, though he had balked at such an obvious display of an infirmity he did not feel. Nicolaa had insisted, declaring it the perfect height for her needlework. She was determined to give him the prettiest scar yet.

"What are you doing? Is it not accomplished? 'Twas a small wound," he said, twitching to get out of the hall and back to his war.

"For a small scar, many stitches are required. Besides, I am removing a small design, most lovely, I had sewn onto your face. It is a shame, truly. Perhaps you would like to keep it?" She grinned, her face just above his, her hands gentle as she smoothed away the last traces of blood.

"Ruthless," he said softly, laughing silently. "Would you have me walk the earth with your mark upon me?"

"Aye,'tis a nice thought," she said.

"And how would I mark you? For you shall not escape this branding."

"Tell me again," she said, her smile soft.

"I love you," he said.

"So I am marked. Your love brands me. Be content with that, I pray you; I do not trust your hand with a needle."

"Nay, I would mark you with my sword," he said, sitting up and pulling her toward his open legs. She nestled within his thighs, her hips against his.

"Ah, would that be Rowland's sword of legend?"

"Do not tell me that even that has found its way into legend for I shall blush like Beatrice."

"Blush? Not crow like a cock?" she said, her eyes wide in amused shock.

"First blushing and then crowing. Would you join me?"

he asked and then said hesitantly, "A man grows lonely within a legend." He pulled her into his arms for an embrace that was as bottomless and full as the sea.

"You will not be lonely," she said, her voice lost in his hair, her breath whispering in his ear. He could hear her in his heart, her words an echo that filled it to overflowing. "You loved, and that was the beginning of the legend, but after Lubias's death you were not loved in return, and so the legend was tragic." She pressed her body against the long length of his and said softly, "I love you."

He knew what it had cost her. She had sheltered her heart against all wounds, her shield against the vulnerability of love impenetrable. She was not unscarred, but he did not need her to be. He would have her be no other than what she was, a woman scarred by brief, hard marriages, and the stronger for her battles. Nay, he would have her no other way. He was blessed to have her at all, this woman who had taught him the depth and scope of a living, breathing love.

He ran his hands up her back, to lose themselves in the red glory of her hair, touching fire and being only warmed by the glow. She buried her face against his neck, and he could feel her tears on his skin. They stood long like that, in the midst of the great hall of Soninges. Finding peace and love and strength in each other. Knowing enough of the world to cherish the gift.

In time, Rowland set Nicolaa away from him, and she nodded her head at the action. It was time, past time, for him to go. The siege had not stopped. The battle still waged, and he must go.

He must go.

Looking into her blue eyes, he said, "Tell me again."

The Willing Wife

* * *

It was just after the morning mass on the following day that King Henry came to Soninges. The mangonels stopped their thunder, and all was strangely still in the cold morning air. Rowland saw him come as he looked out from the curtain wall, and ordered his bowmen to hold their arrows. The king had come. There would be a reckoning.

From his place, he watched Henry, his red hair blazing in the early light, growl his commands. Young he was, not much past Ulrich in age, yet a king in all manner and ways. His wishes were law to those who had sworn to serve him, as Rowland had sworn, as William had sworn, as Jean had sworn. William was with him, and Richard, flanking Henry as he made his will known to Jean and to Philip. As one, they turned and rode toward the gate of Soninges. The gates would be opened. It was the king of all England, ruler of Anjou, Aquitaine, Poitou, and Maine who came. He would be admitted, and then Rowland must needs find a way to explain his actions.

He went down the stairs to the dirt of the outer bailey; the gate had been opened to admit the king, who had commanded in his fierce way that they be opened. Who could disobey the king?

They rode in, King Henry leading them, William, Richard, Jean, Philip, and three of Henry's knights well known to him. None smiled a greeting. It was not an occasion for smiles.

"You have found a war of your own, Rowland, when I have more than enough to keep you occupied," Henry said. "I have not finished with the Welsh. I need you there. What say you?"

"I ask your forgiveness, my lord," Rowland said, facing

his king. "It was not my intention to start a war."

"Yet you have. And over the simple matter of a lawful betrothal," Henry said. "Or is there more to it? William would have me believe so."

William looked at him, his gray eyes as dark as storm clouds, and said nothing. William had done what he could; he had involved the king, which was the only hope in breaking this betrothal. But as to reasons, he had none that would serve a king.

"There is no just cause," Philip said. "The contracts were signed. As Beatrice's father, I have no complaint against Jean de Gaugie."

"And I have no complaint against either Philip or his daughter, my betrothed," said Jean, wisely keeping his temper in check. "I seek only to seal the vows."

"Not for the first time," Richard said solemnly.

Nay, and that was Nicolaa's cause for alarm. The man had taken himself six wives and dug six graves. That was the only reason that would serve.

"Aye, and one of them my daughter, Joanna," the knight, Geoffrey, said. "I had no complaints either, and she was dead within the year."

"So . . . yet women die, as do men. It is in God's hands," Henry said.

"Not if men get there first," Rowland said, jumping before he could gauge the drop.

It was a hard step, to accuse a man of murder, yet had he not already taken that step when he had backed Nicolaa? Was it not what she thought, though she had not said the words? Six wives and six graves and, by all that Agnes said, Jean the richer for every death. He had no proof and never would; he had only the deep fear of Nicolaa that Beatrice would not survive this marriage. No proof, only Nicolaa. The choice was made. The step was not as long or hard as he had thought. Nay, not at all.

"Six wives, all young, just into their bearing years, and each one richer than the next. Is that not so, Jean?" Rowland said, studying the man and his response to such a charge.

"It is so," Jean said. "Am I to be charged for marrying when fathers release their daughters into marriage? Is it not the way of men, and of women, to marry as richly as they may, increasing the wealth for all? Tell me, Rowland, did you not twice marry a land-rich wife?"

"I married where, when, and whom I was bid," Rowland said. "I did not seek out wives."

"Then that is your choice. For myself, I like the married state," Jean said.

"And like it well, by all evidence," William said, backing Rowland.

Two now backed him: Richard, who had given him the words to voice the thought, and William, who would back him unto death no matter what the course. Geoffrey hung by a thread, and might be pushed either way; he had spoken of his daughter, and that might be the name that would stir the wind of doubt.

"Your daughter, Joanna, she was young and well endowed?" Rowland asked Geoffrey.

"Aye to both, and comely as a summer cloud," Geoffrey said, looking at Jean. "Never sick before she went as wife, and then we get word that she was dead and buried, the masses read. I never did get an answer as to what felled her so quickly."

"Now is your chance," Henry said, also looking at Jean.

"I am certain Jean de Gaugie will be glad to tell you how your daughter fell into sickness, and by what manner she met her death."

"I was not with her when she died," Jean said. "I was the sorrier for it."

"And what of the other five? How did they meet their ends?" Henry said.

Jean looked a dog driven into a cold kennel, slunk down and obedient, but far from willing to walk where he was bidden. Rowland could hear the whispers of guilt and fear emanating from the man, coming to his ears like distant surf.

"Am I to answer for what is God's province?" Jean said. "I cannot reach so high as that. I am here to collect Beatrice, who is willing to be my wife as I am to have her. The contracts have been signed. All is lawful."

"As to that," Philip said, his blue eyes troubled, "contracts can be broken. I will not give my daughter into your care with these questions unanswered."

"Come, then, Jean," Henry said, "and let us have them answered. The betrothal contract between you and Lord Philip can be broken upon his word. Let us have your answers concerning past wives. This war is done. Rowland," Henry said, looking to him, "I have need of you in Wales. These private wars you get about you for your own amusement must cease."

"Aye, my lord," Rowland said, bowing, hiding his smile.

"Your lady wife is well? I made you richer by giving her to you," Henry said as he turned to go.

"Aye, sire, I am most assuredly richer by having Nicolaa as wife," he said. He who owned the pearl had all he would ever want or need. He was the richest man in Christendom.

356

Chapter Twenty-two

Twelfth Night

They were gathered in Dornei for the holy days, Isabel being plumped with child. She radiated her happiness as brightly as any fire, and all who sat near felt the warmth of her joy. The tapestry Nicolaa had given her hung in a place of dominance above the hearth. It made Nicolaa smile to see it. It was the only tapestry in sight and, unless she gifted Isabel another upon the birth of her child, would likely remain the only tapestry in Dornei. Yet Isabel had other gifts, the fineness of her table being the most appealing to both eye and tongue.

Cathryn sat with William, her look thoughtful, her body still as slim as a young boy's. He stroked her hand and spoke with her until he coaxed a smile. She would bear fruit, in her season; now was not her time. Nicolaa could see that, and judged that William did as well. For such a loving pair to not produce a child would be a burden most painful for all. She trusted God to see it right. They had been married for just a year, too soon to learn to live with the sorrow of a barren womb.

For herself, she kept a secret knowledge from her husband. A secret that he would not wring from her until they were alone again and back at Weregrave. He had been gone much, busy about his wars, but Henry and the church had deemed it proper to give fighting men a rest during the Christmas season. Tomorrow was Epiphany, and soon all wars would be loosed again, but in the few days she had with Rowland before he went back to battling, she would tell him of her own victory.

Beatrice sat on her left, fingering the stitches of her embroidery. No longer hidden within the solar, Beatrice and even Nicolaa herself sat by the hearth in the great hall and worked their fingers and the wool. Beatrice, her betrothal broken by her father's word, had learned to find calm in her distress. She no longer ran toward marriage, but waited for it, certain it would come in its proper time. That time was almost upon her. She would not much longer be counted among the maidens of Nicolaa's keeping.

Perette was gone, married to distant kin of Rowland's in the Aquitaine. Blanche had found a man of name and rank on the shores of Normandy, and there she contentedly dwelt. Ermengarde, proud woman of reduced means who had refused to marry beneath her worth, had set her eye upon a landless knight in the streets of Dornei and refused to look elsewhere. Did he care that her estate produced poorly and had a leaking roof? Did she care that he brought only his strong arm and his skill to the match? Nay, they cared only for what they saw in each other's eyes. They had married in all haste and she had been smiling ever since. She had finally found a man worthy of her regard, no matter that his worth did not match her own. But in that, she might have been wrong, for he was a most worthy man. Agnes, her hopes on Rowland and what he could do for a woman of her years, waited patiently for the man who would see her value. There were many knights of Rowland's knowing, men he had known in his years of fighting, who would value a woman of Agnes's worth, but it was Rowland who was the impediment. Agnes did not know it, but Rowland had turned away four knights who would have married her before Christmas. For Agnes he would not settle, and judged all men with the eyes of a father. It might be May Day before Agnes was allowed to find her man. Jeanne did not wait patiently, but there were few men of her years with a mind to marry, and if they were not of a mind, then she had no use for them. Her hunger for a man's companionship was still strong; if the man could not match it, of what use the match?

In the months since her marriage to Rowland, Nicolaa found she could understand her grandmother better than she ever had.

The fire burned down, consumed by the cold, wet air of winter, yet the hall was merry. Ulrich played upon his lute, his voice stronger, deeper than a season ago. He had truly become a man. William had knighted him just weeks ago upon the Welsh hills; it had changed him. His tongue was calmer now, if just as sweet with honeyed words, yet he had a bright spirit that could not be dimmed by war or sorrow. It was just as well. The world did not have enough of buoyant hearts and laughing tongues. Beatrice he kept within his orbit distantly, her blond brightness a sun he could not leave altogether for the dark. As to Beatrice, she kept her eyes lowered and her thoughts to herself, which only caused poor Ulrich to circle ever closer, his tongue stilled for fear of causing her distress. In all, Beatrice had found a way to manage him quite well, though Nicolaa was not entirely certain Beatrice had known what she was doing. Still, she had what she desired: a knight of fair looks and fairer tongue who kept his distance and his silence.

The hushed sounds of the hall were broken by the arrival of a messenger from the king.

"I bear a message," he said. "It concerns Lord Rowland."

"I am he," Rowland said from his place leaning by the hearth, where he had been talking to Richard.

"Where may we speak?"

"Here, if the message concerns Jean de Gaugie. All here may know what Henry says on that subject," Rowland said.

"It is of Jean de Gaugie I am to speak," the messenger said. He was a youth, not past fourteen, yet a man about his tasks for all his lack of whiskers. "De Gaugie has been questioned by the king's examiners, put to the ordeal of the hot iron to test his innocence or guilt in the matter of the murder of his wives. He has failed the test. He has admitted to murder, murder six times over, murder for gain. He has been sentenced. The sentence has been carried out. The king's justice has been accomplished."

There was silence after that. Even the logs burned softly and cast no sparks. So she had been right. Her fears had been well-founded. Beatrice had been saved. And Rowland had done the saving.

She looked at him, mere paces from her, and read his eyes. He had saved Beatrice and he had saved Nicolaa, against all counsel, all wisdom, all honor. He had saved them both, though neither of them had yearned for saving. Nay, Beatrice had yearned for marriage and Nicolaa had yearned for freedom. And she had found it, in him.

She looked at him, his dark strength a comfort in a cold world, and watched his eyes. His honor had been restored by Jean's guilt. Yet in her eyes, he had never been sheathed in more honor than when he had defied all the laws of Britain and her king in following the heart of his wife without any proof that she was worthy of his trust. His honor was the stuff of legend, and he had given it to her. It had become torn and muddied in her grasp, yet he had not snatched it back. What man did that? Only Rowland. That his honor was now returned, magnified, was only joy to her.

She looked at him and smiled, holding her secret deep within her heart.

"Your message is delivered," Rowland said to the messenger, looking at her. "Stay and eat, if you may."

"Thank you, Lord Rowland," he said, following Edmund to a stool and a mug.

Rowland left the hearth, his eyes never leaving hers, and she watched his coming. He moved with the stealth and power of a wolf, his eyes predatory and possessive. She grinned her welcome at his approach.

" 'Tis settled," he said. "The matter accomplished."

"Aye," she said, "the king should be well pleased with you."

"The king? Aye, he might be pleased, but 'tis you I want to please."

He reached out and touched a single curl that hovered near her throat. Her skin grew warm at the knowledge that his hand was near upon her. Nay, 'twas no simple knowledge, but one that threatened to topple her off her stool.

"I am pleased," she said, falling into his black eyes, as soft and deep as heavy wool.

"You should be." He grinned. "I have done my part. I have gotten you with child."

Her eyes widened in surprise and then she laughed. "How did you know? I have but missed my courses by a month."

He laughed and kissed her brow, his hand warm upon her throat.

"I heard you," he said against her skin.

Author's Note

The twelfth century was a fascinating time. In many ways it was another world entirely. Medieval man did not look at the world with the same eyes that we do today. He did not yearn for what could not be. He was born into his place in society and he learned to find his contentment in that place.

Marriages among the land-rich, titled nobility were marriages of convenience only. The sole purpose of the marriage was to gain land, increase wealth, solidify power, and produce children. Yet men and women married, and the human heart yearns for love, no matter the year.

It was not uncommon for men to "trade up" in their wives, leaving a wife of lesser power or wealth for one higher up on the social and financial ladder. The church did not approve of this practice, but could do little about it in the twelfth century. As the church increased in power, divorce became more difficult in later times.

Medieval man believed that it was biologically necessary for a woman to achieve orgasm for her egg to be released. In rape cases of the time, a charge that was taken seriously even then, a woman who became pregnant was judged not to have been raped, since she had clearly enjoyed the encounter. What a raped woman would have felt at that decision, I can only wonder.

I hope you have enjoyed *The Willing Wife* and the other books of the trilogy, *The Holding* and *The Marriage Bed*. I have loved living in the twelfth century while writing these books. It is going to be so difficult to leave. Rest assured, I will be back!

Claudia Dain

Prologue

The Texas wind was blowing hard and cold, but he didn't care. All he cared about was that little girl in his sights; she was a woman full-grown, but slight, like a girl, with red hair the color of ripe pumpkins hanging down her back. The wind blew her hair hard, making strands of it whip around her head like straw in a cyclone. She kept pulling at it, tugging those wild strings of hair down with her white hands until she held them like a bouquet.

There was only one reason for a woman to wear her hair loose on a day of such wind: she wanted to catch a man's eye.

She'd caught his.

He'd seen her before. This game she was playing with him was an old one, and he let her lead him around in it, knowing it built her confidence to have him chase after her. Knowing it made her sure of herself. Knowing that soon she'd do something reckless. And he'd be right there when she did.

He'd give her what she was asking for.

Maybe even today.

He got hard thinking of it, thinking of her under his hands, soft and willing. Her mouth telling him yes when he wrapped his arms around her and asked her to marry him.

That was what she was wanting from him, a proposal of marriage, and that was what he'd give her. That, and a few dozen kisses. But she'd be getting more than kisses from him. A whole lot more.

He knew exactly what she wanted. Same thing they all wanted. And he was more than happy to oblige.

He was nothing if not accommodating.

She was a pretty little thing, her hair so bright against the milk white of her hands. She had a spray of freckles across her knuckles that just about matched the color of her hair. She was smiling at him, her eyes blue and round with excitement. He'd arranged this meeting with her yesterday, as she was walking out of church with her folks. He'd whispered to her as she'd passed, her head down as she walked behind her ma, and she hadn't answered. But here she was.

Her folks didn't know about him, not yet. They'd know soon enough. Once she agreed to marry him, they'd know it all.

"You're a pretty little girl," he said, closing the distance between them.

"I'm not a little girl," she huffed, letting loose her hair. It rose up in the air and twisted, writhing and hot against the blue of the sky.

"Is that why you came today? To prove to me you aren't so little?"

"Is that why you asked me out here? To make sport of me?"

She turned her back on him in a sulk that begged to be petted out of her. He accommodated her, giving her just what she wanted out of him. He knew everything about this game they were playing.

He stroked down the wild tangle of her hair, holding the length of it in his fist. It was cool and smooth across the back of his hand.

"Your hair's like slick fire," he said, pressing up against her. "Is your mouth the same?"

She turned in his arms, her hair wrapping around her throat and breasts like a red silk cord. She wanted to give in, but couldn't. He was moving too fast.

"You gonna make me beg for it?" he said on a whisper.

"Would you?" she asked, raising her eyes to his.

"Nah"—he grinned, lifting up her face—"I'm gonna make you beg. More fun that way."

He kissed her then, liking the smallness of her body pressed against him. Her mouth was like fire, after he had tutored her some.

It was her first kiss.

She acted as if she liked it fine. She was pressed up against him, her breasts small and hard and high, and her arms wrapped around him. She wasn't holding anything back, which was just how he liked it.

"You beggin' yet?" he said softly against her throat. That red hair of hers was still wrapped around her, so hot against the white of her skin.

"No, you'd better"—she was breathing roughly—"you'd better—"

He cut off her air with a kiss that had her hanging on to his belt for balance. When he was finished, she laid her forehead against his chest and gulped in air, her fingers still wedged in his belt.

"Are you playing with me?" she whispered, hiding her face from him.

He wrapped his arms around her with a huge smile. This was it. Time to give her what she'd come all the way out of town to get.

"Hell no, darlin'. I'm not playing with you. I want to marry you."

"You do?" She looked up at him. She had the most powerful blue eyes.

"I do," he said. "Will you?"

She bloomed like a flower, right there in his arms. "Yes!"

He kissed her again, sealing the pledge they'd just made between them. She sure seemed to like his kisses.

"I've got a little something for you," he said softly as he ended the kiss. His eyes were gentle as he looked down at her; this was the moment, the perfect moment.

"You don't need to give me a thing," she protested, but she reached out her hand for whatever the gift was that he had brought her. "I'm just so happy right now that I don't need another thing to make it perfect."

Women said things like that. They didn't mean them. He knew that.

He kissed her once more, in parting, while he gave her the gift he'd brought just for her. Just like a flower, she was, just like a flower that bloomed bright and fresh with the sun on it and then was blown down by the first cold wind.

When she collapsed on the ground, her throat crushed like a broken stem, the wind blew hard at her unbound hair; it flew up and twirled against the sky, glistening red against deep blue. No one now to hold it down, to keep it off her face and out of her eyes. It didn't much matter anymore. He studied her for a minute, that pretty hair flying wild in the wind, and then left her.

She'd gotten what she came for.

To Burn
Claudia Dain

He has sworn to battle the empire wherever he finds it, and an isolated Roman villa in Britannia seems the perfect target for his revenge. He and his fierce Saxon warriors will sweep through it like an inferno, destroying all in their path. From the moment he sees her, he knows she embodies all that Rome stands for: pride, arrogance, civilization . . . beauty. She is a woman like no other, fighting with undaunted spirit even as he makes her his slave. She calls him barbarian, calls him oaf, calls him her enemy. Yet when he takes her in his hard-muscled arms, her body trembles with excitement. But will the fire flaring between them conquer him or her? Is the passion that burns in their souls born of hatred, or of love?

CLAUDIA DAIN
THE MARRIAGE BED

It starts with a kiss, an explosion of longing that cannot be contained. He is a young knight bent on winning his spurs; she is a maiden promised to another man; theirs is a love that can never be. But a year's passing and a strange destiny brings them together again. Now his is a monk desperately fleeing temptation, and she is the lady of Dornei, a woman grown, yearning to fulfill the forbidden fantasies of girlhood. They are a couple with nothing in common but a wedding night neither will ever forget. Eager virgin and unwilling bridegroom, yielding softness and driving strength, somehow they must become one soul, one purpose, one body within the marriage bed.

___4933-3 $5.99 US/$6.99 CAN